PRAISE FOR SARAH A. BAILEY

"*Heathen & Honeysuckle* is a second-chance masterpiece. **An absolute must-read.**"

- *USA Today* Bestselling Author Cali Melle

"*Wicked & Wildflower* is romance at its most breathtaking–emotion-packed and **brimming with delicious tension.** Sarah always creates a world you can get lost in, with characters so real it feels like they're sitting next to you, and *Wicked & Wildflower* is no exception. **Simply unputdownable.**"

- Bailey Hannah, author of *Alive & Wells*

"*Pacific Shores* is anything but fictional. It feels like a home away from home in the form of beautiful friendships, relatable characters, and **emotions that burst off the page**. This series is forever cemented in my soul."

- Emily Tudor, author of *The Road Not Taken*

"A perfect blend of **carefully crafted plot** and **irresistible heat**. Sarah is a master at creating relatable characters that you can't help but fall in love with...Her writing is both passionately sexy and **deeply heartfelt**, and *Wicked & Wildflower* is no exception. **Pure perfection.**"

- Ambar Cordova, author of the *Baker Oaks Series*

heathen &
HONEYSUCKLE

heathen &
HONEYSUCKLE

SARAH A. BAILEY

Page & Vine
An Imprint of Meredith Wild LLC

This is a work of fiction. Names, characters, places, and incidents either are the product of the author's imagination or are used fictitiously, and any resemblance to actual persons, living or dead, business establishments, events, or locales is entirely coincidental. The publisher does not assume any responsibility for third-party websites or their content.

The author acknowledges the trademarked status and trademark owners of various products referenced in this work, which have been used without permission. The publication/use of these trademarks is not authorized, associated with, or sponsored by the trademark owners.

Paperback ISBN: 978-1-964264-17-2

For the lost souls still finding themselves.
& for all the good girls who want to be a little bit bad:
You're safe with me. (And Leo).

CONTENT WARNING

Heathen & Honeysuckle is intended for readers 18+ and includes heavy emotional and explicit content.

Detailed warnings can be found at:
www.sarahabaileyauthor.com

Now. May 7th.

This letter is ten years too late. God, I'm sorry. I'm so sorry.

I've always wanted you to know it had nothing to do with you. I missed you so much. I still do. I always hoped I'd get the chance to see you again, if for nothing more than to explain why everything happened the way it did. You deserve more than a letter, more than a phone call, but I'm afraid this letter may be all I have to offer you. I'm afraid that the chance to see you—speak to you—again is quickly falling from my grasp.

I'm getting married in two weeks.

Jackson isn't a bad person. He and I were just both groomed to believe this is our destiny, that we're fulfilling some grand duty by doing this, but he's not my person. He never has been. I know I can't love him, because I've tried. I know I can't love him, because I've witnessed real love already. I've witnessed that all-consuming, soul-deep, once-in-a-lifetime kind of love. I've experienced it firsthand. I know that what I have with Jackson isn't that, and I think, deep down, he knows it too. Yet we continue to orbit each other, preparing for that moment at the altar when we tie ourselves together–and I'm afraid that's when my life, the life I've always dreamed I'd someday find, will cease to exist.

I think that's why I'm writing this: to find somewhere—someone—to give these words to, even though I know I'll never send it to you. Once upon a time, you were the person I told everything to, the person I trusted most in the world. I think maybe you still are. I'm not sure what that says about me—that the person I turn to in my darkest moments, the person I long for when I'm lonely, the person I still trust with my deepest insecurities and my wildest dreams, also happens to be the person I've betrayed most.

~~*Maybe marrying a man I don't truly love and living out my life sentence in a house that has never truly felt like home is punishment for what I did to you. What I did to us.*~~

What a stupid thought.
I'm fine. I'm safe. I'll be okay.

I just needed you to know I'm sorry. I hope you're okay too.

One

Honeysuckle

Then. June 2nd.

I spin around my new bedroom as Kacey Musgraves flows through the speakers. Sea breeze and sun float through the open window that looks out onto the ocean. It smells like salt water and fresh air, like summer in a way that Crestwell, Kansas, never has.

I was so angry with my dad when he told me I was to spend these months with my grandmother in California. I don't know what happened between my parents and my sister. All I know is that I came home from school two weeks ago to find the three of them sitting at the formal dining table, my dad's face red with anger, my mother's pale and withdrawn, and my sister's washed in tears.

Dahlia has always done crazy things—running away, skipping class, dating boys my dad doesn't approve of. When she graduated from high school last year, my parents made her attend Wichita State, thinking it was the best way to keep an eye on her. Something must've happened despite it, though, because when she arrived home at the end of her spring semester, all hell broke loose.

They wouldn't let me speak to her that night, wouldn't tell me what she did or what had happened, only that I'd be going to California for the summer while they resolved the "mess" my sister made.

To my knowledge, they disconnected her cell phone, and the only time I'll get to speak to her is during weekly Skype calls with my mom and dad on Sunday afternoons. I've never gone so long in my life without seeing my sister, let alone talking to her. She's my best friend, the only solid, dependable, constant force in my life—even if she's a chaotic one.

After that night, Dahlia went back to Wichita to pack her things. Mom went with her—to keep an eye on her, no doubt. I spent the last week taking my final exams. The school year ended only yesterday, but Dad had me on the first flight out to San Diego.

Now that I've had time to settle with the news of spending a summer away, of being separated from my sister, being left in the dark about whatever is going on at home, I'm feeling open to the prospect of enjoying my time here. My thought process began to brighten right around the time the clear blue ocean became visible beneath the airplane as we landed.

I've never lived near the beach. Ocean water has only touched my skin a handful of times in my life, mainly on vacations growing up. I've always loved the idea of it, a seamless way of life. Everything seems a bit slower—easier—in small beach towns like Pacific Shores.

My grandmother's house sits on a cliff overlooking the pier at the bottom of the hill. My grandma is hard and strict, closed off and brash, but we've always gotten along well. She seems to see me in ways neither of my parents can—I'm not sure how else to explain it. I have her eyes and her color hair, though hers is now highlighted with silver. I don't have to try as hard to cover my emotions, because it seems as if she'd just see through them anyway. I have no choice but to be honest with her, and somehow, that feels freeing.

Grandma gave me the guest bedroom with the ocean view. She bought a new bedroom set—soft yellow and cream. She said it reminded her of a sunny day, like I do. Yellow is my favorite color, something I don't think I've ever told her, something I know neither of my parents would remember if I'd told them. She just... gets me.

That knowledge, along with the smell of the ocean and the

opportunity that the start of summer provides, gives me a little boost of optimism as I go about unpacking my things.

I'll miss my friends. My parents. My bed. Dahlia. But I have the sun, the sand, new places to go, and restaurants to eat at, maybe even some new people to meet.

I have a swirling feeling deep inside my bones that tells me this summer in Pacific Shores, California, might just change my life.

I startle as something loud knocks against the side of the house beneath my window. Pausing, I wait to see if it happens again. It does, this time seeming to shake the wall slightly, as if something was being thrown against the side of the house. I approach the window, throwing back the beige curtains.

"Whatever music you're listening to sucks, man."

I poke my head out the second-story window, frowning as I settle on the source of the voice. The brightest pair of blue eyes I've ever seen snag onto my hazel ones. A boy with sandy-blond hair, shaggy and thick as it flips up at his ears, grins up at me. Two dimples appear on his cheeks, and I think my heart stops in my chest.

His skin is sun-kissed, the planes of his chest smooth as he stands shirtless at the base of my grandmother's house. A rope necklace hangs at his neck, and he's wearing only a pair of sand-colored board shorts and black-and-white-checkered Vans. He hugs a surfboard to his side, and I can see the black lines of a tattoo snaking around his ribcage, though I can't make out exactly what it is.

"You're not Diane," he says, that mischievous smile still accenting his lips.

"No," I respond breathlessly. "I'm her granddaughter."

He takes his time studying me before responding. "Well, welcome to Pacific Shores..."

"Darby," I say.

He chuckles. "Darby. Welcome to Pacific Shores, Darby."

Taken aback, I blink. "Oh. Thank you..."

"But the music you're listening to sucks. Mind turning it down?"

I feel my nostrils flare, and I consider slamming the window shut in his face and turning my music off completely. I'm not sure why I feel defensive. I have nothing to prove to anyone, and it's not a crime to listen to country music in the comfort of my own bedroom. Still, I feel embarrassed somehow. My first impression of this boy was that he may be the most beautiful person I've ever seen. His first impression of me was that I had terrible taste in music.

He's still grinning playfully as the emotions flash across my face. I take a breath, settling myself before finally saying, "How about I do whatever I want, and you get off my property?"

His brows rise in surprise before he lights up with laughter that reminds me of wind chimes in the breeze. It's so light and childlike, a complete contrast to his looks.

"Okay, new girl has claws." His voice turns a bit rough. "I like it."

"Can you leave so I can listen to my terrible country music in peace? You're trespassing."

He smirks, those blue eyes a perfect match to the ocean horizon behind him. He looks like a photo cut directly from a surfing magazine. "Your grandma's backyard has a shortcut down to the cove—and she loves me, by the way." Something about the expression on his face tells me that's not true. "All I'm suggesting is that if you're going to be living on the beach, you should try out a little Bob Marley. Maybe some Vance Joy? Y'know, fit in with the locals. Just a piece of friendly advice." He winks.

I roll my eyes. "I don't live here. I'm just visiting."

He tilts his head. "Where are you from?"

"Kansas," I say, unsure why I'm indulging him.

He laughs that annoyingly charming laugh again. "Ah, so that explains the accent."

"I don't have an accent."

He slowly raises one brow. "Yeah, you do. It sounds like

you've got honey in your mouth when you're talking."

"And it sounds like you have bullshit in yours. Where's that accent from?" I smile at him before clamping my mouth shut. I never speak like that. I don't know what has gotten into me.

He gives me a smile that is nothing but troublesome. "Yep. Honeysuckle."

"Excuse me?"

"You remind me of honeysuckle. Nectar sweet as honey, like the sound of your voice. But the berries are deceiving—poisonous if consumed." He shrugs playfully. "Beautiful and deadly."

My skin flames. I imagine my cheeks are so red he can see them from where he stands on the ground. Those dimples appear again—taunting and knowing. A whoosh of air leaves my lungs at the intensity of his stare, as if he can read every thought running through my head.

I step back suddenly, slamming the window shut and drawing the blinds.

I swear, I can almost hear the chimes of his laugh fading outside.

Running a hand down my face, I regain my composure after *that* strangely electrifying encounter. I turn around, starting as a figure appears in my doorway.

My grandmother is wearing a floral sundress and a straw hat, her gardening gloves covered in soil, letting me know that she was likely outside, tending to her flowers during the entirety of that interaction with the boy whose name I never learned.

Her arms are crossed as she glares at me. "That boy is a heathen. If you're smart, you'd stay far away from him."

"He certainly is," I respond, knowing I'm nowhere near as smart as she thinks.

Two

Heathen

Now. May 18th.

The bell on the door chimes, letting me know someone is entering the shop. I glance up and find Everett's dark eyes glittering back at me as he enters with a smile.

"I'm here to take over for you, partner."

My eyebrows knit together. "Why?"

I'm on the schedule today until closing. I always work Tuesdays; it's the one day a week I can focus less on my demanding career and more on the reason I went into said career, the childlike passion that once fueled me.

It's my form of therapy, standing at the counter of our shop and watching kids come in with wonder in their eyes, begging their parents for new boards. When people actually recognize me—and not from my *Sports Illustrated* or *GQ* covers, but for my championships and the records I've set. When they ask me for advice because they want to be like me someday too.

That's the only thing fueling me to continue surfing professionally.

My brother's dark brown eyes take on a playful sparkle as he smirks at me. His massive tattoo-clad arm slaps an envelope down on the counter. "You've got mail, and I figured you'd probably like to read it at home."

My eyes narrow. "Am I being sued?"

He laughs. "No. Just...trust me."

I walk around the far side of the counter and take the envelope from his hand, my breath lodging in my throat as I look at the return address.

"Is this real?"

Everett's smile fades, as if he just now realizes the effect she still has on me. "I don't see why it wouldn't be, but you won't know until you open it."

With a pit in my stomach, I brush past him and out the door of our surf shop, making the twenty-yard walk to my apartment on the backside of the building and climbing the stairs.

I'm tearing the envelope apart the moment the front door shuts behind me.

I let the envelope flutter to the floor as I unfold the single piece of paper inside it. The handwriting I remember as well as my own is scrolled across the page, and I feel my heart split open as her words filter their way between the cracks.

Three

Honeysuckle

Then. June 7th.

Water splashes up around my ankles as I kick at the waves lapping up on the shore quietly on this silent morning. The sun has nearly risen, the sky a peaceful shade of teal and orange, dotted with pink and purple clouds. The beach is almost empty, with only a handful of people strolling along the sand.

In the distance, a group of surfers stand in a circle, looking as if they're preparing to go out into the water once the sun has peaked over the mountains behind us. I keep my head down, my sandals dangling from one hand as I scan the sand for seashells. I take a wide berth as I approach the surfers, feeling suddenly uncomfortable. Most of them look to be around my age, and I've always disliked being the odd one out. I decide not to even attempt small talk and just stroll past as if I don't see them.

Musical, chiming laughter stands out from the rest as I pass them. "Honeysuckle? That you?"

The laughter immediately dies.

I lift my head to find five new pairs of eyes planted on me, but the only ones I see are those deep, ocean-blue ones. I'm drawn from his eyes to his mouth as those equally distracting dimples pop up on either side of his cheeks as he smiles at me.

"What are you doing out here so early in the morning?" he asks.

My gaze darts between the others standing around him, a

dark-haired, dark-eyed boy and a girl who looks exactly like him, eyeing me curiously. The girl's curly hair is thrown up into a messy bun, and she's wearing a wetsuit folded down to the waist. Her black bikini—much more revealing than anything I'm allowed to wear—is on display, and she doesn't seem the least bit insecure about it. The boy is looking at Heathen—as I've decided to call him, since I don't know his name—with a smirk on his face.

Two other boys—one with short black hair and brown eyes, one darker complected with bright green eyes, who appears younger than the rest of them—look to me as well. I realize I haven't responded.

"Just taking a walk," I murmur, dipping my head again to hide my face.

"Is your name really Honeysuckle?" one of the twins asks. At least, I assume he and the girl next to him are twins—maybe siblings.

"No, I just call her Honeysuckle because her mouth reminds me of it. Sweet yet dangerous." Heathen smiles. "She lives on Oceanside Drive, just moved in last week."

The boy next to him snorts. "Of course you'd already know what her mouth tastes like."

My cheeks immediately flood in humiliation, and I turn away from the group and the beach behind them. The mountains to the east are suddenly very interesting to me. I take a breath through my nose, willing the redness in my face to fade as I turn back, looking only at Heathen.

Heathen's face straightens into a seriousness I wouldn't have thought possible on him. He shoves his friend so hard the boy falls against the surfboard he has propped up in the sand and tumbles backward to the ground on top of it. "That's not what I meant, douche."

I say nothing, too embarrassed by this group of strangers thinking I was kissing a guy I didn't even know the moment I came to town.

"I call her honeysuckle because of the sound of her voice and her little country accent," Heathen mutters.

The pretty girl tilts her head at me, the movement catching my eyes. "Say something. I want to hear your accent."

"I don't have an accent," I murmur quietly. "All I said is that I was from Kansas, and he decided to run with it, I guess."

The girl snorts. "You do have a little bit of twang in your voice."

My cheeks heat again. I look out to the horizon, as if it's going to tell me something I need to know. "Well, I told my grandma I wouldn't be long, so I should probably get back home." I shuffle past the group of them, around the surfboards they all have propped into the sand. "Nice to meet you all," I say while waving awkwardly.

"I'll walk you home!" Heathen chimes in, skipping up to me and throwing his arm around my shoulder as if we'd known each other for years. He smells like oranges and ocean water.

I shake out of his embrace. "That's fine. I can manage."

His friends laugh from behind us.

"I told you she's dangerous!" he yells back at them, completely unaffected. "You don't have to talk to me, but I'm still going to walk you home," he says nonchalantly, following a step behind me.

"Why?"

"Because now that I know you're walking out here alone, I need to know you get home safely. If I let you walk away and I never see you again, I'll be wondering for the rest of my life if something happened to you. I don't want to have to wonder if I could've stopped it, so I'll at least make sure you get home safe."

I stop and turn back to him. "But if I get home safe today and then get kidnapped and murdered tomorrow, that would be fine, because you weren't the last person to see me alive?"

He deadpans, "That would be awful, Honeysuckle. But... yeah, I wouldn't feel guilty."

"You're strange."

"That's part of my charm."

I don't offer a response.

"Sorry about my friends, by the way. Everett is...an idiot."

"Everett, the one who insinuated you know what my mouth tastes like?" I ask.

I can hear him swallow. "Yeah. Like I said, he's an idiot. His twin sister, Elena, is okay, though. They're basically my siblings."

I continue walking a step ahead of him. "Who're the other two?"

"Zach and August. They're brothers," he says as he catches up to me. I eye him curiously, because those boys looked nothing alike. He laughs. "Zach, the older one, was adopted. August came a couple years later."

I nod absently, and we walk along the beach for a while in silence. I take my time to appreciate the color of the sky and the way it contrasts with the water, how endless the horizon seems, as if I can see the world curving with it. The breeze is constant, but with the heat of the sun, it's cooling. Calming. Reliable. The palm trees flutter above us, and the town begins to awaken. I hear the bells on shop doors as they open and close. The smell of coffee from the boardwalk cafe. Cars zooming along the interstate that runs along the cliffside above us.

We migrate away from the beach itself and toward the residential road up the hill to my grandmother's house. He walks between me and the road, always a step behind, as if ready to intercept something. I realize he's protective by nature. I also realize that and the fact that he surfs and likes to taunt girls he's just met are the only things I know about him.

"I don't even know your name," I blurt. "I've been calling you Heathen in my head."

I hear his footsteps stop suddenly, and I fear I may have offended him. I spin around just in time to see his entire face light up as crackling laughter—the start of a new fire coming to life—erupts from his throat. I can't help but match it, and soon enough, we're doubled over on the sidewalk, breathless.

"Do you know what a heathen is?" he asks.

I shrug. "My grandma called you that. I thought it meant a...

delinquent?"

He laughs again. "Is that what you think I am, honey?"

I look away. "You seem like the type of person who doesn't care much about the rules."

He leisurely places his hands in the pockets of his boardshorts. I find myself thankful he decided to wear a shirt this morning. He's still chuckling as he strolls past me up the hill. "I care about following the right rules, but I guess...yeah, I am a heathen." He turns around and begins walking backward so he can face me. "Do you know the actual definition of a heathen?"

"Something tells me you're going to inform me regardless, so go ahead," I mutter as I trudge up behind him.

"A heathen is someone who doesn't practice an organized religion, although I do suppose your understanding of it would be the more modern definition." He shrugs. "You're not wrong, though. I don't believe in religion, and I don't particularly care for most of society's rules, either."

"You don't believe in God?" I sputter.

"I believe in a higher power. Divine intervention. The Universe. Whatever you want to call it." He turns around, back facing me now. I fail to ignore the muscles in his arms as they flex with each of his steps. "Do I believe that some dude in a white robe is going to smite me because I'm not adhering to the guidelines of an old-ass book? No, not particularly."

I fight the urge to gasp. He speaks of it so casually, entirely without fear. Swallowing, I say, "That's really not what it's all about. It's about being a good human being. Some people take the Bible more literally than others, but where I'm from, we believe that God's only requirement is to strive to be a good human. Help others. Have empathy. Be kind."

"I believe in those rules, too, Honeysuckle. I just don't think I need to be God-fearing to follow them. I'm going to be a good person because I want to be, not because anyone else told me I should be."

We reach the steps of my grandmother's house, and he

turns to face me once more. "I get that," I say. I'm impressed by it, actually, but I don't tell him that. "I've just been raised to be a rule follower—attend church every Sunday, don't curse, be home by curfew, and set a good example. Stay on top of my grades. Always be polite and quiet. Do as I'm told, and don't talk back. Don't offer an opinion on something unless asked, and *never* in front of a man." Heathen's face twists into something like disgust at that. I shake it off and add, "Don't hang around kids who cause trouble..." *Kids like my sister* are the words my father never adds. My finger twists around the gold band on my left ring finger—a nervous tick I've had for years. "Save myself for marriage." My mouth clamps shut. I can't believe I just said that.

Heathen smiles knowingly, eyes zoning in on the ring. "I think you just need to learn the difference between the rules that matter, and the rules that only truly exist so they can be broken." He bends at the waist, waving one arm out to the side in a dramatic bow. "Well, you're officially home. I am no longer responsible for your safety." He straightens and smiles at me, those dimples on full display. "Until the next time I see you, of course."

I wonder why he feels the need to be responsible for such a thing as my safety. I imagine it extends to everyone around him. "You say that like there is going to be a next time."

He shrugs playfully. "I told you I believe in divine intervention, didn't I? I dunno. Got a gut feeling this isn't the last moment I'll be spending with you." He spins on his heel, tucking his hands back into his pockets, as if he's going to leave me pondering those words. "And my name is Leo, by the way. I'll see you later, Honeysuckle."

"If you keep calling me Honeysuckle, I'm going to keep calling you Heathen!" I shout as he walks away.

His laugh chimes back at me, and I feel it in my bones.

Four

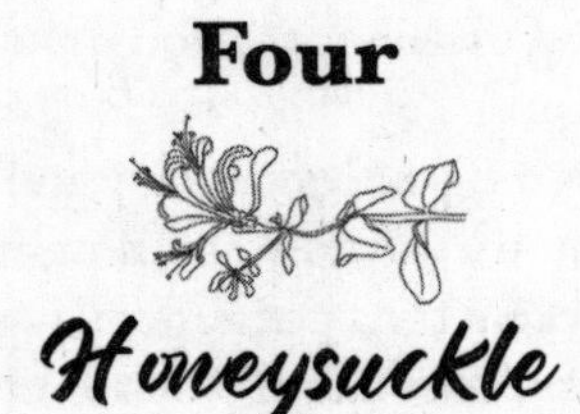

Honeysuckle

Now. May 28th.

I avert my eyes from the magazine cover in the center of the coffee table in my bridal suite. He's inescapable. He's always been inescapable, but today of all days, I need his face completely out of my sight.

I've done a good job of avoiding the covers, bit down on any itch I've had to watch his competitions. His interviews. Old footage. Tabloid claims of polyamorous relationships with models and heiresses.

But of course, today is the day he just so happens to be gracing the three-year-old issue of *Sports Illustrated* sitting on the table in the bridal suite of the church where I'm to be married.

I pull my eyes away from the table, twisting the obnoxiously opulent diamond ring around my finger, hoping it'll calm my trembling hand. The buzz of noise—conversation, laughter, music—floats all around me, but I can't hear any of it.

A woman whose name I can't remember pulls at a section of my hair, twisting it around a large curling iron. I swallow as I catch sight of the white dress hanging on the door.

My hands begin to tremble again.

Jackson's mom glances at me from behind the book she's reading in the corner of the room. A permanent frown seems to be plastered on her face, but I can tell the look she's giving me now is more disapproving than normal. I remove my gaze from her own, catching my reflection in the mirror in front of me. The heaviness beneath my eyes remains apparent, despite the amount of concealer I have on. My cheeks look hollow, and I seem to be sporting the same permanent expression as my soon-to-be mother-in-law.

No, my expression is pain not disappointment.

I force my lips to tilt upward in the smile I imagine a bride should wear on the grandest day of her life, but my eyes can't lie as well as my lips can, and I fall short.

I wonder how I can be in a room full of so many people, and none of them can see the misery behind my eyes. Not my friends from the elementary school I work at—who huddle together in the back of the room, sipping from champagne flutes, hardly acknowledging me. Not my mother. I would've preferred to have had my friends from college, even Maggie—my boss from the flower shop I worked at in Wichita—as bridesmaids, but I didn't get to choose the women who will stand with me at the altar. My mother did.

Save for one person.

Dahlia breezes through the suite doors a moment later, a flush to her cheeks as her chiffon Maid of Honor dress sways back and forth. She waltzes around the room, assembling my jewelry and reminding everyone how much longer they have to get ready.

She's bent over a table, rummaging through a paper bag, when she catches my reflection in the mirror. She stops suddenly, and for a long moment, we watch each other. She reads me better than anyone in this world, and she sees all the words I can't say.

I can't do this.

I know it's not a coincidence that our parents have done their best to keep us apart the last few months. They've always thought she was a bad influence on me. They've been incapable of reining in their oldest daughter since the day she was born. Dahlia has always been rebellious, unwilling to be confined to the expectations of our upbringing. I—for the most part—have always been the opposite.

I know she's been against my relationship with Jackson since it started seven years ago, but I've dumped too much of my life into him, into this town, into my career. They're the only things I have to show for myself, and backing away from them now would leave me with nothing.

Dahlia may not care about her reputation, about pleasing our parents or finding a husband "suitable" by our father's standards, but Dahlia has something worth fighting for. She has Lou, something worth more than society, status, and wealth.

I have nothing at all.

Dahlia doesn't understand that. She's been pushing me since the day I met Jackson to let him go. She knows, deep down, this relationship is nothing more than a business arrangement. Not for a lack of trying, though. I've tried to love Jackson. I think he's tried, too—or at least, he used to. And somehow, I can only blame myself. I think he's always known when he kisses me, when he holds my hand, when he tells me he loves me—he knows I'll never return those sentiments in the same way, that I'm not capable of that anymore.

I can't blame him for giving up after so many years, for finally accepting this arrangement for exactly what it is: a perfect match on paper between two empty souls.

Jackson will get the company he's spent his entire adult life building. My dad will get to keep his business in the family without actually handing it off to my sister or myself. I'll get my childhood home from my parents—their wedding gift to me. My dad's acceptance and approval. Financial security, possibly children to love and care for someday.

And I'll make sure that's enough.

If Dahlia got any whiff of my...hesitation to move forward with these nuptials, she would've done something about it. Stolen me away in the middle of the night. Made me admit the inner thoughts I've been holding inside.

My parents know this.

I know this.

So, I've let her stay away. I let my dad convince me to move out of the house I shared with Dahlia and my niece, Lou, and move back in with my parents as we approached the wedding. My mom claimed it was so she could help me with planning.

It also wasn't lost on me that soon after my engagement, my dad began sending Dahlia to several out-of-state "conferences" as the head of marketing for his real estate development company, not only keeping her away from me, but from her own child. There were few lengths he wouldn't go to get what he wanted, and my marriage to Jackson was no exception.

I haven't called as often as I should. I've told her I was happy each time we've spoken, laughed on the phone, and then I cried after the call ended. I knew if I let her see the truth underneath my mask, I'd have to face it.

Face the fact that I will never love Jackson the way I'm supposed to.

My parents knew I'd never make it down the aisle without her up there with me. Regardless of the man standing at the end of it, if Dahlia isn't there, I won't be either. She flew home from a "business meeting" in Chicago last night, rushing straight to the church this morning.

Now, she stares at my reflection and watches the mask slip off my face. She sees the truth everyone else around me has chosen to ignore—including myself.

Because my eyes can't lie as well as my lips can.

The hairstylist pins the last section of my hair into a roller when Dahlia asks, "Can she take a break while those set?"

The stylist nods, stepping away. Dahlia appears behind me, eyes meeting my own in the mirror as I watch her grab that copy of *Sports Illustrated* off the table and casually slip it into the small trash can near the door. *Thank you*, I mouth at her.

Her face takes on an unreadable expression as she steps up to the chair I'm in and bends so she's at my level. Meeting my eyes in the mirror, she leans in and whispers, "Honeysuckle?"

My body goes rigid as I gasp, choking on the air stuck in my lungs. "What did you just say?"

Five

Heathen

Then. June 15th.

I stare up at the whitewashed, two-story house with hydrangeas in the front yard and a wraparound porch. The home fits in perfectly with the charming older houses along Oceanside Avenue. It's nicer than the house I live in, a little bigger. An ocean view. A backyard that hangs over the cliffside, allowing the green of the grass to clash with the blue horizon of the ocean.

I don't know why, exactly, I'm here. I haven't been able to get those hazel eyes out of my head since the first moment I saw them. I told her she reminded me of honeysuckle because her voice was sweet but her words were poisonous. Truthfully, though, everything about her reminds me of honey.

The way sound drips from her voice—thick and sweet and slow, like you want to savor every word, even the ones that hurt. The color of her eyes reminds me of honey, too. It's easy to say they're hazel, but when the sun hits them—the way they were that morning I saw her at the beach—they appear more like amber. Her golden hair, flowing past her shoulders in thick, straight strands—she's all honey-colored.

I bet her lips taste like honey too.

It's been a week since I left her on the front porch of this house, and I haven't seen her since. I've been spending every day with Carlos and Everett at the garage. Early summer is a busy time. The wealthy are taking out their convertibles and classic cars that have been covered all winter and need a tune-up before going back out on the road. The families need work done before they take off on their summer road trips.

I need to earn my keep, so I work every day in the summer. Nobody in the Ramos family has outright told me I need to work in exchange for my living there, but I know they struggle. I know my free labor and the tips I make to help myself get by are what allow them to continue supporting me in all the ways they can. I owe it to them.

Maybe that's why I'm out here. Sometimes, the house can feel suffocating to me. They try to make me feel like I'm part of the family, make it feel like home. Most of the time, it does, but there are moments when I remember I'm not a Ramos. It's not home. Truly, I don't have a family. I'm alone.

There is something in Darby's eyes that makes me think she feels the same way sometimes. Maybe that's why I'm here, looking for the relief that I'm not the only person in the world who feels the way I do, but I'm also curious about her. Why is she suddenly here in Pacific Shores with her grandma? How long does she plan to stay?

And maybe I'm wondering what her lips taste like.

I quietly sneak around the side of the front yard, silently unlatching the gate. I do this often, and while I'm pretty sure Diane, Darby's grandma, is entirely aware, I try to remain quiet. Diane's backyard has a trail down the rocky cliffside to a hidden cove. Whoever owned the house before her must've made the trail. It's steep and dangerous, but once you're down on that beach, you feel isolated from the rest of the world. It's a private oasis in the overpopulated beaches of Southern California. It's also got a great swell, making it the perfect private surf spot. Tonight, though, I'm not seeking out that cove. Tonight, I'm seeking out the girl who's likely sleeping in the bedroom upstairs.

As I circle the backside of the house, I stop in front of her window. A faint glow illuminates from behind the shut curtains, and I'm filled with hope that she's still awake.

Picking up a handful of pebbles from the ground, I begin tossing them up toward that window. I have no idea where her grandmother's bedroom is, so I try not to make too much noise in case she's on the same side of the house.

After I throw three pebbles, the light in the room suddenly shuts off. Either she's trying to appear asleep, or she's scared. I back up a little bit so I'm on the open lawn, illuminated by the light of the near-full moon. Adjusting to the darkness, my eyes catch movement behind the curtains. I can't see her, but I know she must be peeking through them to see who's throwing rocks at the window. I hold my arms out, waving them to catch her attention, smiling broadly.

Suddenly, the curtain is aggressively swung out of the way, and the window is hauled open.

"What do you want, John Hughes?" she whisper-shouts.

"Who?" I shout back.

Her eyes are so big, rolling so dramatically, I can see it from where I stand. "What are you doing here?"

"Bored." I shrug. "You wanna sneak out and go break some rules?"

"Sneaking out is breaking a rule," she snipes back.

"Okay," I drawl. "You wanna sneak out and then not break any other rules?"

She rolls her eyes again. "No, thank you."

I huff, running a hand through my hair. I feel disappointed, but I shouldn't be surprised. She doesn't even know me. I'm sneaking through her backyard in the middle of the night and asking her to run off into the dark with me. Of course, she wouldn't want to do that.

I'm an idiot.

"Sorry for bothering you. I'll see you later, Honeysuckle."

I turn to walk away when I hear her sweet voice ask, "What's wrong?"

Spinning back to her, I smile. "Nothing's wrong. Like I said, I'm just bored. Thought I'd try to corrupt the new girl in town."

"You're lying," she says, tilting her head at me as if she's reading my features for information she knows will never come from my mouth.

"I'm not lying. I do want to corrupt the new girl in town." I grin devilishly before shrugging it off. "Tough night, but I'm fine. I'll see you later, I'm sure. Goodnight, Honeysuckle."

She sighs. "Hold on."

Before I can respond, the window is slammed shut.

I pace around the backyard for what feels like years, unsure what she meant when she told me to hold on, unsure how long I should wait before I give up and leave. Finally, I hear a door open and quietly click closed before a figure comes jogging down the back porch steps.

Darby's cheeks are a little flushed, her beautiful hair pulled back into a bun. She's got on cotton shorts that show off a distracting amount of her smooth skin and a cropped sweatshirt that gives me the faintest glimpse at her stomach.

My knees suddenly feel a bit weak.

"Hi," she says.

Realizing my gaze has been eagerly soaking up every inch of her body, I snap my eyes to her face. "Hi."

"So, what are we doing?"

I bite my lip, hiding a smile. "Well, I think maybe it's best we ease you into the whole rule-breaking thing, yeah? Since you snuck out, we can keep the rest of the night tame. You wanna go get matching tattoos? Or we could get our tongues pierced?"

Her eyes go wide, and her mouth drops open. She looks like she's trying to say something, but she's just gaping like a fish. I burst out laughing.

"I'm kidding, Honeysuckle. First lesson in corruption: stop being so gullible."

Her mouth clamps shut, and her nostrils flare. It's fucking cute.

She shoves me, muttering something like "idiot" as we sneak around the side of the house and out the gate.

"Let's go down to the pier. Have you seen it with all the lights yet?"

She shakes her head.

We skip down the hill together. "Speaking of tattoos, you have one," she says.

"Yep," I respond.

"I didn't see what it was. I just noticed the one on your side."

"Maybe I'll show you sometime if you're lucky."

I hear her take a sharp inhale, and I can't fight the smile that the sound gives me. I like startling her like that. "So, are you eighteen, then?"

I shake my head. "No, I'm seventeen. About to go into my senior year of high school. I got my tattoo last summer."

"Oh, me too."

I turn around and grin at her. "You got a tattoo last summer?"

She rolls her eyes, but I catch the little tilt of her lips. "No..." She draws out. "I'm going into my senior year of high school too. I turn eighteen on November eleventh."

"I turn eighteen on May second."

Her brow furrows. "How did you get a tattoo at sixteen?"

"I know a guy." I shrug.

She makes a contemplative noise, and we continue walking in silence. As we reach the pier, I hear her gasp. My favorite thing about the Pacific Shores Pier is that it never really shuts down. The shops and restaurants close, but the city leaves the lights on all night. It's not uncommon to find people wandering around the boardwalk after a night out at the bars, admiring it. The Ferris wheel stands tall, lit up in red, purple, and blue. Yellow lights wrap around the rails of the pier, making it look like a landing strip jetting out into the water. All the palm trees lining the boardwalk are wrapped with multicolored lights. The fullness of the moon makes it all seem that much brighter.

I turn to catch the reaction on Darby's face. By the sound she made, I assume she hasn't seen the pier like this since moving here. Her eyes are lit up in surprise, and her pouty lips are parted just slightly, her face a little red from our walk. A stray piece of golden hair falls onto her forehead.

I've always loved the beauty of the boardwalk at night, but I quickly realize it holds no comparison to the golden girl standing in front of me now.

I watch her eyes scan the area, her face lighting up as she takes in all the brightness. "It's beautiful," she says.

"My favorite place in the world," I respond.

Her eyes snap to mine, and a smile breaks out from her cheeks, spreading across her face. She may be the most effortlessly beautiful girl I've ever encountered. I feel my breathing get heavy, and my legs dissolve into jelly again, but Darby just continues to smile at me without a care in the world.

I get the feeling that Darby is the type of person who may care too much all the time. This moment is probably the most carefree one she's had in a while, and something like pride swells inside me knowing I've given her that.

Without another word, I grab her hand, dragging her toward the pier. I'm not taking her to the boardwalk or to check out the Ferris wheel—I'm taking her beneath it. There's a place beneath the pier where the water is calm, and you can often find sand dollars dotting the beach. At night, the lights of the pier shine through the gaps in the boards, illuminating the space. It makes you feel like you're breathing, standing, and walking underwater, somehow protected from the world above you.

I go down there at night sometimes—nights like tonight, when I'm feeling suffocated and homeless and like a burden. Nights when I think too hard about what life was like before I found the Ramoses, when I think too hard about what my life would be like without them.

I like to stare up at those lights through the boardwalk and stick my feet into the water. Sometimes, I'll swim out just to the place where my toes can no longer touch the bottom so I can become weightless, feel like I'm somewhere else for a little while.

Pacific Shores is my favorite place in the world because it's the place that built me, but it also tends to feel like every mistake I've ever made. Every promise I've ever broken. Every disappointment I've ever been to those I love. When I act out, break rules, and generally cause a ruckus, it makes me feel like I'm taking it back a little bit, making Pacific Shores my own, ensuring nobody here forgets me.

I'm sure there are better ways to go about making myself unforgettable than stealing street signs, trespassing on my neighbor's property, and underage partying, but the way I go about things sure is a hell of a lot more fun. Plus, the one rule I do set for myself, the one rule I'm sure to follow, is this: I only break rules that affect me individually. I'll never intentionally do something to hurt another person.

As long as I'm living by that, I can live with myself.

"I'm not going to have sex with you, you know," Darby says as I drag her down the beach and beneath the pier.

"Get your mind out of the gutter, Honeysuckle." As we reach my favorite spot beneath the boardwalk, I let go of her hand and turn to face her. Her body is awash in shades of blue, purple, and gold, an expression of wonder on her face as she spins in a circle, admiring the space. "I'm not trying to seduce you. I'm just showing you a spot I like to come to when the world feels a little too loud. It seems like maybe you need a place like this too."

Her eyes land on me, her mouth forming a thin line. "What makes you say that?"

"You just seem like maybe you're under a lot of pressure. Doesn't sound like you came to spend the summer here at will." I shrug. "Plus, your grandma is a real hard ass, y'know? I just imagine you may need a place to...decompress, like I do. Lucky for you, I'm willing to share my space."

She snorts. "How could you possibly garner all of that about me from two interactions?"

Because I think you're a lot more like me than you're willing to admit, I want to say, but I don't. "I'm an empath."

A small giggle bubbles from her throat, followed by a bright melody of laughter. She covers her mouth with her hand, and I have an urge to pull it away, wanting to see her smile, knowing that I'm the one who placed it there.

Once she gathers her composure, she asks, "Was the world too loud tonight, Leo? Is that what brought you out here?"

Yes. But more than that, I couldn't stop thinking about her. I wanted her to come with me. I can't say that to her, though, so instead, I say, "Have you ever been surfing?"

Six

Honeysuckle

Now. May 28th.

I spin in the chair and look up at my sister, who still watches me with that indecipherable emotion. Glancing around the room to ensure nobody is paying attention to us, she grasps my arm and pulls me from my seat, dragging me out of the bridal suite and into its adjacent bathroom.

She locks the door behind her, grabs my arm, and pulls me into the far corner of the room where a vanity with two sinks, a mirror, and a changing station rests against a far wall.

"You don't have to do this, Darby. It's not too late to call it all off. I know you don't want this. You deserve more. You deserve better, and—"

"No. We're not doing that right now." I shake my head. "Why did you just say that word to me?"

She chews on her lip as she watches me curiously. "I wanted to see your reaction."

I feel my pulse uptick. My ears ring with the nickname I haven't heard in so long. "Why?"

"I was told there was a guy in the church's parking lot asking to speak to the bride's sister specifically. That's why I stepped out earlier." I think back to a half hour ago when our wedding coordinator peeked into the suite and asked for Dahlia. I didn't think much of it, too lost in my own head. "There was a very recognizable man in the parking lot with a bouquet of flowers for you. He asked me to ensure you get them. Away from our parents, he had pointed out." She raises a brow at me and then nods at something behind me.

I turn, gasping as I find the bouquet she mentioned sitting against the bathroom vanity. My eyes narrow in on the white and pink drooping petals, the long yellow needles poking out from the center of the flowers, the small berries on top.

A bouquet made entirely of honeysuckles.

My mind goes to a thousand different places and possibilities, landing briefly on that letter I wrote two weeks ago, the one I shoved into my desk drawer and ensured would never be seen again, making this exact scenario entirely impossible.

It has to be a joke.

My eyes swell. "Did Jackson find out about him? Do this to punish me?" Afraid to touch the flowers, I look back at my sister. "Did Dad?"

Dahlia shakes her head. "No, Darby. I spoke to Leo myself twenty minutes ago. He was the one outside with those flowers in his hand."

Leo. A name I haven't spoken—haven't even allowed myself to think—in years. When I was twenty, just after my first date with Jackson, I broke down one night and told Dahlia everything—every little detail of that summer, of that night, of what happened afterward.

I told her that after I let it all out, I never wanted to speak of it again. Never wanted to speak of him. Of what I did and what I gave up. I've become accustomed to keeping those memories and those feelings locked into a small box at the back of my brain.

The honeysuckles sitting right in front of me feel a lot like a key to unlocking a lot of things I've fought tooth and nail for years to forget. Those flowers feel like confrontation, and yet, they also feel like an escape.

"You don't have to do this," my sister repeats, her champagne-colored dress ruffling as she leans against the wall. "You have a way out now."

On trembling legs, I walk over to the vanity before grasping the flowers with shaking hands. I look up in the mirror, taking myself in. My eyes are wide and red, fighting back unshed tears. My blond hair is tied up into ridiculously large rollers pinned on all sides of my head. My white silk pajamas hang off my frame limply.

"Why are you saying this right now?" I grit my teeth as I turn back to my sister, feeling anger rise in my throat. "I am three hours away from walking down the aisle. The ship has fucking sailed, Dahlia."

My anger isn't just directed at her; it's at him, too. I made a clean break all those years ago, and while I would be lying if I said I didn't hope he'd come looking for me, him showing up now is too late. There's nothing that can be done at this point.

"Why would he show up like this? How would he even know?" I feel a hot tear make its way down my cheek.

"I sent him your letter," my sister whispers. "And I may have added the date, time, and address of the church before I mailed it." I feel my jaw tremble and my nostrils flare. My entire body shakes, and I see her wince.

She closes the gap between us, putting her hands on my shoulders. I fight to shake her off, but she holds strong. "I forgot to sign one of Lou's permission slips, so one morning when I was dropping her off at school, I popped into your classroom to steal a pen. I found the letter in your desk drawer."

"Why would you read it?" I seethe.

"Because you're my sister, you're miserable, and I'm so fucking tired of it, Darby. You've kept that summer locked up for years, but I asked Grandma about it once. She told me she'd never seen you so full of life than when you were seventeen, that you've been dead inside ever since. If she were here right now, I think she'd be telling you not to go through with it. If she found that letter, she'd have sent it. If that man"—she points toward the door—"showed up at this wedding, and there was any chance of you getting out of it, she'd make you take it."

She wipes a hand down her face and folds me into her chest. Only then do I realize I'm sobbing. "I saw his name on it. I had to see what it was. Once I read it, I knew he needed to see it too."

"How did you get it to him?"

"He's got a P.O. Box for fan mail, but I knew if I addressed it with your name, it would catch his eye." She pulls back at me and smiles. "And it looks like it did."

I wipe my eyes, stepping back from her. "I can't believe you did that." I feel my breathing increase again. "He is probably just here to tell me off. I don't...I don't know what he could possibly want."

"Open the card and find out."

For the first time, I notice the small white card tucked into the flowers. With hesitant, trembling fingers, I pull it from the bouquet, and Dahlia takes the flowers from me as I open the envelope.

In writing as familiar as my own, I read his message, tears streaming freely down my cheeks.

Seven

Honeysuckle

Then. June 15th.

"Have you ever been surfing?" he asks. It's not lost on me that he ignored my previous question, which gives me the answer I'm looking for anyway.

His blue eyes may be the brightest I've ever seen, full of light and life, but they're also haunted. He's clearly not comfortable enough to tell me what ghosts he's running from when the world feels too loud, but I don't blame him for that.

I don't have ghosts, but I have wolves, a commanding presence that controls every aspect of who I am. Who I'll become. Who expects me to be part of the pack but not to lead it. To cower underneath an alpha and to never question their motives.

I wonder if he can see the shred of fear in my own eyes that I've only ever thought was visible to myself. I wonder if he sees that fear and sorrow and finds comfort in it, if he thinks his ghosts can dance with my wolves and give us both a reprieve for a moment.

I try giving him what he's searching for when I say, "No. I've never even been swimming in the ocean."

His face twists into something like shock. "What?"

I chuckle, the blue lights above us washing out his features and making him appear truly horrified at my revelation. "This is only like"—I pause as I try to remember—"the third or fourth time in my life I've actually been to the beach. When we went on vacations as kids, I wasn't allowed to swim, because it was too dangerous."

"That's ridiculous," he scoffs. "Didn't your parents ever go in the water with you?"

I laugh at that. "My dad normally had business calls during our vacations, and my mom...she's not the type to want to get her feet sandy or her hair wet. She doesn't like to spend much time outside at all, actually."

"So, what did you do on vacation?"

"When I was young, we had nannies who spent time with us, but they wouldn't take us to do anything too dangerous and risk the wrath of our parents. When I got a little older, my sister watched me, but by that point, I was the one too afraid of our parents to do anything risky, so I just watched her from the sidelines." I bite my lip and look down. "Dahlia...Dahlia could probably surf. She can swim in the ocean. There is nothing she won't try once. She's brave, fearless, and carefree—everything I'm not. It's like God gave her all the courage and gave me all the fear."

"God didn't do that to you, Darby," Leo says immediately. "You were programmed to be afraid of everything. Not because things like surfing or swimming or having fun are scary, but because you're afraid of your parents' reaction if you do them. Your parents likely have their own motives for wanting you to be afraid. Timid. Obedient."

I only shrug in response. He eyes me for a long moment, and I'm not sure if he's waiting for me to say something, or if he's trying to determine what to say himself. Suddenly, he's peeling his T-shirt from over his head and dropping it to the ground in front of us. He empties his pockets of a lanyard with one key on it and a worn wallet, tossing them atop his shirt.

"Come on, Honeysuckle."

"What the hell are you doing?"

"We're going swimming. I'm going to show you that you've got nothing to be afraid of, that there is nothing wrong with getting your feet a little sandy and your hair a little wet." He grins, and a flash of purple light floods his face, his dimples apparent.

"I don't have a bathing suit," I say.

"I'm not going to be scandalized by your bra and underwear, honey. I've seen plenty of girls in plenty of bikinis, which is basically the same thing." He holds his arms out wide. "Beach town, remember? This is California."

"I'm not allowed to wear bikinis."

He runs a hand down his face, muttering something like, "My God." He lets out an exasperated sigh. "I don't want to do something that'll make you uncomfortable, Darby. If you want to go home right now, say the word, and I'll take you. But if I'm being honest, it sounds to me like you've been controlled your entire life. I think you deserve to have some fun. Your parents aren't here. It's just me, and I'm not going to hurt you. I'm a damn good swimmer, and I'll keep you safe."

I swallow. "Isn't there some kind of city ordinance against swimming beneath the pier—at night, no less?"

"Look, I'll tell you my number one rule, and then you can decide if you want to come swimming with me, or if you want me to take you home."

I nod.

"This is what I live by: I only break rules that affect me and only me. I don't ever do anything to hurt someone else. I don't run traffic lights or steal from people. I don't hurt or lie or cheat. I go swimming at night because the city ordinance in place is to protect me from drowning in the dark. I'm a good-ass swimmer, so I'm not too worried about that. Plus, if I drown, the only person I'm really hurting is myself, and—"

"And all the people who love you," I say.

He smiles at me. "That's where you're wrong, Honeysuckle. Nobody loves me. I can only hurt myself."

"If you drown out here tonight, you'll hurt me." His face straightens. "I shouldn't have to witness that, nor should I have to fish your dead body out of the water. I'd be traumatized for the rest of my life."

He stares at me for a moment before he lights up with that

bright laughter. "My point is, there is always a little bit of risk involved. Every time you leave the house, you're at risk of hurting yourself and, therefore, the people who love you. When you boarded that plane to come here, every time you get into a car, whenever you walk down a flight of stairs—you're always a little at risk, so be risky for the right reasons." He holds a hand out to me. "I'll keep you safe, I promise. Live a little, will you?"

I huff. I know what I'm about to get myself into, and yet, I can't stop myself from lifting my sweatshirt over my head. Standing before Leo in only my sports bra is the most exposed I've ever been in front of a boy. Cool air pricks my skin, but it's his gaze that gives me goosebumps.

I can tell he's trying not to stare. He's afraid of making me uncomfortable. I'm walking a fine line here as I strip out of my shorts—thankful I decided to wear a pair of spandex underneath them—and Leo looks out toward the water. Once I'm standing before him, covered only at my breasts and hips, I notice him looking back at me and swallowing deeply. I feel a blush creep up my neck, knowing my body has an effect on him. I don't feel scandalized, exposed, or uncomfortable. I feel appreciated. I think I might even feel beautiful.

He clears his throat, nodding toward the water. "Let's go."

When he extends his hand once more, I take it, his calloused fingers brushing against my own, warm, soft, and rough at the same time. He wraps them around my palm, squeezing gently as he pulls me into the water. The ocean laps gently at our ankles, our shins, our knees as we wade deeper into the water.

I hiss as the water reaches my stomach, suddenly cold and prickly. Leo stops in the water and looks down at me, those dimples popping again.

The world is dimmed where we stand beneath the boardwalk, but not in a negative way—in a calming way. Lights flash around us, blocked out by the cocoon of darkness the night provides. The sound of waves drowns out all others, as if we're inside a bubble, a ship floating through the cosmos, the two of us alone.

"The water gets a little chilly the deeper we go. I normally like to just dive in, get it all over with. Your body will adjust quickly, but if you slowly inch into it, you're just going to make yourself miserable with anticipation."

I chuckle. "So, what you're saying is that I should just jump in without thought and see what happens?"

He smirks. "Pretty much my life motto."

"You're crazy."

Without offering a response, he proves me exactly right as he lets go of my hand, raises his arms over his head, and dives under. I gasp, squinting at the dark waves as I wait for him to re-emerge. My eyes desperately scan the surface, the water so black, I can't see any trace of him.

Finally, he breaks the surface a few feet in front of me. Blue light clashes with his silhouette just in time for me to see him whip his head to the side, his hair swinging out of his face and sprinkling water into the air around him. He leans back, floating as he treads backward and faces me.

"You're never supposed to turn your back on the ocean," I say.

"I'd never betray the ocean," he responds. "We're cool. Best friends. She's been here for me my whole life, and I know she won't turn her back on me either." He smiles.

"You're strange."

"Part of my charm."

I humph at him, but he doesn't take his sight from me, as if he's waiting for me to dive in too. I bite my lip, finally breaking eye contact to look down at the water. I watch a small wave crest and splash over my hips. "I don't want to go so deep I can't touch the bottom," I say.

I hear shuffling and splashing before I feel his body come close to mine, and I look up to see him hovering over me. "I like when I can't touch the bottom. It makes me feel like I'm floating outside this world. Makes me feel like I can disconnect from my own body—my own mind—for a little while."

Like floating through the cosmos.

I sigh, my stomach twisting in knots beneath me.

"Why don't we go out a little farther, where you can't stand, but I can, so I can catch you if you begin to float away?"

"Okay." I nod.

He smiles, grabbing my wrists beneath the water. He pulls on my arms, and I lose my footing, falling face-first into the water. Leo catches me by my shoulders before I can go completely under, but the shock runs through me as I realize my entire body up to my neck is now submerged.

"Told you it's easier to just dive in." I'm pretty certain I can feel him wink at me.

We inch deeper, little by little, until only the tips of my toes touch the bottom. "I can't stand up anymore," I say, though my head continues to bob above the water, my body buoyant from the salt, and Leo's hold on me keeps me afloat.

His hands slide down my arms, warm and rough, and I feel goosebumps erupt with each inch of skin he covers. I've never let someone touch me like this before, and while I know it's innocent, my body lingers on the feel of it, the comfort.

I've been told that touching boys is wrong. Even something as simple as a hug from someone who isn't family, my dad has always been against it. He's told me it's dirty, that touch is reserved for man and wife only, that our urges can overcome even the most innocent of desires, and that we're bound to lose our control—tumbling headfirst into sin.

But Leo's hands don't feel sinful. They feel reassuring, protective, comfortable. Maybe I shouldn't trust him–maybe I'm as horrible and stupid and terrible as they claim my sister to be, but I don't feel any of those things.

I've never thought any of those things about my sister either. No matter how many mistakes she makes or how many rules she breaks, I still love her. I still find her comforting, protective, and reassuring. Maybe that's why I feel safe around Leo, and maybe I shouldn't. Maybe I'm stupid.

One hand wraps around my back. "Is this okay?" he asks.

I nod lightly.

"Kick your legs up and lean back until you're

facing the sky," he says. "I'm going to keep my hand on the middle of your back so you don't go anywhere. I'll hold you steady, and you just float. See if you feel like you're in a different world."

I lean into the secure warmth of his palm, kicking my feet out. The waves roll beneath me, but Leo doesn't let me lose control. I stay in place, swaying along with them. I feel the water glide against my skin as it moves within the water. I feel weightless and light.

I've gone swimming before, but always in swimming pools, with a lot of people around. I was taught to swim at the country club my mom enjoys frequenting back home. I was taught it was impolite and embarrassing to splash too large or laugh too loud. Dahlia never cared, and she was always scolded for it. I didn't want to bring any more negative attention to us, so I padded along quietly or read a book on the steps.

I've never floated like this, with someone holding my back, supporting me and keeping me in place while also allowing me to feel free. I would've never been allowed to get this close to a boy before. In my small town, rumors would fly—like they have for my sister.

I know some of the rumors I've heard about her are true. I know she has an older boyfriend, Jason. I know she and Jason have sex. I know my dad called her a whore when he found out. I know he slammed our front door so hard the glass in the window shattered. He told her she had ruined herself. Yet, I don't think she is a whore or a bad person. I don't think of her as ruined or less than. Still, I know I'd think all those things about myself if I made the same choices she had.

As I float underneath the pier, vibrant colors splashing across the space around me, I can't help but look up at Leo's face. The heathen is staring down at me, a knowing smile plastered across his lips, as if he can already see I've found that other world he speaks of, that world he feels here too.

A world where this isn't wrong, where this moment is just as right as it feels like it is.

With that thought, I inhale deeply and drop my legs, letting my entire body dip beneath the surface. I feel Leo's arm move from my back as I let out all the air in my lungs and sink down until my feet hit the sand below us. Pushing off, I propel myself upward, breaking with the waves and returning to the world again.

I push my wet hair from my eyes and blink, eyes readjusting to the darkness and the harsh flashing lights. Those blue eyes sparkle at me, and those dimples twinkle.

"World feeling a little less loud, Honeysuckle?"

I smile at him as we both tread water, hidden in our world within the waves beneath a sleeping town.

Eight

Honeysuckle

Now. May 28th.

"That letter wasn't supposed to be a cry for help, Dal." I gasp into my hand.

The room feels as if it's closing in on me.

She folds me against her chest. "Then what was it for?"

"I don't know." I cry into her neck, my voice muffled in my tears. "I told myself it was closure, but maybe subconsciously... Maybe I was asking the universe to save me from the wedding I didn't really want."

She chuckles against the side of my head. "Enter me, stealing a pen."

We both laugh, and when I pull back from her, I notice her crying too. She tucks a stray hair behind my ear. She looks older than me now but not in a negative way. She looks regal. Mature. Like she's lived. So different from the wild child she once was.

With our small, two-year age gap, we've spent much of our lives looking so alike we're often mistaken for twins. Now, though, she looks grown up. I feel so young. Naive.

Dahlia's face takes on a solemn, serious expression now. "Why didn't you tell me how you were feeling about any of this?"

"Because I didn't want it to be real." My voice cracks. "I felt like I was in too deep. I'm still in too deep. I thought that, as time went on, I could convince myself to love him." A sob breaks from my throat. "So, I kept hiding it all, and Leo...he didn't feel real to me anymore. He feels like a teenage dream, the story of a first love, not something that still exists. The idea of him felt like a safe place to unload those feelings because he felt like a void I could throw them in. No solutions, but no repercussions, either."

My eyes meet hers—blue, where mine are hazel, though they house the same sadness. We've always been able to feel the other's emotions this way. I felt this despair the day my parents sent me away to spend the summer with our grandma so they could hide what they thought would be her biggest regret, though it turned out to be her highest blessing.

Maybe that could happen to me, too: the suffocation, the hopelessness I feel so deeply when I imagine walking down that aisle. Maybe it's not too late to stand my ground to turn it into a blessing, to be strong like my sister is.

"I don't want to marry him, but I feel like I've waited too long to change my mind."

Dahlia shakes her head. "It's never too late to change your mind, Darby." She begins to slip out of the sleeves of her dress. "I'm going to order you a taxi. Take it wherever..." She looks down at the note in my hand again. "Wherever it is you want to go. If you're not sure where, then take it to Wichita. I'll pay the extra fees for the long haul. Find yourself a hotel and give yourself a break."

My mind is blank of words, of thoughts. I only watch my sister as she shimmies out of her dress and down to her Spanx.

"Why are you getting undressed?"

"We're going to switch outfits. I don't have any casual clothes here, and I figure a formal gown is preferred to pajamas if you're going to run off in public." She shrugs. "Plus, if anyone sees you beelining it toward the back exit, they'll think you're me."

I only shake my head. "No, Dal. I can't."

She sighs. "You need a break. You need to clear your head without the distraction of...everything. Go figure out what's going on with summer boy...or don't. Either way, just do something you want to do without the expectations of those around you."

"What about calling off the wedding? Telling Dad? Jackson?"

Guilt swirls within my stomach.

She huffs. "What if I told you I'm pretty sure he's fucking his assistant? Would that make you feel any better?"

"No?" My stomach drops. I don't love Jackson, but I don't love the idea that I've been being cheated on either. "I need to tell him at the very least. I can't let him stand up there, waiting for me not to show. He'd be humiliated." I meet my sister's eyes. "I know I won't break his heart, but I will embarrass him, and humiliating him will hurt him more than losing me ever would. Plus, his career—this town—is everything to him. I've run away before without an explanation. I won't do that again. I can't burn another bridge like this."

Dahlia grabs my face between her hands. "I'll take care of that. I'll make sure he can sneak out of here before anyone finds out what's going on, but I need to get you the hell out of dodge first, okay? I'll take care of everything else. I just need you to go before you get sucked into a lifetime of misery." She pauses. "Be selfish for once, Darby. Please."

She doesn't realize how deep those words cut, because I've been selfish before. That selfishness included me running away exactly as I am now. That selfishness destroyed me in ways I still haven't been able to overcome. I've always been selfish.

I close my eyes and breathe, taking a moment to compose myself. Coming to a decision, I say, "Okay, but I need to leave Jackson a note. Let me explain myself."

Dahlia grabs the envelope that Leo's note was nestled in and wrangles a pen from the bag she brought inside the bathroom with us. I scribble across the back of the envelope.

You know, neither of us truly wanted this. We both deserve real love. I hope you find it.

\- *D*

"Can you take it to his room along with the ring? I don't want to keep it," I say. "Oh, and please make sure he's pulled away from the rest of the groomsmen when he finds out."

Dahlia nods rapidly. "Yes, yes. I'll treat the fragile man with the utmost sensitivity, I promise."

Dahlia and I make quick work of switching outfits and unpinning my hair from all the rollers. My tension headache instantly lifts while my sense of dread plummets into the depths of my body. I know what I'm doing will have irreversible consequences.

The last time I made a decision like this, it ended with the irreparably broken shell of my former self. Yet, somehow, I feel like running away from this wedding today may be the last chance I have at ever finding a way to piece myself back together.

"What will everyone think of me, Dal?" I ask as we sneak down the back hallway of the church to the door that will lead me outside to...wherever I'm meant to go next. I don't think further than my current step. I don't think of anything beyond him. I wonder how he felt about the fact that I was just hours away from marrying a God-fearing man in a big white church.

"They'll think you're the sweet, simpering good girl who was corrupted by her evil, spinster sister who's bitter about her lacking love life." She smiles sweetly.

"That's not funny, Dahlia."

"No, it's not, but that's how I'm going to spin it." She shrugs casually, as if further ruining her reputation is of no consequence, as if the very thing I've been most afraid of my entire life is hardly an afterthought to her.

I pull her arm, shoving us back into the corner of the stairwell near the back door. "You cannot do that," I hiss. "You can't do that to yourself. To Lou."

"I'm trying to protect Lou from this very type of pressure. Never in her life will she feel the need to do something that makes her unhappy for the approval of me or anyone else. You being strong and brave right now, Darby, is the exact kind of example I want to set for my daughter."

Well, that does it.

I'm crying again.

My sister's eyes are a piercing blue flame. "I don't give a shit what anyone in this town thinks of me. I don't give a shit about upsetting Mom and Dad. You've overcorrected my mistakes your entire life. You've been the golden girl because I've been the black sheep." I notice tears beginning to well as she blinks hard and looks away. "I can't help but feel like the reason you were mere moments away from going through with a wedding you didn't want is because of me. It's my fault you've felt so much pressure to make up for all my wrongs."

"No, Dahlia. I never..."

"Yes, you did, so let me make up for it now, okay? I'm already spoiled goods, so I'll handle everything here. You go, Darby. Go find yourself, and know that Lou and I will be here, waiting at the end of the road. I promise."

"Lou," I whisper. "I didn't even get to say goodbye."

My niece was in her chair when we snuck out of the bridal suite, getting fully pampered by the stylists as the flower girl. I know she was in heaven when I stepped away, and I can't help but feel guilty. I feel like I'm abandoning her.

Dahlia pulls me into her arms. "I know. I'll make sure she knows how much you love her, and I'll make sure she understands why you've left." She chuckles against my neck. "And I'm going to go steal the photographer for a photo shoot of her in her dress anyway. She'll be so excited she won't even miss you." We laugh through our tears as she pulls away and levels her face with mine again. "It's time for you to go. Don't worry about anything else. I'll take care of it."

I take a deep breath, reaching for the handle of the back door. Stepping over that threshold will inevitably change my life forever. I may never be able to show my face in this town again.

My father may very well want nothing to do with me after the humiliation I'm about to cause him. Yet, as I gaze back down the hallway that leads to the altar, there is no part of myself saying I want that. I don't want to be tied to a man who sees me primarily as a business transaction. I don't want to be a breeding mare, a homemaker in a house that has never, for one second, felt like home to me.

No, I don't want that.

"Call me wherever you settle for the night so I know you're safe."

I nod, stepping out the back door into the church parking lot. The ride my sister ordered for me waits at the curb. I slide across the leather interior, and cool air blasts me from the front seat.

"Where to, miss?" a woman with a slight southern drawl asks.

I pull the card from my purse, rereading the note he left me.

Meadow Creek Inn. Room 616.

Four squeezes, okay?

Heathen

Nine

Heathen

Then. June 21st.

"You really are a heathen," Darby says as she follows me down the hill toward town. "It's illegal to jump from the pier."

I wave her off. "Honeysuckle, we do this every single Saturday. It's why we go early in the morning—so we don't corrupt any tourists, yourself not included. It's our ritual, and you should feel honored I'm inviting you to join."

She huffs, and I fight a smile as I realize she continues following me anyway.

"If my grandma finds out, she'll kill me."

"Didn't you say your grandma is at her knitting club today?" I ask, even though it's something I already know. In a totally not-a-stalker sort of way, I know Diane Andrews's schedule pretty well. I didn't know she was in a knitting club per se, but I know she leaves her house between nine o'clock in the morning and noon every Saturday. Most weeks, she leaves again around four in the afternoon and returns before seven.

We use the times she isn't home to sneak through her backyard and down to the hidden cove, though I haven't been down there since Darby got to town. My friends think it's because I'm protective over the area, but I'm not sure that's true. I told her about it already, but she hasn't brought it up again, and neither have I. It's because I know that trekking down to the cove is dangerous, and I don't want her going down there by herself.

Darby and I have gone back to my spot at the pier three times since I first showed it to her last week, and she seems to grow more comfortable with me each time we go, sharing more bits and pieces of her life in Kansas—who she is. I share parts of myself with her too. The more I get to know her, the more I realize what kindred spirits we are. Our upbringings couldn't be more different, but somehow, we've ended up with similar struggles.

She calls hers wolves, and she calls mine ghosts.

I've never put a title on those thoughts before, but ghosts seem to be the right word. Literal, even.

My spot beneath the pier has always been my way of escaping those ghosts, but I never really felt like they left me. I just felt like they were waiting on the shore, watching me. The moment my feet were planted back on dry ground, they'd invade my mind again.

But with Darby, it feels like she scares them away. She's daylight to their darkness. They disappear when she's around, and I don't find them creeping back in until I'm alone in the black of my bedroom, hoping sleep will take me before they do.

It doesn't always.

I haven't told Darby all the reasons for my ghosts, and I don't think she's told me every aspect of her wolves either, but we've shared enough to understand each other. To form a budding friendship, even. I've found myself beginning to trust her in a way I've only ever trusted Everett, possibly even with parts of me I haven't shown him.

I told her I live with the Ramoses, though I haven't told her why, and she hasn't asked. I think she can sense me, read me, knows how deep I'm willing to go and doesn't push me any further than that, just like I didn't push her any deeper into the water that first night we swam together. Not until I let her figure out for herself how big a risk she was willing to take.

Every day I spend with her, I go a little deeper, trust her a little more. I think she does with me too.

Today is the first time I've invited her to spend time around my friends, though. They can be a bit of a reckless bunch, and I didn't want to scare her away. She's opened up in the three weeks she's been here, and I didn't want to send her spiraling back inside herself.

Darby may not be willing to participate in all the crazy shit my friends and I get into. I doubt she's going to be willing to jump off the pier with us today, but I trust her enough now to at least come. I trust her enough to know that no matter what stupid shit my friends say around her, she'll still open the window later tonight when I throw rocks at it. She'll still smile at me with that golden grin and chase away the ghosts that haunt me with her sunlight.

Secretly, I hope she'll hit it off with my friends, my family. Maybe even Elena, who's the closest thing to a sister I've ever had, who's just as secretive and silent as I am in my darkest moments. Elena needs a friend who can help her escape her shell, and I think Darby may need that, too, but in a different way.

I know Darby is only here for the summer, that she'll eventually return to Kansas, but knowing she's only temporary doesn't make me want to be around her any less. If anything, it makes me want to savor every moment a little more.

"Why do you jump off the pier every Saturday?" she asks.

"When we were twelve, Everett dared me to jump off the pier. One thing to note about me, Honeysuckle, is that I am physically incapable of turning down a dare. It's not in my DNA." She lets out an exasperated laugh as she trails behind me. I still can't believe I convinced her to sneak out of her grandma's house again this morning. "Anyway, Everett dared me to jump from the pier, which is super high up. Plus, there's a thousand-dollar fine for anyone caught jumping from it.

"So, I waited until that Saturday. We all went down early in the morning, before the shops began to open, when there weren't any people around. I jumped because I'm a badass, of course."

"Of course," Darby chimes sarcastically.

"Then, I dared Everett to do it. The next weekend, we went back, and he did. He then dared Zach, who dared Elena, who finally dared August. Week after week, we returned, and one of us took the leap. Then, we mutually decided that the next person not to jump from the pier would be the loser. We've been coming every Saturday morning for five years."

"What happens to the loser?" Darby asks.

I pause before glancing back at her. "I have no idea, Honeysuckle. We never talked about it."

She snorts, a small giggle bubbling from her lips. I smile at the sound of it. "So, should I assume someone is going to dare me to jump off the pier, then?"

I shake my head. "No. I told my friends to leave you alone."

We reach the boardwalk, the sun bright behind us, glistening on the widespread ocean, making it appear blue and gold at the same time. The palm trees are a vivid green as they sway in the breeze, the smell of sand and salt and sunscreen overwhelming my senses.

"Why do you want to bring me with you then?" Darby asks.

I stop walking, allowing her to catch up to me before I reach back for her arm and spin her around so she's facing me, a ray of sunlight flowing directly onto her rosy cheeks. Her skin is already more golden than it was when she arrived just weeks ago. A few freckles dot the bridge of her straight nose and the apples of her cheeks. Her eyes look like pools of honey, molten beneath the warmth of the sun as they blaze through my own.

She's waiting for me to say something, I realize, as I watch her tongue slide between her pouty lips, swiping across her bottom one before she pulls it beneath her teeth. I find myself smiling, watching her eyelashes flutter before her eyes dart away from mine.

"I want to bring you with me because you scare my ghosts away, Darby."

Her head whips sideways so she's looking at me again. She lets her bottom lip go, and her mouth hangs open slightly. It's shock I see on her face now—shock and surprise at my revelation. I can't believe I admitted it either.

Without allowing her to respond, I grip her wrist and drag

her down to the far end of the pier.

"Hi, Honeysuckle," all four of my friends drawl simultaneously.

I've already begun to receive shit from each of them about the apparent crush I have on the new girl in town. I don't care, though. I can't help myself—and none of them can blame me anyway. They've seen what she looks like. They're looking at her now, shooting me shit-eating grins because they see exactly what I see.

But I've also seen so much more. I've gotten to know her, so what they don't understand is that my attraction to her runs far deeper than they realize.

"Hi," she says shyly.

"I'm just showing Darby around the pier today, so leave her alone," I warn.

"You're looking beautiful this morning, Darby." Everett grins, winking at me.

I sigh, closing my eyes and looking up toward the sky as if I'll find the answers there.

"Oh. Thank you?" Darby says questioningly.

"Stop being a fucking creep," Elena adds. I open my eyes just in time to watch her shove him aside and step up to Darby. "He's not trying to be weird; he just has zero game when it comes to girls, and he's trying to fuck with Leo."

August busts up with laughter, and Elena's mouth twitches slightly as Everett shoves him. "Stop pretending like you think she's funny. You know she isn't funny."

Zach—a year older than Everett, Elena, and myself, two years older than August—rolls his eyes at all of us. "Stop fucking around and let's get this over with before it gets crowded." He nods toward Darby. "You jumping or what, new girl?"

She bites her lip and looks toward me, as if I'm supposed to save her. My heart hammers at that revelation.

"God, you are such an asshole," Elena mutters.

Elena and Zach have some weird, secretive, on-again-off-again relationship they try to hide from Everett–who is either a complete idiot or pretends to be oblivious to. It's exhausting for the rest of us to; August particularly loathes watching them.

Apparently, today is an off day.

"You love it," Zach rasps sarcastically.

Elena bares her teeth before Everett yells at everyone again. We finally get to stripping our clothes and throwing them into the waterproof bag Zach will jump with.

"You should try it," Elena says to Darby as she tugs her denim shorts off her legs. Darby seems to be watching the way both Zach and August stare at Elena as she undresses. Her eyes pull back to mine, wide and unsure. "It's not that scary," Elena adds. "It can be fun. Just saying." She smiles.

Elena has always had trouble making friends with girls. She can be a little aggressive, intimidating, and extremely antisocial around those she doesn't know well.

Growing up with a mega-social twin brother, she found herself falling in line with his friends and has never much cared to extend beyond the four of us, though I wonder if she wouldn't mind having a girl she could relate to from time to time.

Elena glances at me and winks as if to say: *I'm playing nice for your benefit.*

I walk over to throw my shirt into Zach's backpack when I brush past Darby and whisper in her ear, "I won't pressure you to do this, but I think you'd have fun if you did." I shove my shirt into the bag before turning back toward her. "And I'll keep you safe. I promise."

Her eyes roam my body, and I watch them snag on the tattoo that stretches across my ribs and abdomen. She drinks in my chest and my shoulders before finally resting on my face. As she shoots me a sly smile, I watch her fingers find the button on her shorts and pop them open.

"If I jump, I want to know the full story of your tattoo. How and where you got it and what it means."

I take a breath, knowing that there are meanings surrounding my tattoo that I've never disclosed to anyone, not even Everett. Yet, somehow, I can't say no to her. I want her to be with me when I leap off the pier today. I like that she's curious about my tattoo and that she cares enough to know these things about me.

I don't want to feel so strongly about that realization, but I can't help myself, so I smile back at her and nod. "Deal."

"She's taking the dare, you guys!" Everett shouts out. The rest of my friends cheer alongside him.

Five of us become six as we climb over the railing atop the pier and balance on the handrail. Darby stands on one end, Zach on the other, Elena, August, Everett, and myself in between. Without realizing it, Darby's hand stretches toward mine, and I take it greedily.

She looks at me, those honey eyes swirling with fear and anticipation—but also excitement.

I squeeze her hand four times. *I'll. Keep. You. Safe.*

We jump together, free-falling into the abyss.

Ten

Heathen

Now. May 28th.

I pull my head from my hands as the light rasp of knuckles on the hotel room door rings throughout my skull. Thoughts like: *why did I come here? and this is a mistake* vanish immediately.

I all but leap from the bed, striding across the room and throwing the door open. All thoughts empty from my head as I stare into the eyes of the woman whose sunshine used to light my life. The woman whose absence left a gaping black hole in the middle of my chest for much of the past decade.

We stare at each other for so long I think the sun fades across the sky, the moon rises, and the sun follows it again. Flowers bloom and die in the moment we take to soak the other in.

Long dark lashes fan out above those eyes—still pools of honey, though the gleam that used to brighten my world seems to have faded now. Her eyes look as haunted as I imagine mine do. The freckles I once loved so much appear to be covered by a dusting of makeup now, as if they're something to be hidden away. Her golden hair falls thickly around her shoulders in large waves. Her body is wrapped up in a sparkling, cream-colored dress that runs the length of her long legs. Cheeks flushed, eyes wide and red-rimmed, she studies me just as intently as I study her.

I watch her tongue scrape across her bottom lip, and a familiar hammering erupts in my chest. She pulls that lip beneath her teeth, giving me a look I know all too well, the kind of expression that makes it feel like I'm saving her.

"You came," she whispers, breaking the silence.

My hand flexes at my side, fighting the urge to reach for her, an instinct I've had since the day I met her.

"You needed me."

With those three words, her bottom lip begins to tremble before her face crumples entirely. She falls against the doorway, but my arm snaps out and wraps around her waist, tugging her against my chest. I guide her back inside the room, shutting the door with my foot.

"Honeysuckle," I murmur into the top of her head as I sit back on the bed, holding her against me.

Sobs rack her body harder at the name. I don't know what else to do than to press her head against my chest. She smells like fresh florals, the same shampoo smell I've remembered for so many years. Her body shakes, her hand fisting my T-shirt as I rock her side to side.

I don't know how else to help her right now, how else to soothe her. I don't know what's causing this reaction—if it's seeing me, hearing me tell her that I crossed state lines because I thought she needed me, or if it had more to do with the man she's supposed to be walking down the aisle to right now.

I don't know how I could possibly explain to her—explain to myself—the hurricane of dread that stormed through my body the moment I read those words. *I'm getting married in two weeks.* How wrong those words looked when it came to her. How I knew, if there was any possibility of getting her away from that wedding, I'd do whatever I had to ensure it didn't go through. How awful and selfish that made me feel.

I'll never be able to admit to her how it felt to imagine her walking down that aisle, marrying a man we both know she'll never love the way she loved me.

Having her in my arms feels like the last ten years of my life have suddenly been erased.

I've split my lifetime in two: before Darby and after Darby.

I haven't allowed myself to savor the blip of time that *was* Darby.

Not until this moment.

It hurt too much, and it was always too raw. So, I locked that summer away in its own private corner of my soul.

Darby's hand flexes against my forearm, as if I'm the only thing anchoring her to this world, and it suddenly feels a whole hell of a lot like something inside me is being set free for the first time in a while. Another part of myself tells me to catch it, smother it, stop it before it destroys me.

"Leo," she whispers against my chest, and I realize there's no point in fighting. She's always had the key to my heart.

She always fucking will.

I glance down at the same moment she tilts her head up, our eyes clashing like ocean waves against the sand. She studies my face for a long minute before her eyes flash with an unreadable expression. She looks around the hotel room, as if realizing her surroundings for the first time.

Suddenly, she's detangling from my arms, standing up and stepping away.

I stay on the bed, hopelessly watching her as she begins to pace across the floor.

She braces a hand on her forehead as her long dress shuffles with the movement of her legs. "Oh, God..." She sighs. "The guests..." She reaches the window, turns around, and walks back toward the bed, her eyes glued to the floor. "The flowers... The money..." She stops, turning to face me head-on. Her hands frame her face as she pulls her hair back. "My father."

I can see her blinking back tears as she looks up at the ceiling.

"I can't...I can't believe I did that..." She hides her face, and I see her chest heave. "Oh, God... I have to go back. I have to... I have to..." She looks around the room, as if she'll find answers there.

I feel helpless. I don't know what to do. I can only watch her pace the floor in an opulent gown that looks nothing like a wedding dress, but I'm too afraid to ask her about it in the midst of her breakdown. As if some outside force begins pushing me, I stand up from the bed and step into her.

She starts as I brace my hands on her forearms, holding her in place. "Darby," I say in a rough enough tone that she snaps out of her head and looks into my eyes. "Did you just notice how you didn't mention yourself? That you didn't mention him? You feel like you need to do this today because of the money that's been spent on it. Because of the people who are watching. Because of your father. It's not because you want this, not even because you think he wants this. It's because you feel obligated." I hold her in place as she panics. "Has anyone actually asked you if you want this? Asked you how you feel about all of it?"

She stills for a moment before giving her head a shallow shake.

"Then you don't owe them a goddamn thing."

Her eyes slowly flutter shut before she falls against my chest again. That instinct takes over, and I tug her into me. I can feel her panicked breaths, her heaving chest expanding against my own. "Breathe for me, honey." After a few long moments, she begins to calm. "What do you want right now? What do you need?"

Her words are muffled against my chest as she murmurs softly, "I need to get out of here."

That hurricane re-emerges in my stomach. "Out of this hotel room? Or out of this town?"

"Town," she says with a sigh, and I instantly settle at the sound of it.

"If you could go anywhere in the world right now, Darby, where would you go?"

She pulls back to look at me, emotion still bright in her eyes, though tears no longer fall. "I want to go to Pacific Shores. I want to go home."

Eleven

Honeysuckle

Then. June 21st.

Elena twirls around in the sand, shaking out her hair all over August like a wet dog. He laughs, blocking her with his T-shirt as he tries to put it back on.

Zach hovers close by, glaring at them both. Everett is digging around the shared backpack for something, and Leo walks back toward me, our clothes in his hands. I still don't own a bikini, and while I've gotten comfortable around Leo in just a bra and shorts when we're at our spot beneath the pier in the middle of the night, I still make sure to wear a one-piece any time I'm in public.

My bathing suit today is burnt yellow with ruffled sleeves. I bought it last year for a pool party I was attending, hoping for my dad's approval, since it didn't have a sloping neckline or midriff cutout. While he did ultimately approve of the suit, my sister told me I looked like a toddler taking swim lessons for the first time.

Leo approaches me with my T-shirt and shorts in hand, smiling as he extends them to me. He doesn't look at me any differently than he does when I'm in nothing but my undergarments. He never looks at me like I'm wearing too much or not enough. He always looks at me like he approves of all of it.

"That was amazing," he says to me, dimples popping. His blue eyes strain under the direct sunlight, but the way it reflects on them makes them appear identical to the sparkling water behind us—the same, ever-changing shade of blue. Even the ripples and the waves appear to be present within his irises.

"Yeah," I say breathlessly.

I didn't even realize I reached for Leo before we jumped, not until he grabbed my hand and squeezed it as we leaped. He never let go. Even after our bodies hit the water, in that stillness beneath the surface, he held onto me as we let the air leave our lungs and paused underneath the waves, letting the world fade away, knowing we both needed that moment.

He held my hand as we swam back to shore.

Leo laughs as we redress. "You feelin' like a heathen now, Honeysuckle?"

I swallow. "Yeah, a little." I let out a breathy chuckle. "I feel like I gave into the peer pressure they're always warning us about."

"Oh, please. We weren't telling you to do meth, Darby," Everett grumbles as he throws his arm around me and turns me away from Leo.

Once everyone is dressed, we begin making our way back down the boardwalk. Elena and the brothers walk together in front of Everett and me, and he's still keeping an arm around my shoulder as Leo trails behind us.

"New girl can hang, though," Everett says.

I chuckle, feeling lighter than I have before around this group. "Thanks, I guess?"

"Are you coming with us to Milo's party tonight?"

"Darby doesn't want to go to a party," Leo says roughly from behind us.

Everett clicks his tongue, finally letting me go as he skips ahead of me and then turns around to face us. "Think about it, Honeysuckle." He winks. "It'll be fun." His voice draws out as he turns back around and catches up to his sister.

"Who's Milo, and why don't I want to go to his party?" I ask.

Leo chuckles, running a hand through his sand-colored hair. "Milo is a guy we go to school with. He's got mega-rich parents and a super nice house up on the hill." He nods toward the cliffside directly in front of us, higher than the one my grandma and Leo live on. "His parents work out of the country often, so he has a lot of parties." He clears his throat. "Honestly, Darby, I hate that you used the word peer pressure back there.

"I think you've been far too sheltered, and I want you to know what it feels like to have fun. I think you should know this town is a lot different than the one you've grown up in. And yeah, you might be sneaking around your grandma, but I've known her for years, and I've got a gut feeling she's a lot more understanding than your parents. I think this summer could be a good time for you to learn how to live without the fear of someone breathing down your neck and making you second guess everything you do."

I open my mouth to respond, but he continues before I can, "But I hate that word: pressure. I don't ever want you to feel like I or my friends have pressured you into doing something you don't want to do. The party is going to have drinking and rap music—which I'm sure your dad hates—and people will probably be hooking up. Getting loud. Being reckless. It might be too much for you, and I'll be damned if you get into a situation you don't want to be in and then blame me because you think I've coerced you into it."

I take a moment to gather my thoughts and soak in his words. We continue walking back down the boardwalk and toward our houses, but we're walking so slowly the rest of Leo's friends have already disappeared, gone their own ways.

"If I go to this party, will I be expected to drink? To...hook up?"

He huffs a laugh. "Of course not. But you're from out of town, and you're..." He waves his hand at me. "You look like that."

I frown. Is he referencing my swimsuit? Do I actually look like a toddler?

"I look like what?" I ask defensively.

He sighs. "You're beautiful, Darby. You'll get a lot of attention. You don't have to do any of those things. In fact, please absolutely do not hook up with anyone you meet at that party. I'm begging that of you." He laughs roughly.

I'm more focused on the fact that he called me beautiful than anything else. I feel my face heat under those words, under his blue-eyed gaze. I think about what he said about me deserving to have fun and being too sheltered, using this summer to live without fear. Maybe it could be a time for me to figure out who I really am, who I want to be once I leave Crestwell, Kansas.

"But you'll keep me safe, right?" I ask.

He stops suddenly, and I walk right into him. Stumbling back, he spins around and grips my forearms. His eyes pierce through me as he says, "Yes, Honeysuckle. Whatever you want to do, whatever you want to experience, I'll keep you safe. I've got your back. I won't let anyone hurt you, and I won't let you hurt yourself. I'll do my best to ensure you don't get caught doing anything less than appropriate by your parents' standards—I'm good at not getting caught, by the way."

I laugh at that. "You'll do all that just because I chase your ghosts away?"

He licks his lips, pulling his bottom one beneath his teeth as if he's contemplating something. My eyes are fixated on his mouth, and suddenly, I'm very curious about what it tastes like. I've thought about kissing before—what it feels like, why people seem to get so caught up over it. It always seemed so simple to me.

I've never imagined kissing a specific person, though. I've thought about my first kiss, what would happen and how it'd make me feel, but there was never a face attached to the fantasy. I imagine that may be about to change as I watch Leo's lips glisten in the sunlight, full and pink and soft.

I think I've stopped breathing.

"No, Honeysuckle. I'll do all that just because I like you."

Twelve

Honeysuckle

Now. May 28th.

"Then let's get you home, Honeysuckle." I feel the warmth of his breath as he speaks against the side of my head. He smells like the ocean breeze I haven't experienced in years, and he feels like taking a deep breath after being underwater for far too long.

I panicked as I took the elevator to the sixth floor then paced up and down the hall for ten minutes before finally knocking. My stomach was on the floor as I waited to see his face again, to see his reaction, but I froze the moment I met those blue eyes.

He looks so different from the seventeen-year-old boy who whisked me off my feet those years ago. He looks like a man now—taller, broader, more defined. He has a sharper jaw, slightly darker hair, and eyes that have seen and done things his younger self could've only imagined, a soul that seems to understand real heartbreak peering down at me through those eyes.

I dissolve beneath them. I lose all my composure, and with an involuntary reflex, I reach for him, for the boy who kept his promises. Who kept me safe. Who made me feel alive and free, real and raw.

As he holds me now, I realize he's no longer that boy. He's a man. A man I betrayed and abandoned. A boy I broke. I don't deserve to be held by him.

I scramble back from his arms, and he immediately gives me space. I look down at my feet, unable to meet his eyes. "No, I can't.

I'm so sorry. I shouldn't be here."

My heart is racing again, as if his lack of touch sends me spiraling back into that panic.

"You're safe with me, Darby," he whispers quietly.

I shake my head. "No, I know... I just..." I finally find the courage to look at him. "I don't understand why you came. I don't know what I'm supposed to do, what *we're* supposed to do."

His face softens as he rakes his gaze along me. "Well, first, you should change out of that dress. I hope that's not what you planned on getting married in."

I can't help but let out a small laugh. "It's my sister's bridesmaid dress. She thought it would be better to escape in this than my pajamas." I laugh again; it sounds so stupid.

"I think the pajamas would've been preferable, although anything is better than the wedding dress itself."

A giggle bursts from me. "Oh yeah. My dress was all tulle, with a high neckline and long sleeves in the middle of June. It had a three-foot radius around the skirt, and I looked like one of the evil stepsisters from *Cinderella*."

"Sounds like I would've hated it."

I snort. "You would have. It was hand-picked by my father."

Leo is quiet for a moment before he says, "I came because you needed me, because I promised you that I'd be there for you if you asked. I came because you deserve better than this." He pauses until I finally meet his eyes. "I'm here to be whatever you need from me. You want to go home? I'll take you home, Darby. I've got a car. I'll find a plane. A submarine. I don't fucking care. Just say the word."

"I can't ask that of you, Leo."

"Ask what of me, Darby?" He lets out an exasperated laugh. "I already came all this way. You'd be doing me a disservice if you didn't at least let me entertain the idea of coming to your rescue."

I chew on my lip, crossing my arms as he towers over me, his eyes searching my face for some kind of answer. The whole interaction feels too uncomfortable to fully register. I still don't feel as if my brain is fully comprehending where I am, who I'm talking to, what I've done. I have no way of knowing how I'm supposed to handle this situation. How am I supposed to talk to him, address our past, move forward from it?

The inability to confront my demons activates my flight response. It tells me I'm not supposed to be here with him, with anyone. The only instinct in my body shouts that I need to get away from all of it.

Willing all the courage I have left, I look into the eyes of the boy whose heart I broke and ask, "Can you take me to the airport?"

Thirteen

Honeysuckle

Then. June 21st.

The music roars as we pull up to the mansion in Zach's Toyota Camry. He's the only one of the group with a car. Apparently, Elena and Everett's dad owns a mechanic shop, where Leo and Everett both work during the summer, so they have cars they borrow and swap out from time to time, but neither of them has something to call their own. Zach and August share the Toyota, but since Zach is older, it's really his car.

Leo doesn't have a car for the same reason Elena and Everett don't, since he lives with them. I'm curious about his history with his own parents, but I haven't pushed him on that yet, just like he doesn't push me any further than I want to go when I speak of my own.

I always thought the house I grew up in was big and elaborate, but it's nothing compared to the place that stands in front of us now. It looks like a miniature White House, with columns in the front and grand double doors at the entrance. Music blares from inside so loudly I swear you can hear it for miles.

Gravel crunches beneath the car as it comes to a stop in front of the house, and Zach turns off the engine. We all climb out, and I find myself sticking to Leo's side. He doesn't seem to mind as he wraps an arm around my shoulder and tucks me into him. "The guys here are going to give you a lot of attention, attention you may not be comfortable with. So, tonight, you're mine, Honeysuckle. I won't let anyone come near enough to touch you—not unless you ask me to."

"I won't," I promise. The only person I want near enough to touch me is him. The fact that he just called me his and made that kind of claim on me—even if just to protect me from other guys—has my stomach doing kickflips in a way I've never felt before.

He lets out a sigh that sounds like relief, and my stomach flips at that too.

I went home after our jump from the pier before my grandma returned from her knitting club. I went to the farmer's market with her, and she asked me a lot of questions about Leo and how much time I've been spending with him. I mumbled answers that weren't lies but weren't the whole truth, either. She warned me again to keep my wits about me but didn't press further. I can only hope she won't tell my dad about it, that she won't realize I've snuck out again tonight.

The pebbles hit my window around ten o'clock. My grandma has always been an early riser, so she goes to bed early. Luckily, her bedroom is on the first floor, behind the dining room. The staircase and the backdoor are both on the other end of the house, so it's not difficult for me to sneak downstairs and out the back without making enough noise to wake her.

Zach and the rest of Leo's friends were waiting in the car for him to get me. They parked a block over so my grandma wouldn't be woken up by the sound of the engine or slamming doors.

I wasn't sure what teenagers normally wore to house parties, so I decided to go with a blue cotton dress dotted with daisies that cinched at my waist with a drawstring bow and flowed out down to my knees. I curled the ends of my hair and let them rest thickly past my shoulders. I notice Elena is wearing a pair of shorts and an old band T-shirt, and I suddenly feel overdressed.

I tug at the end of my dress, trying to adjust it.

"You look beautiful," Leo whispers into my ear. "Another reason I'm going to have to go all neanderthal on these other guys tonight." He laughs against my head.

"I feel overdressed," I murmur, looking at Elena, who has her arm looped through August's, Zach following at her heels.

Leo traces my line of sight before chuckling. "No, you're perfect. Trust me. She is underdressed."

The house smells sour as we walk inside, like stale beer. The music continues to blare, fading into the background behind the noise of people shouting and laughing. There are bodies around each corner, but most pay us no attention, though some stop to greet Leo. Some girls give him a one-armed side hug because his other arm is wrapped around my shoulders. Guys fist bump him as they eye me curiously—sometimes with interest, but Leo only holds me tighter when they do. He keeps me close, casually introducing me to others, though I don't pick up any of their names.

A tall dark-skinned boy with hazel eyes and curly hair down to his shoulders makes his way toward us. He's wearing jeans and a Bob Marley T-shirt with no shoes, a bottle of some kind of beer in his hand as he extends his fist to Leo. "Hey, man. I haven't seen you all summer. Glad you made it up tonight."

Leo returns the gesture. "Hey, Milo. How have you been?"

"I just got back from Greece, so I really can't complain." Milo flashes a wide grin. "How's the surf here?"

"Been out there every day. Waves get choppy in the afternoons, so we've been surfing in the morning. It's going damn good, though," Leo says.

"You better keep at it if you want my dad to sponsor you when you're a professional someday." Milo winks, giving Leo a slap on the back.

I didn't know he wanted to be a professional surfer.

Milo's gaze finally finds me tucked beneath Leo's arm. His eyes rake up and down my body before a small smile creeps up on his face. "Waves not the only thing you're riding this summer, Graham?"

I frown—not only because of what he just insinuated, but because I also realized I didn't know Leo's last name.

"Watch it, Sanchez," Leo warns. His tone is light and playful, but at the same time, invited no room for negotiation. It's a dare for Milo—or anyone else—to make another comment about me. "This is Darby. She's visiting for the summer, and you're going to be nice to her." Milo's brows raise before he glances at me and looks me over again, a smile hinting at his lips. "She'll be going home with me—only me—tonight."

I catch Everett smirking from the corner of the room. Elena and August are talking with two people I don't recognize near the kitchen, but I think I catch a glimpse of a knowing smile on their faces too.

Milo shoots Leo a shit-eating grin while simultaneously sticking his hand out toward me. I return the shake as he says, "It's so nice to meet you, Darby. We've been waiting for someone to put our boy here on a leash."

I turn toward Leo, searching for an explanation for that comment. He only huffs and rolls his eyes.

As if manifesting from thin air, a beautiful brunette appears next to Milo. Long legs are accented by long hair that flows past her waist. It's pin-straight and voluminous at the same time. Her green eyes are bright as emeralds, and her skin is deeply tanned.

"Hi, Leo," she says with a strenuously fake smile, a false chirp and glitter to her voice. While she greets him, her gaze is on me, soaking in my skin, my eyes, my face, the dress I have on, my height, my lack of curves. Disappointment highlights her face at every piece of me she studies.

"Amaya," he says just as strenuously. "How has your summer been?"

She shrugs, as if she couldn't care less about the conversation. "Fine. And yours?"

"It's going well." He clears his throat. "This is Darby."

Her gaze flicks up and down my body again. "Nice to meet you," she says in a tone that sounds like it is certainly not nice to meet me.

"You too," I murmur.

She tosses her hair behind her shoulder and turns away. "Are you coming, Mi?" Her fingers trail down his arm sensually.

Milo huffs a laugh. "My bedroom is going to be occupied tonight, but if you guys need a place to...be alone, you can use any of the upstairs guest bedrooms." He winks, gripping Amaya's hand as they walk away.

Leo and I turn to each other at the same time. He looks uncomfortable, embarrassed, maybe slightly pained. For some reason, it makes me laugh. "Excuse my language, but what the fuck was all that?"

His eyebrows skyrocket into his hairline before he begins laughing, too. He takes a moment to compose himself before finally saying, "I'm so sorry. Amaya is...my ex. I guess. I don't really know." He runs a hand through his hair. "I expected her to be here tonight, but I didn't expect her to act that way. I'm really sorry."

My mouth drops open. "She was the last girl you dated?"

He shrugs. "She's the only girl I've ever dated, really."

I let out all the air in my lungs. "She's beautiful."

"Beautiful and mean, Honeysuckle."

I look at him, expecting his eyes to be following the girl he might've once loved as she leads another guy up the stairs, but he's only staring at me. "You called me beautiful and deadly."

He smiles. "Deadly in a good way."

We don't speak again as he takes me around the party, introducing me to a few more people. I'm offered a red cup, and I take it, not wanting to be rude and decline. Leo pulls me away from the guy who offered it to me and tells me it's rum punch.

I've been told not to drink alcohol, but I've also been told not to sneak out. Not to hang out with boys who don't believe in God. Never to attend a party like this. I figure adding one additional item to the list of Things I Should Never Do won't hurt. Plus, Leo makes me feel safe. So, I take a sip.

It's good. Like, really good. So, I take a few more sips. Next thing I know, my cup is empty. I ask Leo for another. He looks at me like he wants to say no, but he doesn't. He gets me more. I drink that cup too.

Guys continue to ask me questions, Leo continues to be territorial, and the more I drink, the more my belly fills with warmth, and my chest flutters as I watch him shove people away from me. I like it so much I might be sick over it.

My head starts to get hazy, and I think it might be the alcohol, but I also think it might be Leo. He seems to glow when he laughs, and it feels like bells chiming in my soul. Even in the dim lighting of a house party in the middle of the night, his blue eyes sparkle the way most eyes only do in sunlight. My body is extra warm in all the places he touches me: his arm around my shoulder, his hand at my waist. He's never not touching me, and I savor that.

I want to know what it feels like to be touched by him everywhere, all the time.

I wonder if Amaya knows what that feels like.

Suddenly, my stomach flips.

"You said people come to these parties to hook up?" I ask Leo as we migrate to the corner of the living room next to a grand fireplace. The couches are littered with kissing couples. Some people dance in the middle of the room. Outside, there are people swimming, and others play drinking games in the kitchen.

He waves in front of us at the couches. "Clearly."

"Is that what you do?" I ask. "What you used to do with Amaya?" I can't stop myself from saying her name with disdain. Leo looks at me with surprise. "No, Darby. I've never hooked up with anyone at any party." He huffs a laugh. "That's precisely why Amaya and I didn't work out, why none of my flings ever tend to work out."

"So you have *dated* more than one girl?"

He chuckles, taking a sip from the beer in his hand. "Not really. I've had a few I've been interested in here and there, but Amaya is the only one I really tried to make it work with, and even then, it wasn't enough."

"I've been on one date," I find myself saying. "My dad will only let me date boys from church, and only once he's met their parents and both families have spent chaperoned time together." I gulp from my red cup, feeling a bit of liquid run down my chin before I wipe it away with my hand. "William—that's his name—and I have gone to church together for years. He finally asked me on a date. He picked me up in his Subaru and had his shirt tucked in." I'm not sure why I included that detail. "We went to the movies. He's always been polite and kind to me. Always a gentleman. He opened my door and bought my tickets and my popcorn, complimented the dress I wore."

I sigh. "About halfway through the movie, he put his arm around me. I didn't think too much of it, but then his hand started to trail a little lower than it should. Next thing I knew, he was cupping my breast." I don't miss the way Leo's eyes briefly dart to my chest before meeting my own again. "I kept adjusting myself to shrug it off, but he moved each time I did. I didn't say anything. Maybe I should have." I take another sip. "Then, on the drive home, he put his hand between my legs, trying to...rub me. I finally told him he should keep both hands on the wheel, that I didn't want to distract him." My skin feels numb as I think back on the memory. "He laughed and pulled over into an empty parking lot about three blocks from my house. He shut the car off and leaned over the seat, putting his hand between my legs again—more firmly that time. He brought his lips to my neck, told me he'd been waiting forever to touch me, to finally have a piece of me." I shiver. "That he couldn't wait to know what I feel like."

Leo's nostrils flare, and I notice his fingers turn white from how hard he's pressing into his beer bottle. "What did he do to you, Darby?"

I swallow. "Nothing." I shake my head. "I got out of the car before he realized he hadn't locked it, and I ran away. I hid behind the shrubs in someone's yard until he drove off, and then I ran home." Leo lets out a sigh of relief. "But the next week at school, he told everyone we had sex anyway. The rumor flew around town like wildfire, and by the time I got home that day, my mom had already heard. She knew the rumor wasn't true, because as soon as I had gotten home from the date, I told my parents everything. They could tell I had been running. I was dirty from hiding in the bushes. I was distraught and upset. They believed me, thankfully."

"Of course they should believe you."

I shrug. "It's not that easy with them. Anyway, they made William write an apology letter to be published in our congregation's newsletter, as well as the school paper. It didn't matter, though. People at school called me a prude. They still make fun of me, saying I'm a tease because I let him pay for my movie and my food but didn't 'give him anything back.'" I put up my fingers to air-quote the words. "They say I'll die a virgin." For some reason, I snort out a laugh at that.

I look at Leo to find his face is red, his jaw tight. He's still squeezing the bottle so hard it looks like it could burst. He looks downright infuriated. "I'm sorry," I whisper. "I didn't mean to upset you. I shouldn't have said anything."

His eyes meet mine and immediately soften. "I'm not upset with you, Honeysuckle. Never with you. I'm fucking disgusted that a boy thought he was entitled to your body, that he assaulted you, and when that came to light, it was turned on you."

"My parents were really just concerned with my reputation." I shrug. "The rest of it was swept under the rug."

We'd been standing shoulder to shoulder beneath the hearth when he suddenly steps in front of me, blocking out the rest of the room. The rest of the people in it. The rest of the world. "You need to understand that the only person with authority over your body is you, you and whomever else you allow. No one is entitled to your body, nor are they entitled to what you do with it. That includes your parents." His blue eyes blaze, as if it's important to him that I absorb every word.

"What do you mean?"

He covers my hand with his own, running his thumb across the ring on my left hand. My purity ring. "If you want to save yourself for marriage, I think that's great, but if you're telling yourself you need to do so because your dad told you to, or because you're afraid of being punished by your religion, that's not okay either." He sighs. "Any choice you make in life surrounding your body, Darby, you need to ensure it's yours."

My head is hazy, my mind heavy behind my eyes. I feel as if my mouth begins to move on its own accord as I speak. "I don't know what I want, honestly. I've always been a little afraid. My sister... She fell in love with a guy who wasn't deserving of what she gave him. He took from her until he sucked her dry. He's still sucking the life from her, I think." I look away from Leo, down at my feet. My toes are painted light pink, because my mom says it's a good color for my skin tone. I kind of wish they were yellow instead. "He breaks her heart again and again, and I can't help but think it hurts a little extra because she gave him...everything." I lift my head again, suddenly feeling heavy in my chest too. I miss my sister. My parents still won't tell me what she did. "I don't want to make the same mistake."

"Me either," Leo says.

"What do you mean?" I repeat.

He shrugs. "I think sex can be casual. I think every encounter comes with a vulnerability we open up for that other person, but with enough time and experience, we're able to process that differently—become less affected by it." He grips the back of his neck. "I think as long as two people go into it wanting and expecting the same thing, casual sex is great. But I also think that when you don't know how to block out that vulnerability—when you haven't learned how—it's impossible for sex to be meaningless.

"I think that when you allow yourself to be that raw—especially for the first time—it can feel like giving away a little piece of your soul. I think you can only learn to block that level of vulnerability with experience. So, when that happens for the first time, it's impossible not to give a piece of yourself away to that other person, a piece of you they keep forever."

I feel every word he says deep in my bones. I let them settle there, realizing just how similar Leo and I truly are, how his words seem to effortlessly explain the feelings I've never known how to voice—how to process. His eyes dance around the room, but mine burn straight through him, wanting—needing—to soak in every word he says, as if I could live off his voice alone.

Finally, that sapphire gaze meets mine. I feel the air leave my lungs at the intensity of it. He's always so intense when he looks at me, as if I somehow amplify every emotion he has. I think he may do that to me too.

"I haven't found anyone I want to give a piece of my soul to yet...and I don't want to take anything from someone else that I'm not willing to give back," he says finally.

I can only nod. Words gather on my tongue, but I don't know what they are or why I can't say them. I can only look at him. Study the planes of his face. The strength of his jaw and the small bump on the bridge of his nose. The way his eyebrows are slightly darker than the rest of his hair because it's kissed by the sun. I think all of him was kissed by the sun. I think he's beautiful.

"Stop looking at me like that, Honeysuckle." His voice is rough.

"Like what?" I ask, suddenly breathless.

His full lips part on an inhale as his tongue snakes out to rake across them. Maybe it's whatever I've been drinking, but I realize I very much want to know what that lip feels like between my teeth.

"Like you're wondering what a piece of my soul feels like."

I gasp, turning away before the blush I feel coming can completely surface. My eyes land on Elena across the room—she's smirking at me.

I watch her stride across the space between us. "You're drunk."

"No, I feel great."

Leo chuckles from behind me.

"Because you're drunk," she counters. "Come on, let's go dance."

I turn to look at Leo, and he smiles, dimples popping. "You don't need my permission. If you feel like dancing, go dance." He leans a little closer, whispering in my ear, "Just remember, Honeysuckle: if another guy touches you, I'll remove his arms."

Something about the tone in his voice tells me that threat isn't only for my benefit.

Elena laughs, long dark hair swaying as she pulls on my hand and drags me to the center of the room.

Fourteen

Heathen

Now. May 28th.

I open my mouth to tell her yes, to tell her again I'll literally do anything she wants. I know I shouldn't say that. I know it shouldn't be true. She looks at me as if she sees all the thoughts in my head, anyway, as if she knows she shouldn't be asking for my help, either. She knows I shouldn't be offering it.

But here we are: me offering the world on a platter, and her handpicking what she wants to take. It's such a familiar feeling it's hard for me not to grasp it and let it guide me. Then, I remind myself that I don't know her anymore. I had one summer with her, and this man had an infinity with her in comparison.

She was hours away from marrying someone else, belonging wholly to someone else.

While I only ever got pieces of her.

Another familiar feeling washes over me as I melt into her hazel eyes, the feeling that you've been longing for something your whole life, and you didn't know what it was until it was right in front of you. Like you've been missing a piece of yourself, but you had no idea what part until you suddenly find it.

There's so much to be unpacked between us. I'm not even sure if it's worth reopening at this point. We both have wounds that have clotted, and any conversation between us outside of the direct situation at hand could be dragging a serrated knife across a puckered scar.

Before we can even begin to consider how to approach our past, we need to get her out of that ugly-ass dress and out of this hotel, away from this town before her father comes looking for her—which I expect to happen any moment now. It sounds like he hasn't changed on that front.

I open my mouth to tell her just that when I hear a chiming coming from her dress.

She fumbles, sticking her arm into what I now notice is a big-ass pocket and fishing out her cell phone. She slides her thumb across the screen and presses it to her ear. "Dal?"

She raises a hand against her chest, her breath increasing as I hear a muffled voice speak a thousand miles a minute.

"I'm going to go get on a plane. I'm going to go to Pacific Shores. Grandma's house. Just...to get a break and figure out what I'm supposed to do next. Two weeks tops. Just tell Dad I'll call him when I'm ready."

She nods. "Yeah, I know." After a moment, her face drops slightly, and she looks at me. "Yeah...I am." Her brows knit at the center of her forehead. "I guess?" She slowly pulls the phone away from her ear and holds it out to me. "She, um, wants to talk to you."

I take her phone and press it against the side of my head. "Dahlia?"

A perky voice on the other side pipes up. "Oh, hi! I'm so happy she went to the hotel. She was hesitant, but I was pushing her. I knew you wouldn't come all this way just to tell her she's a raging bitch."

"Why would I ever say that to her?"

"She thought you were going to tell her off."

"I'd never do that," I rasp.

She laughs. "I know. Tell Darby that, not me." She clears her throat. "Look, I told Darby my dad is disappointed, and that Jackson left the church. I don't want to freak her out, but the truth is, all hell has broken loose here. Jackson is already on the way to my parent's house to see if Darby's there. My parents are still at the church, but they're losing their minds." She sighs as her voice lowers almost to a whisper. "They're hellbent on finding her and making this wedding happen. Jackson and my dad are humiliated. There's an hour before the ceremony is supposed to start. They've got all the guests here waiting. They'll drag her down that aisle by her fucking hair if they have to." She swallows, and I can feel the emotion pricking at her voice through the phone. "It's only a matter of time before Jackson realizes he can track her location on her phone, so as soon as we hang up here, I need you to turn her phone off. Take her to my house and have her pack a bag. Quickly. Then drive her to Wichita and get her on a plane. Get her the hell out of dodge, Leo. Tonight."

I nod. "I will."

I hear fumbling on the other end of the line. "Tell me your phone number."

I oblige, rattling it off as Darby watches me from the side of the room curiously.

"All right, please have her call me later. If I need anything from either of you, I'll call too."

"Got it." I hang up and Darby reaches out, but I don't hand her phone back. I power it off and slip it into the pocket of my jeans.

She watches me with an open mouth as I stride across the room, grab the one backpack I brought with me and the rental car keys, and sling my jacket over my shoulder. I press against the hotel room door and crack it open. "Let's go."

Darby's eyes narrow. "What was all that about?"

I flash a smile at her. "Operation 'Get Honeysuckle The Hell Out of Dodge.'"

Fifteen

Heathen

Then. June 21st.

I watch her blue dress flare and lift as she twirls around the living room in Elena's arms. They're the only two people at this party still dancing, and they don't seem to care at all. Darby is definitely tipsy, and I finally cut her off after her third mixed concoction.

I've never seen another person look so carefree, and as much as it makes my heart soar, it makes my chest drop in equal measure because I realize that never in her life has she had the ability to feel this way, and after this summer, she'll go back to that small town, to those judgmental people and her overbearing parents.

It's why I'm dead set on making this the best summer of her life.

Then, I'm a little afraid that once she leaves, I'll end up waiting around for her to return someday. That is, if she ever does.

I watch a stocky, sweaty guy with greasy hair that's far too long and eyes that stare far too intensely at Darby's legs walk up to her. He must not attend our school, because I don't recognize him.

If the shove he gives Elena isn't enough to set me off, the hand he places on Darby's waist as he spins her around to face him will.

She's still smiling, not realizing it's no longer Elena touching her as she turns around. She recoils as she finds the guy standing in front of her—touching her against her will. Elena is behind him, fuming. She's closing the distance between them, pushing him away as I maneuver toward them.

"Back the fuck off," he snaps at Elena.

Darby steps back from him, but her eyes are hooded. She's too drunk to really stand up for herself—if she even knows how.

"I'll fucking kill you where you stand," Elena barks back. *Dramatic.*

I brush past Elena and shove him by the shoulder he was touching Darby with. As he stumbles back, I wrap my arm around Darby's hips and spin her so she's tucked beneath my own. She sighs with relief as she settles into me. Her body feels limp in my arms, as if she's having trouble standing straight.

"Did she give you permission?" I ask.

"What?" he seethes.

"Did. She. Give. You. Permission? It's a simple fucking question. Did you ask if you could touch her? Did she say yes?"

He only scowls in response.

I smile. "That's what I thought. Get the fuck out of here." I wave him off. "Oh, and if I see you shoving my sister—or any other woman—like that again, I'll also kill you where you stand."

Elena snorts. She's always been hard and brash, probably the last person who needs any kind of protection. In fact, I know for certain she can kick my ass herself. Guys like that, though, aren't capable of understanding that a woman can be stronger, smarter, and meaner than them. I'd rather not have Elena get into a situation where she needs to defend herself, so I'll make my threat because I know it may weigh more than hers does.

"You get the fuck out of here with that shit," Elena mutters.

I knew she'd say that.

I laugh. "I will, actually. I'm going to order us an Uber and get her snuck back into her house before she passes out."

Elena pouts. "We were having fun."

"Yeah, we were having fun," Darby perks up from beneath my arm. I glance down to find the biggest set of honey eyes gazing up at me. She sticks her bottom lip out, and I swear to every god I don't believe in that if she keeps looking at me that way, I'll give her everything she's ever wanted.

"You can't even stand up straight, honey." I chuckle. "Do you even know where you are right now?"

She nuzzles her head against my chest. "I'm exactly where I want to be."

Oh fuck. That sentence feels like a prayer being answered.

I look at Elena, giving her a pleading expression. She knows me well enough to read my face, and she nods at me as she says to Darby, "Maybe you should let Leo take you home. Doesn't bed sound nice right now?"

Darby nods sleepily, and I mouth a thank you to Elena as I turn Darby toward the entrance. Our ride is a few minutes out, but it's warm enough that we can wait outside. As we reach the front door, I hear footsteps coming down the grand staircase and Milo's voice ringing out, "Are you leaving, man?"

I flash a smile at him. "Yeah. I'm going to take her home." I nod at the girl in my arms.

"Are you coming back after you put her to bed?" Amaya asks.

I shake my head. "I don't think—"

"No, because he'll be in bed with me," Darby says nonchalantly.

Several mouths drop open, including mine. I look back and forth between her and Amaya, who's now scowling. Milo is grinning. Elena is cackling in the corner. I don't know where Zach is, but August left a half hour ago, looking all pissed off. I was too caught up in Darby to bother asking him why or where he was going. Everett, I'm sure, is upstairs with some girl—or guy. There's no telling who he'll end up with at the end of the night. There are other people in the room, but I'm not paying attention to any of them.

"You sure that's a good idea in her...current state?" Amaya asks me in a sickly sweet tone.

Darby laughs. "Oh, I don't mean like that. I don't have to sleep with Leo in order to...sleep with him. Y'know?" She shrugs. "He likes it better in the morning, anyway."

A look of pure fury crosses Amaya's face, and Darby laughs

again.

Suddenly, there's a slow clap from the top of the stairs. We glance up to find Everett at the top of the stairs, smiling down on us with his wicked smile and sex-mused hair. "I think you've officially been corrupted, Honeysuckle."

Darby laughs, eyes wild as she slowly raises her hand to flip him off. There are tears in my eyes from laughing so hard as I lower her hand and pull open the front door. A blast of cool sea air hits me as I spin Darby around and lead her out of the house. I can only shrug at the rest of them as I follow my golden girl into the night.

My golden girl.

God, she is starting to feel that way.

I have the Uber drop us off a block away from Darby's house so we don't risk the sound of the car waking her grandmother. I'll have enough trouble getting her into the house without making too much noise.

She won't stop laughing. At everything.

My shoes. The way my hair flops onto my forehead, apparently. Our Uber driver, an older man named Henry, was absolutely smitten with her as she rambled on about how much she loved Cheetos. Henry even stopped at a gas station so I could buy her some.

As we turn the corner to her grandma's street, the only sounds are our feet hitting the pavement and the crunch of her eating. She silently extends the bag to me, and I fish one out.

I don't even like Cheetos.

I just like her. I like that she's sharing with me, so I'll force it down simply because she offered it.

She finishes the bag off as we reach her house. I pluck it from her hand and silently stuff it into the trash bin set at the end of her grandma's driveway.

"Quiet for me now, okay, Honeysuckle?"

"Are you coming inside?" she asks.

"Can you make it to your room on your own without making noise?"

She smiles, her eyes glistening playfully. She shakes her head. *Liar.* The car ride and the Cheetos sobered her up enough that she could make it up the stairs and to her room without a sound, but apparently, it didn't sober her enough to stop her from wanting me to sneak into her bedroom with her.

"You know it's not a good idea for me to come in, right?"

She shrugs. "Sneak out after I fall asleep?" She asks the question in such an innocent way, her eyelashes fluttering with the words, as if she can't bear to hear me say no.

I don't think I could. I don't think I'll ever be able to say no to her.

"Okay."

She bites her lip, hiding the smile I know she wants to take over her face. On instinct, I find my hand on her chin, my thumb tugging on that lower lip and removing it from her teeth. "Don't ever hide your smiles from me, Honeysuckle. I need to see every single one, especially the ones I put there." I move my hand to cup her cheek. "Show me every smile, and I'll do whatever you want, yeah?"

She giggles, and it feels as if I'm being blasted with a burst of light. I can't help but return it.

I grab her hand, leading her behind the house and through the gate until we reach the back porch. I pause, listening for any sound from inside the house and checking the windows for any source of light. There doesn't seem to be any, so we silently climb the steps to the glass door.

"Leo, wait," she whispers. She places her hand over mine on the doorknob, halting me. "I want..." She takes a breath. "I've never kissed someone before." *Fuck.* Why does that knowledge make my heart stutter in my chest? "I've never really wanted to, honestly," she continues. "But... I think I want to kiss you. I..." She looks at me, hazel eyes shimmering in the moonlight. "I want you to kiss me."

It feels like one of those moments where you suddenly realize you'd been longing for something your entire life, but you weren't sure what it was until it was standing in front of you. It's like how I imagine it feels when an artist picks up a paintbrush for the first time, or a writer gets their first story down on paper.

It's like you know you existed before you found it—that thing, but you don't know how you lived before it. You suddenly can't imagine yourself being whole without it.

The only thing that's ever come close to that feeling for me is surfing, but in truth, I've never lived my life without surfing. I got on a board for the first time with my mom when I was four years old. I know it's something I can't live without simply because I've never had to.

Now, I'm not sure how I've lived this long without kissing Darby. I'm not sure how I'll continue existing without it, not now that she's put it out on the table, that she's told me she wants it. Wants me. I can't imagine why.

It's probably because she's drunk.

She's drunk.

I drop my forehead against the glass door of her house. "Honeysuckle, baby," I groan. This physically hurts. "You know I can't kiss you when you're intoxicated. You're not even sure you really want it."

I turn back to face her, expecting to see sadness, but all I see is pure determination.

"I dare you." She smirks triumphantly. She remembers I told her I can't turn down a dare.

Goddamnit.

"Darby," I whisper defeatedly. I want her so badly, but I can't do it, not when she's like this. I can't stand the idea of her regretting it in the morning, not something as big and important to her as her first kiss. I won't be something she regrets.

I pull her into me, and her smile widens, believing I'm giving her what she wants.

I don't. For the first time in my life, I turn down a dare.

I give her the only thing I can right now as I press her against my chest, brushing my lips across her forehead, inhaling the scent of fresh flowers, the smell of her shampoo.

When she steps back from me, disappointment is plastered on her face.

I'm wrecked.

She clears her throat and nods, reaching toward the handle. "Goodnight."

I watch my golden girl step inside alone, shutting the door in my face.

I'm obliterated.

Sixteen

Honeysuckle

Now. May 28th.

Leo puts the rental car in park as we pull up to the curb outside my sister's familiar craftsman-style home with the blue shutters and the yellow door. Dahlia, Lou, and I chose those colors together. I look at the rose bushes I planted beneath the kitchen window and the fence that leads to my garden around back. The hanging planters overflow with late-spring blooms. The house belongs to the three of us, the closest thing I've ever had to home here in Crestwell, Kansas.

I knew it couldn't last forever. I knew that, eventually, I'd get married and move out, or she'd meet a man, he'd move in, and the space would become too crowded. But staring at it now, I wish I had just a little bit longer, a little more time with the three of us together.

I sigh, unbuckling myself as Leo cuts the ignition. Sitting passenger while he drives was a strange comfort I didn't know I missed. He swivels in his seat and faces me. "I can come help you if you want."

Things are still painfully awkward between us, like we're walking on eggshells, and we're trying not to let them crunch beneath our feet so as to not bring attention to how shattered the two of us became.

"No, it's okay." I shake my head. I notice the flash of concern in his eyes. "I'm leaving behind more than just my relationship with Jackson." I swallow the lump forming in my throat. "I just... I need a moment to myself."

I grip the door handle, and as it swings open, Leo's arm flashes out, grasping my other hand. I'm halfway out of the car when I pause and look down at the place he holds me. "Don't start rethinking your decision, Darby." My eyes travel up his arm until they meet his face. Those blue eyes blaze into me with the same intensity they did at seventeen. "Please...don't marry him." He drops my hand and looks away.

"Why are you doing this, Leo?"

With his gaze still glued on the windshield, he says, "Because I keep my promises."

I don't say anything more as I step back from the car. I quickly make my way up my sister's driveway and input our pin to the keypad on the door before slipping inside. The house smells like my sister, like fresh air and her favorite fabric softener.

I brush my fingers along the walls of the hallway, looking at the pictures of us together, of us and Lou throughout the last decade. There aren't any photos of our parents in her house. I asked her about that once, and she told me her relationship with our mom and dad was no more than a business arrangement, and she didn't keep photos of any of her other coworkers.

My parents allowed her to have Lou and go to college. My father set her up with a career in his company. In exchange, she allows them to play the part of doting grandparents in front of the masses, though behind closed doors, their resentment seeps through the cracks of our carefully constructed family portrait.

I stop at the doorway to my old bedroom, thankful I decided to leave some things here until after the wedding. Knowing time isn't on my side and that Leo is waiting in the car, I make quick work of packing a duffel bag with enough clothes to get me through at least a week and changing out of Dahlia's dress and into a pair of leggings and a crewneck.

My mind races back to the last time I packed a bag so briskly, to all the questions I left unanswered, all the hurt I caused. I know, eventually, Leo is going to want answers to those questions. I know I owe him that, and maybe that's why I told him not to come inside, why I needed a moment for myself.

He thinks it was so I could think about Jackson, but truthfully, Jackson became the furthest thing from my mind the moment I handed that ring over to my sister. Earlier, actually. Jackson became inconsequential to me the moment I learned Leo had arrived in Crestwell to crash my wedding.

He has a tendency to do that, the heathen—completely eclipse my life until nothing of it remains except for him.

I'm zipping up my bag and heading for the door when something catches my eye: the old wooden jewelry box on the dresser. Dahlia gave it to me for a birthday years ago. I don't wear jewelry often, and I know my mother doesn't like that box, so I didn't take it with me when I moved back in with my parents a few months ago. I didn't want to risk her donating it without telling me.

I think back to the man sitting outside. To that summer and the way it changed my life. To my grandmother and the friends I made and lost. Everything I lost. The way I lost myself.

I take a deep breath and open the box. In the bottom-most compartment is the small necklace I'm looking for. I cried the day I took it off, feeling like I had no right to wear it. I still don't deserve it, but for some reason, despite all I've done to him, Leo's here, for me, without hesitation or question. Maybe I could use this as a second chance, a way to ask for the forgiveness I've so desperately needed, to make myself deserving of all the future love I hope to receive. A way to find my way back to myself, to piece all the shattered parts of my being back together.

My eyes grow heavy as I slip the necklace into a side pocket of my bag and quickly make my way back to the front door. After locking it behind me, I shuffle down the porch steps and back into Leo's black rental car. I shove my bag into the backseat and shut the door with a sigh.

I can feel Leo looking at me, but I don't return it. I don't want him to see the tears silently falling down my cheeks as the emotion surrounding today's decisions suddenly washes over me.

"Got everything you need?" he asks.

I nod. "Let's go." My voice is hoarse, just on the brink of cracking.

From the corner of my eye, I see one hand leave the steering wheel and reach out toward my face before stopping midair. It's as if his instinct is to wipe my tears, but he's thought better of it. Instead, he pulls his hand back and turns the ignition.

"One condition."

I take a deep breath, the day's weight hitting me like a truck. I have no interest in playing games or attempting to lighten the mood right now. Everything feels entirely too heavy as I take one last look at my sister's house.

"What, Leo?" I finally turn to face him, letting him see my broken face.

A small smirk accents his features, dimples as familiar as my own heart appearing on either cheek. "Give me one smile."

I don't know how he knows.

How, after so many, many years apart, he can instantly read my shift in mood. The heaviness in my bones. The hurt inside my soul. I don't know how he knows that one glimpse of those dimples and the flash of those eyes—blue like the ocean water I haven't felt in far too long–is enough to settle the raging storm in my body.

But somehow, he does.

So, when I smile back at him, it doesn't feel forced at all.

It's as if the smile I give him is what he needs, and he grins back before pulling out onto the road. I give him quiet directions toward the interstate that will lead us toward Wichita and the closest airport, and once we're well on our way, I settle into my seat and attempt to get comfortable.

"Do you want me to get our flights booked or something?" I ask, trying to break the awkward tension floating over us.

He pulls his phone from the center console and unlocks it.

"Sure. Pull up the airline app I have saved. I'm a rewards member there."

I nod, still not understanding why he hasn't returned my own phone to me but feeling too tired to ask. I'm surprised that he's just handed over his phone without a second thought, as if he has nothing to hide.

Jackson never did that. He's never allowed me to just have access to his phone, not even for something as simple as booking a reservation or checking the time.

"Flying into San Diego or Los Angeles?" I ask.

Leo shrugs. "Preferably a direct flight, whatever we can get on quickest. Everett can pick us up from either airport."

I swallow a sudden lump in my throat. "How is Everett? And...everyone."

"He's good."

"Is he still a slut?"

Leo bursts with laughter. "I mean...he prefers his men to have beards and his women not to, but that's really his only standard. So, yeah. Still a slut."

I snort.

"He owns the garage now that Carlos retired. We also own a surf shop together on the boardwalk."

"Amazing," I breathe. A professional surfer and a business owner in the town he's always loved—it sounds like all of Leo's dreams ended up coming true.

Something I always hoped for him. Something I know wouldn't have happened if I hadn't left him the way I did. That knowledge seems to calm a ten-year-old storm I didn't know was thundering in my heart until it stopped.

"What about Elena?" I ask.

He's quiet for a moment after that question, as if he's not sure how to answer. He chews on his lip before turning to face me briefly. "Have you heard of the author Violet Rose?"

"Oh, yeah. She's pretty big in the Dark Romance genre." I don't read much romance anymore, don't find much time for reading at all, actually. My reading these days has been limited to *James and The Giant Peach* and *The Bridge to Terabithia* for the fifth-grade classes I teach. But when I'm at the bookstore, I like to look around at the sections I used to enjoy reading so much. The name Violet Rose is a familiar one. "Wait, that's Elena? Like, *Elena* Elena?"

He smiles proudly. "Yep. She started writing in college. Her third novel really took off, and the rest is history."

"Oh, my God. That's amazing. I had no idea." I sigh. "What made her choose the name Violet Rose?"

"I'm not sure exactly." I expect Leo to smile at that, but he frowns. "Her middle name is Rose. August came up with Violet. Not sure why." His tone is solemn.

All of them ended up doing incredible things with their lives, and as much joy and excitement as I feel for each of them, I can't ignore the small dark corner of my mind that reminds me how little I have to show for the last twenty-seven years of my own existence.

"And you all still live in Pacific Shores?"

Leo clears his throat. "No. Elena actually lives in New York City right now. She moved about two years ago." He says it in a way that sounds like a sore subject, and given my own soreness surrounding Elena, I decide not to press.

"Wow, an author and a professional surfer in the same family. Carlos and Monica must be so proud of you guys."

He smiles softly. "Yeah. They are." It feels forced. "And you're a...teacher? I think your sister said something like that when I met her outside the church."

"Yeah. Fifth grade."

"Do you like it?"

I shrug. "Yeah, it's good."

"But it's not flowers?"

I look at him then, hating that he can read every expression on my face. "I worked at a flower shop all through college in Wichita. Maggie's."

He smiles at that. "Why didn't you stick with it?"

I pick at my nails, looking down at my lap.

Because my dad told me not to.

The last few years, he's taken an interest in local politics, thinking it would help to have a daughter with the school district.

"There weren't any jobs available in Crestwell after I graduated college. My degree is in education, so it made the most sense."

He lets out a contemplative hum, and I'm desperate to change the subject. "Isn't taking off on a whim to crash a wedding kind of bad for your work schedule?"

He laughs at that. "I'm not too worried about it." He shrugs. "I'm a couple days behind on my gym routine, and I'll need to make up for that this week once we get back to California. I've got a competition at the end of July in Huntington Beach. But I'm not quite as competitive as I used to be."

"Set too many records, and now you're bored?"

He glances at me and raises a brow. "Just..." He sighs. "It's become so demanding. I have an agent, a PR team, a personal assistant. There is always some kind of sponsorship they want me to take on. A new competition they want me to enter. A new record they hope I can set. I don't feel like I'm doing it for the same reasons I started. The love for it I had as a kid seems to fall farther from my grasp with each passing day."

I think back to those quiet mornings on our beach, the way he moved through the waves. I remember the reason he was so drawn to them and the person who led him there. The way he looked so fluid and peaceful, as if he were part of the ocean itself.

"The world is just a little too loud now?" I ask.

He lets out a breathy chuckle. "Yeah. Something like that."

"You ever go down underneath the pi—"

He shakes his head. "No, Honeysuckle. I've never gone back."

Guilt and sadness wash over me at that. "I'm sorry, Leo."

"Don't be sorry." He shakes his head. "Don't apologize. You've had a long day. Why don't you try to rest before we get to the airport?"

I only nod, unsure how else to respond, how—or when—to address the past between us. I lean my head against the window and close my eyes.

Before long, I feel my head growing heavy as sleep takes over.

Just on the cusp of consciousness, I feel his hand reach over and pull something from my grasp. His warm fingers brush against mine, lingering for a moment too long.

I savor the feel of his skin, fighting the hollowness left in his wake when he pulls away.

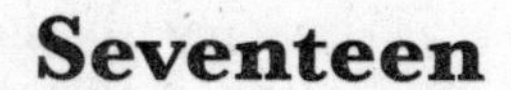

Seventeen

Honeysuckle

Then. June 22nd.

My head is pounding behind my eyes as I come to consciousness.

Haziness lingers as I open and blink around my room. Soft light filters through the closed drapes in front of my window. I turn over, realizing my legs are rubbing together, and my middle feels constricted.

I throw off the covers and glance down. I'm still in the blue dress I wore to the party last night.

The party last night.

Oh, God.

My memory suddenly floods back, along with my cheeks, as the humiliation settles in. I danced. I made a snarky remark to that girl—Amaya—about Leo sleeping in my bed. I asked him to sleep in my bed, to kiss me.

He rejected me.

Red-hot humiliation turns to white-hot rage.

I'm never speaking to that boy again.

I can't. It's too embarrassing. I'll never be able to look him in the eye again.

Groaning to myself, I kick the sheets off the rest of my body and roll out of bed. I'm running a hand down my tired face as a knock sounds at my bedroom door. "You missed church this morning, Darby," my grandmother chimes. "You best get downstairs to Skype your parents. They're calling in ten minutes!"

"Shit," I mutter. *Shit*? I never say shit. "Okay!" I shout back. "And I'm sorry! I was up late last night...reading."

Grandma laughs as her footsteps fade back down the stairs.

I make myself busy washing my face, brushing out the knots from my hair, and changing into a clean pair of clothes, a blouse and skirt that would be deemed church-appropriate. I have no idea if my grandma will lie for me about attending, but I've got to at least try.

I prance down the stairs and into the dining room just as she meets me in the doorway with a cup of coffee extended toward me. "Thank you," I murmur. "Why didn't you wake me?"

"You looked exhausted." She smiles at me behind her own mug. "In last night's dress and all."

"I..." I trail off, unsure of what to say.

"You smart, sunshine?"

I bite my lip. "Not as smart as you think I am, I'm afraid."

She chuckles. "You at least havin' fun?"

"I..." I don't know how to tell my grandma that I was having the time of my life with the heathen she believes I'm stupid to be around. "Yes."

"Good." She nods. "Everyone should have some fun at seventeen, sunshine. Fun and dumb often go hand in hand, and down here is a much better place to be seventeen and stupid than Crestwell, Kansas."

Unsure how to reply, I find myself saved by the bell as the laptop set up on the dining room table begins to chime. I race around the table—excited at the prospect of talking to Dahlia. I accept the call and see both of my parents' faces come on screen.

My mom's botoxed forehead is pulled tight with a blond bun tied behind her neck. Her green eyes seem drained. My dad seems to be missing more dark hair than he was when I saw him just a month ago. At this rate, he'll be bald within a year. The crinkles around his eyes crease as he smiles at me. "Hi, sweetie," he says in a tone far too chipper for him. "You look like you just got back from church."

"We did," Grandma peeps from behind me.

"Hi, Mom," he says in a monotone, much closer to his typical voice.

"Hi, Dad." I smile. "Mama." My mom gives me a strained smile back. "Where's Dahlia?"

My mom's eyes swivel toward my dad, as if she's waiting for his cue to speak. He glances back at her with unspoken permission. "She's sleeping. Not feeling well." My mom adjusts in her chair uncomfortably. "Tell us about your week, Darby."

Disappointment washes over me for the second time in twenty-four hours.

"Is she okay?" I ask.

This is the fourth week in a row I haven't been able to talk to Dahlia. The first time, I was told she was still not speaking to my parents, though I wasn't sure what that would have to do with me. The next week, I only spoke to my mom; she claimed my dad and Dahlia were out of the house. Last week, they told me she stayed back at church—which I immediately didn't believe—and promised me I would talk to my sister this Sunday.

I'm not one to contradict my parents' guidance, but... "This is the fourth week in a row I haven't been able to talk to Dahlia, and I'm—" My dad frowns at the camera. It's his *stop-talking* face. My mom's expression just looks afraid. I feel my stomach churning, and my throat feels strained and tight as I choke out, "Is she... sick?"

My mom's face softens at my fear. "No, no, sweetie. She's going to be okay."

My dad lets out an annoyed sigh. "She did something very, very bad, Darby. Part of her punishment is that she doesn't get to speak to you." My mom adjusted again. "She doesn't get to speak to anyone. Not until she...fixes the issue."

"What did she do?"

My mom only shakes her head, a clear indication I'm not to ask for details. I won't be provided with them. I drop my eyes to the table.

"We sent you to spend the summer with your grandmother because we think you need a...break from Dahlia's influence. Plus, we thought you would have some fun there," my mom says lightly.

"You're a good girl, Darby. You're across the country, still attending church, taking your online summer classes, minding your grandmother. We thought you deserved a summer away, somewhere nice like Pacific Shores."

"And Dahlia doesn't deserve that?" I ask, feigning innocence.

Dad's nostrils flare. "No. She doesn't."

I chew on my lip, deciding it's best not to argue. "When will I get to speak to her?"

"Once I've decided she's learned her lesson." His voice invites no room for argument or questioning. His tone tells me he's finished with this conversation. Like the good girl I'm supposed to be, I clamp my mouth shut.

My mom launches into questions about the weather and the beach, how my classes are going. I tell them everything is great and fine. All the while, my insides twist and turn with thoughts of my sister, what she possibly could've done, and more importantly, if she's truly okay.

Another bell saves me. This time, it's the doorbell. My parents listen intently as Grandma strides over to the entry, and I hear it creek open. Hushed voices go back and forth before my grandmother returns to the dining room.

"Elena is here to take you to the beach," she says.

My mom's face lights up, but my dad's remains stern. She gushes over the prospect of me having a friend while my dad asks simple questions about her family and social status, whether or not she's good enough to befriend me. I wince, knowing she can likely hear everything he says from the doorway.

"She's great. The family is great. Been my neighbors for years. Now, let the girl live, will you?" Grandma finally interrupts.

Dad's nostrils flare, but he concedes. I say my goodbyes to my parents before meeting Elena at the door. "Hey," I say.

"Do you want to go to the beach with me today? The boys are

pissing me off." She leans against the door with her arms crossed. Her curly brunette hair is thrown into a messy bun, tendrils framing her face. Red bathing suit straps peek out behind her black tank top and denim shorts as she picks at her nails.

"Sure." I find myself smiling. I've never been good at making friends. My parents heavily police whom I spend time with. They only approve of a few girls from church whom I truly don't have much in common with. I have a few girls at school I like, but I'm not normally allowed to spend time with them outside of class.

Plus, boys are making me mad today too.

"Let me go upstairs and change."

She nods before sticking a hand into the bag slung around her shoulder and pulling out something black. She hands it to me. "I've been noticing you looking at my bathing suits. It sounds like you've never been allowed to wear bikinis or something. I just thought maybe you want to take one for a spin, so I grabbed an extra, if you want."

I blink. "Oh...wow. I..." I don't know what to say.

She just shrugs. "You don't have to. Just thought I'd offer. Either way"—she hikes a thumb over her shoulder—"I'll be waiting out here."

I tug uncomfortably at the tight strap of Elena's swimsuit as we walk side by side down the hill and toward the beach. My grandma only winked at me as I walked out the door and told me to be back before dinner.

"Why are boys pissing you off today?"

She snorts. "The audacity."

"The audacity to do what?"

Elena looks over at me, lowering her large black sunglasses so I can see her caramel-colored eyes. "Just the audacity. The general audacity to fucking exist and believe they deserve to breathe the same air as me."

"Wow," I breathe. "I wish I had that kind of confidence."

"I'm not confident, Darby. I'm just in love with a person who doesn't see my value."

She sighs but says nothing more as we continue down the hill. I wonder to myself who she could be referring to, because the only people I ever see her around are her brother and his friends.

"Are you...um..." I swallow.

"I am definitely not referring to Leo."

I nod. "I'm sorry. Whoever it is you are referring to sounds like a...fucking idiot." A giggle bursts from my throat as I clamp my hand over my mouth.

Elena looks at me with a grin. "You don't talk like that often, do you?"

I shake my head.

"It's not a crime, you know. Fuck is my favorite word. It's got like...endorphins or something. It's physically therapeutic to say."

I make a mental note to research the validity behind that statement.

We both pause to take off our sandals as we reach the beach. Walking barefoot through the sand, I say, "I mean, it's not like I think I'm going to hell or something for a curse word. It's just... I was taught it was impolite. Not ladylike."

Elena scoffs. "Fuck being ladylike."

I purse my lips and shrug. She only laughs at me.

We find a spot near the waves, and Elena pulls a blanket out of her bag, spreading it along a flat place in the sand. She takes her clothes off before lying back on the blanket in just her bathing suit. I opt to keep mine on.

I hear attention gathering in murmurs and gasps from around us. Elena groans. "He must be out there again."

"Who?"

"Leo." She doesn't sit up. She's lying on her back, eyes closed through her glasses as if completely unaffected.

"Leo?"

She turns her head to look at me. "Yeah? He's like...the best young surfer in Southern California. People come from all around to watch him, but he'll catch the attention of regular beachgoers sometimes, too, if he's having a particularly good day."

My gaze snaps to the horizon. I don't need to look long or hard to find him among the dozens of other surfers dotting the waves. Many of them stay back, closer to shore, where the waves are smaller. Only a handful are farther out on the horizon. I know him immediately from the blond hair and from the stature of his lean, muscular body, from the orange board he was holding the day I met him.

I watch him hop up on the board, bending at the knees and leaning back, arms spread wide as he glides through the water. It's as if the ocean parts for him, as if he's in control of the waves, bending them at his will as he flies through them.

He leans to the side, and his board tilts up, cutting over the top of the wave before flipping back down as he skims the crest. All of my breath leaves my lungs as I watch him move within the water. The white of the wave begins to crest, tunneling over him, and I'm holding my breath, my stomach tying into knots as I watch it swallow him whole.

I realize my hand is clutching my chest, my other hand gripping Elena's elbow. I think she's laughing at me, but I can't hear through the ringing of anxiety in my ears. Finally, I see Leo's head pop up from the surface of the water. He climbs back onto his board and turns back to the other surfers behind him, lifting both his arms above his head in triumph.

Both those in the water and those on the shore cheer for him. Elena sticks two fingers between her lips and lets out a deafening whistle. His head snaps sideways and toward our direction. He lingers for a moment, watching us. I can't help but feel like he's staring right through me, though I know it isn't possible. The beach is far too crowded, and he's too far away. He can't tell me apart from any other beachgoer.

I feel like I'm still holding my breath as I watch him paddle toward the shore before hopping off his board and making his way back to the sand. He carries his surfboard to an area where towels and umbrellas are tangled in a mess on the ground. After setting his board down, he keeps his focus on Elena and me as he walks toward us.

For some incomprehensible reason, I take my shirt off. Elena's eyebrow rises from behind her glasses as I lean back on my elbows with more of my body on display than ever before. Two black triangles cover my chest, tying behind my neck. I shimmy out of my denim shorts, leaving only a matching black scrap of fabric covering my lower half, too.

As Leo reaches us, I notice his nostrils flaring. His gaze soaks in every inch of my body. I've been around him in my sports bra and shorts during our nights at the pier, but I've never shown this much skin before. Those moments were also in the dark of the night, away from the lingering looks of others. Now, I'm on display for anyone to see, bright in the sun. As if realizing that, too, he frowns.

I frown back. He rejected me last night. He gets no opinion on how I choose to show myself off to the world now. I raise my hand to shield my eyes as I look up at him. "Can you move? You're blocking out the sun, and we're trying to tan."

Elena snorts.

Leo turns to her. "Leave." Nodding back the way he came, he adds, "Go sit near our stuff. Everett's in the water, and he'll be back soon."

"Don't tell me what to do," she spits. "We hate men today, so leave us alone."

Leo looks back at me, and I can see the concern in his eyes, the sadness. He crosses his arms and kicks out a hip. I watch a bead of water run down the center of his chest, along the ridges of his muscular stomach, before disappearing behind the band of his shorts. I force my eyes to look away. "I promised if you jumped yesterday, I'd tell you the story behind my tattoo," he says.

My eyes fall back to the ink that stretches across his ribs. It's a large circle, like something in between a swirl and a wave. I can see the shades of blue and the caps of white, detailing it to look like a cresting ocean wave, but the circular shape of it almost looks as if it's swallowing itself. The design stretches tight at the place where he crosses his arms, and I can see it runs from just below his arm to just above his waist, stretching from his back to his stomach.

Elena clears her throat. "Did you, by chance, pack any of those wine coolers I like?"

He nods. "In the green water bottle. I poured the watermelon one in there for you. Was hoping you'd change your mind about coming down here today."

She smiles. "Just had to make a pit stop." As she scrambles to her feet and slips her shorts over her legs, I notice her glance around. "Zach isn't down here, right?"

Leo rolls his eyes. "No."

She bites her lip, giving me a small smile and a wave before walking off. Leo takes her spot next to me. "I'm sorry...about last night."

"I don't want to talk about it," I say.

Leo nods, looking straight out in front of us—at the ocean. "I got the tattoo in memory of my mom."

I look at him, but he doesn't do the same. "She..." I trail off.

"Yeah. When I was eleven. I moved in with the Ramoses when I was twelve." He props his knees against his chest and clasps his arms between them. "She taught me how to surf. We spent every weekend, and every day we could during the summer, down here on this beach. She worked at the hospital as a nurse's assistant. She worked overnight shifts, came home exhausted and drained, and before getting even a moment to herself, a minute of sleep, she'd wake me up and take me down here, put me on the front of her board, and teach me how to ride the waves like I was one." He swallowed hard. "After I lost her...this was the only place I felt close to her. It felt like a little part of her never really left the water. When I'm on my board, she's there too, still standing behind me, holding me steady.

"I got the tattoo as a reminder of that. That when I'm out

there"—he nods toward the horizon—"she's still with me. That she might be gone, but I think her spirit remains with me, and I feel it most when I'm in the water. I chose the circle because it becomes a wave that never ends..."

"Even though her life did, the connection between you two never will."

"Yeah," he says, voice cracking.

"I'm so sorry, Leo." He turns away from me, trying to hide that he's wiping his eyes. I reach out and place my hand over his. "I think that's beautiful. I'm also sorry if I made you feel pressured to tell me. I had no idea it was something so personal to you."

He looks at me now, his blue eyes bright with sunlight and unshed tears. "I didn't feel pressured. I've been wanting to tell you every time I'm around you, Honeysuckle. Just didn't want to make you feel differently about me." He flips over his hand in mine so our palms touch, and he squeezes my fingers. Four times. "You're the easiest person to talk to. You make me want to tell you everything, every thought running through my head. I feel lighter each time I open up to you."

"Because I chase away your ghosts."

"Because you chase away my ghosts." He nods. "But I'm also afraid of you seeing those ghosts up close, Darby."

"I'm not afraid of that," I find myself saying, fully aware that I'm supposed to be upset with him.

"That's because I'm not finished with the story yet."

I squeeze his palm now. Four times. "Go on."

"Let's go put our feet in the water," he says, standing up and reaching his hand out toward me.

I remind myself that he rejected me last night, that I'm upset and hurt. But something tells me I'm hurting much less than he has for so many years, that I may have inadvertently opened some kind of floodgate for him. I may have caused him to expel emotions he's been holding in for a while, so I take his hand and let him pull me up.

We maneuver between the many, many people spending this

Sunday afternoon at the beach as we make our way toward the waves. Leo never lets go of my hand. He holds tightly as we sink our toes into the water, watching intently as it crests and breaks over our ankles.

"I wanted to go to a football camp that summer. It was the summer before sixth grade, and I wanted to play football at the junior high school that fall," he tells me. "Except, I forgot I would need cleats. So, the morning the camp was set to start, I woke up early and waited for my mom to get home from the hospital. She only got off a couple of hours before it started. I begged her to take me to get the cleats as soon as the store opened. She'd been up all night working, but she used to stay up all night and then take me surfing, so I didn't really take into consideration how tired she would be..." He sighs.

"Leo, where was your dad?"

He runs a hand through his hair. "My dad and I never really got along. He was an alcoholic who couldn't hold down a job, and I was the kid he never wanted. His inability to be sober to help provide for our family was a point of contention for him and my mom. Apparently, it wasn't an issue before I came around, according to him."

I squeeze his hand again, four times. *You're safe with me.*

"Don't get me wrong, he was still a good dad. He wasn't a mean drunk or a violent drunk. He just wasn't ever sober. He didn't like to work, content to stay at home and take care of me. The only problem was that we really couldn't afford for him to do that, so he was always working odd jobs and getting fired for coming to work intoxicated." He shakes his head. "Whatever. The point is, he was passed out after a night of drinking, and I couldn't ask him to take me to get my cleats. I begged my mom. She was so tired, and I felt so guilty for forgetting until the last minute." We'd been walking through the waves, but suddenly, Leo stops, staring straight ahead and looking out to the horizon again. "They said it must've been sheer exhaustion, possibly falling asleep at the wheel, that caused her to swerve across lanes and into oncoming traffic."

My stomach leaps into my throat, a gasp flying from my mouth. He only swallows, as if numb to that reaction.

Leo leans to his side, lifting his arm so that the tattoo along his rib cage comes into full view. "She was killed immediately on impact. I was stuck in the car with her body until first responders showed up, but I ended up walking away with nothing more than a gash right here." He points to his side, to the tattoo itself.

I lean in, letting my gaze study the blue ink, noticing for the first time the puckered line through the middle of it. I find myself instinctively reaching out to touch it with my free hand, but I think better of it, pulling my arm back to my chest.

"It's okay. I don't mind if you touch it."

I lift my eyes to his, finding sincerity and sorrow in their blue depths. "I was in the front seat, but I didn't notice her dozing off. We had the music playing. It was companionable silence, the kind my mom and I always had. I just wish I would've talked to her. Said something. Noticed she had started to fall asleep." He lets out a dark laugh. "Or that I would've just remembered to get my fucking cleats before the camp."

"Leo..." His grip tightens on my palm, and I run my other hand across his side, the scar rough against my skin. We both tremble at the touch. "I'm so sorry. I... I don't know what to say."

He looks at me, eyes glistening with emotion. "Tell me it's not my fault."

I pull my hand from his and bring both up to his face. Standing on my toes to level my gaze with his, I say, "It is not your fault. Please"—my own voice cracks—"don't think that. Don't ever think that." He glances away, attempting to drop his head, but I hold it firm. "It breaks my heart to hear you think that. You don't want to break my heart, do you, Heathen?"

"Never, Honeysuckle," he whispers.

What he doesn't know is that I needed to hear those words too. I need to know he didn't have any intention of hurting me when he rejected me. I refuse to allow some boy I hardly know to break my heart, but I can't pretend he didn't leave a crack in it when he walked away last night.

"Leo?" I ask, still cupping his firm jaw between my hands.

"Yeah?"

"Where is your dad now?"

I drop my hold on him, but he catches my hands in his own. "His drinking got worse after my mom died. Despite everything, he loved her. He loved her a lot more than he loved me, I think. He saw it as my fault. He was so broken without her, irreparably so. He couldn't forgive me, and he couldn't support us both, either." He took a deep breath, closing his eyes. "So, he dropped me off at Everett's one Saturday for a sleepover. He never came back."

"Leo," I breathe.

He opens his eyes and looks at me, a small hint of a smile on his mouth. It's not enough to make his dimples pop, but enough to let me know he's trying. "He finally called Everett's mom a few days later and told her he was going to Texas, that he was sorry to 'leave the kid' with her. The Ramoses took me in without question, gave me their spare bedroom that very day, and never looked back."

"Leo," I say again. "Please, listen carefully to what I say next." He nods. "Your dad does not deserve you. What happened to your mom was an accident and not your fault. I'm sorry he abandoned you. I'm sorry he left you to grieve alone." He gives me a closed-mouthed smile. "I'm also very thankful you found the Ramoses, but I hope you know that they are lucky to have you, too, and...and so am I." I take a deep breath. "Lastly—and this is the important part—I need you to understand that your dad is a fucking asshole."

That closed-mouth smile becomes a full-blown grin before he begins thundering with laughter. He runs his hands up my arms, and in one swift movement, he tugs me against his chest. He cradles the back of my head with one hand while wrapping the other around my back.

"You're something else, Honeysuckle." He chuckles into my hair.

And with that, he grabs me under the arms and lifts me into the air. Before I have the chance to protest, he's tossing me out into the waves.

Eighteen

Heathen

Now. May 28th.

The only sounds are the roar of the rental car whipping down the interstate and Darby's soft, heavy breath filtering from where she sleeps against the window.

It ignites something in my chest to know that she still feels safe enough with me to fall asleep here. After the day she's had, the adrenaline pumping through her veins, there's no doubt she's exhausted. But I also know it must mean something that alone with me is the place she feels she can finally rest.

It's all so strange, being back in her proximity. It still feels like I'm staring directly into the sun, but where her light once gave me warmth, it's now only a reminder of how badly I was once burned.

I know she has reasons surrounding the way she left things all those years ago. I know her family likely has some part in it. It destroys me to see how much she's fallen back into her role of submissive, timid, perfect daughter, how far back into the wolf's den she crawled. That's likely why it was so easy for me to hop on a plane and fly halfway across the country to reach her.

Our past could be damned if it meant getting her out of a lifetime of being controlled by her father and marrying a man just like him.

Despite this, I want an explanation from her. I crave it. I can see the guilt plastered across her face every time she looks at me, and that destroys me too. I plan on asking her about it when we get back to California, once she's across state lines, away from her family and from that man. Once she has a chance to dip her feet back into the sand, into the ocean waves I know she loves so much, I'll ask her.

We'd always been able to open up to each other effortlessly, since that very first night we spent together underneath the pier, sharing bits of ourselves, little by little, until there was no piece of our souls left untouched.

I've already found it incredibly easy to fall back into that same pattern. When it came to talking with her about my career and my struggles with it, her instant understanding, her ability to listen, to simply acknowledge me without trying to offer me a solution or a different way of thinking was invaluable. I missed having someone who could so effortlessly recognize my feelings and thoughts.

Opening up to her is as simple as breathing. She's the easiest person to talk to, those deep hazel eyes burning through me like she's hanging onto every word, like I fucking matter. That's the way Darby Andrews has always made me feel, and until I wrestled my way right back into her life, I had no idea how empty I was without her.

I take the next exit off the interstate, turning onto a narrow highway as I follow a sign toward the airport. I reach across the console with one hand, lightly shaking Darby's shoulder to wake her.

"Hey," I whisper as she begins to stir. Finally, she turns to face me, and her eyes flutter open, big and bright and golden. "Hi, Honeysuckle." I smile. "Sleep well?"

She gives me a soft, tired smile as she stretches her arms. "Where are we?"

"About a half hour from the airport. Did you get the tickets on my phone?"

She sits up straight, her eyes widening. "Oh, no. I totally forgot. We started talking about Everett and Elena, and—"

"It's cool." I pull my phone from the console. "You wanna

try to book them right now so we can get a head start once we get there? Or, if there aren't any immediate flights, we can grab dinner or something. Have you eaten today?"

She laughs as she snatches the phone from my hand. "I haven't eaten a single thing today, but to be honest, I don't have much of an appetite." She begins typing away on my phone. "Also, why are you holding my phone hostage?"

I shrug. "Dahlia told me that your fi—ex-fiancé can track your location. She wanted to make sure I kept it turned off."

Darby snorts. "Why don't we just turn my location off then?"

I look at her from the corner of my eye. "Honestly, Darby... he's probably been blowing up your phone. I think your sister was a little afraid that if you saw his calls, his text messages, any communication from your parents, you'd feel obligated to go back to them..." I sigh. "And I'm a little afraid of that too."

She's quiet for a moment, continuing to work through booking our flights before she lets out a breath and pauses. "I know. You're both right, which is why I haven't caused more of a fit about you taking my phone. I think...I think I probably need the break."

"Once we're home, and you have the chance to get some distance, you can give them a call to start working things out."

I look at her then, seeing the emotion in her eyes at that word.

Home.

She doesn't respond to me, but after a moment of fiddling on my phone, she turns and starts rummaging through her bag in the backseat. She finally turns back to face the front, and I notice a pale pink wallet in her lap.

"No, Darby. Just use my credit card." I reach into my back pocket and pull out my own wallet before tossing it onto her lap. She immediately throws it back at me.

"Leo, you flew across the country, rented a car, and booked a hotel room so you could break me out of my wedding because I wasn't brave enough to do it myself. The last thing I am going to do is ask you to pay for my plane tick—"

"Don't ever say that again."

"Excuse me?"

"That you aren't brave. Don't ever say that again." I look at her just in time to see her mouth clamp shut. Her nostrils flare in the same cute way they used to when she was younger. "I didn't do anything but show up in case you needed me. The decision to leave, the decision to risk everything you've built for yourself, to stand up to the people who've been controlling you all your life, was yours. Today, Darby, you've given up your entire way of living. The comfort of wealth, of security. Your family. All in the spirit of finding happiness. That's one of the bravest things a person can do, Honeysuckle. You didn't need me for that. You would've figured it out all on your own. I'm just here to help however I can."

I take my eyes off the darkening road only briefly to look at her. The sun is setting behind my window, casting her beautiful face in golden light. I see the shimmering of unshed tears glittering inside her eyes.

"I owe you so many explanations, Leo."

My hands tense on the steering wheel. "You don't owe me anything, Darby. The past doesn't matter anymore. It's behind us now. Let's just work on getting home."

She seems to swallow any words she has left to say before silently turning back to my phone in her lap. She unclips her wallet and begins to fish through it. "Well, I'm still not allowing you to pay for my flight..." She trails off as she begins frantically flipping through her wallet, taking out every card and stuffing it back in.

She dives into the back seat and pulls her large duffel bag into her lap, rapidly searching through it. "Oh, no..." She continues digging through the bag before going back to her wallet. "Oh, God."

"What's going on?"

She throws her head back against the headrest before letting out a frustrated sigh. "My fucking wedding planner has my driver's license." Her face falls into her hands. "I gave it to her yesterday for some kind of collateral she needed with the caterers or...something. I don't even remember." She begins stuffing things back into her bag before tossing it behind her. "Which means I can't get on an airplane. I have no I.D."

I chew on my lip. "All right. It's okay. We'll figure something out."

She shakes her head, still hiding her face. "Look, Leo, I appreciate you coming all this way. I mean...flying across the country for this, for me? It's more than I ever could've asked or expected of you. It's been... I'm glad we got to catch up. Clear the air. Find closure..."

There is no closure here. All she's done is rip me back open.

"But just...can you drop me off at a hotel or something? I'll pay for your flight home. I promise I won't contact my dad or Jackson. I just need a night to myself, and then I'll call Dahlia in the morning, and..."

"No, Honeysuckle."

"What?"

"No. We're not doing that. I asked you where on Earth you wanted to go, and you said Pacific Shores. I'm taking you to Pacific Shores. I'm taking you home, Darby."

She's stunned into silence, and I continue driving toward the airport, even though I know that's no longer an option. I think we both realize I'm just driving until we can figure out where we're supposed to be going. All I know is that there is no way I'm just leaving her here by herself.

After fifteen minutes of tense, awkward silence, she finally drops her hands from her face. "Leo..." She lets out an exasperated sigh. "This is ridiculous. We can't..."

She trails off as our attention is snagged on something outside the windshield. I immediately take my foot off the gas, coasting by the used car lot as if we're moving in slow motion. As soon as it's in the rearview, I turn to her with a shit-eating grin.

"What year do you think that model was?" she asks.

"Looked to be about a seventy-six."

"Cherry red," she says on a breath.

"Cherry-fucking-red, Honeysuckle."

Before she has the chance to respond, I'm whipping a U-turn in the middle of the highway and beelining it back down to the car dealership. I pull into the parking lot, stopping the car right in front of the bright red 1976 Mustang they have on display in front of the building. A big sign in the window lists it as *like-new* condition for twenty-five thousand dollars.

"What the hell are you doing, Leo?"

"You don't have an I.D., so we can't fly, and we need to get to California." I pull the key out of the ignition of the rental car and turn to face her, giving her my widest smile. "We'll drive."

Her mouth drops open in disbelief. "You're just going to buy that car? Right now?"

I laugh. "Do you know how long I've been looking for a 1976 Mustang convertible in this kind of condition?" I open the door, and she immediately follows me into the parking lot. The dealership is twenty minutes from closing, but I can see one man sitting at a desk inside. Darby catches up to me as I lazily throw an arm around her shoulder. "When the divine is trying to intervene, Honeysuckle, I'm going to fucking listen."

I'm smiling to myself as I hold the glass doors open to the small town used car dealership. Darby brushes past me as she steps through and out into the budding summer air.

The flat horizon is a deep orange, fading into pink and purple before dissolving into a midnight blue sky, the scattering of stars becoming present.

I've got a folder in one hand, with the title to my new Mustang, the car I've been dreaming about owning—right down to the specific year, model, and exact color—since I was a teenager, the key dangling from my fingers in the other.

The salesman helped us get our bags from the rental car before I handed him over the keys. When I offered to pay full price for the Mustang with a check right then and there, I found there was little he wouldn't do to close the deal. He's going to return the rental car for me, allowing Darby and me to head out of town directly from here.

Darby has hardly said a word. She stared after me with wide, shocked eyes as I signed a twenty-five-thousand-dollar check and handed it over to the salesman as if it were nothing more than a simple transaction. That ignited something inside me, the way she seemed almost impressed by it. I've worked my ass off to spend money like this, to become so much more than the homeless orphan she once knew.

Yet, she said nothing, and she continued to say nothing as I signed the paperwork, got the keys, and loaded our things inside the new car. As we part ways with the salesman and climb inside the Mustang, a thick tension coats us both.

"Tell me something, Honeysuckle," I say.

Her eyes seem to glow in the twilight as she glances at me. "Hmm?"

"I need you to be honest with me. Once upon a time, you and I were good at that, you know?"

"I know," she murmurs.

I nod. "If you're uncomfortable around me, I understand it. I understand it was a big gesture for me to come here today. I know it was likely a lot more than you asked for, probably more than you would've wanted from me." Thus far, being cordial hasn't gotten me far. Small talk has been nothing but awkward, and the lack of confrontation surrounding our past has only been painful. So, I opt for honesty. "When I got that letter, Darby...it scared the shit out of me."

Her brows knit together at the center of her forehead, her face taking on a beautifully concerned look.

"It was desperate and heartbroken. You seemed so...guilty." I sigh. "Like you thought you deserved to be treated the way you were, deserved to essentially be sold off into marriage against your will because of what happened..." I trail off, realizing I'm not even sure I understand the whole of it. I still have no idea why she left me all those years ago.

I shake my head, continuing, "It is important to me that you understand that isn't true, that you understand you deserve happiness and love and fulfillment, regardless of the past." I notice her eyes seem to be glossing over, but she doesn't let her tears fall. "It seemed like you forgot everything I asked you to remember, Darby, all those conversations we had. I just... I couldn't stand the idea of you being stuck like that."

In truth, I couldn't stand the idea of her marrying another man. Loving another man. Having his last name and bearing his children.

But that was something I'd never admit to her, something I couldn't even admit to myself.

Night takes over as we sit in the dark cab of the new-smelling car. The parking lot is empty, only the emerging light of the moon illuminating us. My entire body goes onto alert as Darby slowly reaches across the center console, placing her hand over mine. Her skin—familiar, soft, and warm—brushes against my own. Feelings I've repressed for so many years I forgot they existed seem to resurface at her touch.

"Thank you, Leo," she whispers. Her smile is light, fading just as quickly as it appears.

I flip my palm, wrapping my fingers around hers, squeezing them four times, reminding her that she is, that she always has been, safe with me.

"If you want me to find you a hotel in Wichita, say the word, and I'll take you there. If you want me to drive you back to your sister's, I'll take you there instead. If you want me to take you back to your fiancé and watch you walk down to aisle to him, I'll hate every fucking second of it, but I'll do that too.

"But if you want to go home to Pacific Shores, start over, start fresh, figure out what you want to do next on your own terms, then let me take you there. I don't want you to feel like a burden, or like I'm doing you a favor. I made the decision to come out here all on my own. I needed to be here, and I needed to know I'd offered you a way out, an escape. I needed that for me." I sigh. "And now, I've found my car." I smile at her. "I've got to get it home somehow, so I've got no choice but to drive. You'd be doing me a favor if you helped keep me company over the next few days."

The brightest smile she's given me since I stormed back into her life spreads across her face. Just as she opens her mouth to say something, my phone begins buzzing in my pocket.

I pull it out as Dahlia's name flashes across the screen. I hold it out to Darby. "It's your sister."

She snatches it from my hand in a flash, sliding her thumb across the screen and pressing it to her ear. "Dal?" She nods frantically, though I can't make out what's being said on the other end of the line. "Yeah, so funny story about that. I actually don't have my I.D. on me." Her sister responds as Darby grabs my backpack from the back seat and ruffles through it, finding her phone and powering it on. "No, we're going to drive." I watch her phone light up, and a moment goes by before it floods with notifications. Darby sighs. "Yeah, he called me about a thousand times." She nods. "Yeah, I'm turning my location off now. No, I'm not going to respond, but I'll have my phone on me if you need me, okay? I'll text you with updates on where we are." She scrolls through her phone, nibbling on her lip as she looks through the messages. "Don't tell anyone where I'm going. I don't want Dad or Jackson, like...showing up at Grandma's house and trying to drag me back here. I just... I need time to figure things out." She closes her eyes and leans her head back against the seat, letting her phone fall into her lap. "Yeah, I love you, too. Tell Lou I love her. Okay, bye."

She hands my phone back to me.

"Lou?" I ask.

"My niece..." She swallows, her tone sounding almost pained. "Dahlia's daughter."

I nod. "Is everything okay?"

"Yeah." She sighs. "Jackson is just blowing me up, telling me he can't believe I've done this to him, how humiliated he is." She bites her lip. "Begging me to come back." She hangs her head.

I can almost feel for the guy. I know what it's like to wake up and find out Darby Andrews disappeared from your life. I know the kind of irreparable, gut-wrenching, soul-crushing heartbreak that comes with losing her, though I think he's devastated for very different reasons than I was, and that makes me hate him.

"What do you want to do, Honeysuckle?"

She looks at me as if she's hoping I'll make the decision for her. So, I do. I reach out and snatch the phone from her hand. Unwilling to look at any of the man's messages, I simply swipe across her screen and delete the entire conversation with him. While I'm at it, I delete the voicemails he left her too. I notice there isn't a single communication from her parents.

"It's not worth looking at, Darby. You'll reach out to them when you're ready."

She only nods.

I sigh. "Look...we can just forget about our past, okay? You've obviously got much bigger shit going on in your life than the fling we had at seventeen. We can make this drive together, get you away from that shitshow of a wedding and fraud of a relationship, and maybe we can try...starting over? As friends?"

Her face straightens in a way that spells devastation, and I already regret everything I've just said. I know none of that is true. I know it was never a fling between us. It was so, so much more. By the look on her face, she knows it too.

But I don't know how else to explain to her that she doesn't need to worry about me, worry about our past, the answers she thinks she owes me. Because if she has that pressure, she won't leave here with me. If she doesn't leave here with me, she may go back to him.

I don't know how to tell her how badly I don't want that, but trying to work around those words only caused me to fuck up more.

"I just mean..." I shake my head. "A clean slate. Get to know each other as the people we are now without the pressure of—"

"I understand, Leo," she cuts me off.

I don't think she gets it at all.

In an attempt at not digging myself a deeper hole, I simply ask, "So, you'll come with me?"

I watch her throat move as she swallows. Finally, she nods. "I'll come with you."

I give her a smile that feels all too fake. She returns it with her own unconvincing grin. I start up the new car, and it roars to life beautifully. Flipping on the headlights, I pull out onto the highway as Darby searches for directions on her phone.

"How long do you think you can go tonight?"

The way she phrased that question goes straight to my groin, and I shake off the very unwelcome feeling she stirs inside me.

"A few hours before I get too tired."

She types away on her phone for a moment. "All right, I've booked us two rooms in Garden City. It's about three hours away."

"Okay," I say. "And you can use my credit card for that. For anything. I don't—"

"Shut up, Leo."

My lips twitch at that. "All right, Honeysuckle."

Nineteen

Heathen

Then. June 22nd.

"You've got to stick your feet out in front of you."

"But then my head goes beneath the surface."

I laugh. "No, just take deep breaths. There is enough salt in the water to keep you afloat. Here"—I reach my hand out to her—"hold my hand and stretch your other arm out wide."

Darby does as I say, her beautiful golden hair floating behind her. She's got her legs kicked out in front of her, her chest toward the sky, and her arm outstretched toward me. With each breath she takes, her chest lifts, and I'm entranced by the beads of water that run between her breasts. The sunlight reflects off the droplets, casting her beautiful body in a golden glow.

I'm thankful my lower half is hidden right now.

I mimic her position and hold her hand just as a large wave comes toward us. "Don't freak out!" I shout. "We'll roll right over the top of it. If you can't see the white water cresting, then we're fine."

Just as I promised, we float over the top of the rolling wave with our feet kicked out first. My stomach lifts as we drop down the back side of it. "Doesn't it make you feel like an otter?"

She doesn't answer me because she's laughing too hard.

My stomach lifts at that too.

We've been in the water for hours. The sun is beginning to lower on the horizon, casting the world around us in a golden hue.

I didn't want to talk about my ghosts anymore; I just wanted her to know they existed. I didn't want to kiss her last night, because I knew I wasn't good enough for her, and I needed her to see that, too.

I've shown it to her, and if she chooses to kiss me now, that's on her. I'll happily and greedily take anything she's willing to give me.

I can tell she's still upset, still sheltering herself, but she told me she didn't want to talk about last night, so I figured the next best thing was to simply try to make her smile. Make her laugh. Show her all my ghosts and let her chase them away with her sunlight. Then, maybe she'd understand just how much her presence is beginning to mean to me and why I wouldn't risk that over one drunken kiss.

I drop my feet below the surface and tread water, turning to look at her. She follows suit, dipping beneath the waves and popping back up, pushing her hair back out of her face. The freckles on her cheeks seem to twinkle like stars in the setting sunlight. Eyes of molten honey crinkle in the corner as she smiles at me. "I'm pruned!" she calls out.

"Me too." I smile back.

"I've got to get home for dinner."

"All right." I nod toward the shore. "Let's go get dry."

We wade out of the ocean, and she trails behind me as I walk back to the blanket she and Elena brought down to the beach. It's much emptier now than it was earlier in the afternoon. The vacationers have meandered back to their hotels and rental houses to prepare for dinner and the nightlife the area has to offer. The afternoon wind brought a choppiness to the waves that made for poor surfing conditions, so the surfers dispersed, too, including my friends, it appears.

The only people left on the beach are a few small groups dotted across the sand, either sleeping, reading, or walking along the water.

Darby reaches me and begins to wring out her hair with her

hands. I try not to let my gaze linger on the curve of her hips, the dip of her waist, or the two dimples on her lower back, but she makes it really fucking hard with the way she's bent over in front of me right now.

She suddenly snaps up and looks at me, brows furrowed.

Shit. I think she said something. "What?"

She blushes. "I said, I just realized I forgot a towel." She huffs, distractedly searching for her clothes on the ground. "And stop looking at me like that."

"Like what?"

She pops a hip and places her hand on it, giving me an exasperated look. "Like you're wondering what a little piece of my soul feels like."

All of the air leaves my lungs, every last breath. I choke on nothing.

She flicks a brow before tossing her hair behind her shoulder and muttering something like, "I'm going to go rinse off." Her hips sway with each step she takes, only making this harder on me.

"Darby, wait!" I jog after her, but she ignores me.

She reaches the outdoor showers sporadically located along the boardwalk, and I catch her arm just as she reaches for the handle to turn it on.

"You really believe I didn't want to kiss you?"

Her nose scrunches in annoyance, and I smile because it's cute, which only makes her scrunch it harder. "Yes? You told me no. You left." She holds up a hand. "Which, I get it. I understand. I'm not upset because you're...not into me. I mean, it's..." She sighs. "That's my problem to deal with. What I'm mad at you for is all the mixed signals. I've never done this before, Leo. I'm not used to being flirted with for fun.

"So, when you...treat me the way you do, get all protective over me. Tell me that I'm pretty, that you like the sound of my voice. When you touch me the way you do, when you tell me that I chase away your ghosts and take me to your secret places...that means something to me. That's not something I've ever done with any other person before. So..." She waves her hand in the air. "It's whatever. Just... No more of that."

"I've never done any of that with anyone else either, Darby. It's important to me that you understand that. I've never taken anyone under the pier before. I've never told anyone about my tattoo, not even Everett and Elena."

Her face straightens at that declaration.

"So, all of this"—I wave my hand between us—"means something to me too. That's exactly the reason why I didn't kiss you last night."

Her tongue swipes across her bottom lip. "I don't understand."

"I said no because you were drunk. I was afraid you'd regret it in the morning, that you were only asking because you were intoxicated. Not because it was what you wanted. Not because you wanted me." I run a trembling hand through my hair. "Because it's crazy to me, Honeysuckle, that someone as beautiful and golden and good as you could want someone like me. I couldn't kiss you until I let you see all of me, all of my past. Who I really am—an abandoned orphan from the wrong side of the tracks with nothing going for him, who will never be good enough for you. It's impossible for me to believe that, after seeing that, you still want me."

Her expression softens immediately. She steps into me, pressing a hand flat against my bare chest and backing me up until I hit the metal of the outdoor shower. I'm looking at her eyes, and she's staring at my lips. I feel her breathing get heavier, every expansion in her chest brushing against my own.

We reach for the handle to the shower at the same time, her fingers brushing over mine, eliciting a reaction in every atom of my body. We twist the handle, gasping as cold, fresh water pours over us both.

"Well, I do. I do want you, Leo. And for someone who tells me I should stop letting other people control me, that I should make my own decisions and live life by my own rules, you sure like to tell me what's good for me."

I can only nod. "You're right." I think she's right about everything. She could tell me that up is down and down is up, that the sky is neon green, Jack Black is the President, and pigs have wings. Who would I be to argue with a single word that comes out of that beautiful mouth? She just told me she wants me. She said it like it's a simple fact of life, as plain and permanent and pure as our feet on the ground, as the sky being blue and grass being green.

Something as unbelievable and far-fetched as the flawless and fierce creature in front of me telling me she's chosen me? Who am I to doubt even the most impossible things in life?

"You know what I've decided?" she asks. I watch water cascade down her perfect face, a droplet falling from her bottom lip and onto her chin. I wonder what kind of god I need to pray to to let me lick it off.

"Tell me," I beg.

"I've decided that you are good for me. You've changed me more—made me better—in one month than anyone else in my whole life. You make me feel free. You make me feel beautiful and safe and smart, and that makes me want to kiss you." Thank God. "And I've never done this before. So, do you know how hard it is to tell someone that? How good they make you feel and how much it makes you want them and have them turn you down? It's pretty traumatizing for this being my first experience at...all of this. You tryna traumatize me, Leo? Are you trying to break my heart, Heathen?" she repeats her earlier question.

So, I repeat my earlier answer. "Never, Honeysuckle."

Her lips part, and I move one of my hands away from the shower handle and up her arm. I can feel goosebumps spreading across her skin. She's still looking at me with molten eyes and full lips as water pelts us both. I bring my hand around the back of her neck and hold her there, tilting her face back slightly. My other hand grabs her at the hip.

Her hand finds itself on my face, brushing my soaking hair off of my forehead before running down the length of my cheek and brushing across my jaw. She drags her thumb along my bottom lip, swiping away the water gathering there.

"Tell me this: would you have dared me to kiss you if you weren't drunk?" I ask.

She gives a slight shake of her head. "Probably not, but only because the alcohol made me courageous, not because sober me wants you any less than drunk me does."

"How are you feeling right now?"

"Afraid." She looks rapidly between my lips and my eyes. "Of rejection."

I grip her hip tighter, pressing my thumb into the soft flesh just below her bathing suit. I pull her into me until our bodies are flush together. One hand of hers is on my chest, the other on my arm. I lean forward—never breaking my gaze from her eyes—until my lips hover just over hers.

"Dare me again, Honeysuckle," I whisper.

"Dare ya, Heathen," she breathes.

I drop my mouth to hers, delicately at first. I'm mindful that it's her first time, so I guide her through it. Feathering my bottom lip between both of hers, I move my mouth against hers. She lets out a small gasp, and it's innocent, yet somehow, the most erotic sound I've ever heard.

I use the hand on the back of her neck to press her against me tighter, and I open my mouth a little wider. She takes everything and then some when she snakes her tongue through her lips and into my mouth. I groan at the taste of her. I let her lips move freely against me, let her lead the way. She can take everything from me, move as fast or as slow as she wants. I'm at her mercy.

I swipe my tongue across her bottom lip, tasting her for the first time.

She doesn't just taste like honey. She's sweeter. Her lips taste like the answer to every question I've ever asked. Her lips taste like finding faith, like realizing you believe in God for the very first time. Because how could I not? When she presses her beautiful body against me and runs her warm, delicate hand down the length of my torso, exploring me—savoring me—how could I not believe that God created her just for me?

Water drenches us both, separating us from the rest of the world. Anyone could be walking by, could be watching us, but it again feels like we're on our own planet. It's just the two of us here in this moment, water cascading down around us, her lips tasting like life, her skin lighting mine on fire.

She lets out another moan, which elicits one from me too. I dig my fingers into her hips again, knowing she can feel the reaction of my body by how tightly we're pressed together. She doesn't seem bothered by it, though. She rolls her hips into mine, and I hiss at the friction. It almost seems as if she wants me as badly as I want her—which I didn't think could be possible—as she wraps her arm around the back of my neck and pulls us even closer, like she's desperate for every inch of her skin to line up with every inch of mine.

She pulls my bottom lip beneath her teeth and nips on it, making me downright feral.

I bring up both hands to cup her face and kiss her harder. I kiss her with everything in me, and she takes every bit of it—she throws it right back. Sounds sweeter than honey and softer than clouds fly from her mouth, and I swallow them like they're water and I'm a dying man.

"Leo," she moans, and I'm ready to lose myself.

"Fuck," I respond.

She finally pulls away from me, her eyes fluttering open slowly, blinking through the pouring water and the daze of passion. I cup her cheek, running my thumb across her lip.

"Wow," she says breathlessly. "I've clearly been missing out."

I smile down at her. "No, baby. That's something you only find once. Something you'll only ever know with me."

"I guess you were worth the wait, then." She smiles back.

Twenty

Heathen

Now. May 30th.

Somewhere inside the red rocks of the Utah desert, thunder rumbles through the world outside the car, but it's nothing compared to the frigid air of the space between Darby and me.

I'm not sure she's said more than a few words to me in the last day.

She was silent on that first night after I bought the Mustang. I had a feeling I'd said something that upset her, but two days of brooding made me wonder what was genuinely running through her brain. I can't find the courage to ask her, though.

She mapped out our route yesterday morning and booked our hotel for the evening, ending the day just outside of Denver. The moment I parked the car, she was tumbling out of it like she'd been suffocating. She refused to have dinner with me in the hotel bar and wouldn't share breakfast with me this morning. Lunches have been painfully awkward pit stops. Any time I'm driving, she's got music blasting from the earbuds in her ears while she devours books on her Kindle like it's nobody's business.

I tell myself it has nothing to do with me. She just ran away from her *wedding*, from her family, her friends, and her career, from everything she's known. There is bound to be some unchecked, unbalanced emotion that comes with that, and I'm the only person around for her to take it out on.

But I also can't stop thinking back to the look on her face

when I told her I'd all but forgotten about our "summer fling," as if it weren't the most all-consuming kind of love I've ever experienced. As if I haven't been walking through life like a corpse searching for the feeling she gave me ever since.

As if I'm not well aware that nothing—no one—has ever come close to her.

The look she gave me at that moment made me feel like she was thinking all the same things, as if she were just as ruined as I was by our past. But if I allow myself to ponder that, I'll wonder why she left me. I'm not sure I can bear the answer to that question, which is part of the reason I don't allow myself to ask. Not yet, anyway. Not while the two of us are trapped in this car together for three more days—part of the reason why I suggested we forget our history in the first place.

At least until we both have more space. Oceans of it.

Having her close to me brings up feelings I've spent a long time trying to forget. I can't face the truth of that heartbreak in addition to her proximity. It's simply too much. Yet, I know there is no other place I'd rather have her be than right here, right beside me.

So, we resolve to silence instead.

I want to give her space to brood, to think about her life and her future, but I also can't stand the broken look on her face every time her eyes meet mine. I want to give her space, but instincts deep inside my soul compel me to try to comfort her. Solve all her problems. Make them mine. I don't know how to walk this tightrope with her.

Another clap of thunder roars around us, loud enough to drown out the music I have filtering through the car stereo. "Fuck," I mutter as the approaching storm shakes the car.

The sky directly above us is still clear blue, vibrant as the sun bounces off the bright red rock formations all around us. But up ahead, the clouds are thick and dark, encroaching on us like a predator to its prey, readying to swallow us whole.

"That's about to get fucking ugly," I murmur to myself.

"What?" Darby pipes up. I glance over to find her looking back at me, one AirPod removed from her ear.

I nod toward the windshield. "That thunderstorm is headed our way."

She follows my gaze, gasping as her eyes grow wide, as if she's only just realized. "Damn."

I laugh to myself. "Are you just now noticing? Have you missed the earthquakes of thunder that have been shaking the car every thirty seconds for the last fifteen minutes?"

Just as the words leave my mouth, thunder rumbles again.

She lets out a whoosh of breath. "I guess I've been really absorbed by this book."

"Which one?"

She clears her throat. "Um, *Tied Up In Temptation...*"

"Hmm." I hum, trying to hide my smile. "One of Elena's filthiest."

She gasps again. "You've read this?"

"I read all of Lele's books." I shrug. "She's my sister, and I want to support her."

"By reading about the girl who falls in love with her serial killer kidnapper?"

In reality, my stomach is in my throat as I think back to the novel Elena published a few years ago. Everett refuses to read her books, claiming they're far too erotic for him to even associate with his own sister. In a way, I agree, but I wanted to make sure she felt supported when she was just beginning her career.

The thought of Darby sitting so close to me reading that... I glance at her again, noticing for the first time the way her legs are clenched together, the flush spreading across her cheeks and down her neck. Fuck.

I shake those thoughts away. "Look, personally, not my kind of love story, but to each their own. Her writing is incredible."

Darby snorts, the first positive sound she'd given me in over a day, if not a sarcastic one.

"What?" I muse.

A small laugh erupts from her lips, and I realize I'd do just about anything to make it happen again. "I just can't imagine you reading smut."

I bite my lip, thinking of the best way to keep her laughing like that. "You know, I especially loved the part where he's got her tied up in the basement, and he uses the chains to—"

"Leo," she breathes, doubled over as she hides her laugh. "God, you're still a heathen."

"Yes, I am." I smile. "And, Darby"—her head snaps up to look at me—"I told you not to hide your smiles from me."

An emotion I can't read flashes across her face as her smile fades, and she nods. Silence fills the air between us once more as the approaching storm begins to devour us.

"Leo," she whispers.

"I know, Honeysuckle. I know."

My knuckles are so tight they're beginning to ache. I'm driving less than thirty miles per hour down the interstate. Windshield wipers are at full speed, and yet I can't make out the road more than a few feet in front of me. We've hydroplaned multiple times.

The only good thing is that there are hardly any other cars on the road right now. I'm not worried about crashing into someone else—I'm just worried about rolling my car into a ditch.

I'm worried most of all about the person next to me, about harming her.

"Are you buckled?" I ask.

"Yes," she responds. I glance over and find that she's gripping the handle above her with one hand. The other is dug into the end of her seat. She's breathing heavily. She looks afraid.

"Fuck this," I mutter. I'm not putting her in danger.

Through the pounding rain, I'm able to make out a sign that reads there is a rest area a fourth of a mile up the freeway. I slowly move into the right lane, both of us holding our breath as the car slides across the slick pavement again.

"What are you doing?" Darby asks as I exit the freeway and crawl into the parking lot of the rest area.

"I can't see shit, Darby, and I'm not going to risk getting us in an accident. We're just going to have to wait out the storm."

She lets out an exasperated breath as she throws her head back against the seat. Expecting her to argue with me, I wait for her response. Instead, she only nods.

After I make it to the rest stop and get the car parked, we both take a moment to catch our breath. Rain pelts the car around us, blocking out all sounds other than the thundering water and our breathing. The windows begin to fog, enclosing Darby and me into our own world, where it's just the two of us. It's reminiscent of another place where we once spent our time together, though, back then, it was the place I found peace. Now, my mind rages with chaos.

She's silent, eyes glued to her Kindle.

I clear my throat awkwardly. "So, how far into the book are you?"

She sighs, shutting off the e-reader before turning to face me. "We don't have to do this, Leo. We don't need to make weird small talk and pretend that any of it matters."

All of it matters.

"What's going on, Darby?" I ask. "I don't understand what I've done to make you so..." I wave my hand between us, realizing I don't have a word to describe her behavior right now. "I thought we agreed to start over as...friends."

Her nose scrunches in that annoyed expression I used to find so endearing. I hate that I still find it cute as hell, because I know this moment is tense. I hate that her beautiful face still makes me want to smile. I hate that I can still track every freckle that dots her nose. I hate that I still want to kiss them, that I still remember exactly what it feels like to have her against me and how hollow it feels to have her sitting right next to me now yet so far away. To know that I'll never hold her that close again.

Her eyes soften, and I wonder what kind of expression I must be giving her. I wonder if my eyes are disclosing how desperate I feel in her proximity. If those windows to my soul are wide open and calling out to her. I wonder if she's tracking my lips the way I'm watching hers. Remembering how soft and smooth they felt against me. Remembering all the places I've kissed her, all the places I've touched her.

I wonder if, like me, she's thinking about how the kind of connection the two of us once had is something that can't be replicated. Can't be forgotten. Can't be moved past. There can't ever truly be friendship between us, because Darby and I were once intertwined stars. At one time, we burst with light, threading through each other and forging together, though, in reality, we were both dying suns. Now, there's nothing left of us but stardust floating through the cosmos in the dark.

"Did you mean it?" I find myself asking. "What you said to me that night?"

Her eyes don't leave mine. They blaze right through me as she whispers, "Yes."

"Then why'd you leave?"

I promised myself I wouldn't ask. Told myself I didn't want to know, but the longing in her face is threatening to tear me apart, and I can't stop myself from yearning for the answer to the question that has haunted me for ten years.

Her honeyed eyes shudder as she breaks our contact.

"I need a moment," she murmurs. The roar of the outside storm comes to life as she throws the passenger door open and steps out into the pouring rain.

The wind howls, water pelting me sideways before she slammed the door behind her. The rest area is an empty parking lot with one building containing two sets of bathrooms. There is a small grass area with one towering tree in an otherwise barren desert landscape. I can just make out her figure running toward the bathrooms as I'm throwing open my door and going after her.

Wind whips through my hair, thunder roars through my

skull, and water drenches my body as I jog through the downpour behind her. "Darby!" I shout just as she reaches the women's restroom.

She pauses, seeming to take a deep breath, before turning around to face me, squinting at me through the falling rain as I reach her.

"Stop running away." I pant, catching my breath.

She throws her arms out wide. "Clearly, running away is what I do, Leo." She refuses to meet my gaze as she adds, "Run from the things that haunt me."

"What does that mean?" I ask, taking a step toward her.

She shakes her head, still glancing down at her feet. "Remember when you told me about your ghosts? About the ghosts that haunted you after you lost your mom? The way you blamed yourself?"

As she finally lifts her head toward me, my stomach bottoms out. There is so much sorrow, so much pain in her eyes. Water runs down her face, and I can't help but wonder if there are tears mixed into it. The storm raging above our heads is nothing in comparison to what brews within her gaze.

I nod.

"Well, I have ghosts now too."

"What ghosts?" I rasp.

"I can't..." She shakes her head, looking away. "I can't right now."

My heart feels like it's falling right out of my chest and onto the ground in front of her. An offering. I'm ready to get on my knees and beg her for the explanation I've been needing for years, but I can see the pain etched into her face is raw and real. Whatever happened, it tore her apart, maybe even more than it destroyed me.

She moves to step back from me, but it's as if a force outside my control takes over, reaching my arm out and grabbing hers, pulling her into me.

She falls against my chest, tense at first before settling. One arm snakes around my back while the other holds onto my chest, twisting into the now-soaked fabric of my T-shirt.

"I'm not afraid of your ghosts, Darby. You don't owe me an explanation. You don't owe me anything at all. But if you ever find yourself in a place to share your story, I'll be here to listen."

She doesn't respond, but I can feel her nod against me.

I give myself one final moment to savor the feel of her. The honey and floral scent of her shampoo. The soft curves of her body I used to think were created to fit the hard lines of my own. The warmth of her hand against my stomach, the other on my back. The way the top of her head rests perfectly below my chin.

She begins to pull away, and I let her, despite every instinct inside me begging me not to. Just briefly, she looks at me, her eyes still storming with so much emotion. We're in a small, covered alcove outside the bathrooms, but the rain blows sideways, coating us both in moisture.

I watch the water cascade down her soft cheeks. A droplet falls from the tip of her nose and onto her lips, lips that once made me believe in miracles and fate and two people being destined for one another. Looking at those lips—at her—feels like a tragedy now, like loss and longing and the death of faith.

Her lashes flutter, catching my attention as my gaze drags up to meet her eyes. Her brows pull together as she searches my face for something.

"Leo," she breathes. "Stop looking at me like that."

"Looking at you like what, Honeysuckle?"

"Like you know exactly what my soul feels like, and you've been incomplete without it all this time."

I do. I have.

I let my eyes fall shut and step back into the rain, finally putting that space between us. When I open them again, she's still beneath the awning, staring back at me through the downpour with devastation on her face.

"There's still a lightning storm out here. The safest place is in the car. I'll be waiting for you there, but please don't stay outside too long."

I turn around without waiting for her response and walk slowly back to the Mustang, uncaring if I get soaked in the process.

I'm staring out the driver's side window as I hear the passenger door open, and she slips inside a moment later. The only sound is the echo of rain pelting the hood.

"For what it's worth, I really did love you," I whisper.

"My word is worthless...but I loved you too."

Twenty-One

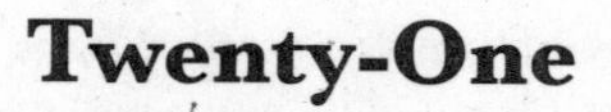

Honeysuckle

Then. June 30th.

I never knew being with another person could feel this way.

Sometimes, I unknowingly brush my fingers across my lips because I can still feel him there. I wonder if there will ever be a time in my life when I don't feel him there anymore. Every kiss he gives me is different than the one before it. Some are soft and delicate, feeling like the very first moment his lips touched mine. Others are hard and desperate, like the moment he realized I wanted more from him.

All of them are warm and delicious. All of them taste like mine.

I realize I'm rubbing my lip again as the sea breeze whips through my hair, tangling in the fingers resting on my face. The sunrise is pink and lavender this morning as I stare out at the soft, peaceful horizon. One lone surfer straddles his board out there on the waves. My surfer.

We migrated from our late-night walks to the pier to early-morning ones along the beach, where I watch him surf. We've spent each morning of the last week together this way. He then goes off to work in the garage that the Ramoses own, and I spend my days with my grandmother and in my online advanced-placement classes. Some evenings, I'll find him throwing rocks at my window, and I'll sneak out to spend time with him and his friends—our friends, it's starting to feel more like.

He's got his hand on me every moment we spend together. Even in public, it's always on my lower back or wrapped in my own. When we're alone, it's his lips that can't ever seem to leave my skin. He's always kissing my mouth. Or, he'll kiss my forehead, my hands, my shoulder, as if he can't get enough of me. But he never goes further than that, never further than what I've given him permission to do, places I've told him I want him to touch.

And the truth is, I want him everywhere. All around me. All the time.

He won't push for that, though, not until I'm ready. I feel myself barreling toward that with each moment I spend with him, feel myself falling into him faster and harder with each day that passes. It terrifies me, but not enough to try to stop it. Sometimes, it feels like I'm tumbling head-first into heartbreak, and I can only find it in myself to enjoy the freefall.

I watch Leo lie flat against his board and paddle out into the sea, as if he sees something I can't. Finally, I notice the wave coming for him. He flips his board around just as it crests, lifting him. He pops up as he ascends into the sky with the water, cutting sideways and gliding along the length of the wave as it crashes around him. It tunnels over Leo, but he rides through it before the wave finally crashes completely. He coasts out the far end and gets swallowed up by the water, his board slowly sinking back down into it.

Once his head pops up above the surface, and he climbs back onto his board, I send him a shout. He turns back toward me, and I shoot him a thumbs up. He throws me back the "rock-on" sign, with his hand fisted and only his pointer and pinky fingers in the air—though his thumb is sticking out too.

Elena told me Leo was one of the best surfers in the region, and though I know next to nothing about surfing, I believe that. What he does out there on the water is mesmerizing. It's majestic. Magic.

I understand what that Milo kid was talking about at the party last week when he was asking Leo about surfing. Leo isn't just another kid out there, catching waves on the weekend. This is his entire life. It's what he was meant to do.

I wonder what that must feel like—being destined for something.

A small while later, he comes back to shore. His tall, strong body drips with salt water as he makes his way toward me. The sun hasn't quite risen over the Pacific, and the world remains quiet with the sound of crashing waves and chirping birds as the morning's soundtrack.

"You're amazing," I say.

"And you're beautiful," he responds, bending down to press a wet kiss to my lips.

I laugh, pulling away as he shakes water all over me. "I'm serious. I don't understand how you can do that and make it look so effortless. It doesn't seem like it should be possible to do that."

He beams at me, those dimples appearing on his cheeks. "Do you want to learn how?"

"Leo." I roll my eyes. "There is no way I could ever learn how to surf like you do."

"Honeysuckle, nobody can surf like I do," he says, like it's the obvious answer. "But I can put you on my board. Teach you how to ride." He gives me a slow, mischievous smile.

"I'm sure you could." My voice produces a tone much rougher than I intended.

He raises his brows at me, and suddenly, my skin feels too warm, too tight.

I jump up from where I'm sitting and pull my T-shirt over my head, revealing Elena's black swimsuit again. Shimming out my shorts, I say, "Okay, fine. Let's do this." In reality, I think a splash of cold saltwater would do me well right now.

Leo's swallowing up my body, hardly noticing as I rip his orange surfboard from his hands and begin stalking toward the water. As he jogs after me, he places a warm hand at the center of my back, and a flood of chills roll down my spine at the feel of it.

He snaps the black strap of the bathing suit. "Have I ever told you how much I like this on you?"

"You don't have to. I can tell by the way you can't stop staring at my chest."

He pulls me tighter against him, and I stumble over the awkwardly large surfboard I'm trying to hold. "Can you blame me?" he whispers against my ear.

He chuckles at the physical shivers his proximity gives me, the goosebumps he no doubt feels erupting from my skin as he kisses my neck. I run my free hand down his chest, hovering dangerously close to the waistband of his shorts. "No, I can't," I murmur.

He groans. Reaching over and knocking the surfboard from my hand, he spins me so I'm pressed against his chest. Snaking both arms behind my back and grasping my backside, he presses his mouth against mine. It's a quick kiss, but I feel his tongue dip into my mouth, and I open for him on instinct. He swallows the moan I let out at the feel of him before he pulls back.

"You taste like honey," he rasps.

I hum against his mouth. "You taste like corruption."

He laughs, grabbing the board from the ground and stepping into the water. He walks until he's waist deep, small white caps crashing over his stomach. He stands at one end of the surfboard and holds his hand flat against it. Nodding to the opposite side of him, he says, "Get on."

"If you let me drift out to sea, Heathen, I swear to God..." I realize I can't think of a threat.

His dimples flash at me. "You're safe with me. Always."

I brace my arms on the surfboard and hoist myself over. It wobbles beneath my weight, but Leo holds it still. I sit straight up, straddling it with my legs hanging off either edge.

"All right, lay on your stomach." I inch my hands toward the top of the board and lay flat. "Okay," Leo says. "Now, you're going to paddle."

"No!" I yelp. "I don't want to float away alone."

He laughs. "I'm not going to let go. I'm going to hold you in place, and you'll just see what it feels like to paddle against the waves."

He stands behind me as I put my hands in the water and begin to paddle. I feel the water cutting through my fingers, flowing past my body, but I don't go anywhere.

"Good girl." I giggle at that. "Normally, you'd paddle out past the break. Then, once you see a wave coming that you want to ride, you start to paddle back toward the shore, hopping up once you feel the wave begin to swell. Then, you spread your legs wide and bend at the knees to keep your stance steady, riding the wave back to shore."

I nod. "That sounds great, but I don't think I will be trying that today."

He laughs again. "How about I hold the board here, and you just try popping up in place?" The board rocks beneath us again, and I give him a wide-eyed expression. "Most first-time lessons take place on the sand, but you're getting special treatment since you're with an expert."

I huff a laugh as I brace my weight on my arms and, in one quick movement, jump up until my feet are beneath my knees, and I'm crouched on the board. "Someday, I'll be able to tell people that the famous professional surfer Leo Graham gave me personal lessons once."

I wait for a wave to pass beneath us before I stand up straight on wobbly legs. I throw my arms out side to side as I sway, attempting to keep my balance. Leo looks up at me, his blue eyes sparkling with sunlight and his smile. "Hope I can teach you more than just surfing lessons, and I hope it's a lot more than once, Honeysuckle."

I click my tongue, still standing above him. "That an innuendo, Heathen?"

He shrugs playfully. "Maybe."

"Not sure what you think you could teach me, virgin," I clip back.

"Beautiful and deadly, that mouth," he says as he gently

pushes the surfboard and removes his hands. I squeal as I begin to lose my balance. He waves at me, smiling wickedly as the board floats away with me on it.

A wave crashes over me, and I tumble off the surfboard and into the ocean.

Water rushes through my nose and mouth as I become submerged. I feel my feet hit the ground, and I plant them, pushing off and toward the surface. Breaking it, I gasp for air, wiping salt water from my eyes as I blink around me.

The surfboard floats right next to me, attached by the cord strapped around my ankle. Leo's dimples are on full display as he swims toward me. "Look at you, baby! Riding a wave all by yourself. You're a natural."

I roll my eyes, pushing my sopping hair from my forehead. "You're annoying."

He only smiles at that. He grabs the board and holds it steady before hoisting himself over the top of it and straddling it. Holding out a hand to me, he says, "Come on."

"We can't both fit."

"It's not a wardrobe door, Darby. It's made to float. Trust me."

I snort at his lame *Titanic* reference and take his hand. He pulls me up onto the board, and I swing my leg over until I'm mimicking his position. We sit parallel to the horizon, both straddling the surfboard and staring at each other.

"Is this summer everything you hoped it would be when you got here?"

I smile. "I had no expectations of this summer when I arrived. I was mostly just concerned for my sister." I sigh. "I still am. I still haven't been able to speak to her. So, in that regard, things aren't great." Leo frowns. "But I didn't expect to meet any friends here, either. I'm normally pretty shy. It takes a lot to get me out of my shell, and the last thing I expected was some bad boy surfer to come break that shell right open the way you have." Leo's palm lies flat against the board in between us, and I cover it with my own. "And that part is better than anything my imagination could've cooked up."

The smile he gives me is bright and genuine—grateful. The smirk it morphs into is mischievous and playful. "You think I'm a bad boy?" he asks, flicking a brow.

"In my world, definitely."

"Do you...like bad boys?"

"Shut up." I laugh, shoving at him. "You're the best kind of bad boy because you've got a good soul." My hand is still pressed against his chest, and as I move it away, he stops me, covering it with his own.

He squeezes it four times. "That's the best thing anyone has ever said to me."

My eyes swell at that admission, and I find myself at a loss of words. I move my hand from his chest to behind his neck, tugging him into me. He meets me halfway, sealing our mouths together. His lips are salty and sweet and full and soft as he kisses me like he'll die without me.

"Leo," I breathe, realizing maybe it's me who kisses him like I'm the one about to die. "What are we supposed to do when summer ends and I go back to Kansas?"

"What do you want to do, Honeysuckle?" he asks against my lips.

"I just don't ever want to stop kissing you, stop hanging out with you. I want you..." I can't finish the sentence. The truth is, I just want everything from him, anything he's willing to give me, whether that be his friendship, his heart, or all the pieces of his soul.

I can't finish the sentence, but I'm not sure it matters. I'm not sure how he can give me anything when I'm two thousand miles away.

"I want it all too, Darby," he says. He raises his hand to cup my face. "I don't think it matters what promises we do or don't make on this beach. I'll be stuck on you, regardless. So, you can go back, and I can stay here, but I'll still be yours."

My eyes suddenly feel heavy, and my lips tremble as I speak.

"Me too."

He runs his thumb across my lip. "What about next summer? When you're done with school?"

I shrug. "My parents want me to go to college somewhere prestigious. They've never seemed too particular about where I go, though. I could...say I want to come back out here to be close to my grandma. Maybe I could go to UCLA or something."

"As long as the ocean stays exactly where it is, I can stay here too." He smiles.

"You'd wait a whole year just for me to come back?"

"I think I might wait my whole life for you to come back, Darby. Something tells me there would be no point in trying to move on from this, because I'd end up searching for you in every place I go, in every person I meet, aimlessly wandering until I find you again."

I close my eyes, letting his words soak into my skin, into my bones, my soul. I want them tattooed there, want to remember what this feels like. This moment. This feeling. His breath, his skin, his kaleidoscope eyes. I want him branded on me.

His grip on my chin tightens slightly, and I let my eyes flutter open. "You have to promise me something, though, Honeysuckle."

"Anything," I whisper.

"When you go back to Kansas, you need to promise me that if you're ever feeling unsafe, if you're ever feeling like you're about to break, about to lose yourself completely, you call me. Text me. Email me. Send letter by messenger pigeon. I don't fucking care.

"Do not go back to the girl you were before you arrived here. Do not be obedient. Timid. Submissive. You're not just the honey, Darby. You're the whole damn flower. Do not forget you have poison berries. You have strength, resilience, and an independent mind. You do not need to conform to anyone else's way of living. Okay?"

I nod.

He squeezes my jaw four times, reiterating a word with each press of his fingers against my skin. "You're. Safe. With. Me."

Letting his hand slide from my jaw and to my chest, his hand hovers just over my heart. "Day or night. If you need me, I'm there, no questions asked. I'm always going to protect you. Until the end of time."

I have no words to respond with, so I give him the brightest smile I can muster. "I'm so lucky I found you, Leo."

"I don't think luck had anything to do with it, Honeysuckle. This"—he wiggles his finger between us—"is divine intervention."

Twenty-Two

Honeysuckle

Now. May 30th.

My fingers brush against the skin of my lips as I stare down at my phone screen.

Things have miraculously been less awkward since our moment at the rest stop. The storm lasted another two hours after we both climbed back into the car, soaking wet and emotionally devastated. He only smiled at me and asked if I wanted to play checkers with him on his phone.

We set it horizontally on the console between us, one end facing me and the other facing him. I won seven times, and he won five. We laughed the entire time, and I felt lighter than I had in years. We didn't talk about our past together, about the two of us. We were content to find common ground, even though we both knew it wouldn't last forever.

He told me more about his career, all the places he's traveled, the records he's set, the trophies he's won. I told him about my time in college and how I went into teaching. I talked to him about my life with Dahlia and Lou.

I know Leo deserves more than I'm giving him right now, but I can't read him now the way I was able to when I was younger. There are moments when he tells me to forget about our "fling" like it was nothing to him, and then there are moments where he's looking at me with so much longing I'd think he never moved on from us at all. He's guarded, much more so than he was at seventeen, and I can't help but think I'm the reason for those walls.

I also wonder if I'm the one who can cause a crack within them, and that's what's happening when his eyes take on that glassy hue and zone in on my lips like he's remembering what they feel like.

As for me, I've never forgotten what it feels like to kiss him. I still feel him there every time I touch my face.

Which is what I'm feeling now as I read Jackson's most recent text message for what feels like the hundredth time.

You know I love you, Darby. Please come home. I need you, babe. Please. I'm begging.

The sad part about it is that I don't believe him, because this is the first time he's told me he loves me since I left. All the messages before this one have consisted of, *You're embarrassing me* and *You're making us look like a joke* and *Get your ass back to the church immediately. Stop causing a scene.*

Something tells me he and my father have spent hours poring over the note I left him, analyzing it like it's another one of their business contracts, determining that the best way to make me come back is to convince me that Jackson's loved me all along.

The only thing Jackson has ever loved is his career, being my father's right-hand man, the certainty that a marriage to me would bring him when it comes to taking over Andrews Development when my dad retires.

My father has always wanted to keep the business in the family but never had the belief that my sister or I were capable of running it ourselves. Which is fine by me because I have zero desire to manage a construction company, to be the owner of half the land in Crestwell, Kansas.

That company made my father heartless.

My heart may be the only part of me I still feel like is mine and mine alone. I'd never risk that.

My dad knew the best way to keep the business inside the family, without having to hand it over to my sister or myself, would be to hand it over to someone we'd marry. He also knew that Dahlia would never conform enough to allow him to hand-pick the man she weds. But I, on the other hand, have been groomed for just that since the day I was born, since the moment he realized he'd never have a son.

I sigh.

"Where's your head at, Honeysuckle?" Leo asks beside me.

I pull my eyes from my phone and look up at him. On the flat, empty stretch of highway, he takes his gaze off the road to briefly focus on me.

"Um, just...checking my messages."

I watch his throat work as he swallows. "Is everything okay?"

"Yeah," I breathe. "He's just... He's been begging."

"And you feel guilty?"

I shake my head. "I feel bad because I *don't* feel guilty. I don't believe him."

"Do you love him?" he asks.

I blink at Leo, and his head immediately swivels back out to the highway, as if he didn't mean to pose the question.

"I've tried." I look back down at my phone. "When we first started dating, everyone loved him. My parents, my friends, my coworkers. He was perfect on paper: good-looking, educated, generous, and kind. I knew it was an arrangement; he wasn't in love with me, but you know... Things could be worse. It made me feel selfish to think that wasn't enough for me. So, I tried..."

"To force it to be enough?"

"Yeah..." I sigh. "And it never was."

"I know the feeling," he says quietly.

We fade back into silence, knowing that the moment cut a little too deep. Only the sound of the rumbling highway remains.

I didn't return Jackson's message. I texted Dahlia to let her know we'd gotten stuck in a storm and didn't reach Richfield, Utah, today as we planned. Then, I turned off my phone, too afraid that the next time Jackson calls me, I'll answer.

Rain started pouring again just as the sun was setting. Leo wasn't willing to risk getting caught in another storm in the dark, so we made a small detour into Moab, the closest town off the freeway with an abundance of hotels due to its proximity to Arches National Park.

Apparently, the amount of hotels didn't matter when the congestion of summer tourism outnumbered them.

"I've got one room available," the receptionist says as her fingers click across the keyboard in front of her on the other side of the counter from where Leo and I stand, exhausted and still damp.

It's the sixth hotel we've walked into since pulling into town. I had to cancel the reservation I made for the hotel in Richfield. Service in the area wasn't strong enough for me to book a room in Moab online, so we've resulted in walking inside a number of lodges and inns trying to find two beds for the night.

Leo glances at me from the corner of his eye. I bite my lip. I know he's waiting for me to make the decision.

"How many beds?" I ask.

"Two queens."

It's possible we could find another hotel with two rooms, but I'm exhausted and in desperate need of a long, hot shower.

Without allowing myself to read Leo's expression, I quickly say, "All right, we'll take it."

Before I have the chance to sort through my wallet, Leo is smacking his credit card across the counter and paying for the room. The receptionist hands us over our keys and a pamphlet on Arches. Leo takes both, as well as my bag, hiking it over his shoulder as I follow him to the elevators.

This is the point in the evening when I've snuck off to my own room, wallowing in self-pity, ordering several orders of french fries from room service and talking to my sister until I pass out the last two days.

Tonight, I won't have that option.

Neither of us says anything as we take the elevator up to the fourth floor. To *our* room.

Leo enters ahead of me, flipping on a light as he holds the door open with his shoulder. The room smells clean, at least. To my right is a sliding door that leads to a small bathroom with a sink on one side, a shower with a clear glass door covering only one half of it on the other, and a toilet at the back. To my left is a closet, and in front of me is a standard hotel room with yellow floral-printed comforters on each of the queen beds that sit against the sage green walls. On the far end of the room are paneled windows that look out to the parking lot and the towering red rocks behind them.

The view is actually beautiful. The sky is clear now, the moon illuminating the rocks in a soft, blue light. I imagine it's stunning in the daytime.

Leo clears his throat behind me. "Which bed do you want?"

I'm afraid to turn and look at him, so I keep my gaze glued on the windows. "I don't care."

"I'd prefer to be closer to the door if that's all right with you."

I nod because, despite everything, I think I still know him down to his bones. Leo prefers to be closer to the door because we're four floors up, which means a threat-by-window is unlikely, but if someone were to break in our door, they'd have to go through him before they got to me.

He's protective by nature, by trauma, which is likely why he refused to drive through the storm today. He knows what it feels like to lose someone in a car accident, to believe it's his fault, even when it isn't.

Despite everything, his driving force is to keep me safe.

To keep his promises.

That realization has the room suddenly feeling much too small, too tight, as if I can feel his presence all over me, even when he's several feet away. I hear him slowly come up behind me, throwing his backpack onto his bed before crossing the room to gently set my bag down onto mine.

"I am, uh, I'm going to go move the Mustang to the backend of the parking lot so I can see it from the room. You know how people like to break into classic cars."

I didn't know that was a thing, but I said, "Yeah."

"If you want to shower now, I'll shower when I get back?"

"Sure." My eyes catch the mirror in the corner in front of me. I study myself. My blond hair is in a messy braid that falls down the side of my shoulder. My deep red Kansas City Chiefs crewneck hangs off me loosely, still damp with rain. My white sneakers are muddy with red dirt. My eyes are tired and bloodshot. My face spells exhaustion, both emotional and physical.

But my gaze is pulled to the man behind me. He looks just as tired as I do, but his blue eyes still sparkle just as brightly as they always have. He doesn't seem to notice the mirror, doesn't seem to notice me watching him as he rakes down my body. I notice the way his fists clench at his sides, as if fighting the urge to reach toward me.

I understand that instinct, because it takes every ounce of my remaining strength to keep my back turned to him.

His jaw is tense, full, soft lips tight, brows furrowed as he studies me. It's longing I see on his face, a mix of devastation and desire. It's the same waring expression in his eyes when our conversations move rapidly from laughing like no time has passed to heavy silence when one of us says something a little too deep.

Suddenly, his eyes snap to the mirror, to my own. He doesn't look away, and neither do I. He opens those windows to his soul, letting me see everything swirling within them, the cracks and bruises and wounds that haven't healed. The truth he didn't speak out loud earlier, but that I knew was there anyway.

Both of us have attempted to give ourselves to others over the years, and we've both fallen short each time.

No other person, no other love—no other soul—will ever be enough for either of us. And now, as we stare into each other through the mirror, we can see the reason behind it all.

I feel his eyes in every atom of my body. I feel him all across my flesh, goosebumps rising as he burns through me. I feel the intensity of that sapphire gaze covering me like a fog. Like a cloud. A downpour. A thunderstorm roaring all around me. Drenching me. Choking me. Drowning me.

I lower my head, breaking the moment, unable to breathe.

Leo doesn't say anything as he backtracks out of the room and leaves, the door clicking shut behind him.

I find myself rushing through my shower because all I can think about is Leo sitting in the room by himself, waiting for his turn. I don't want to leave him in his cold, damp clothes. I wash my hair, my face, and my body, only savoring the warmth of the water as I rinse. I change into a pair of cotton shorts and a large T-shirt, ringing out my wet hair before pulling it up into a lazy bun.

I'm normally a little too insecure to be around someone as beautiful as Leo without makeup, especially with the hormonal breakout I've got going on right now, but at one point in my life, I allowed the man I'm sharing a room with to intimately know every inch of my body. He's seen me with and without makeup, seen me washed in tears, with food in my teeth and sand in my hair, and back then, he loved me all the same, thought all of me was beautiful anyway.

Jackson didn't think that way about me, I don't think. He's seen me bare-faced, but he's also always inspected what I've worn to a public outing, had no problem telling me if he thought I had too much makeup on or not enough. Before Jackson, it was my mother who said those things to me. I guess, over the years, it made me a tad self-conscious.

But I also know I snore, and I have no choice but to sleep in the same vicinity as Leo tonight. So, if he's going to hear me snoring, then seeing me bare-faced should be the least of my concerns.

I gather my dirty clothes and my toiletry bag, sneaking back out into the main room. Leo's sitting on the edge of his bed, scrolling through his phone as he drags a hand through his wet hair. It flops onto his forehead as he lifts his head to look at me.

His eyes roam across my body again, lingering on my legs before meeting my face. "Shower's all yours," I say hoarsely, having trouble speaking through the blaze in his stare.

He nods, and we pass each other awkwardly as he makes his way toward the bathroom, and I make my way toward my bed. As I set my things down, I glance over my shoulder to find him pulling off his shirt as he enters the bathroom.

I get a glimpse of his shoulders, the flex of the muscles along his stomach, the strength of his arms as he lifts them over his head. I catch just a flash of the ink across his bare chest, the sight of which has my heart seizing in my own.

I can't help but listen to him move into the bathroom, the shuffle of clothing as he undresses. I remember the freckle on his upper ribs I used to press my mouth against. I wonder if his skin is still bare and smooth, or if he now has a dusting of hair. I think about the veins in his hands, the way they used to look as they ran along my skin.

I think about his tattoos again. My throat suddenly grows thick, my eyes heavy.

Deciding I need space and fresh air until I'm sure he's fully clothed again, I bend down and pull my wallet from my purse before walking toward the door. I pause, rasping my knuckles against the bathroom. "I'm going to go grab some drinks from the vending machine. Do you need anything?" I ask.

"Water," he says gruffly before clearing his throat. "Please."

"Okay." My voice cracks because I'm now imagining him naked, only a door separating me from the sculpted planes of his athletic body.

Shaking off the unwelcome wave of desire, I slip out of the

hotel room.

I'm quiet when I return with two sodas and two bottles of water a few minutes later. I hear the roar of the showerhead behind the door.

It's as I'm setting the drinks down on the mini bar that I freeze, because I hear a rough, strained "Darby" from inside the bathroom. It almost sounds pained.

I step up to the door, pressing my ear against it as I place my hand on the knob, wondering if something could be wrong, if he heard me re-enter the room.

He lets out another groan, that one deeper than the last.

Without much thought, I shove the door open, my own protective instincts taking over as I step into the bathroom.

All of the breath leaves my lungs, all of the thoughts leave my head, and all the air inside the room seems to dissipate as I take in the sight before me.

He's leaning against the shower wall, his spectacular body on full display as the glass door covers only the half of the shower where the water cascades from the head, the other end left wide open. His body presses against the tile as his head is thrown back and his jaw slack.

Thick veins in his neck work as I watch movement in his shoulders. My gaze soaks in every detail of the man I've spent countless nights dreaming about when I've closed my eyes. He's broader than he was when he was young, more toned. Lean muscles are cut and defined from years of balancing on a surfboard and wading through water.

But my eyes are snagged by the thin chain around his neck and the unmistakable gold ring looped through it, hanging at the center of his chest, pressing against the tattoo across his heart.

There is no way.

I swallow thickly. It's not possibly what I think it is, but my heart stops all the same. It cracks open, falling to the floor along with my jaw. I can't stop watching him, drinking him in.

Water storms against his chest, beads of it cascading down

his form. My traitorous eyes follow a droplet as it slowly runs down the length of his stomach, pooling at the place where his hand meets his—*God.*

Veins in his forearms flex as I watch him pump himself, long, thick, and hard as steel. Suddenly, my mouth is very, very dry. It's nearly mesmerizing as I watch him pleasure himself.

Until his hand stops moving.

My eyes shoot to his face to find his own now open, glued to me, watching me. He doesn't seem startled, doesn't seem embarrassed. No, he seems almost...assessing, as if he's trying to gauge my reaction. Meanwhile, that's what I'm doing too.

Because we definitely just crossed a line, and I think we're both trying to figure out if the other is going to take a step back to their own side, or if we're about to throw all caution to the wind.

I swallow. "I–I'm sorry... I thought..." My eyes flicker to his cock again, and I lose all coherency. "I thought I heard my name."

I bite my cheek, allowing myself one last glance as I slowly step through the threshold of the bathroom, but before I can shut the door, I hear him softly murmur, "You did."

I lift my head to meet his gaze. "What?"

He doesn't shy away. "You did," he says, louder this time. "You did hear me say your name. The name I've been moaning every time I fuck my fist for the last ten years."

A sound leaves my lips at that, but I'm not even sure what it is. It kind of sounded like a moan, an involuntary noise, followed by an involuntary reflex to run my eyes down his beautiful body again.

My teeth drag against my lips as he pumps himself once more, then freezes, as if he didn't realize he'd been doing it until I was focused on it.

"Darby," he rasps. I look at his eyes again. "Do you ever think of me?"

I feel my face go red, but not with embarrassment. With need. With desperation. "Yes," I whisper.

"When?"

"Every time I close my eyes."

He lets out a groan at that, his head falling back against the tile as his cock twitches in his hand. I can't look away. I know I should step out. Let him finish. Pretend this never happened, that those admissions never came out of either of our mouths. But I can't. I can't, because I feel like I've just received the answer to a question I didn't know I'd been asking.

"Will you show me?" he asks quietly, his bright blue eyes blazing through me with such ferocity I'm not sure how I'll survive the night without touching myself anyway.

My tongue flicks out across my lip, knowing Leo just crossed that line, invited me to smash those boundaries with him, and I know the logical part of my brain is out to lunch because no part of me can say no right now.

"Yes."

His chest is heaving rapidly, and I feel my thighs clench together, feel my body flood with heat as I watch his hand resume its earlier motion. My gaze bounces rapidly between his eyes and his cock.

"Take off those shorts." He nods toward the bathroom counter across from him. "Sit your pretty ass on that counter and slide your panties to the side."

Oh, my God.

Part of me wants to say to hell with all of it and strip off the entirety of my clothing so I can step inside the shower with him, but clearly, he's trying to keep some sort of boundary in place, and I don't want to risk making him uncomfortable.

I do as he says. His eyes smolder as he watches me slowly slip out of my pajama shorts and pad across the bathroom before hiking myself onto the counter directly in front of him.

My mind is still stuck on the ring around his neck as I watch it bounce with each inhale of his rapid breath. He licks his lips, eyes zoned in on the center of my thighs. "Spread your legs, Honeysuckle."

They spring open, as if he's got control over all my movements.

I watch his hand move quicker now, pumping his cock at a rapid pace. The ache between my own thighs is unbearable now as I slide a hand across my leg and slowly pull my underwear to the side, baring myself for him.

I hear his breath hitch. "Fucking beautiful." His voice is rough and raspy, just as I remember it. "Are you wet right now?"

I run a finger through my center, knowing he can hear the evidence of my arousal as I gather the wetness on my finger before moving it up to circle my clit. It's answer enough.

"Fuck."

I can't decide what's more erotic: the hungry look on his face, the fervor in his eyes as his gaze devours my body, or the sight of him fucking himself as he watches me. The knowledge that he thinks of me while he does it. Imagines me the way I've always imagined him.

I don't know where to look, because the sight of him is too much. The water coats his body and makes his tan, smooth skin glisten. His muscles flexing as he works himself. The ridges of his cock, knowing it's hard for me. The way his jaw flexes as he watches me circle myself faster, searching for the release I've needed for so long.

Wishing it was his hand, his fingers. His mouth or his cock. Just wishing it was him. Needing him. Desperate for him.

I slide my hand down to my center, slowly slipping one finger inside myself. He groans as he watches me. I pull out and then add a second finger. Pressing my thumb against my clit, I begin pumping into myself faster and faster, feeling the pressure build. The buzzing in my center is beginning to reach its peak.

"Leo," I moan.

"Baby. Fuck. Darby. Yes," he chants, the words nearly unintelligible through the gruff roughness of his strained voice.

My skin grows tight, my body tensing as I inch closer to that euphoria I'm so desperate for. I feel my legs begin to clench around my arm when Leo growls, "Keep those fucking thighs open."

My stomach flutters at his demand as I spread my knees,

moving toward the edge of the counter and angling my hips upward so I'm even more bared for him than I was before. He makes a noise of approval.

I'm still watching his cock strain against his hand, watching it pulse as he fists his hard length. His arm is trembling as he moves, his opposite arm flat against the shower wall. The scene in front of me is so raw, so intimate. The band within my body is beginning to snap, but I yearn for something more. I don't know what that more is. I think it might be him.

"Leo," I whimper. "I need...I need—"

"I know, baby. I know," he moans.

The sound of his voice sends me tumbling head-first into that oblivion I've been craving.

My head falls back against the bathroom mirror, my eyes flutter shut as I feel my body lift out of my throat, and my mind begins to scatter. Toes curling, I know I'm about to lose myself.

"Eyes on me, Honeysuckle. I want you looking at me as you come."

"Fuck." My head snaps up, gaze landing on him just as my climax tears through me, cleaving my body apart. My hips buck against my hand shamelessly as I feel myself tremble and tense around my fingers, wishing it was Leo I was clenching.

His eyes glow with desire and lust as he watches me. That blue-eyed stare rips me to pieces, his mouth parting in ecstasy. He moans my name, fisting his length one final time as his release erupts from his tip, landing on his stomach. My own pools in my palm, my hand still pressed against my center.

I'm not sure there are words to describe the potency of the air between us, crackling with energy and passion. My entire body feels warm as I catch my breath. Water pelts Leo's body, washing away his release. I pull my hand from between my legs and let my knees close. The room feels heavy as we both come down from the clouds, and the reality of our actions settles over us.

Taking a deep breath, Leo runs his free hand through his hair. His gaze lingers on the place where my teeth sink into my bottom lip, and mine is still focused on the ring around his neck.

"Did you mean what you said? That you think of me every time you close your eyes?" His voice is strained.

"Yes," I say, soft but clear.

His eyes blanket with something that resembles agony, and I wonder if mine look the same, because the realization dawning on him is one I came to as well.

He turns, pressing his forehead against the shower wall as the water pounds against his back.

I don't say the words, but he does. "All we are is lost time."

I can't keep the emotions at bay anymore. I feel tears trickle down my face. I'm not embarrassed by what just happened—I'm only wrecked by it.

I silently slide off the counter, not bothering to pick up my shorts from the ground as I exit the bathroom and crawl into bed. I face the wall so I won't have to watch him when he re-enters the room. I hear the shower shut off, and a moment later, the bathroom door opens. I make no effort to quiet the tears that soak my pillow.

Footsteps near, but I don't turn around. I don't acknowledge them as I feel the mattress dip behind me.

"Honeysuckle," he whispers just above my ear. I don't respond. "Can I lay with you?"

There is no taking back the mistakes of our past, no way to right our wrongs or reverse our regrets. The heavy weight of that is nearly unbearable and has been unbearable for years.

Knowing he needs this moment as badly as I do, I nod.

The sheets lift as he crawls in beside me, wrapping one strong arm around my waist and tugging me against him. His knees line up with mine perfectly, our hips flush together, as if made just to fit the other. He nuzzles his chin over the top of my head, allowing his lips to lightly brush against my temple.

And finally, I tumble into a dreamless sleep.

Twenty-Three

Honeysuckle

Then. July 7th.

"So, what exactly happened on your first date?" Elena asks as she tugs a brush through my thick hair.

"It's really not worth repeating," I mutter.

"Must've been bad to get Leo all worked up."

I wave a hand. "He's dramatic."

She snorts. "True, but you know he's never taken someone on a date like this before? He pays such close attention to you that he actually remembers exactly what clothes you have in your closet and described to me the exact dress he wants you to wear tonight."

A blush creeps up my neck.

"I've never seen him this way before, Darby. It's...cute. But also weird."

I laugh. "Well, I've never exactly felt this way either."

Elena is quiet for a moment, twisting my hair around a curling iron. "I'm glad you guys found each other, that you get to experience this kind of...thing when you're young."

"Are you saying you've never been in love?" I ask, knowing that's not true.

"I think there is a difference between love and infatuation. Infatuation is dangerous. Obsessive. Toxic, like holding matches when you're covered in gasoline. You know you're going to destroy yourself—destroy each other—but you do it anyway, just because you wonder what the burn feels like."

"Wow," I breathe. "Intense. So...why keep going back?"

"Because I can't stay away," she murmurs.

I'm fairly certain she's talking about Zach, but she doesn't use his name, so neither do I. "Is it hard? Being so...intertwined? Between your relationship and the mutual friendships floating all around you?"

She nods thoughtfully, focusing on my hair. "It's devastating, but for how awful it is ninety percent of the time, that ten percent is..." She huffs. "There aren't words. Like there is this little world where only the two of us exist, a language that only we can speak. When he touches me..." She shakes her head. I can see chills roll down her spine at the thought of it. "It's a touch only he can provide, a feeling only he can produce. And in those quiet moments, there is so much passion, so much love." I meet her eyes through the mirror. "There is love. I promise."

I hold my hands up. "I believe you. I can see it."

"That love outweighs everything else, and I don't know if we'll ever be capable of getting it right. If we'll ever learn to love without the hate. If we'll ever be able to heal without hurting. But for those moments when it's just the two of us...I'll fight my whole life for that."

Our eyes meet in the mirror again, and hers go wide, as if just realizing what she's said. She shakes her head. "Wow. I cannot believe I just dumped all that on you. I'm sorry."

"No." I shake my own head. "Please, dump on me."

She snorts, and we both bust up with laughter.

"I just mean...I've never had girlfriends either, Elena. I think this is what girls do. So, you can tell me about your feelings any time. As long as I can dump all over you, too."

An hour later, I'm descending the stairs in a sundress and a pair of white sandals with a small heel. Elena curled my hair and clipped it half up. She dusted blush on my cheeks, mascara on my eyelashes, and a swipe of gloss on my lips. My dress is a pale yellow with thin straps over my shoulders, tied at the top with a bow. Buttons line the center of the dress from my chest to the hem. It's cinched at the waist and falls down to my mid-thigh.

I say goodbye to Elena as she leaves, and she lets me know that Leo will be by in twenty minutes to pick me up. I shut the door and startle as I find my grandma sitting at the dining room table, staring at me.

"Hi," I squeak.

"You look like you got plans tonight." Her eyes scan me as she drops the Kindle in her hand down onto the table.

Ignoring her observation, I ask, "What are you reading today?"

She smirks behind her glass of white wine. "I'm not telling you anything."

I smile. "Then I'm not telling you anything, either."

"Sit down." She nods toward the other end of the table.

I huff but take a seat.

"Where are you going tonight?"

I bite my lip. "Are you going to tell my parents?"

She rolls her eyes. "Have I told your parents about any of the other nights you snuck out? Did I tell them when you were hungover that morning? Or about the boy I've caught tromping through the backyard more often than normal?"

I gasp, realizing she's been privy to everything that's been happening over the course of the last month.

She snickers. "I'm not an idiot, sunshine. You're also not as stealthy as you think you are, not even a little bit." She shrugs. "I told you I wanted you to be dumb and seventeen, and I also think your dad is a bit of an asshole, so I'm not going to say anything." I let out a sigh of relief. "But I also need to make sure you're being safe. Because if something happens to you, that's when we're going to have a problem."

I study my grandmother for a moment. Her face is so similar to mine I wonder if she looked just like me when she was younger.

I wonder if all she wanted at seventeen was to be young and dumb too. I wonder if she had a Leo.

"Why haven't you told my parents anything? Why aren't you holding me to the same standards they do?"

She slowly lifts her glass of wine to her mouth. "Because when I was your age, I wanted all the things you want right now too. I didn't get them. I listened to my dad. Went to the college he told me to go to. Married the man he picked out for me. Had the babies and the house, watched my husband make money and own a successful company—none of which was given to me upon his death. No, it all went directly to your father, who still controls all of my finances. I let it happen, though. I sat quietly by and watched forty years of my life pass. A life that wasn't mine." She takes a slow sip. "Your sister is different; she was born kicking and fighting, and she'll make it through this too. But you, Darby, you're just like me. I don't want you living a life that isn't really yours."

As her words filter through my being, I feel my heart break for her. "I'm so sorry."

"Don't be sorry for me, child. I don't want that either." She smiles. "Just...don't make the same mistakes, all right? I'm protecting you now, but I can't protect you forever, and not from everything. Eventually, you're going to need to start standing up for yourself and putting your foot down with your dad. I hope this summer will teach you how to do that."

"Me too," I whisper. "I'm going on a date tonight. My first date with a boy back in Kansas, it...didn't go well. Leo wants to try to make up for it. I think he's just taking me to dinner."

She nods. "That boy is a heathen, but he's got a good heart, and he's been through a lot."

"He has," I respond quietly.

"What are you going to do about him when you go back home at the end of the summer?"

"Hope I get to come back someday." Hope is all I have.

Grandma gives me a sad smile. "You know, my back is getting bad." She swirls her wine around the glass. "It's hard for me to get up and down the stairs these days." She's lying. She's the most in-shape seventy-year-old I've ever met. "Maybe...maybe I'll need you to stay around here to help me out." She glances up at me with a glimmer in her eye. "That is, if you wouldn't mind finishing out your senior year of high school here."

I grin back at her. "I was thinking about applying to UCLA. It would be a lot easier to do that if I were already here." I shrug. "Y'know, campus tours and stuff like that."

It was unlikely my father would agree to something like that, even if he weren't already upset with me, which he very much is. This past Sunday, he refused to let me talk to Dahlia again. I've tried calling her phone myself, but it goes straight to voicemail each time.

I told my parents I wasn't interested in speaking with them until they could either tell me what was going on with my sister or let me talk to her myself. My dad fumed, asking what had gotten into me. I felt like I saw a little sparkle in my mom's eyes at my defiance. Regardless, I told them to call me when I could speak to Dahlia and hung up.

I haven't heard from anyone since. Tomorrow is Sunday, and I'm hoping I'll get a call from Dahlia then, but I'm not expecting it. That's what most of my life is when it comes to my dad—hope without expectation. I can hope he'd let me stay with my grandma next year, hope he'd let me go to school here in California, hope he'd let me talk to my sister, hope he'd give me freedom.

But deep down, I know better than to expect any of it.

"Be safe and have fun tonight." Grandma winks at me, rising from the table and walking out of the room with her wine glass in one hand and her e-book—probably those romance ones about cowboys I know she likes—in the other.

I've never really had a role model, nobody I particularly looked up to and wanted to be like, but I think I may want to be like her when I'm older, in her house on the cliffside, overlooking the sea, spending her days tending to her garden, attending the farmer's market, sitting on the porch reading steamy romance books and drinking wine.

I can only hope I'll have a lifetime of love to go along with it, a person to hold my hand in those rocking chairs. Maybe a career I love, too.

I take a glance around my grandma's dining room, noticing the flowers that bloom all along the window sills outside, imagining what it would feel like if this were my house. My home. I realize it's the closest thing I've ever felt to home before.

"Grandma!" I shout, catching her attention before she heads outside.

"Yeah?" she calls back.

"Can you show me your garden sometime this week?" I chew my lip. "Do you think I could plant some flowers somewhere?"

A cackle of laughter rings out before I hear the back door shut.

I smile to myself as a knock clammers from the front of the house. I brush my fingers through my hair and smooth out my dress as I stand from the table. I tell myself I'm not nervous, but butterflies flutter in my stomach, and my heart leaps from my chest as I pull the front door open and find him standing there.

He's smiling at me with his boyish dimples and eyes of pure blue. His hair is brushed out of his face, and he leans against the doorway with one hand in his pocket, the other holding a bouquet of flowers. His skin is golden beneath his white short-sleeved button-down and a pair of black shorts. His Van-clad feet are crossed at the ankles.

As my eyes roam back up his body and reach his face, I realize he's doing the same to me.

"You are, without a doubt, the most beautiful person I've ever laid my eyes on."

I glance down at my feet, feeling the blush that rushes to my face. I bite my lip to hide how much his words make me want to giggle.

"None of that." He clicks his tongue. "I told you not to hide your smiles from me."

I lift my head and let him see it—the way he makes me feel. "I just don't know what to say," I finally murmur.

"Say thank you."

"Thank you." I nod toward the bouquet in his hand. "You brought me flowers?"

"Honeysuckles."

I laugh as he hands the flowers to me. They smell sweet and light. "How did you find a bouquet of just honeysuckles?"

"I didn't." He shrugs. "My neighbors have a bush in their front yard, so I snuck over in the middle of the night and picked them for you."

"Leo." I look up from the flowers and to his face. "You could've gotten in trouble for that."

He smiles, dimples deepening on his cheeks. "Worth it."

I rush forward and kiss his cheek. He's the one blushing as I pull back. "Thank you," I say. "They're beautiful and perfect."

"Just like you."

God, he is not real.

I walk into the kitchen and fill a vase with water before dropping the flowers inside of it and meeting Leo back at the front door. He takes my hand, leading me down my grandmother's porch steps and to some kind of black classic muscle car I can't put a name to.

I look at him, eyes wide and mouth gaping. "What is this?"

"I may or may not have borrowed one of the cars from the shop for tonight."

"Borrowed as in..."

"As in, Carlos doesn't know I've borrowed it, but it'll be parked back in the shop tomorrow morning in the same spot it was in when he left today."

"That is incredibly reckless."

He pulls the car door open and motions for me to get in. The seats are bright red leather, and the interior is immaculate and classic. "You're worth the risk." He winks as he shuts the door and walks around to the driver's side.

He slips a pair of sunglasses over his eyes, and the sun hits him at just the right moment that I swear, he could be in a movie montage. It's like he's moving in slow motion, pulling the keys out of his pocket and opening the door.

My body seems to vibrate with need for him.

"Where to now?" I ask as he turns on the ignition.

"The best night of your life, Honeysuckle."

Twenty-Four

Heathen

Now. May 31st.

She snores.

Darby snores. She's been lying on my arm all night, and her knee is in my balls. I swear to God, I've never felt more content.

I never got to have this moment with her when we were younger. We had nights where she'd fall asleep in my arms on the beach, or sometimes in my bedroom on the rare occasion I could sneak her in, but we never truly got to spend a night together. We'd always have to sneak back home before her grandmother woke up.

I've never had the chance to experience her sleeping deep enough to be snoring in my ear or kicking me in the knee.

I'm not sure I slept at all last night, but at this moment, my soul feels more rested than it has in years. Her cheek is flat against my chest, her legs bent in between mine, her arm thrown over my waist. Her heavy breath splays across my neck with each noisy exhale.

I can't help but wonder the last time she slept so deeply, the last time she didn't have something weighing on her. Was it the last happy moment she spent with me? Before whatever happened, happened? Before she met him and was forced into a relationship she wasn't confident in, planning a wedding she didn't want, and living up to the unreachable expectations of her family?

I wonder if he's ever gotten to wake up next to her, gotten to feel her breath against his neck, and if he cherished it the way I am right now.

She told me she'd lived with her sister up until her engagement and that she moved back in with her parents to plan the wedding. It sounds like she's never lived with her fiancé. Ex-fiancé. I'm sure it has something to do with the small-town values of her family. It makes me wonder if there are other parts of her he's never seen, moments he's never experienced with her.

But I don't let my thoughts run down that road. I'm not sure I could live with the disappointment of the probable reality.

I realize now that it doesn't fucking matter. It doesn't matter why she left. It doesn't matter what happened in our years apart. Every move I've ever made has been plastered in the tabloids. I'm sure she knows exactly what my history looks like, and I can't imagine the pain that must've put her through, especially now that I know she's been missing me in the same ways I've been missing her.

Every time I close my eyes.

That one simple sentence destroyed me.

All this time, I believed she moved on with her life. Was happy without me. Had possibly even forgotten me. I was the one who couldn't escape the girl who got away, the one who allowed a summer-long relationship to haunt me for over a third of my life. I'd always thought there was something fundamentally wrong with me because of it.

I always thought that if she loved me the way I loved her, she would've come after me. She would've responded to me.

Her phone number had been disconnected, all her social media accounts deleted. I'd tried to find her for months afterward, tried to remind her that I was still there. Still hers. And I thought I had. I thought she'd known and just didn't care, hadn't responded.

I thought that if it had been her parents keeping her away, she would've come to find me after she turned eighteen. Thought she would've come when her grandmother's health took a turn. When she died.

But Darby never did.

The only conclusion came to was that she had moved on. And while I could've—should've—gone after her like I had promised I would, I was afraid to face the reality of my fears, afraid to see her again and watch her turn me away.

Though now, I wonder if those wolves had their claws in her so much deeper than I was aware of, that her father had such control over her that he wouldn't let her return, even when her grandmother was sick.

Disgust coats my throat at the thought of it.

I drop my head, looking at her as she's curled against me. Long lashes fan out across her cheeks, freckles glowing in the morning light that filters through the window. Her golden hair is splayed out across her pillow behind her, pink lips pursed in her sleep, heavy breath blowing through them.

Undiluted anger rages through my body.

Rage toward her father. Her mother. The man she almost married, whose name I refuse to say, even inside my own head.

She deserves so much better than all of them.

She deserves me.

I decide I don't give a fuck what the last ten years have been like. I only care about the next ten, about having her in my life in whatever capacity she'll allow me. I only care about taking that pressure off her shoulders, that hurt and that heartache. I care about giving her the wild freedom I know she was once capable of feeling when she was with me.

I softly press my lips to her forehead, unsure if she'll allow me to continue touching her this way once she wakes, unsure of exactly how we're going to address the events of last night.

I don't regret it, not at all. I wasn't embarrassed. It wasn't awkward, not like so many of our moments have been since I showed up in her town and asked her to leave her wedding with me.

No, for the first time since being back in her life, it felt right: the way she soaked in my body, the way she bit her lip, the way her eyes flared with lust. Watching her come undone for me, moan my name—that felt like coming home.

But in the daylight, things might be different.

Regardless, I'm determined to give her whatever relief I can, give her the opportunity to feel like she can breathe again.

My kiss didn't seem to stir her, so I slowly untangle my legs from hers, already rethinking my decision as I lose the warmth of her body.

She hums in her sleep but otherwise remains dead to the world.

I know she turned her phone off yesterday, stressed out from the messages she was receiving from her ex. I decide I'm going to try convincing her to keep her phone off for the rest of today as well.

Hell, I'm going to try to convince her to throw it away, get a new number, and never think about him again.

I pad across the room on silent feet when my eyes snag on a pamphlet that sits on the corner table where the room keys are. I pick it up and flip through it. Towering, picturesque red rock formations spring up from the dry, arid land, accented by bright blue cloudless sky on every page.

I walk over to the window and peek through the curtains without opening them completely, so as to not flood the room with brightness and risk waking her. Sure enough, all evidence of yesterday's storm is gone. Only a beautiful clear sky remains.

Even from our hotel room, the landscape is stunning.

I chew my lip, contemplating our options before finally coming to a decision. I grab my phone from the bedside table and shoot a text off to Darby's sister.

Her phone is off, and I'm going to try keeping it that way. Booking a second night in Moab to check out Arches today. I think she needs it.

A moment later, my hand buzzes with Dahlia's response.

Thank you for taking care of her.

My chest soars at that.

I scribbled a note on the pad at the desk, letting her know that I've gone downstairs to grab us breakfast and will be right back.

When she was seventeen, she loved iced vanilla lattes, which aren't an option at the complimentary breakfast bar in our hotel, so I went for the next best thing: hot coffee and a shit ton of french vanilla creamer packets.

I toast two bagels and remember she doesn't like butter, but she loves peanut butter. So, I grab a to-go container of that as well. Lastly, I grab an apple for myself and an orange for her because she always said she loved the smell of citrus.

I also stop by the desk and extend our stay by one night.

I try to be quiet as I re-enter the room, but with my hands full, the door slams behind me. I quickly realize it doesn't matter, because she's already awake.

She's sitting at the edge of the bed we slept in with her hair a splayed mess. Her hands hold the note I left at her knees as she reads over it.

Her head slowly lifts, and I try to prepare myself for the regret I may see on her face, prepared for her to be upset, or even angry, about last night.

Instead, her eyes brighten, and she gives me a soft, sleepy smile.

My heart stops right there in my chest.

Her silky voice has it beating again. Thundering. Pounding. "Hi."

I smile back at her. "Hi, Honeysuckle."

"I slept in."

"That's okay," I say.

"How far are we going today?"

"We're not going anywhere."

Her brows furrow as she cocks her head, but she doesn't reject the idea. She only looks to me for an explanation.

I just shrug casually. "I want to check out Arches National Park if that's cool with you. I already let Dahlia know."

She blinks a few times, looking around the room. "I mean..." She opens her mouth, closes it, then opens it again. "Don't you have things you need to get back to? In Pacific Shores?"

Technically, I haven't told Lynn, my agent, or Kate, my PR manager, that I've gone out of town. I'm supposed to be training for the Huntington Beach competition in July, but truthfully, a week off probably won't do much damage.

As for the surf shop, Everett is fine without me. August doesn't let me in anymore, even when I try, and there isn't anyone else in my life I'd like to be with than Darby.

"Nothing so important that I can't spend the day here with you."

She blushes, looking down at her feet. After a moment of contemplation, she nods to herself. "Yeah." She lifts her head, and I watch as her eyes sparkle with amusement. "I guess I can carve a day out of my imploding life to go look at some rocks with you."

My stomach flutters, and my chest lifts with ease.

It's so easy with her.

When we finally lift the pressure of the rest of the world off each other and allow ourselves to just be.

It feels like we've been wearing masks, the mask of two people who were never connected. Who had healed and let go and moved on. Who weren't still affected by the first person they'd ever loved. When we faked those emotions around each other, things were tense, difficult, and painful.

The moment we allow ourselves to remove those masks, to see the other for who we are—who we've always been—it suddenly feels like seeing light at the end of darkness.

I hand her the coffee, bagel, and fruit I brought her, and she quietly nibbles on it while I get dressed and ready for the day. Then, she gets ready herself while I stare out the window and watch the sun reflect off the mountains.

"All right, I'm ready," she says.

I turn to face her, and all the air leaves my lungs.

She's so fucking beautiful.

Hair split into two braids that hang off her shoulders. A pair of denim cut-offs that accentuate her beautifully long legs. Pale yellow sneakers that somehow complement the maroon-colored cropped T-shirt that shows just a hint of her midriff.

"Where to?" she asks as I realize I haven't responded. I've just been staring at her, shamelessly devouring her with my eyes.

I compose myself, smiling as I say, "Best day of your life, Honeysuckle."

Twenty-Five

Heathen

Then. July 7th.

The sun sets behind Darby's head, illuminating her in an otherworldly glow, almost as if she's wrapped in a halo. A fucking angel. An angel sent straight from heaven to pull the heathen from me. Sent to give me faith. To make me believe in miracles and fate and God.

I called Tyler, a server and fellow surfer friend of mine who works at the Seaside Sunset, the nicest restaurant on the pier, and asked him to reserve the best table and the best time of day for Darby and me. He owes me a favor because I took the fall a few months ago when we got caught smoking weed on the beach, and he was afraid of his mom finding out.

He came through, because it's by far the most beautiful dinner I've ever had in my life. Something tells me it's got nothing to do with the view, though. It's got everything to do with her.

Tyler comes by and clears our plates, winking at me as he walks away. "Are you having fun?" I ask her.

She reaches across the table and grabs my hand, squeezing four times. "Best date I've ever been on."

"It's nowhere near over yet, honey."

I pay the bill and hold her hand as we exit the restaurant and make our way down to the other end of the pier. She asks to stop and watch the sun finish its descent over the Pacific. I oblige, of course, because I can't say no to her. She stares out over the horizon, admiring the sky. I stare at her because I wasn't lying when I said she was the most beautiful thing I've ever seen.

I don't just mean people. I mean everything. In comparison to the sky, the stars, the flowers, and the trees, even the ocean waves—she outranks them all.

Once the world finally flashes from light to dark, she looks at me with a smile. Despite the fading daylight, she remains shrouded in brightness, the most golden thing in existence.

I take her hand, leading her to the ice cream shop at the edge of the pier. A bell on the door chimes as we enter, and Ruby smiles brightly at me. Ruby is the owner of the entire building, which holds her ice cream shop, Sweet Rue's, a gift shop, a snack shack called California Fish Co., and the apartment above the gift shop. Ruby is also Everett and Elena's mom, Monica's best friend.

"Hey, Ruby," I say as we enter. "This is Darby. She's Diane Andrews's granddaughter."

"Well, I would have guessed that. You look just like her." Ruby beams at Darby. "It's nice to meet you."

Darby tucks a piece of hair behind her ear. "Nice to meet you too," she murmurs.

"What's your favorite flavor of ice cream?" I ask Darby.

Her hazel eyes glow as she shrugs at me. "Vanilla?"

"Vanilla?" I scoff. "There are like forty flavors here, and you're going to tell me you want vanilla?"

"I'm not really allowed to eat ice cream at home," she mutters. "My mom tells me that sugar tends to go straight to our bellies. It's in our genes or something. So, we don't really keep it in the house."

Fuck. I hate her parents more every day, I think.

I suppress an eye roll, but she catches my expression anyway.

"When I was a kid, though, I liked vanilla."

Ruby gives me a strained smile, excusing herself through the door that leads to the back of the shop. I face Darby, placing my hands on her shoulders. "Darby, you have control over your body, remember? You can eat whatever you want, whenever you want to. I understand your mom might be trying to instill a sense of importance over your health, but she's going about it the wrong way. Eat healthy because you want to be strong and live a long time, not because you should give one single fuck about how soft your belly is. That's ridiculous."

She opens her mouth like she's about to say something, but then she closes it again.

"I'm going to love your body no matter what," I promise her. "So, that means you should too. I will take personal offense if you hate something I like so much. Understand?"

"I understand," she murmurs, looking down at our feet.

I huff. The priorities of her parents are enraging. She deserves so much better than them. "Ruby!" I shout. Her head peeks out from behind the door a moment later. "Can you get a sample of every flavor?"

She raises one brow at me before shaking her head with a breathy laugh. "You kids will be the death of me."

"Okay, yeah, the huckleberry cheesecake is my favorite flavor. This might be the best thing I've ever tasted," Darby says, slowly pulling the spoon from her mouth.

Ruby went to the back again, and the shop was empty, since it was technically closed. She agreed to let us stay until we finished our samples, with the agreement I'd mow her lawn this week.

A trace of ice cream lingers on Darby's bottom lip. I lean into her, swiping it away with my tongue. It tastes like fruit and cream—sweet but not nearly as sweet as she is.

"Disappointing." I lick my own lips. "Because your lips are the best thing I've ever tasted."

She doesn't hide her smile from me this time, but she does burst with laughter. "That was really cheesy."

"Yeah, well, you make me a melted puddle of emotion,

Honeysuckle. It's your fault."

She blushes. Looking down at the table in front of us, littered with dozens of empty sample cups, she asks, "Should we help Ruby clean up?"

I nod. She picks up the cups and throws them away as I dart behind the counter and grab a rag and cleaning solution. I go ahead and wipe down all her tables, take the trash out of all the bins, and tie them up. I shout my gratitude to Ruby through the back doorway and let her know I'll take her trash out. She reminds me it won't get me out of lawn mowing duty, and I promise her I'll see her in a couple of days.

"You're not a bad boy, after all," Darby says as I toss the garbage into the dumpster behind the shop.

I laugh as I walk her back to our stolen car.

"Do you want to try something kind of risky?" I ask her as I take a right onto the freeway ramp.

"Is it illegal?" she asks.

"Yeah." I shrug. "But it's unlikely we'll get caught. Even less likely that we'll harm anyone."

"Is the risk worth the reward?" She says it in a nonchalant way, as if it's a perfectly normal conversation to be having, whether or not to commit a felony in a stolen car. As if she weren't scared to wear a bathing suit in public less than a month ago.

"I've truly corrupted you, Honeysuckle." I smile.

She laughs, bright and lively. "Just answer the question."

"Yeah," I chuckle. "The risk is worth the reward."

I drive three miles east on the interstate before taking an exit and turning left. I follow that road down to the near end of it before taking another left. At the end of the next road is one final right turn onto a dirt road.

Darby twists in her seat, facing me. "Where are we?"

"An old dirt road. Isn't this what you country girls are into?"

She gives me an overexaggerated eye roll but begins to burst with laughter. "You are so lame."

I grin back. "You love me."

The world seems to momentarily stop spinning. All the air in my lungs, all the oxygen in the car, seems to be sucked out of it as I realize what I just said. I should probably look away, but I can only stare at her. A faint smile remains on her face, but her eyes spell shock.

Finally, she lets out a small hum and glances out the window. "Yeah, maybe I do."

I sigh in relief, turning back to the road. I begin to lower all four of the windows on the car. The wind whips through Darby's hair, roaring through the cab. I'm forced to raise my voice when I say, "When you tell me you love me for the first time, Honeysuckle, I want you to look me in the eye. I don't want to ever hear the word maybe in that sentence either. When you say that to me, I want you to mean it."

Even through the howl of wind as I pick up speed down the dirt road, I hear her gasp. Smiling to myself, I press my foot against the accelerator, bringing the 1978 Chevy Nova closer to full speed. Gravel whips beneath the car's tires as Darby grips the grab handle above her window. The faster the car goes, the more it feels like my stomach is lifting out of my chest.

I hear Darby begin to squeal as we reach the end of the road. I let my foot off the gas and yank the steering wheel to the right. That squeal becomes a full-blown scream as the car begins to spin. Her body falls across mine at the force of the movement, and her hair flies across my face.

Finally, the car comes to an abrupt stop, the cab still shaking slightly over the wheels. Darby looks at me with a flushed face and a heaving chest. I can't help but imagine all the other ways I could make her blush and breathless.

"Oh, my God," she gasps. Her hair stands in a hundred different directions. "That was incredible."

Shit. I imagine all the different reasons I could make her say that.

"You wanna go again, honey?"

She gives me a coy smile and a nod. I return it, reaching out to crank up the radio before I release the emergency brake and throw the car back into drive.

I repeat the same motions, speeding down to the far end of the road before whipping around in circles, though I don't let the car stop this time. I continue to spin us before taking off down the dirt road again. "Summer" by Calvin Harris blares through the stereo of the old car.

I glance in Darby's direction, seeing her eyes closed and her head tilted back. She has one arm stuck out the window, her hand making waves through the wind. Her other is folded behind her head. She looks so free. So fucking beautiful. Pride blooms in my chest, knowing I'm capable of making her feel so safe, safe enough to close her eyes and let go of her worries while I drive ninety down a dirt road in a stolen car in the dark.

I reach over and place my hand on her thigh, squeezing four times.

A silent reminder that she's always safe with me.

Her eyes flutter open, and she smiles at me, and it's almost as if I can physically feel my heart leave my chest and hand itself over to her. As if I've got no control over it at all.

"You're a good driver!" she shouts over the roar of the wind and the engine.

"Perks of working in a garage." I shrug.

"Do you want to be a mechanic when you're older?"

I laugh. "Not at all. I just work for the Ramoses as a way to repay them for all their hospitality, for taking me in. I like cars as much as the next guy, cars I'd love to own someday. I sure as hell have fun doing shit like this, but no, they're not my whole life."

"What's your dream car?" she asks.

I slow down a little so I can hear her better. "Probably a 1976 Mustang. Cherry red. Basic, I know, but one of the first cars I worked on with Everett and Carlos was a seventy-six Mustang. It was the first time after being left by my dad that I felt like I had a man in my life I could trust, a man who actually cared. It stayed with me." I swallow the sudden lump in my throat. "And red was my mom's favorite color."

"I bet your mom would be really proud of you," Darby says, and I feel my chest constrict.

I huff a laugh. "Yeah, I'm sure. Committing felonies on a Saturday night and corrupting the pretty new girl in town."

"You're kind. You're brave and smart. You're a hard worker, you're empathetic, and you care deeply for those in your life. You've made me brave. You've given me safety, protection, and comfort I've never felt before. You've made me feel alive for the first time in my life, Leo. That's something she'd be proud of." She places her hand over the one I have still resting on her leg.

"Thank you," I say. "I didn't know how much I needed to hear something like that until you said it. You seem to always know what I need." I smile at her. "That innate ability to chase my ghosts away."

She runs her thumb back and forth across my knuckles. After a few silent minutes, I decide to take her home. The night has turned more intimate than speeding down dirt roads, and all I really want to do is keep talking to her.

"Is what happened to your mom the reason you're so protective?" Darby asks suddenly.

"What do you mean?"

"I mean, the second time we met, you said you had to walk me home because you didn't want to feel guilty about something happening to me if you never saw me again." She chuckles. "Then, at that house party, you didn't even want someone looking at me, and you were protective over Elena. You're always encouraging me to do reckless things, but at the same time ensuring that my safety comes first."

"First of all, Honeysuckle, I made up an excuse to walk you home because I thought you were pretty and wanted a reason to talk to you. At the party, I didn't want anybody pawing at you because you deserve better, but again, it enrages me to imagine any other man touching a single millimeter of your skin. That was me being more possessive than anything else." I sigh. "But yeah, I'm pretty protective by nature. I know what it feels like to watch the person you love most in the world die right in front of you and know that you likely could've done something to prevent it. I don't want to ever feel like that again, but more so, I don't ever want to lose someone I love like that again."

"Leo." She leans across the center of the car and rests her head on my shoulder. Her warmth immediately sinks into me, chasing away my chill. "I'm so sorry you had to live through something like that."

I'm comforted by her acknowledgment. She doesn't try to change my mind, my trauma, doesn't tell me it'll get better, because she knows it won't. She simply acknowledges that it exists, and somehow, that's the best reaction she could give me.

"It doesn't feel so bad now that I have you, Honeysuckle," I whisper against her hair, pressing my lips to the top of her head.

"Nothing feels quite as bad when I'm with you, Heathen," she says into my chest, and that's when I feel it: the moment I know for certain that my heart no longer lives inside my body—it now lives inside the palm of her hand.

My heart, my soul, the entirety of my being—they all belong to Darby.

"Do you want to go home? Or, do you want me to show you another secret spot?" I ask.

"I want to do anything that'll keep this night from ending," she answers.

I press another kiss against the top of her head, thanking all my lucky stars for my girl of gold.

Twenty-Six

Heathen

Now. May 31st.

"It's so beautiful out here," Darby says.

I glance at her, face tilted toward the sun and freckles on display. Her eyes are closed as direct rays of light dance upon her cheeks. Her golden hair shimmers where it rests on her shoulders. Smooth, lightly tanned legs are propped up against my dashboard, and light-pink toes wiggle to the beat of the song I am playing.

Traffic is at a near standstill at the entrance to Arches as we inch, one-by-one, through the park gates. The crowds are to be expected in early summer when the weather is still pleasant enough for hours of hiking. I'm thankful I thought to take the top off the Mustang this morning.

"It's really beautiful," I respond, knowing I'm staring at her, that I haven't taken a single second to take in the scenery around me, because she's all I see anyway.

She cracks one eye open to look at me, as if checking for the direction of my gaze. I notice her lips twitch slightly as she finds my eyes on her. A small blush accents her cheeks.

"Leo." She sighs, turning her face toward the sky again.

"Honeysuckle."

"When you were getting breakfast this morning, I searched your name on YouTube. I wanted to see videos of you from the competition, setting records." She swallows. "I never allowed myself to search for you before. I'd seen you...in magazines and online, but I never allowed myself to *look*."

"Yeah?" I breathe.

She nods. "But this morning...I just wanted to see." She keeps her eyes closed but turns to face me. I can't help but notice the small smile on her face. "You know the first result that came up when I searched your name?"

Goddammit.

I sigh.

She laughs. "That botched commercial where you're talking about how much you love footlong sandwiches." She drops her legs and bends over as she continues laughing. "But you never, not once, use the word 'sandwich.' You just keep saying, 'I love a good footlong after a rough day out on the waves.'"

She's got tears in her eyes as she cackles maniacally.

I'll never live that goddamn commercial down. It's what I get for not reading the script thoroughly and just reciting what they had held up on a board in front of me.

The musical tone of her voice makes a small chuckle burst from my throat too. As long as she's laughing, I don't care if it's at my expense.

She clears her throat as she calms down, and I realize she's picking at her fingernails now. "I watched a lot of your competitions, though. You really are amazing."

I give her a soft smile. "Thank you, Honeysuckle."

"And dating someone like Milan Hampton, that must've been wild."

I actually do laugh at that, her way of bringing up my past.

I've been seen throughout the years with the heiress to one of the most famous luxury hotel brands in the world, which has always caused a stir in the media. I'd be lying if I hadn't thought about Darby seeing me on the cover of the tabloids with Milan over the years. That guilt has always eaten away at me a little.

I glance at her and raise a brow. "I've never dated Milan, Darby. We've always been friends. We're still friends."

Her mouth drops slightly. "But I saw so many articles..."

"When someone is as famous as Milan, any person she's seen with is a scandal. I met her at a gala I was invited to by one of my sponsors about a year after I began surfing professionally. We hit it off and..." I decide not to finish the sentence. Truthfully, Milan was an on-and-off hookup over the years. Both of us were hung up on people from our pasts, which made it easy to get our physical needs out of the way without the other person expecting something more.

She's a good person and a good friend, though.

"But we never dated. She and I spent a lot of time together because nobody knew my name. Nobody cared about me, and it gave her a bit of a break from the spotlight until simply being seen with her made people search my name." I shrug. "I needed money, so when I was offered brand deals and was asked to model, I felt like I couldn't say no. I felt like I had something to prove. Then, over the years, it stopped becoming about surfing, and..."

I realize I've started rambling. I'm talking completely off-topic, but Darby's hazel eyes are bright and patient as she waits for me to continue.

"My point is, it was always casual. I've never been in love with her, and despite what you may have read in the headlines, I've never once referred to her as my girlfriend. We really are friends, though, sometimes business partners when my agent tells me to take her to dinner with the proper branding on my body."

She frowns slightly. "I'm sorry, Leo."

I attempt to give her a comforting smile. "It helps to be out here. Nobody here knows my name or recognizes my face, like it doesn't matter so much out here as it does in Southern California. It's been a nice break."

She smiles back. "Well, at least something good came out of my runaway-bride act."

I find the courage to reach across the center of the console and brush my thumb across her hand. "I think a lot of good things are going to come out of this, Darby."

"Careful, Honeysuckle!" I shout from the bottom of the rock.

"Leo," she huffs, "I've gone hiking before."

I pause at the bottom of the steep embankment, hand on a hip. "Don't be silly, Darby. You've lived your whole life in Kansas. You don't even know what mountains are."

She slowly steps around the rocks and roots, closing the gap between us as she mutters, "Heathen."

When she reaches me, I outstretch my hand to help her jump the last few feet down onto the flat ground. We've been hiking through the red rocks for hours as we explore Arches. The bright color of the formations clashes with the piercing blue sky, illuminating the world around us in vibrancy. Despite it, she's still the brightest thing out here.

We've just finished the three-mile round-trip hike to Delicate Arch, the most famous landmark of the National Park. The sun is beginning to lower on the horizon as we silently make the trek back to my Mustang.

"That was pretty incredible, though. One of those things you've seen a million times but never actually realized was real."

I nod in response.

"I'm glad we spent the day here," I say as we reach the car.

"Me too, Leo." She smiles at me from the passenger side as I unlock the door. "I just realized another good thing to come out of all of this."

"What's that?" I smile.

"You finally found your dream car."

I found my dream girl again, too, but I don't say that out loud.

As we slowly drive out of the Park with the top down, the setting sun against our faces, and the wind blowing through Darby's hair, I notice a peaceful smile on her flushed cheeks.

I can't help the fluttering inside my chest as I watch her. She looks so carefree, so happy.

The look on her face stirs something up inside me enough that once we make it to the exit of Arches, I don't turn left toward town and our hotel. Instead, I turn right.

She whips to face me, amused confusion highlighting her face. I only shrug, smiling back at her as I fly down the highway.

Cars become fewer the farther away we drive, until we're the only vehicle on the one-lane road. I pull up my phone, deciding to play a song I know will keep her smiling.

Just as the beginning of the song begins to play, Darby's beautiful face lights up with laughter. She props her feet up on the dash again, lifting her hands above her head to feel the wind blow through them as her hair flows behind her.

I press my foot against the accelerator, bringing the car to full speed just as the beat drops on "Summer" by Calvin Harris. I feel Darby's light laughter in my bones, my chest soaring with the speed and proximity of the beautiful woman next to me.

I allow myself, for the first time in ten years, to feel every emotion coursing through my body, to relive the perfect moment from the perfect night all those years ago, the moment I knew I'd well and truly given my heart away to the girl in my passenger seat.

I realize now that I've never had it back. I've been wandering the earth with a hollow chest all this time. I know that my heart—my soul—has been sitting right here, in the palm of her hand. Blood spreads through my veins again for the first time. It feels like life is being breathed back into me as I watch the sunset over the red rock canyons, illuminating the girl of my dreams in a golden glow.

Twenty-Seven

Honeysuckle

Then. July 7th.

"Beef jerky? Really?" I curl my lip at Leo as we reach the checkout counter.

"What's wrong with beef jerky?" he asks as the cashier rings up our items.

I got Cheetos, a red Slurpee, and a bag of M&Ms. Leo got one Slim Jim. I frown at it. "Why aren't you getting anything else? Something sweet?"

His blue eyes sparkle as he snakes a hand around my waist and tugs me into him. "I've already got something sweet. Honey-flavored." His fingers dig into my hip, the same place he always grabs when he kisses me.

I roll my eyes as the cashier snorts. "That was lame, wasn't it?" I ask him.

He has a light smirk on his mouth as he nods at me. Leo only smiles, completely unaffected by the stranger and me making fun of him. He presses a kiss against the side of my head as our items are bagged up.

"All right, one last drive with the windows down, and then I've got to return this to the shop. We'll walk to the secret spot from there. It's not far." I laugh. "Okay. Let's put on some music again."

"Way ahead of you, Honeysuckle." The screen of his phone lights up his face, and a moment later, a beeping noise chimes through the stereo of the car. "Elena, Everett, and I all share the same account, and we've spent years cultivating the perfect playlist for every situation. This is the driving-with-the windows-down-in-a-stolen-car-with-a-beautiful-girl playlist."

Somehow, I don't believe that's what it's called.

The windows lower as Leo backs out of the parking space. He places his hand on my headrest and turns around, looking out the rear window as he throws the car in reverse.

I'm not sure what about it sends butterflies straight to my stomach.

Drums begin to beat through the stereo, with the sound of snapping and the soft strum of a guitar. It sounds like music that would be playing in a diner in the 1950s.

"What is this, Jersey Boys?"

Leo scoffs. "Jersey Boys is the musical, Darby. The Four Seasons is the name of the band. And they're incredible, by the way." He turns out of the store parking lot and begins flying down the residential road, wind whipping through my hair. "But this is the Arctic Monkeys."

I lean my head back, propping my feet onto the dashboard. I let the night chill run along my skin and feel it wash away by the warmth of Leo's hand on my bare thigh. I let my hair blow across my face, let the sea breeze invigorate my senses.

The song says something about belonging to another person for eternity until the sun no longer shines and the rivers run dry. I've never much related to love songs, but as his thumb runs across my skin again, I can't help but feel like the music speaks to me directly.

I suddenly wonder how I'll ever belong to anyone else again now that I've experienced what it feels like to be his.

We pull into a gated parking lot; Leo punches a number into the keypad, and the gate slowly slides open. He pulls into a space at the far end of the lot and shuts off the engine. Using some kind of tool attached to his key chain, he pops open the dash and begins to mess with something.

"I'm adjusting the miles to look like the car was never driven tonight," he says with complete focus. "Can you make sure there isn't any trash in here? No fingerprints on the windows and shit?"

For the first time, I realize we did actually steal someone's car. I step out and begin to check the windows, laughing the entire time.

After he's finished, Leo steps out and walks over to the side of the building, grabbing a hose. "What are you laughing at?"

"We stole a car," I choke out between giggles.

"We borrowed a car. We're literally putting it back exactly the way we found it right now. Stealing it would mean we intended to keep it."

I only laugh harder.

Leo washes away the dust that settled on the exterior while we were racing down the dirt road, then runs the keys back inside the shop before relocking it. Lastly, he pops the trunk of the car and begins digging around inside. He pulls out a duffel bag full of blankets and pillows. "I wasn't sure if you'd want to go to the beach at some point, so I wanted to be prepared," he says.

He places our snacks in the bag and hoists it over his shoulder.

We stumble out of the parking lot in the dark, and Leo closes the gate behind us. He takes a right on the main road, and I follow him up the hill.

"This is our road," I say. It's the same road he and my grandma both live on.

"Yep."

We continue to climb until we're standing back in front of my grandma's house. He smiles at me, squeezing my hand four times as he begins toward the gate that leads to the backyard.

"Are you taking me down to the beach you were headed to the day we met?" I ask.

"Yeah," he responds in a hushed tone. "I haven't been in a while. Been spending all my time with you."

"Why haven't you taken me?"

He stops at the edge of the yard where the grass meets the

cliff. There is a little gap in the lavender bushes that line the property, and I can barely make out the flattened dirt that leads between them and down the steep face of the cliffside in the dark.

"It's not the safest hike down, and I didn't want to risk you trying to do it alone when I'm not with you." Leo drops the duffel bag at my feet. "Don't protest, or we aren't going down there." He pulls something out of the bag and stands in front of me. A small band dangles from his fist with something heavy on the end of it.

It takes me a moment to figure out what it is.

I snort. "A headlamp?"

"It's dark, it's steep, and it's dangerous. I'm going to go before you; you're going to step where I step, and if you fall, you're going to fall into me."

"Yes, sir." I salute him playfully, snagging the headlight from his hand and strapping it to my forehead.

I turn it on to find him smirking back at me, one dimple popping in the corner of his mouth. "You look cute."

I roll my eyes and flick my hand toward him, motioning for him to begin the descent. We take the climb slowly, and he asks me how I'm doing no less than a dozen times. His foot slips once, and he stops to watch me walk through the same section to ensure I don't slip too.

Finally, we make it to the bottom. He hops off a rock and down onto the sand, extending an arm to me and helping me climb down. I take the light off and hand it to him as he sets the duffel bag down on the ground.

The full moon sits against the horizon, illuminating the world in shades of blue. The waves are quiet and peaceful as the low tide laps against the shore. A light breeze blows through my hair, the palm trees making music as they shuffle in the wind.

Rock faces surround us on three sides, towering toward the sky, forming a secret cove. The cliffs drown out the sound of the interstate above us, the noise of the city around us, truly creating a secret slice of paradise that exists only for him and me.

"It's beautiful," I whisper, as if too much noise may disturb the sea and the wind.

A flicker of light illuminates from behind me, and I turn around to find Leo setting two small lanterns into the sand, producing a faint glow along the beach. He's laid out a fluffy white blanket and two pillows propped up against a log. Our snacks are piled in the center of the blanket.

He smiles, holding his arm out to his side in the direction of the setup. "M'lady."

"Pulling out all the stops tonight, aren't you, Graham?"

"I told you I was going to give you the best night of your life. You should know by now that I keep my promises, Darby."

"I know," I say. I step up to him and tug at his hand until he tumbles onto the blanket with me. "This is the best night of my life."

He sits back against the pillows, and I straddle his legs, resting mine on either side of his hips. I cup his face between my hands and lean in so my mouth hovers just above his.

"Truly?" he asks.

"Truly."

I press my mouth against his. His lips are soft and warm, and he lets out a groan at the ferocity of my kiss. I open for him, and he delicately slips his tongue into my mouth. Caressing me with rough hands, he runs them down my back and along the bare skin of my shoulders. He tastes like a saltwater breeze, and I'm overwhelmed by his familiar citrus and sand smell.

I want to soak him in, soak in this moment, grab hold of it, and never let it end. The way his body aligns with mine, and I feel him everywhere. The way he tastes like something that was always meant to be. The way his hands feel against my skin and his lips feel against my mouth. The way his sounds of need echo through my body, bouncing off the walls of my chest and ringing through my soul.

Because the most beautiful boy I've ever seen, with bright blue kaleidoscope eyes, ended up being the kindest, purest, most genuine soul I've ever met. He ended up being the person I spent my whole life needing but never had, and now, I can't imagine ever living in a world where he doesn't exist. Knowing that he needs me just as much as I need him feels like the answer to every prayer I've ever sent up to the sky.

"Leo," I whimper against his lips. "I need you to know..." I sigh as his lips move from my mouth and across my jaw down to my neck. "I need you to know that you've changed me." He pauses, but his mouth still rests against the hollow of my throat. "I'm not the same person I was when I got here a month ago. I didn't think it would be possible to grow so much in just a number of weeks, but you've made that happen. You've made me brave. You've made me want to find myself, figure out who I am and what I'm meant to do in this world."

His lips drag against my throat as he lifts his head. Those blue eyes glow like sapphire stars as he looks at me. "You've changed me, too, Honeysuckle. You've made me understand what it feels like to be found. Seen. Heard. Valued. You make me believe in myself in a way I've never had before. You make me feel like I'm worth something."

I feel my eyes begin to swell at his admission. His mouth covers mine again, his hand moving up to the back of my neck. "I don't know if I used to believe in divine intervention, but I think I do now," I say between his lips. "I believe I was destined to find you so you could teach me all of this."

"I know we were," he says into my mouth. Pulling away, he looks up at me with shining eyes. "I lost so many pieces of myself when I lost my mom. I've been so afraid to give any more of myself away, only to lose it." A smile accents his features. "But I've never trusted someone the way I trust you."

"You deserve to be protected, too, Leo. I'll do that. I'll

protect whatever pieces of yourself you choose to give me. I'll cherish them." I lean into him again, tracing his jaw with my mouth. "You were my first kiss. My first date. My first true, real best friend. You make me feel so safe, Leo." I sigh against his skin. "I want you to be my first everything. I want to give you a piece of me too."

I feel him gasp. I can feel his heart thundering in sync with my own, creating a drumming in our chests. "Darby," he breathes. "Are you..." He swallows, shaking his head. "I wasn't expecting... I don't expect any of this from you. I would never expect that from you. All I wanted to do was give you a perfect night, the first date you deserved."

I smile because I know what he's saying is genuine. That's why it's so easy to give myself away—because he's not demanding it, not expecting it. The choice is mine. I'm in control of who I give this piece of myself to. It's a decision I come to on my own, and I know that no matter what else happens the rest of this summer—the rest of my life—I want to keep this moment in time locked away into permanence, a chord that will forever connect the two of us to this moment, keeping it perfect and safeguarded.

I can't think of a better way to do that than to give him a little piece of my soul and to be gifted his in return.

I pull back so he can see my face clearly. "I want to be yours. I want you to be mine."

"You already are, and so am I," he whispers, as if afraid to disturb the night.

"We don't know where life will go after this summer—after this night, even. I want—need—to know that when the dust settles, all of this was real. That you are real. I want a piece of your soul. Maybe that makes me selfish, but I don't care. I need to know a part of you will always belong to me, and I want to give you that, too."

His eyes blaze through mine, so intense that I feel him in every bone, in every nerve ending, from my toes in the sand to the tips of my fingers tangled in the hair at the back of his neck.

"You don't need a piece of my soul, Honeysuckle. You already own the whole goddamn thing."

I feel as if my heart could burst right out of my chest. I know that words won't do the moment justice, so instead, I pluck the gold band from my left ring finger. I grasp his hand from where it rests on my shoulder and slip the ring onto his pinky. "Then show me."

His eyes zone in on the purity ring that now rests on his own finger. We've never addressed it before—not directly—but I've seen him look at it. He knows enough of the history of my family to know that a ring on my left finger was clearly there as a symbol of my virtue, a virtue I no longer care about maintaining. I think I only preserved it so heavily because fate knew I was waiting for him all along.

His eyes dart back to my face, and in a flash, he surges forward to capture my mouth again, kissing me furiously and with purpose, as if I just broke some type of seal. His hands knot themselves in my hair as mine reach down and grab the hem of his shirt, lifting it in a silent request.

He pulls back from me and tugs it over his head, letting it fall into the sand. Chest heaving, Leo pauses and takes me in. I'm still sitting on top of his lap, though now I'm sure my hair is a mess, my lips swollen, the straps of my dress hanging limply at my arms.

"You're so fucking beautiful," he rasps. "The moon wraps

around you in the distance like a halo. You're glowing." He drags his fingers across my collarbone. "An angel. An angel and her demon."

I close the gap between us once more, feathering my lips over his. "A honeysuckle and her heathen."

He laughs, gently lifting me and laying me flat on my back. He hovers over me, kissing me everywhere his lips can reach, whispering affection into each inch of my skin he devours.

None of it feels wrong. No moment with him ever has. Everything with him feels so incredibly right, so meant to be. I have no interest in living in a world where I'm punished for the love I give and the love I receive back. I have no interest in living in a world where this moment in time is wrong, because the only thing it feels like to me is destiny.

He takes his time with the buttons on my dress, undoing them one by one from top to bottom. He makes me promises as he kisses his way back up my body. He tells me I'm beautiful again as we both work to remove the remainder of his clothes.

Finally, he hovers over me, sliding his hands up my arms until his fingers interlace with mine. He squeezes my palm four times. *I'll keep you safe.*

Underneath the full moon, against the backdrop of the
ocean waves and the rustling trees...
Our souls intertwine.

Twenty-Eight

Honeysuckle

Now. May 31st.

"Who knew drive-in theaters were still a thing, huh?"

"I like it. I feel like I'm in an old movie. Plus," I say between bites of my burger, "this is the best food I've eaten in a long time."

Leo looks at me with an amused smile. "What? No good burger joints in small-town Kansas?"

I shrug. "There are, but I was never...encouraged to eat this kind of food." I take another bite anyway. "I was told it goes straight to my thighs."

Leo scoffs. "So, ice cream goes straight to your belly, and burgers go straight to your thighs?"

I only give him a closed-lip smile. He responds with an eye roll as he swirls a french fry in his chocolate shake and hands it to me. I dip a fry in my strawberry shake and pass it to him.

"I can't believe you remember that."

"I remember everything about us, Honeysuckle," Leo says quietly.

I turn my head and gaze out at the headlights in the field beyond us, the towering projection screen in front of us—anywhere but his face, at the emotion I know I'll see there.

We're getting dangerously close to crossing another line.

"I also remember telling you that only you have control over your body. I distinctly remember telling you that you needed to love your body exactly how it is, and that I'd be personally offended if you disliked something I love so much."

His use of the present tense has my head snapping back in his direction. Looking for a sign of a slip-up that he didn't mean it that way, I only see sincerity.

I don't know how to respond, so I just stare at him. He doesn't shy away from it. If anything, he seems to encourage it by the way he smiles at me.

My eyes roam along his straight nose, soft, full lips, and strong jawline. They run along the veins in his neck, his smooth skin. Finally, I snag again on the chain around his throat, the way it dips below the collar of his shirt.

"I told you earlier I was watching some of your videos," I whisper, seeing him nod. "They call you Heathen. The announcers. Your fans. It's written on all your boards."

I don't say it, but I also noticed he was wearing that exact necklace at every competition, in every interview.

He swallows, brows knitted at the center of his forehead. He licks his lips as if he's contemplating something before he pulls his phone from the center console. The screen brightens his features as he types into it.

He hands his phone to me as a video begins to play. It's a short dark-haired, middle-aged man in a Hawaiian T-shirt and khaki shorts, standing barefoot in the sand with a microphone in his hand. Leo jogs toward him, dripping wet and shirtless. His lean, toned, and tanned body is on display as he stands before the interviewer in a black wetsuit folded at the waist and an orange surfboard with that nickname written in giant letters down the side.

The way the water drips down his stomach reminds me of the way it looked last night as I watched him in the shower, the way his hands... I shake that thought away as the interviewer begins speaking. Leo sits beside me silently.

"Mr. Graham, you set another record here today at Mavericks. How does it feel?"

Dimples pop on either side of Leo's cheeks. He looks younger here, but not by much. Both of his tattoos are on display when he faces the camera. "I've dreamed of surfing Mavericks my entire life. Despite years of training, you're never quite prepared for what the waves are going to throw at you. It feels like fate was definitely on my side today, and I'm just lucky to be here."

"Humble as always, Heathen," the reporter laughs. "Speaking of"—he nods toward Leo's board—"it sounds like you've got a new business venture on the horizon. Want to tell us a little about that?"

Leo laughs, and I know it's a professional laugh, not his real one. Not the one that sounds like wind chimes. "Yeah. I'll be opening up a surf shop with my brother back home in Pacific Shores. We're looking at launching later this year, and we hope to see you out there." He winks at the camera, and I imagine all hundred and twenty thousand viewers of this video swooning at that exact moment. "Heathen's on the Boardwalk."

Leo looks like he's about to walk away when the reporter claps a hand on his shoulder. "Tell me more about this nickname: Heathen. Where did it come from? How does it relate to your identity as a surfer?"

My eyes flick away from the past Leo on the screen to the one sitting next to me now. The movie plays in front of us, but we're not paying attention. His eyes meet mine, sparkling with some emotion I can't place.

"It's a nickname given to me by someone special, but it's also a representation of what my friends and I were like as kids. My brother and I wanted to pay tribute when we decided to open our own business in our hometown."

"And how about those two necklaces you've always got on? Are those a gift from someone special too?"

Leo's hand reaches up to brush against the twine necklace around his neck, accented with seashells and a small stone in the middle. It's different from the one he wore all those years ago, but I don't have to wait for him to answer to know who it's from.

"My sister made this one for me, actually. She likes to add crystals for protection and to ward off negative energy."

He chuckles. "I think this is her way of telling me to stay safe, reminding me she loves me."

His hand then slides down to the gold ring hanging at the center of his chest. "This one is..." He swallows. "It's special. A good luck charm."

The reporter smiles knowingly. "Any chance that one is a gift from one of the girls we've seen you out and about with lately? Maybe an heiress in particular?"

The smile on the interviewer's face is hungry, predatory, as if he thinks he just unearthed a major scandal. It's gross, honestly.

Leo's eyes shutter on the screen as he clears his throat. "My personal life remains personal. Thanks for coming out."

He stalks away without another word, and the video ends. I pass his phone back to him without looking at him. We sit in silence for what feels like years.

"You don't wear one of Elena's necklaces anymore," I say for some stupid reason. We both know it's not the necklace I'm really asking about.

"I spend so much time in the water that they don't last very long." He looks down at his lap. "And she hasn't made me a new one in years." His voice nearly breaks at that.

"Just for you? Or for Everett, August, and Zach too?"

Leo lifts his head, and it's devastation I see on his face—not the same expression that he gives me when we're talking about our own past. No, this is something more permanent.

I realize for the first time that he hasn't mentioned August or Zach since he's been back in my life. Maybe they're not friends anymore.

He opens his mouth and closes it several times, as if he's wanting to say something but doesn't know how. So, I change the subject for him, finally addressing the thing that's been haunting me. "The necklace you do wear, that ring... Is it mine?"

"Yes," he whispers.

"You've been wearing it all this time."

With the soft nod of his head, I feel as if some gate inside me has just opened, flooding me with every feeling I've repressed for all these years. Suddenly, I'm drowning in it. Drowning in him.

"Why, Leo?"

"It was a good luck charm at first, when I was sure that you were coming back. When I thought that you were still mine. It made me feel close to you, the same way the ocean makes me feel close to my mom." His jaw flexes, and he refuses to meet my eyes. "Then, it became a reminder that you were real. The longer time went on without hearing from you, I began to believe I had made us up, that you couldn't have loved me the way I thought you did. The way I loved you."

My eyes sting with tears at his words, at the loss of faith he faced when I left. That he could've ever believed what we had wasn't real. That he needed a physical reminder of it to know it happened.

"It represented a piece of you that would always belong to me. If I couldn't have you. If I never got to see you again. If you..." He sighs. "If you went on to marry someone else, love someone else, give the rest of yourself to another person..." He reaches up to grab the ring hanging at his chest. "I'd have this. I'd have this piece of you, this reminder that at one point in time, you were mine. It's a reminder that I know what love is. That I have been loved, even if I'm not anymore."

I feel the pounding ache in my chest, the hot tears streaming down my face, the tightness in my throat. I physically feel the crack through my soul and the breaking of my heart as he speaks those words to me, as I realize just how broken I'd made him.

All this time, I thought it was just myself I'd destroyed. I'd learned to live with it. My own kind of punishment. I never imagined he was hurting just as much as I was, that the way I abandoned him would echo so deeply and for so long.

He still won't look at me, and I can't blame him. I wouldn't want to look at me either, but I can't stop staring at him, taking in the perfection in his features and the permanent light in his eyes. The way he's endured all that life has thrown at him, the way he's fought his ghosts, including the ones I left behind, how he still comes out of all of it with a smile, with kindness and care...

That realization only slices deeper.

"I was supposed to protect you," I choked through my tears. I feel them dripping off my chin and onto my chest, but I don't wipe them away. "I was supposed to be your person. You gave me pieces of your soul, too."

He finally lifts his head to look at me, emotion glistening in his eyes. A desert chill rushes through me, and I'm not sure if it's the breeze in the open night or if it's the look on his face.

"I took a piece of you you'd been afraid to give away, and then I left you. I broke you, Leo. I broke you, and you saved me, and..." A sob wrenches from me, loud enough to drown out the sound of the movie playing in the space around us.

I cross my arms over my chest, trying to hold in the despair tearing through me, knowing I deserve to feel every ache and cut so deeply they scar.

"I don't understand why you don't hate me, Leo." My head falls into my hands, hiding my face as I'm overcome with it all.

I hear shuffling before the scent of citrus and the sea engulf me. Strong arms grab my own, pulling me sideways until I'm flush against a warm, hard chest. His heart beats rapidly against my ear. His breathing is heavy against my body, his fingers rubbing smooth, soft circles along my skin.

"Was there a reason for it, Darby? A reason you left? A reason you never came back?"

I nod against his heart.

He brings his lips to my temple as he hushes my sobs.

"Will you tell me those reasons someday?"

I nod again.

He pulls back so he can look at me, and I realize silent tears have been falling down his cheeks too. Now, he only smiles at me softly. "Then for now, it's enough."

He continues to brush his hands up and down my arms, and despite the warmth of the summer air and his skin on mine, it gives me chills. I find myself unable to comprehend how he's here, sitting in front of me, saving me from the mess of my life and taking care of me when I'm the one who ruined him. Who ruined us. Who ruined everything.

I can only stare at his beautiful face, his eyes that shimmer underneath the moonlight, and his boyish smile—the one that has made me weak in the knees since the moment I met him. I can't help but wonder what brought him to me at seventeen and what brought him back at twenty-seven. I think about how I used to call him mine, and I wonder how I ever let him go.

"Stop looking at me like that," he whispers.

"Like what?"

"Like I own all the pieces of your soul. Like you've been incomplete all this time without them."

I can't stop looking at him that way, because that's exactly what's happened. He's owned every piece of me since I was seventeen, and I only now realize how lost I've been since then.

"This moment is the most complete I've felt since that night on the beach all those years ago," I whisper.

He lifts a hand, running a thumb along my cheek and across my bottom lip. His mouth tilts up into a smile as he studies my face. "Me too, Honeysuckle."

Twenty-Nine

Honeysuckle

Then. August 1st.

"So, it's the time of day you were born, like down to the minute, that determines your rising sign. Then, your sun sign is your most-known zodiac sign, which is based on the day of the month you were born. Your moon sign is determined by which sign the moon was in at the time of your birth, and that makes up your big three."

Elena furiously types away at her phone. "This app will also tell us your Mercury, Venus, and Mars placements, plus all twelve of your houses, which kind of act as a map of your life. But for now, we can focus on your big three so as not to overwhelm you."

I feel incredibly overwhelmed by her rapid masterclass on astrology, but I don't tell her that. I tell her the day, year, and time I was born as she quickly plugs all of it into the app on her phone.

The day is at its peak, the sun beating down onto the top of our heads, the sand warming beneath our feet. Leo and Everett sit on the horizon on their boards, but Elena chose to stay back with me as we swap books on the beach.

"Okay, you're a Scorpio sun, obviously." She hisses. "An Aquarius moon. Yikes. And," she draws out, "a Cancer rising." Elena takes on a contemplative look as she nods at her phone screen. "A lot of conflicting shit going on up there, huh?" she gestures toward my head.

I just shrug.

"I'm a Leo sun, Pisces moon, and Aries rising, which sounds concerning, but I've got my shit on lockdown. I am one with myself." She gives me a cool smile.

"Oh, God, is she going on about that astrology shit again?" a voice sounds from behind us.

Elena closes her eyes and sighs. "That, however, would be my Achilles' heel."

Zach plops down into the sand behind us and lazily throws his arm over Elena's shoulder, tugging her against his chest. "Don't let her get you all worked up over the stars and shit, new girl," he says, smiling at her. Elena rolls her eyes but fails to hide the tilt of her lips and the blush of her cheeks.

"He's a Capricorn sun. He doesn't know what the fuck he's talking about."

"I like hearing you talk about it," August says softly as he joins us, taking a place on the other side of Elena.

"And that is because you are a little Libra angel." She leans over and kisses Zach's younger brother on the cheek. August instantly blushes.

Zach scoffs, though his arms remain wrapped around Elena, his grip tightening possessively. He presses his lips to the top of her head, but his eyes are on his brother as he does it. August looks away.

Elena grabs her backpack, fishing through it before pulling out a small bag. "I don't know if you've noticed the boys and I all wear these little rope necklaces?"

I nod. I had noticed Leo's the day I met him, noticed that he never took it off.

She opens the bag and pulls out a necklace: twine-colored rope braided together with a small black stone nestled in the middle. "I make them," Elena continues. "The stone is Black Tourmaline. It's a protection crystal." She hesitantly holds the necklace out to me, as if this is something she doesn't do often. "It'll protect you physically from harm, but it also protects your energy, keeps negativity away from you."

Zach runs a thumb along her arm, but I notice August is the one smiling at her now, looking at her as if she hung the moon.

August is wearing a necklace, too—his with green rope, but the same black crystal as my own necklace. I notice that Zach's neck is bare.

As if he notices my observation, Zach laughs. "She took mine away from me a few months ago when she got angry and decided she'd like me to get hit by a car."

"I gave it back," she scoffs, rolling her eyes.

He shrugs. "I forget to put it on sometimes."

August rolls his eyes at that.

I take the necklace from her and immediately tie it around my neck. "Thank you so much. It's beautiful." I smile at her. "Really, I feel honored. I've never had a friend do this for me before."

"I've never really had a friend before, period," she says timidly, smiling back. "Plus, now that you and Leo have done the deed and all of that, we have to make sure we protect his precious treasure at all costs." She smirks.

I look away, feeling heat rise on my skin.

All three of them laugh. "I'm sorry, I forgot you get scandalized. I won't make any more jokes about you guys totally getting it on." I glare at her, and she laughs again. "Okay"—she clears her throat—"that was really the last one. Sorry. We're pretty open about things here, and I forget not everyone is like that."

"Yeah, Elena is a real open book." Zach winks at her.

"I'm going to go get in the water," August says as he stands up. Zach watches his brother walk away with a concerned look on his face.

Elena pretends to be oblivious to the weirdness of the interaction.

We spend the next hour talking more about our favorite books. Mine are mostly classics and young adult fantasies. Elena's are mostly thrillers and oddly dark romances. Our tastes couldn't be more different, but somehow, I want to read everything she loves, and I think she wants to read all my favorite stories too.

Zach eventually gets up to join the boys in the water, and I notice him meet Leo on the sand, taking his board from him as Leo begins to make his way over to us.

He shakes the water out of his blond hair and then runs one of his muscular hands through it. I never used to think hands could be attractive, but sometimes, when I watch Leo's run along my skin and study the veins in them, I decide that hands can definitely be beautiful. I'm enamored by the way he can make me come undone with only those hands. The way it feels when he grabs my hips, how he guides me with the press of his fingers against my skin when I move atop him. The extra squeeze he gives when he loses himself, as if he wants to brand his handprints into my skin.

In the near month that's followed that perfect night on our beach, Leo and I have spent our early mornings and our late nights wrapped up in each other. Whether in our place on the pier, or our private cove, or even a few evenings in his bedroom when he sneaks me through the back door of the house, we explore each other's minds and souls—each other's bodies. He's made me feel more things with that body—with those beautiful hands and his soft mouth—than I even knew were possible before I experienced them.

"Hi, beautifuls," he says with a smile as he reaches us. His eyes snag on my neck. "Elena made you a necklace?" He squats down to my level and reaches out, brushing his fingers across the rope. "Look at you." His eyes meet mine, and he grins. "You're one of us now."

I can't help the smile that blooms back. Elena knocks her leg against mine, her way of giving affection. I do feel—for the first time in my life—like I belong, like this family made a place just for me, and even when I leave them at the end of the summer, my spot won't be filled by anyone else. I'll always belong here with them.

Shaking off the sudden prick of emotion, I say, "You were amazing out there today."

One dimple appears in his cheek as he smirks. "Are you my

reward for doing well?"

Elena gags. "Take it elsewhere."

"I've gotta work this afternoon anyway." He flips her off. Nodding at me, he says, "Walk me home?"

"Yeah, I'm helping my grandma plant a new wildflower garden today." I lean over and wrap my arms around Elena's shoulder. She stiffens briefly before returning it. "Thanks for being my friend," I whisper in her ear.

"Don't make it a thing," she responds with a choked laugh.

Leo pulls me from the sand, and we walk hand in hand back up the hill that leads to both of our houses. "Wildflower garden?" he asks as we make our way down the boardwalk.

I shrug. "I like flowers. If I'm going to try staying here—living with her next year—I want to have my own mark on the house. I also want something that reminds me of Dahlia here, too. She's beautiful and wild and colorful."

"So are you." He wraps an arm around my shoulder and presses a kiss to my forehead. "Can you plant honeysuckles too?"

I laugh. "Maybe. I want to plant all kinds of flowers. I want to make beautiful bouquets I can line the house with. I want the whole place to bloom."

Two ocean eyes pin on me as he runs a thumb across my skin. "You're pretty amazing too, Honeysuckle."

Thirty

Honeysuckle

Now. June 1st.

We were supposed to make it to St. George, Utah, today, but instead, we're not even one hundred percent sure *where* we are.

I was looking at our route on my phone as we left the hotel in Moab this morning when I noticed we had to pass fairly close to Bryce Canyon National Park.

Knowing that yesterday was one of the best days I've had in years, I wasn't quite ready to let go of the feeling I was having here in the mountains, in the car with Leo. In bed with Leo, honestly.

Once we got back to our hotel room last night, one bed remained empty, just as the night before. Neither of us addressed that. We didn't say anything at all. We took turns readying for bed, and he lay down in what was supposed to have been his bed while I brushed my teeth, but I climbed in right next to him. He held me all night in comfortable silence.

I woke up this morning to find him sleeping soundly with his arms wrapped around my waist, one hovering dangerously close to my breast while the rest of his body molded to mine, his cock pressed into my back—rock hard.

It was a struggle not to shift my weight so he would be cupping my chest or to grind my backside against him like a cat in heat, but I endured. I have no guilt about being close to him, sleeping in bed next to him. I wrote Jackson a note, and my intentions to end my relationship were abundantly clear when I made the decision to leave my wedding. Plus, if my sister is correct, he's been unfaithful anyway.

But when—if—Leo and I cross that final line, I need him to, first and foremost, be awake. Secondly, I think, for the sake of both our fragile hearts, we need to understand what it means and where it'll lead. I'm not sure either of us is quite ready for those conversations, for those decisions.

So, this morning, I quietly slipped out of bed and got him breakfast. As we began our drive toward St. George, my own memories of that place began to resurface, making me uneasy. With that, mixed with the carefree feeling I've been having on this trip with Leo and the urge to deny what a mess my life has become, I found myself looking to extend our trip a little longer.

I asked Leo if he'd mind taking another detour so we could spend the day in Bryce Canyon, and he obliged without question.

I know Leo has responsibilities—huge responsibilities—back in Pacific Shores. I know it's unfair of me to ask him to table them day after day because I'm simply afraid to confront my own issues, but the genuine smile on his face when we hiked through the bright red canyons and drove along the sprawling vistas made me feel less guilty.

He looked at me like there was no place else in the world he'd rather be, and I realized I felt exactly the same.

I've spent the majority of my life working to please other people, to be praised by other people. It felt good to put myself first—to put Leo first. It felt a little like we were making up for lost time, getting to know the new versions of ourselves. That feeling stirred up something deep inside me, as if, for the first time in a long time, I was doing something I was meant to do. The universe or divine intervention or God or whatever you want to call it smiled down at the two of us and said, "This is what I've wanted for you all this time."

After spending the day in Bryce Canyon, Leo suggested booking a hotel closer to the National Park so we could stay to watch the sunset over the cliffside. He found a tiny town, complete with one motel, one gas station, and one bar, not far from the entrance to the park.

As we pull up to the parking lot of the motel, a bright pink neon sign blinds us, but some of the lights are out, so instead of it reading: *Canyon Motel* and *Vacancy,* it read: *any Mo* and *Vacan.*

I snort. "Charming."

"Look, it had four stars on Yelp." Leo laughs.

The building is painted a bright teal, but the paint is faded in several places. There is only one row of about fifteen rooms stretching from one end of the property to the other. Every door is painted yellow, and a few of them are missing numbers. There is a small office on the far end of the building with a flickering light illuminating over a sign that reads: *Reception* but has the *P* missing from it.

"Those reviews are definitely left by the skinwalkers out here trying to lure people into their flesh-eating claws."

"Don't be silly, Darby. Skinwalkers live in Appalachia. You're thinking of Bigfoot."

We're both laughing as we step out of the Mustang, and Leo covers the top, triple-checking that the car is locked.

"Do you want to go grab food first?" I ask, hitching my thumb back toward the small, equally run-down dive bar across the street. "I feel like once I go in that room, I'm not going to want to leave for the rest of the night, and I'm starving."

Despite it being early summer, being this high in the mountains gives way to a frigid chill after the sun sets. I wore a pair of thin leggings today, and my tank top is doing very little to protect me from the whipping wind that prickles at my arms.

I know that once I have a hot shower and a warmer pair of clothes, the day in the sun and the soreness from the hiking is going to hit me, and all I'll want to do is pass out.

"'Course." Leo smiles. He places his hand at the small of my back as he leads us across the street and into the bar.

It's exactly what you'd expect to find from a southwestern, small-town pub. Faded wood lines the floor, a black bar top straight across from the front doors, a bundle of tables to the right, and a small dance floor with an old-school jukebox to the left.

Dark walls are covered in license plates from all fifty states, along with a bunch of other random Utah-themed paraphernalia. Multicolored string lights line the ceiling of the building, along with a few dimmed lamps hanging over the booths and tables and two small spotlights at the center of the dance floor.

The bartender motions for us to sit wherever we want, and Leo maneuvers us to a booth in the back corner. We somehow enter an in-depth discussion on the existence of Bigfoot while we look over our menus—I'm not an idiot, so I know for certain there is no such thing, but Leo claims that being born on the West Coast and *not* believing in Bigfoot is considered a war crime.

The bar is decently busy. It appears that some bikers traveling throughout the country visiting National Parks have made a stop here. Couples in their fifties and sixties litter the dance floor together and take over much of the bar. I can't help but smile at them.

"Honeysuckle," Leo says, breaking me from my stare.

"Yeah?"

"You never came to visit your grandma after she got sick."

I look up at him in confusion, wondering where that statement came from.

He turns toward the group of older people in the bar laughing together, appearing carefree and happy. "Was it because of me? Did you miss the last years of her life because you were trying to avoid me?"

"No, Leo." I shake my head. It hurts my heart that he's so convinced I didn't want him that I would've avoided my own family to stay away from him. It breaks me that he can't see how little control I had, how little control I've always had over my life.

His eyes meet mine, blue kaleidoscopes. "You didn't even come to her funeral."

I cock my head. "Yes, I did. Her funeral was held in Crestwell. That's where she's buried." I sigh. "I didn't know her health had begun declining. I was never close with her growing up, not until I came to stay with her. We didn't talk much. She came to visit a few times over the holidays after that summer, but our relationship was a little strained after I left." I feel emotion rising in my throat. "I guess she and my dad decided it was best not to tell Dahlia or me. He says it was so we wouldn't get scared, but in reality, I know it was to avoid me ever going back to Pacific Shores."

Leo's eyes shudder, undiluted anger flashing across them. "Why would she agree to that?"

"My dad has control over *everyone*, Leo. Grandma included." Plus, there were other reasons why my relationship with her fell apart, but I'm not ready to dive into those yet.

"Is that why you never..." He trails off, shaking his head.

Before I can ask him for clarification, another thought dawns on me. "What did you mean when you said I didn't go to her funeral?"

He shrugs. "We had a funeral for her in Pacific Shores, too. The whole town came." He reaches across the table and grabs one of my hands. "She was really loved there. That was her home."

I find myself rapidly blinking back tears. My grandma and I had a tough relationship before I came, and especially after I left, but outside of Dahlia, she was the only person in my family I felt understood me. I always hoped we'd have the chance to work things out.

Sometimes, I even wondered if it was her lack of trust and disappointment in me that made things so strained, or if it was my father's influence.

Though, I guess I'll never have the chance to ask her, to try to work it out. I block out those thoughts often, but when they arise, they always break my heart.

Our conversation is cut short when my phone begins to ring. I've gotten better at keeping it on silent, since Jackson's calls haven't relented, but Dahlia had texted me earlier today, letting me know she would be calling this evening to check in.

Leo nods at my phone, encouraging me to answer.

"Hey, Dal."

"Hey, where are you?" she responds.

"Somewhere in the middle of Utah." I chuckle, hoping it doesn't sound as forced as it feels.

She hums. "You two are taking an awfully long time to complete a...what? Two-day drive?"

I smile at Leo. "I think we're both trying to avoid our responsibilities for a moment. But we'll be in California the day after tomorrow."

"Well, speaking of that..." Dahlia sighs. "Dad figured out you're going to Grandma's. I mean, I won't admit to anything, but I think he finally put enough information together to assume that's where you're headed."

I nervously begin chewing on my fingernails as Leo stares after me with concern.

"I overheard him in the office today talking to a realtor. He's trying to get her house sold and cleared out immediately so that you won't have a place to stay. I think he might put a freeze on your trust account so you only have your own savings. He's hoping that'll be enough to get you to come home."

From reeling from our conversation about my grandma to now being wrecked with this news about my father, my emotions begin to boil over. I feel my face heating with anger, my stomach funneling with despair, my eyes spilling over with tears I'm no longer able to hold in.

I move the phone away from my mouth. "He's selling my grandma's house," I whisper across the table to Leo.

That rage takes over his features once again. He clears his throat, excusing himself as he stands from the booth and steps outside the front doors. I watch him through the window as he pulls out his own phone and presses it against his ear.

"I'll figure out something, Dal," I say.

"I know you will," she agrees. "Do you need me to send you some money?"

"No." I bite my lip. "I think...I think subconsciously, I've been building up to this for a while, knowing that, in some way or another, I'd have to stop relying on Dad and Jackson. Or, maybe I just didn't want to be indebted to them. I don't know." I hear her grunt her agreement on the other side of the line. "I've been saving up for years. I have enough to get a small apartment, and as long as I can find a new job before the summer is over, I'll be fine. I don't need him. Them. I don't need anyone."

"Damn right, you don't. That's my girl." I hear shuffling. "Do you want to talk to Lou? She's right here."

"Of course, I want to talk to Lou. What kind of question is that?"

My sister laughs warmly, and I feel a little more settled than I did a few moments ago. I continue watching Leo through the window as my niece rattles on about her last week of school and the camps she'll be attending this summer.

Leo re-enters the building, but instead of making his way back to our table, he goes to the bar. I watch him greet a few of the bikers crowding the area before speaking with the bartender briefly, a gleam in his eye as he turns back toward me.

I tell my sister and Lou I need to go, letting them know I love them and I'll call soon. Leo reaches me just as I end the call, but he doesn't sit down.

Instead, he holds a hand out toward me. "I'm so goddamn tired of seeing you cry. Let me make you smile." I give him a bemused look, eyes flicking between his face and his outstretched arm. "Dance with me, Honeysuckle. Please."

A soft song begins to flow through the room. A few couples link arms in the middle of the dance floor and begin to sway to the music that sounds more fitting for a 1950s diner than a motorcycle bar in the middle of nowhere.

I can't help the bubble of laughter that bursts from me, and the smile that highlights Leo's face is just enough to have me rise to my feet and take his hand.

He twirls me around as he leads me to the center of the floor. The sickly sweet melody floats around us as he brings one hand around my waist and holds onto my own hand with the other.

He pulls me into him, resting his chin on the top of my head as we slowly spin in circles. Butterflies flutter in my chest, but it's my heart that flies away from me as the chorus of the song begins to play.

Something about being sweet as a honeysuckle and falling in love with the same person over and over again.

I let my eyes close, my face falling into his neck.

"You listening, Darby?" he whispers against my temple.

"Leo," I breathe. It's all I can say. There aren't words for the way it feels to be wrapped in his arms, the warmth of his breath and the caress of his hand along my side. The way he tightens his hand around mine in four quick motions, speaking the secret language we developed so many years ago.

"I asked you a question, baby. Are you listening to this right now? You get it?"

I nod against his shoulder.

He pulls back to gaze down at me, his eyes bright and pleading. "Tell me what you're thinking about right now."

We continue moving slowly on the dance floor, everything around us fading until it's just the two of us. I see the honesty in his eyes. I see the hope on his face. The quiet determination in his stare that existed all those years ago. The idea that he and I were something special.

Though now, I see something guarded in him, too, something that didn't exist before I placed it there. For all he's lived through in his life, it was my abandoning him that put up those walls, that made him unable to trust others, to give himself away.

And it's me coming back that's given him the determination to try again.

As that realization settles in me, I decide to be honest too. "I'm thinking I want to dare you to kiss me."

His brows raise, a soft surprise on his face as a light laugh leaves him. He removes his hand from mine and cups the back of my jaw, tilting my head upward.

Running his thumb along the back of my neck, he lets his lips hover just over mine. "You know what it means when I kiss you, right?"

"Yes," I whisper.

I've always known what it means to kiss Leo Graham. I've known what it's like to find him, to lose him, and to find him again. I know what life is like with him and what life is like without him.

I think back to a conversation I had with Elena over that summer, what she said about there being a touch only he can provide, the feeling of the rest of the world fading out until only the two of you are inside of it.

How it's worth fighting your whole life for that feeling, knowing it'll never exist with someone else.

I'll never get the past back. I'll never right my wrongs or forget my mistakes, but I've spent ten years without him, always grasping for and never quite finding the life I was building with him. I spent ten years hung up on two months, convincing myself that the older I got, the less it would hurt, the more it would fade.

That never happened, because when my brain fought tooth and nail to convince me otherwise, my heart and soul always knew. It was him. It's always been him. Maybe I can't take back the past, but I can fight like hell for our future.

The stars in his eyes are bright as he looks down at me with so much hope in his sapphire gaze as he inches closer.

"Dare me, Honeysuckle."

"I dare you, Heathen."

But I don't wait. I've been waiting my whole life for him. I run my hand up his arm so I can cup his face and pull him into me.

And finally, *finally*, I find my way back home.

Thirty-One

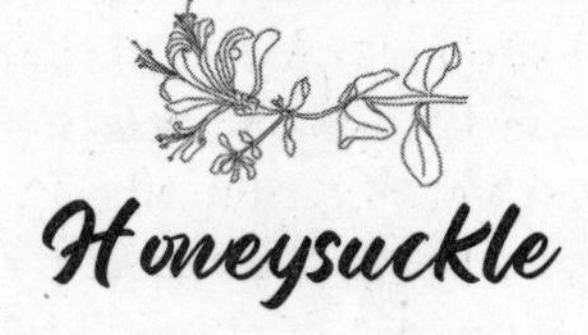

Honeysuckle

Then. August 9th.

"I'm scared," I say as we walk hand in hand through the waves beneath the pier.

Leo squeezes his palm against mine four times. "What're you scared of?"

"Leaving you." I look out into the darkness. Glimpses of water flash through the multiple colored lights that filter through the boards of the pier above us. "Leaving all of this."

Leo doesn't say anything, but he gently tugs me forward. Away from the pier and down the empty beach until the lights no longer touch us.

"Look out there." He points to the horizon I know exists but can't see. "All you see is darkness, right?"

"Right."

"But you know the ocean is out there. You know that when you wake up tomorrow morning and look out your window, the same sparkling blue horizon line will be there, just like every other morning."

I nod.

"Because you have faith in it. You know it's always there, even in the dark when it can't be seen." He drops his arm and runs his hand up my arm. "Tell me what you hear, Darby."

I let my eyes flutter shut. "I hear the waves." The loudest sound around me as they crash against the shore. "I hear the wind in the trees. I hear your breathing."

"Right. You can't see the water, can't see the wind, but you hear them. You know they're there, a constant. They're factual. Reliable." I feel his fingers crawl across my collarbone before coming up to cup my cheek. "I'll be that for you too."

I open my eyes to find him staring down at me, two sapphires glowing in the night. They're like a beacon to me. No matter how dark it is, they'll always be shimmering brightly, the stars I need to find my way home.

"Even if you have to leave, I'll be here, as reliable and sure as the waves crashing against the sand. As the wind that rattles the tree branches. As the air in my lungs—the heart that beats in my chest. Only for you, Darby.

"When you go back to Kansas, it might take some time before you can come back, but I know you will. You'll find your way home to me, and I'll be here. Whenever you begin to doubt that, I want my voice to be the thing you hear in your head, telling you this. I want you to hear me—feel me—even when you can't see me."

He runs his thumb across my cheek, and only then do I realize he was wiping away a tear that began to fall down my face.

"I'll keep you safe. I'll wait for you. I'll always protect you, even if it has to be just inside your own head for a little while."

He grips my chin, tilting me upward and planting a soft, warm kiss against my mouth.

Words gather at the tip of my tongue, three of them, but I don't know how to say them. I never have. I'm not even sure I've ever said them to my parents. We don't speak that way to each other. The only person I've ever been openly affectionate with is my sister. The only person I've ever told I loved. Who's ever said it to me.

I feel them—I know I feel them, and yet, I can't let the sweet little phrase come out of my mouth.

So, instead, I kiss him harder, more fervently, trying to show him those words, that emotion, if I can't express it with my voice.

He laughs against my mouth. "If you really want to make

things permanent, we could go get those matching tattoos."

My stomach flutters. I know he's joking, but I suddenly can't imagine a better way to show him how I feel, a better way for me to be able to leave Pacific Shores than to know that his skin will forever be scarred with my memory.

"Let's do it."

He gives me a bemused look. "Darby, I was joking."

"I'm not," I counter. He bites his lip, and it hits me then. I realize that the only tattoo he has is one for his mother. His skin has already been scarred by a woman he loved and lost, and maybe it's too much to ask him to do that again. "You know what? Never mind. That was stupid. I—"

He puts his fingers over my lips. "I can see your brain working, Honeysuckle. Stop thinking I don't want you forever, because I promise you, I do. I just didn't think it would be something you'd ever actually want to do."

"I do," I breathe. "I want something to represent this summer—represent you—that can't ever be taken away from me. Something that's just mine."

Thirty-Two

Heathen

Now. June 1st.

I don't hear the music anymore, the song that felt like it was written just for her the first time I listened to it. I don't hear the claps and whistles from the other patrons in the bar. I don't see the low lights, and I don't smell the food.

I hear her soft whimpers against my mouth. I hear the rapid beating of my heart. I feel the soft, warm skin of her neck, the curve of her waist beneath my hands. I smell her shampoo, floral and honey like it's always been. I taste her lips, sweet and soft.

My grip on her tightens as she slips her tongue into my mouth, savoring the impossible feel of her flesh on mine. The reminder that she's real. That we're real. We've always been real.

After ten years of drought, my soul is experiencing its first rainfall, and I almost don't care that it's happening inside a crowded bar.

Almost.

"Honeysuckle," I groan into her mouth. "Baby."

She hums, leaning into me as I pull back. Her eyes flutter open as a satisfied smile crosses her face.

"I wanna kiss you all night, Darby, but I've been waiting ten years for this moment, and I didn't expect it to happen in public." Still cupping the back of her neck, I bring it forward and run my thumb across the length of her bottom lip. "Let's get the fuck out of here."

She giggles, giving me an enthusiastic nod.

We're both laughing as I jog over to our booth, and I slap a hundred-dollar bill down onto the counter, leaving our dinners half finished. A few of the motorcycle gang members cheer us on as I push open the restaurant door with Darby's hand in mine.

We laugh the whole way across the street and into the office of the motel. She loops her arm through mine, resting her head on my shoulder, as if it's the most effortless thing she's ever done.

I make quick work of paying for our room and swiping the keys. What I haven't told Darby is that, unlike our last hotel, this one is nowhere close to fully booked, but I won't be spending any nights away from this woman ever again.

I let her enter our hotel room first, wrapping my arms around her waist and trailing my lips along her neck as she takes in the room. I don't give a shit what it looks like. She's the only thing I'll be looking at tonight, anyway.

"Leo," she whispers, throat vibrating against my mouth.

"Hmm?"

"There's only one bed."

I chuckle. "Yeah, baby. We're only going to need one from here on out." She spins around and looks up at me. I brush a wild strand of golden hair from her cheek as she studies my face. I know all she'll find here is amused confidence. "We've slept in the same bed the last two nights, Darby. I don't see how this is different."

She swallows, her eyes casting downward briefly before lifting back to mine. She crosses an arm over her chest. "It feels different."

I run my thumb across her cheek as she instinctively leans into my touch. "Maybe it is, then. It's no accident this time, Honeysuckle. Not because of a lack of rooms or options. Tonight, I think we've both finally realized the only place you belong is right here next to me."

Her eyes soften as her brows draw together. She lets out a small huff of air, leaning against my chest. "I don't understand how you don't hate me."

"I'd never hate you, Honeysuckle," I say, running my hand

along the back of her head. "I promised I'd always keep you safe. I'll always be there for you. I came out here to keep that promise, and I've also realized I never fell out of love with you, either."

She tilts her head up, hazel eyes sparkling with unshed tears. "I don't hold anything you said to me at seventeen against you. We're not kids anymore. You're not beholden to those promises. You're allowed to hate me, Leo. I was awful to you."

I feel the flash of confusion across my face. I know better now than to assume that each decision she made when she left was her own. I know now just how controlled she's been all these years. The situation is awful, yes, heartbreaking and unfair, but I don't know what she thinks she's done that could ever validate hating her.

It almost makes me angry that she could be so beaten down, she could believe I'd ever hate her, that I could ever do anything besides love her. The feeling is hot, burning my throat as I realize I don't think Darby really understands what love even is.

"I mean every single fucking thing I've ever said to you, Darby. I still mean them now."

A tear spills over her cheek as her bottom lip trembles. I quickly swipe it away with my thumb. "How?"

I take a moment to look at her, to study her glowing eyes and golden hair. The freckles on her cheeks are on full display after days in the sun, no longer being covered up and hidden away. I study the color of her nose and the slope of her neck, which fits so perfectly in my hand, the way her fingers twist into the fabric of my T-shirt and hold tightly, like I'm her life raft in a raging sea.

I want to ask her the same thing. How could she ever possibly question why I'd do anything other than love her?

"Was it real, Honeysuckle? The way you loved me then. The way you're looking at me right now. Every laugh, every secret told, every smile you've given me. What you wrote in that letter."

"It's all real," she whispers. "It has always been real."

I cup her face in both hands, wiping away tears as they fall from her face and swallowing back my own emotions. "Did you look for me in the dark? Did you try to hear my voice?"

"I tried." She nods. "But I think your voice got drowned out by the howls of wolves."

"I know, baby. I know." I lean down, pressing our foreheads together and caressing her jaw. "That's why I'd never hate you, Darby. I know you fought for us. You're still fighting now, fighting enough to reach out to me when you were on the brink of breaking. You're strong, Honeysuckle, and you're resilient. You found your way back home, and I don't care how long it took for you to get here, only that you're here now."

"But aren't you angry with me for not fighting harder? I could've been more defiant. I fell back into my old rhythms so easily, Leo." Her voice cracks against my chest. "I promised you I wouldn't. I broke the promises I made. I..." She trails off as a sob rushes through her. My chest tightens at the sound, my instincts screaming at me to make it stop because my body can't stand her tears. "Aren't you angry about that?"

I sigh, pulling back so she can see my face, so she can see the raw emotion in my eyes. Sliding my hands down both her arms, I grip her biceps and begin walking her toward the wall of the motel room next to the bed. "Yes, Honeysuckle. I'm so fucking angry with you for breaking my heart." She hits the wall, and I brace my arms against it on either side of her head. "Destroying my soul." I lean in deeper with every sentence. "Obliterating me into irreparable pieces."

She lets out a shaky breath, tears still streaming down her face. I drop my head, running my nose along her cheek. "But you're here now, wanting me."

"I do," she whispers. "I always have."

I nod against her head.

"So, either you left all those years ago because you decided I wasn't good enough for you, and that's going to destroy me all over again." I run my hand down her neck and cross her collarbone, letting the strap of her tank top fall off her shoulder. "Or, you left me all those years ago not because you didn't love me, but because some force outside the two of us kept you from me, and that'll destroy me too." I repeat the motion on her other side.

"Or...you never came back because you thought you weren't good enough for *me*, and that would destroy me most of all." My lips follow my hands, trailing along her throat. "I don't want to be destroyed tonight, Darby," I whisper against her sweet skin. "Damn the past. I just want to be put back together."

She swiftly grabs my head and pulls it to level her face. Her honeyed eyes are bright. "Then show me what I've been missing. Show me what can only be found with you."

My mouth is on her, hot and wet and needful as I press her into the wall. My hands roam her body freely, marking every dip and curve I've been desperate to touch since she walked back into my life just days ago. I finally take the reins off my thoughts and let them wander to all the places I've dreamed of touching her. Feeling her. Tasting her.

I didn't let myself dream about it, not with her so close and somehow so far at the same time. Not when I thought I'd never get to feel her against me again. It was too raw. Too painful.

But now, as her lips move against mine, her tongue slips into my mouth, and those soft moans swim through her lips, I let it wash over me. Let myself savor it. Own it.

A whimper escapes me as our tongues dance together—hot and needful. Kissing her feels like a breath of air after a decade underwater, like weaving through waves after so many years with my feet on the ground. Like floating after drowning.

I let my fingers brush along her skin softly, reveling in the goosebumps that trail behind my touch. I slip her tank top farther down her arms, and she lifts them so that the straps fall off her completely, folding her shirt in half.

I pull away from her mouth and look down to see her chest bared to me. Dusty pink, puckered nipples heave with her heavy breath. The athletic fabric of her top being tight enough for her not to need a bra beneath it allows nothing to separate me from her body. I slowly move my hand down her chest, lifting my face to search her eyes for permission.

Her cheeks are flushed, eyes sparkling, lips swollen as she raises an impatient brow at me, arching her back so her breast fits against the palm of my hand.

I throw my head back and let out a moan as I feel her harden beneath my touch. I brush my thumb across her nipple, and she lets out a soft sound of need.

"You're so beautiful, Darby," I whisper.

I bend forward, bringing my lips to her breast as she lifts her hand to cup the back of my head and press me against her.

"Needy girl," I murmur as I flick my tongue across her peak. I palm one breast while I wrap my mouth around the other and suck hard before pulling away.

She writhes against me, whimpering my name and arching into my touch. I can't get enough of it—her taste, her touch, her sounds. Knowing I'm the one making her feel this way. Seeing her just as desperate for me as I've always been for her.

I run my hands down her sides, dipping into the back of her leggings to grab her ass as I kiss, suck, and nibble across her chest.

Her fingers meet my forearms as she reaches between us and begins to tug off the shorts I'm wearing.

"I don't have any condoms," I groan against her skin as the realization overcomes me. "But I get a physical before the competition season every year that includes a full STI panel, and everything came back fine. I haven't been with anyone since." I kiss my way up to her neck, straightening so I can see her face. "But if you're not comfortable with that, we don't have to—"

"I haven't been with anyone since you, so I'm good too," she says breathlessly. My heart falls to the floor. "I'm not on birth control, but I can get an emergency contraceptive tomorrow on our way out of town." She reads my face and blinks. I have no idea what expression it's giving off, but it's enough to make her pause. "If you're not okay with that—"

"You haven't had sex with anyone except me?"

She lets out a huff of laughter. "Yeah. So, you know, I'll

probably be a little rusty." She cups my face with her hand, giving me a soft smile. "But you've always been good at teaching me."

Fuck. That can't be real. She can't be real. My stomach flips, and suddenly, I feel like I can't stand up straight. I lean into her touch, unable to believe it.

Darby. My honeysuckle.

My first love.

My *only* love.

"What about...what about him?" Her fiancé, the man she was supposed to marry.

"My dad made me do this whole born-again-virgin thing, made Jackson agree to wait until marriage when we began dating." She shrugs. "But it worked out because I wasn't comfortable giving him that when I still felt like I belonged to someone else." She tucks her free hand beneath my shirt, the warmth of her skin skating up my chest until it hovers over my thundering heart. "And I've always been yours, Leo."

I don't have words for the way she's made me feel, for the need that courses through my veins. The instinct to claim her. To love her. Hold her. Remind her what it means to be mine.

My mouth crashes against hers, a surprised whine falling from her lips as my tongue sweeps in. I grasp behind her thighs and lift her, her legs crossing behind my back as I spin us and carry her toward the bed.

I lay her down atop it, grabbing her shirt, which is bunched around her midsection, and peeling it over her head completely. "I want to see every inch of your skin tonight, Honeysuckle. Taste it. Savor it." I kiss my way down her chest, through the valley between her breasts, along her stomach.

A desperate moan rips through her as she brings her hands to my head, running her fingers through my hair. Dipping my fingers into the waistband of her bottoms, I tug her leggings off her body in a swift movement, throwing them to the floor behind me.

"Leo," she whispers as I turn back to her, ready to devour her body like it's my last fucking meal. Her chest is heaving, her hair splayed out around her like a wild golden halo. Her nipples are hard and pointing at me, skin flushed, eyes hooded with desire and something else I can't register.

I study her face, watching as her gaze drops down. I follow it and realize what she's looking at. Peeking out just from the band of her yellow lace underwear is dainty cursive in black ink.

My breathing increases, my lungs feeling hollow as I run my thumb across that spot on her hip, pulling her underwear aside.

Heathen.

All the air leaves my lungs as I drop my head onto her chest. I can feel her pulse against my skin, her soft hand brushing the nape of my neck. I place my hand over that spot, over her tattoo, gripping her hip and squeezing softly.

"Darby," I whisper, not knowing what else to say.

I've thought about that tattoo so often over the years, always wondering where on her body it was, if she still had it, or if she ever got it done at all. There was always a part of me that believed she never had it to begin with, that she'd faked it and left before she'd ever have to own up to that fact.

I've been itching to ask her about it since she knocked at my hotel room door, but it felt miniscule in comparison to all of the other things we've both been going through.

As I look at it now, her skin scarred with the reminder of me, it's hard to imagine anything feeling more important than this: the nickname that's made me hundreds of thousands of dollars, that's made me a household name in my sport, that's plastered along the side of my business. It all started here with her. She's carried it with her—carried me with her—all this time.

She's always been mine.

I trail my lips along her stomach to her hip before pressing them against that tattoo, letting them linger there. Finally, I lift my head and smile at her. Her eyes are wide, anticipating my response.

"It's beautiful. Much better placement than your ass."

She lights up, beautiful laughter flowing from her throat. She lifts up on her elbows and bites her lip bashfully. "Do you want me to show you why I got my tattoo right there?"

My cock jumps in my shorts at the seduction dripping from her voice. I now realize that I'm face to face with her beckoning heat, her nearly naked body fully on display for me. I've been hard since we were dancing in the bar, but now, it feels painful. I know if I get inside her now, I'm going to embarrass myself.

I kiss her tattoo, grasping her underwear with both hands and tugging them down her body. Once they're on the floor with the rest of her clothing, I grab both her knees and spread her wide.

Her beautiful, pink pussy is wet and gleaming.

I lick my lips, bringing my eyes to hers. "Yes, baby. But first, I need a taste of your sweet little pussy. I'm going to remind you exactly what it feels like to be mine."

Thirty-Three

Heathen

Then. August 9th.

"Your tattoo guy is August?"

"Yeah?" I say it like it's obvious. "He's wanted to be a tattoo artist his whole life. Very talented." I take my shirt off and turn sideways, lifting my arm to show Darby.

"He did the tattoo for your mom?"

"Yep."

"He's like...fifteen."

"I'm sixteen, Honeysuckle." August's voice chimes from across the garage as he digs through a box. "And I'm a born talent. A prodigy. The best the world has ever seen."

Darby snorts. "What are my honest-to-god chances of this getting infected?"

"There is always a chance of infection, regardless of where you get it done. Proper aftercare is essential, and I'll walk through it with you when we're finished." He stalks over to us, setting a bunch of his equipment down on a table. "I'm no less sterile than any other tattoo artist. The only thing I lack is a license and a shop."

"Right," she drawls. "Because you're a minor."

"A minor with a God-given talent."

She blows out an exasperated breath. I'm laughing at her. August, serious as I've ever seen him, claps his hands together and asks, "Who's first?"

Darby raises her brow at me, looking a little nervous, as if to say *that needle looks huge.* I smile at her, giving her knee four quick squeezes before hopping up from the chair I'm sitting in. "Guess it's me."

I lie down on the black bench. Like the rest of August's equipment, it was bought illegally online. Most of it was purchased and used by other amateur artists or artists who just don't give a shit that they're selling to a minor. His parents have no idea about his operation here. He only gives tattoos to those he trusts, those he knows won't rat on him, even if their ink is found by their parents.

His parents rarely use the garage, so he keeps all his equipment stored in boxes disguised to look like old toys.

"What are we doing?" August asks me.

"I want 'honeysuckle,' right"—I swirl my finger in the air before pointing it right at my chest—"here." The tip of my finger lands right over my heart.

I hear Darby quietly gasp.

The corner of August's lips tilt up. He shakes his head, dark curls bouncing with it. "Like the flower?"

"No, Augustus. The word. Like her name."

His brows rise, and that small smirk becomes a full-on grin. He picks his glasses up off the tray next to him and slips them on, wide, square frames that make his green eyes seem huge. "You guys are fucking crazy." He laughs to himself as he begins assembling his equipment.

"C'mere, baby." I reach my arm out toward Darby. She scoots her chair a little closer so she's sitting right at the edge of the table. "I need you to let me squeeze your hand when it hurts."

"Okay," she says quietly.

I turn my head toward her. Golden strands of hair fall into her face as she smiles at me, her honeyed eyes glittering with unspoken emotion.

She jumps at the buzzing sound as August begins inking my chest. The pain is sharp and stinging, and a burn radiates across my skin. Particularly painful pinpricks flare whenever he makes a curving motion, but I keep my face straight, smiling right at Darby as her eyes grow wide, watching the nickname I gave her only weeks ago be forever branded on my body.

God, we're stupid.

Stupid and reckless and mad. But I think we may be all those things in the name of love, the kind you only get to experience once. Maybe it's not smart love. Not sensical. A teenage dream. But fuck, it's real. It's real and raw and all-consuming, and damn if that's not a good enough reason to ink her name right over my heart, because no matter how old I grow or how my life pans out, this summer girl has changed me.

I've changed her, too. The girl I met two months ago would've never dared to get a tattoo, especially not one for me. Maybe I corrupted her after all, though I think I might've helped her find herself instead. I think she's got a bit of a wild side but has grown up with a whole lot of fear, like a spooked animal. She needed a little coaxing and a lot of care and love. Now, she glows. She laughs. She dares.

She dares to fall in love with someone her parents would never approve of, to choose someone who'd be forbidden if we were ever found out. She dares to give me all these little pieces of her, pieces she knows she can't take back, pieces she'll never be able to give anyone else.

I've given her all my broken pieces too.

So, maybe we're stupid, but we're also brave. We're looking down the barrel of disaster and choosing to love hard despite it. That's something worth remembering, something worth scarring ourselves with.

We don't talk, but Darby squeezes my hand the whole way through. Soon enough, August is done, and he has me sit up from the bench slowly as he applies ointment over the cursive lettering that now spells *Honeysuckle* right over my heart.

Darby's cheeks are bright red as she leans into my body and admires the work done. "It's beautiful," she says.

"Your turn, baby. Don't wimp out on me now, or that'll be really embarrassing."

She pulls her eyes from my chest and looks up at me, smiling softly. "Okay, but I don't want you to see it until I decide you can, so you have to leave or something."

I shake my head. "Ain't no fucking way I'm leaving. We're doing this together, Honeysuckle."

She huffs. "Fine, but I don't want you seeing it right away. I want it to be a...surprise."

I shoot her a grin. "As much as I'd love to see my name on your ass, I am not letting Auggie here go anywhere near it."

She gasps, looking in the other direction. August pretends he didn't hear me as he cleans up the station and resets it for Darby's tattoo, though I can tell he's blushing.

"That is not what I'm doing," she finally says.

"We can blindfold him and have him face the other way. He can just reach back and hold your hand if you want," August finally says.

"Can we gag him too?"

His head snaps up, a grin spreading across his face at Darby's snark. He looks at me as if to say, *she fits in well here*. "Whatever you two get up to in your private time is your business."

Darby turns back to look at us, nostrils flaring, cheeks crimson. Her arms are crossed as she gives us an exasperated eye roll and grumbles something like, "Insufferable."

Just then, the door that leads into the house opens, and Zach comes strolling into view. He pauses momentarily, as if he wasn't expecting to see us, then continues over to one of the chairs surrounding the tattoo table and plops down. We all watch him, waiting to gauge his reaction to my new ink, but he's oblivious as he pulls a joint out of his pocket and lights up.

As he takes in a long, deep puff and exhales, his eyes finally zone in on my chest.

He erupts in a fit of coughing, and August and I burst out laughing. Darby's arms are still crossed, but she watches him with a bemused glimmer on her face.

"Shit, dude. You got your girlfriend of five minutes' nickname tattooed on your fucking chest? That's next level."

I smirk. "She's getting one too."

Zach's eyes go wide as he looks at her. "Damn." He laughs to himself, taking another hit. "You two are really in deep." He holds the joint out to Darby. "You want a hit? It'll help with nerves."

She looks at me with an unsure expression. I hop off the table and pluck the joint from Zach's hand, taking a puff. "He's not wrong, but you don't have to if you don't want to."

"I've never done that before," she murmurs.

"C'mere," I say, the joint between my lips.

I take another drag, holding the smoke in my mouth as I hand the joint back to Zach. I don't inhale but instead pull Darby toward me. I grab the back of her head and press her lips against mine. She opens immediately, and I blow all the smoke from my mouth and into her own.

I run my tongue along her bottom lip, getting one quick taste of her before pulling away. "Close your mouth and inhale like you're swallowing it." I see her chest expand, eyes widening before she opens her mouth and begins to cough.

"Wow," she says as she catches her breath. "That was...kind of hot."

The rest of us laugh as I pull her against me, kissing her again.

"All right, Honeysuckle, I'm ready for you," August says.

I've been kind of possessive of that nickname for her, but now that I know it belongs to me, I don't mind sharing it. I kind of like my friends calling her that, like they're familiar. Like she belongs here with us. Like it's just who she is. Elena has always been our prickly pear, but Darby is our honeysuckle.

"Blindfold," Darby says to me.

"This is dumb."

She frowns. "No, it's important to me. I want to show you my tattoo when..." She shakes her head. "When it's the right moment."

I raise my brow. "But it's definitely not on your ass?"

She rolls her eyes. "Definitely not on my ass."

I huff as August comes up to me and ties a strip of an old T-shirt around my eyes, knotting it at the back of my head before walking me over to one of the chairs and sitting me down. "Why does Zach get to see and I don't?"

"Good point," Darby says. "Zach, you have to face the other way, too."

I hear him snort. "Whatever. It's not like I care about seeing your ass, anyway. I'm just here to smoke."

I hear things being arranged in the garage and the soft whispers of August and Darby, likely discussing the tattoo I'm apparently not allowed to see yet. I'm entertaining this because I think it's cute that she wants to make the reveal something special for me.

In the darkness, I reach my arm out. A moment later, a soft, small hand envelops my own. It tenses as the buzz of the needle starts up again, and Darby hisses in pain.

I squeeze her hand four times, but I can feel the tension radiating off her.

"What're you thinking about, Honeysuckle? Sometimes talking gets your mind off the pain. Talk to me."

She giggles. "Hey, Zach?"

He only humphs in response.

"What's up with you and Elena?"

I'm the one who hisses now. We all know better than to bring up Elena to Zach. He's incredibly secretive about their not-so-secretive relationship. We all know they hook up. We all know they torture each other, that he won't make them official for whatever reasons he has, but he won't let her be with anyone else either. She can't let go of him no matter how many times he hurts her, and Elena can hurt him right back.

But we don't fucking talk about it. It's too sensitive for Everett, and neither Elena nor Zach open up to anyone about it.

So, it's the elephant in the room that we've just adopted into kind of a...group pet.

But by the sound of her giggling, I think the weed may actually be making its effect on Darby, or she's just got the placebo effect going on. Either way, she doesn't seem to give a shit that she just popped the lid on our group's largest can of worms.

To my utter surprise, Zach laughs.

He laughs.

The last time I asked him about Elena—after his car ended up suspiciously keyed—he threatened to pull out my balls and wrap them around my neck.

Must be the weed.

"Elena and I are..."

"Like fire and gasoline?" Darby chimes. She must be more interpretive than I realized.

"No. They're worse, like a force of fucking nature." That was August's voice.

I hear Zach let out a breathy laugh. The needle continues to buzz, but Darby isn't gripping my hand quite as tightly.

August continues, "She's like a bolt of lightning, and Zach... he's a..."

"What? A dead pine forest?" Zach snorts.

"Yes. They fucking destroy everything around them, screaming and fighting like you've never seen two people who hate each other more."

"Crying behind closed doors," I add. I turn my head to where I know Zach is sitting. "She cries a lot, man. Makes me want to kick your ass sometimes."

"It's not always my fault," is his response. I swear, I hear August scoff.

"I know." I nod. "And I can't tell the difference between

your fuck-ups and hers, and she won't tell Ev or me shit, so we never know whether or not to kick your ass."

It's like I can feel Zach smirking at me now.

"Once it starts, it's impossible to stop," August says.

"Eventually, you think the fire has died out, but as soon as the air gets dry again..." Zach laughs at that, and August practically growls. "It's like we're just waiting to see where it's going to strike next, what else they're going to burn."

"She does tend to have me in a chokehold." Zach's voice is gruff. He's been laughing, but I can tell he's hitting his limit. He's oddly protective of his and Elena's weird-ass dynamic. I assume everyone must be giving him the same perplexed look I am when he says, "You know...like smoke?"

I can't help the laughter that follows that dumb fucking metaphor. "Booooo." I cup my hands over my mouth and draw it out.

Suddenly, the blindfold is pulled back over my head, and I blink at the light. August's dark eyes are brimming with flame as he snaps his gloves off his hands, muttering, "She's done."

He takes off into the house.

Another odd piece to this puzzle I can never seem to figure out. I'm not sure I even want to.

❧

"When do I get to see it?" I ask, wrapping my arms around Darby's waist in the backyard of her grandma's house and nuzzling my face into her sweet, vanilla and floral-scented neck.

"I can take the bandage off in three days, so I'll show you then." I feel her smile against my cheek.

"Wait, so does that mean no..."

She giggles, nodding.

"For three days?"

"You survived seventeen years without it, Leo. I'm sure you'll be fine."

"I also survived seventeen years without you, Honeysuckle.

Doesn't mean I ever want to live without you again."

I hear the air leave her lungs as she presses her back into me, tilting her head sideways and pressing her lips against my jaw. Her hands cover mine where they're wrapped around her middle.

"Me either, Heathen."

Sweeter words have never been said, I think.

I kiss her goodnight and wait until she gets inside before I stumble home, high on weed, drunk on her lips and her skin and her words.

I think the honey-eyed golden girl might be in love with me.

And I know for certain I'm in love with her.

Thirty-Four

Honeysuckle

Now. June 1st.

The first swipe of his tongue through my legs sets my blood on fire.

I can't control the sound that flies from my mouth, the way my body bows off the bed. I can't control the arousal seeping from between my thighs as Leo holds them open, his tongue flicking at me again, playful and taunting.

It's been so long since I've felt anything besides a vibrator or my own hand between my legs. I've forgotten what the warmth of someone else's skin feels like against my own, the feeling of being filled with someone else, both physically and emotionally. That feeling of floating, of being lifted into the clouds.

Exactly the way it feels when Leo wraps his lips around my clit and sucks hard, using one finger to tease my opening.

Maybe this feeling only exists with him. Maybe sex isn't like this for other people, or maybe it is. I don't know. I don't really care. All I know is that I don't want to go another ten years without this feeling. Without him.

He looks up at me, his sapphire gaze searing into mine, and I see the longing there. Heat seeps from my stomach, fluttering through my chest and up my throat, releasing my body on a moan as he watches me. His eyes tell me how he feels, what it means to him to have me back in his arms, against his body, as if he's been thirsting for my taste all this time. As if he'll die without it.

His tongue works at me in deep strokes, savoring every inch

of me he can devour, teasing as he watches me with each slow flick, a smirk on his face at every moan I let out. His hands are calloused and rough as they run along my inner thigh, yet his touch is soft as he holds me open for him. He takes my nub into his mouth and sucks again, watching me as I writhe and fall apart beneath him. His eyes flare as I cry out his name, like he's been waiting all his life to hear that sound.

He slowly slips one finger into me, curling slightly and pulling back before pushing in again. He's gentle with me, but I want more. I want him deeper. Faster. Harder. I press my hips against his face, angling my body to force his finger deeper.

"Fuck, baby," he groans against my center. "I'm trying to go slow, but you're making that hard for me."

"Don't go slow," I bite out through heaving breaths. "I didn't magically grow back my hymen. Fuck me with your fingers, Leo. I need it."

"Goddamn." He pulls away from me and sits up on his knees at the end of the bed, pulling his shirt off in one swift motion. Smooth, tanned skin and lean muscle glow in the moonlight, filtering through the hotel room blinds. It's almost as if I can feel his beating heart behind the ink spelling out my nickname. His eyes darken as his gaze soaks me in—naked and bare for him. His lips glisten with me, and his tongue darts out across them before he sucks his bottom lip between his teeth.

The expression on his face is purely erotic.

"You want me to go harder, Honeysuckle?"

"Give me everything, Heathen."

A glint of challenge sparkles in his eyes as he grabs both of my knees and leans forward, lifting my hips and spreading me wide. His gaze doesn't leave mine as he slowly lowers his head, hiking my hips just slightly higher, and spears his tongue straight into my core.

My head falls back onto the pillows, my fingers digging into the mattress as I call out his name. He ruthlessly fucks me with his tongue, my legs tightening as warmth blooms through my stomach, and I feel myself inching toward that edge.

His tongue leaves me empty, but it's quickly replaced with two fingers. "You can suffocate me with these pretty thighs, Honeysuckle. In fact, between your legs is the only way I want to go." He pumps into me fast and hard, curling his fingers and hitting just the right spot. "But you better keep those eyes on me, baby. I want you to watch as I give you everything you've been missing."

It's an effort to open my eyes and lift my head, my body heavy with lust. Ocean-blue eyes meet mine as he lowers himself between my legs once again. One soft flick of his tongue hits against my clit before his mouth is on me, devouring me completely.

His fingers don't stop moving, the sound of my wetness echoing throughout the room, drowned out only by the sound of my moans. He sucks my clit into his mouth again, nipping at it gently with his teeth.

My eyes are hooded, fighting to stay open, to keep watching him. My legs are thrown over his shoulders, toes curled as his broad back muscles work, moving rhythmically with his thrusts. I follow his arm down to where his hand is splayed across my thigh. The veins in his arm run up into his hands. Long, thick fingers and wide palms sear my skin with heat where he holds me open.

My moans are growing louder, my body trembling and writhing beneath him. I feel my arousal dripping down my legs and onto the bed beneath us. My stomach tightens as the center of my legs buzz and spark. That heat spreads throughout my core, and I know I'm close.

Leo's eyes are still glued to me, his other hand still pumping into me relentlessly. I feel his tongue press flat against my clit, increasing the pressure as his finger curls deeply and his other hand squeezes my leg hard. Four times.

That's all it takes to have me tumbling right off that ledge, to have stars bursting behind my eyes and my soul scattering into oblivion.

My fingers knot into his hair, my entire body clenching as my orgasm tears into me. I feel my release coating his hands and hear the sound of it as he continues to work at me while I float back to Earth. He doesn't stop, and he doesn't hold up. He slows his pace, letting me ride it out below him until I'm boneless and sated.

"God, Leo," I whimper.

Long lashes flutter upward, blue eyes blazing through me. "I've never been much of a believer, baby." He presses a kiss to my center. "But *fuck*, I'll gladly kneel before you, worship at your altar." I feel his lips move along my inner thigh as he whispers, "Pray for the salvation that can only be found between your legs."

He sits up, bringing his lips to my hip, to my tattoo, and plants a kiss there too. He lifts, sitting back on his knees as he towers over me. He runs the back of his palm down my stomach, resting it at my hip as he whispers, "You look so beautiful like this, Honeysuckle. You're my fucking dream."

The sincerity—the longing—in his words have me springing up onto my own knees and crawling toward him. Surprise flashes through his face briefly, but before he can question what I'm doing, I'm on him.

I'm kissing his lips and tasting myself, dragging my mouth down his neck and across his chest, feeling the chain of his necklace. The ring at the base of it is cool against my tongue. I suckle his skin at the tattoo sprawled over his heart. "It's my turn to show you what you've been missing," I say against his skin, pressing my hand to his chest and guiding him to lean against the headboard.

I push him back onto the pillows with confidence I don't really have. I haven't had sex in ten years, and the last time I did, Leo and I both had no clue what we were doing.

I don't let myself think too hard about why he's so good at eating pussy now.

But what I remember was how comfortable things had been with him, how explorative and open we could be with each other. The way he guided my body to do what he needed, the way he treasured me, always putting my pleasure first.

Those memories are my driving force as I reach for his shorts and tug them off him, tossing them to the floor with mine. His cock springs free, huge and commanding. I slowly reach for him, gliding my hand up his length and along his ridges, swiping away the moisture gathered at his tip.

"Do you know what I remember most about sex?" I ask softly.

He's nearly panting as he watches me sit between his legs, pumping his cock with one hand while I guide my other along my chest, playing with my nipple. "What, baby?"

"I remember the way you used to guide me. Show me what you like. What felt good." He brings one hand behind his head, propping it up, while the other reaches out to grab my breast. "You never made me feel like I was doing something wrong." He brushes a thumb across my nipple, and his jaw is tight as he watches me touch him and explore him. "I love the way you taught me how to pleasure you. Just you. Only you." His stomach tightens, and his legs tremble beneath me as he nods. I smile. "So, I'm going to need you to do that for me again, okay?"

"Baby," he lets out through rapid breaths. "Everything you do is fucking perfect."

I swing my legs over each side of his hips and straddle him. Positioning his cock with my hand, I hover over him. "Are you sure you're okay with this?" I ask.

He grits his teeth, throwing his head back. "Fuck, Darby. Yes. This is everything I've ever wanted."

I drop down onto him. I'm so wet he slides inside me easily, but he's so big, the pressure is intense, so I move slowly. "God, I'm so full," I whimper as I take him deeper, feeling him everywhere.

He grips my hips with both hands, holding me still as his hips inch upward. "You don't have all of me yet, baby."

"Shit."

"You can take it, Honeysuckle." I drop down a little more. "Just like that. We'll make it fit. You were made for me."

We let out a simultaneous groan as I seat myself completely. "So tight," he says through clenched teeth.

I rock back and forth slowly, letting my body adjust to his size. He's watching me, eyes rapidly roaming all across me, as if he doesn't know where to look, as if he's trying to memorize the moment.

I slide my palm down my side until it meets the place he's holding onto me. I cover my hand with his and squeeze. "I love the way you use my hips to guide me, to move me in the way that feels best for you," I whisper. "I love the way you hold me here when you kiss me, the way you squeeze my hip when you hug me. Four times, to remind me I'm safe with you." His hips buck at that, and he hits a spot so deep, it has me quivering. A moan falls from my parted lips. "This is always the spot you hold onto when you come. The spot you hold onto when I'm coming on your face too."

"Fuck," he hisses.

"I don't know if you've ever noticed that, but it's the place your hands are always drawn to. You've marked it with your touch, and I've made that permanent with ink."

"Honeysuckle," he whimpers, gripping me harder as he rocks my body back and forth on top of him. I feel him so deep, all the way into my soul. The brush of his thumb across my tattoo sends chills up my spine.

I catch his eyes as they roam from the ink to the place where our bodies are connected. He lifts me slightly, and we both look at where I'm gripping his cock, watching as he raises me up and slowly slides me back down.

The buzzing in my body is deeper and more primal than before. I feel the sensation between my legs, up through my chest, all the way into my toes, tension winding up and pulling tight.

I lean forward, flushing our bodies together as I bring my face to his. His hands slide across my back, holding me to him as he begins to thrust upward, gradually picking up his pace. His hands dig into my back, running along the length of my spine. My hair covers both our faces like a curtain, blocking out everything except the two of us—the breath we share, the sounds we make, the movement of him inside me.

I let my hand feather along his jaw and across his full lips. I let myself fall into the depths of his ocean eyes. I lose myself in his heat, in his voice as he whispers sweet nothings against my neck.

I feel him in every nerve ending.

I feel him in my veins.

The scar tissue left on my torn-apart soul rips open, and he pours in.

Our heartbeats drum together like the beginning of a song only our bodies can sing. Slow and soft. Golden chords flow through us, tethering our souls. The lyrics are his name, leaving my mouth in rapid breath as his hands skim along my skin.

"You're so beautiful," he whispers into the night. "An angel." He lifts a hand from my back to cup my face, pushing my hair from my forehead.

I moan at his words, sealing my mouth to his. He moves his hand to the back of my neck, tangling in my hair. I rock my hips back, becoming desperate for the pressure of him deep inside me. He meets me with a delicious rhythm, our kisses becoming carnal as he nips and bites my lips, whimpering into my mouth.

"You're incredible, baby," he says before taking my lip between his teeth. He tightens his grip on my hair and tugs hard, my head snapping up as he slowly drags his teeth across my mouth.

His tongue glides across my jaw and down my neck. I shiver as he grazes his teeth against my sensitive skin, following it with his lips and tongue.

I feel myself getting close, my legs shaking and tightening over top of him as I continue to grind.

"Take it, Honeysuckle. Take what you need. Take everything." He bites lightly onto my shoulder, sending a quiver through my body. "Every piece of me belongs to you anyway."

Those words send me tumbling through the stars. He holds me tightly, letting go of my hair as I fall onto his shoulder, crying out his name. He continues fucking me straight through my orgasm, letting me ride out every wave of pleasure that cascades through my body.

I collapse on top of him, limp and satisfied. He's still hard, still moving inside me as he chuckles against my ear. "That's it, baby." His hands splay across my back as he hooks his legs on either side of my knees and flips us so smoothly his cock doesn't even leave my body as he rolls atop me.

His hair—slightly darker than when he was younger—falls into his face as he gazes down at me, bracing his arms on either side of my head to hold himself up.

"That was hot," I pant.

"I'm about to show you what it's like to fuck a surfer." He rolls his hips against me, hitting that spot deep inside. "Balance," he breathes. "Fluidity. Endurance," he huffs with each thrust, each precise, delicious movement.

"Arrogance?"

He laughs against my lips. "Confidence, Honeysuckle."

I run my hand down the length of his chest, grasping onto the ring that hangs around his neck. It swings back and forth with each motion, slipping through my fingers as he relentlessly fucks me. "It's so good."

"And you take every inch so well, baby. You're such a good girl."

Those words flow through me, but not in the way he intends. I preen at Leo's praise, but not those two words together. My father has always called me a good girl. The good girl I was had become the worst version of myself.

I think the best version of me is the one who belongs to Leo Graham. No part of my actions is good in the eyes of the traditions I was raised in, but every piece of me feels perfect in this moment.

I feel wild. I feel free. I feel like myself.

"Leo," I whisper, tugging on the chain around his neck and pulling his mouth to mine. "I don't want to be a good girl anymore."

The laugh he lets out against my lips is salacious and stimulating. "You wanna be bad, baby?"

"Just for you."

"Fuck." He pulls out of me swiftly, sitting back on his knees. His cock is glistening with my wetness as it presses against his abdomen. He points to the floor next to the bed. "Then why don't you get on your knees and taste what a bad girl you are?"

God, he is not real.

I'm not sure what kind of noise leaves my mouth, something between a whimper and a plea as I scramble off the bed and onto my knees in front of it.

He steps off the mattress, towering over me as he fists himself in one hand. "You want to taste how wet your pussy is for me?"

Heat shoots between my legs.

I nod.

He positions his cock in front of my mouth as he roughly says, "Suck, honey."

He slowly guides his length between my lips. I give him questioning eyes, needing him to tell me what to do next. I haven't given a blow job since...well, since the last time I gave Leo a blow job, and we both know I had no idea what I was doing back then.

"Play with it however you want to, baby. I've been dreaming about you on your knees for me. Everything you do is perfect." I hum, running my tongue up his length, the heady taste of my own arousal coating my tongue.

I bob my head up and down his cock, licking along the ridges of his shaft and hollowing out my cheeks.

"Just like that. That's good." His words give me confidence, so I begin moving a little faster, adding my hand to his base, pumping where my mouth can't reach. "Filthy fucking girl. You love the way my cock feels down your throat, don't you?"

I moan at that, nodding my head.

"How do we taste together, Honeysuckle?"

I suck hard and pull away. "Good."

"That's right, love." He grips the back of my head, holding it in place as he moves in and out of my mouth. His eyes flutter shut, and I watch his throat work as he swallows, soft sounds of need floating from his lips. His legs tremble beneath my touch, and I realize how much I'm making him feel, how lost he is in me, in the feel of my tongue, the sight of me on my knees for him. The view of him—all strong, hard lines and cut muscle, the flex of his stomach as he pumps into my mouth—has me nearing that edge for the third time tonight.

Unable to help myself, I skate one of my hands down my body, slipping between my legs. I strum my clit lightly with a finger, moaning around his cock at the feel of it.

His head snaps down to look at me through hooded eyes. A sinister smile spreads across his face as he watches me touch myself. He opens his mouth to say something, but we both pause as a buzzing sound erupts through the room.

I glance over the light illuminating from the nightstand, realizing it's my phone ringing. Leo catches it, too, looking back at me as he gruffly commands, "Do not stop touching yourself. Do not stop sucking my cock."

He leans over, stretching out his arm so he doesn't have to change his stance, and grabs my phone. A dark laugh rakes along my skin. "It's him."

I pull away. "Jackson?"

He gives me a pointed look. "Do not say another man's name when your mouth is wrapped around my dick." The demand in his tone—the authority and possession—have me rubbing myself faster. I give him a soft smile before taking him into my mouth again. "Should I answer it? Let him know you're busy right now? Should I let him listen while I fuck your pretty little throat?"

I absolutely do not want him to do that, but honestly, I'm thankful he hasn't let this ruin our moment, grateful he's not intimidated by Jackson's constant calls. I like that he's running with it, making it a game to heighten our own pleasure, because we both know that nothing outside the two of us matters right now.

I'd be lying if I said the taunting in his voice, the thought of that kind of control, of someone hearing us, doesn't turn me on. Knowing that I'm on my knees for the man my father hates, the one man I was never supposed to end up with, has my core seeping. My fingers brush against my clit harder.

Hi, daddy issues? It's me, Darby.

Leo's eyes are deep blue, flaring as he smiles sharply. "You like that, don't you? That get you off, baby? The thought of your ex listening to you on your knees for another man?"

I moan.

He laughs darkly. "You are a bad girl, Darby. A dirty fucking girl." Tossing my phone back onto the nightstand, he growls, "He had years of your time, and he did shit with it. You're mine now, and I want you all to myself."

He grips beneath my chin, holding my head still as he pulls out of me. Leaning down to press a soft kiss to my mouth, he whispers, "Get on the bed. All fours."

He grabs beneath my arms and lifts me, all but throwing me onto the mattress. I crawl forward, hiking my hips up and baring my backside to him. He runs a palm down my back and over my ass. "You're a goddamn masterpiece."

He slides his hands down the back of my legs and to my ankles, gripping and tugging me to the end of the bed. My feet hang off the edge, and I feel his strong hand come to my hip, squeezing the skin over my tattoo as he positions his cock at my entrance.

We both moan as he slides into me effortlessly, already deeper than before. As the front of his thighs hit the back of mine, he reaches a spot that has my toes curling and my hands grasping at the sheets as I cry into the mattress.

He begins a punishing pace, fucking me hard and fast. The sounds of our bodies joining echo throughout the room, mixing with the wet sound of my arousal and the cries of his name falling from my mouth.

It's erotic and raw.

It's everything I've always needed and didn't know I'd been missing. It's something I know with certainty will never be found with anyone else.

I lift my head from the mattress and realize for the first time the mirror on the other side of the room. With our horizontal position across the bed, I can now watch him as he fucks me. My hands grip the sheets so hard my knuckles are white. My hair falls off my shoulders, splaying across the bed. My ass is high in the air, shaking with every slap of his flesh against mine.

Leo's god-like body towers over me, the muscles in his stomach working as he moves inside me. His hands are tense, the veins that run down his arms on display as he grips my ass and spreads me open.

My eyes travel up to his face. His jaw is tight, the corded muscles in his neck straining. He's got his bottom lip sucked between his teeth as he concentrates on fucking me. His eyes are bright, wide, and glued to the spot where we're joined.

Every movement has my body spasming around him as foreign sounds leave my mouth. I feel nearly detached from it as I watch him fuck me, no control over the ecstasy coursing through my veins or the screams coming from my voice.

Leo's so focused on the pleasure he's bringing us both he hasn't even noticed the mirror across from him.

"Are you watching yourself fuck me?" I ask, my voice thick and hoarse from my screams.

His head finally snaps up, noticing the mirror as he meets my eyes through it. He looks like a dark god as his deep-blue pools burn through me as his body works inside me. Rough. Hard. Fast.

"Yes, baby," he groans deeply.

"What does it look like?"

"Fuck." He kicks his head back, a moan working out of his throat before he looks at where we're joined again. "It looks so goddamn good, Honeysuckle. It looks like coming home." He continues fucking me, panting through each thrust. "It looks like finding heaven." He pulls out slightly. "It looks like divine intervention and aligning stars." He pounds into me, causing the bed to shake. "It looks like your beautiful pussy was created to fit my cock..." My body trembles at his words. "Just mine."

"It's yours. It's always been yours."

"Tell me I'm your last. Your only," he whimpers, voice raspy and cracked.

Those words ring deeply, and I know exactly what he means by them. I know there are other conversations to be had, but in this moment, with him so deep in my body and my soul that I know there's no escaping it, I find myself saying, "Only you."

He leans forward and brings a hand around my neck, pulling me up against his chest. With my back to his front, we both take in my body—entirely on display—through the mirror. He grips my jaw with his fingers, bringing his lips to my ear as our eyes clash through our reflection. "When I watch myself fuck you, it looks like coming home. But when you tighten around my cock, honey—" My body clenches at his words, his breath against my cheek. "*Fuck*. It feels like finding faith."

I lose myself then, my body going slack in his arms as a cry tears through me. He sinks his teeth into my neck, continuing to fuck me as he holds my hips against him.

He thrusts deep, pausing there as I pulse around him. He lifts my head where he grips me at the jaw, tilting my face so I can look at him without the reflection of the mirror. "Do you want to see it, baby? Want to see what we look like joined together so beautifully?"

"Yes," I pant.

He pulls out of me again, leaving me painfully empty when I was so close to another release. Flipping me at the hips, he leans in and grabs around my waist, hoisting me up into his arms.

As if he could read my mind, he chuckles against my lips. "I'm dragging this one out. I'm gonna let you come again, but this time, we're going together."

He carries me, lips trailing along my jaw and across my neck as I cling to his hips with my legs, around the bed and toward the mirror in the corner of the hotel room.

Setting me on my feet, he spins me again so my back is to him, and we both face the mirror. Our naked bodies are sweat-slicked, glistening in the moonlight. My cheeks are flushed, and my breathing is heavy. Our tattoos line up perfectly in the reflection, dainty black scrawl across my hip matching the writing on his chest.

The ring—my purity ring—he's been wearing all these years as a reminder of what we once shared glitters in the soft light, catching my eye, a token he wore because he was sure he'd never find what we'd had again. He needed a reminder he was capable of being loved.

I shiver as his hands slowly skate up my body, lingering on my hips and breasts. He drags a thumb across my nipple, sending a sensation through my nerves that gathers in my core.

"Look how beautiful you are, Darby. Look at yourself like this," he whispers against my cheek. I find my own face in the mirror, taking in my bright eyes, my pink cheeks, my swollen lips. There is a color to me I don't think has existed for years, a golden, glowing hue that can only be found with him. "I need you to know that every fantasy I've had over the last ten years, every memory of you, is no comparison to what stands in front of me now. You are more beautiful, brave, resilient, and enchanting than I ever could've dreamed. Having you in my arms now was worth every moment of longing and every minute of heartbreak, every second I waited for you." His other hand brushes against my tattoo as his lips meet my neck. "I'd wait ten years for you again. I'd wait a million more seconds to see you like this, and every single one would be worth it."

I realize I'm smiling. I'm looking at myself and seeing beauty because I'm no longer searching for flaws. I let my eyes flicker to him, but our reflections aren't enough. I turn my head at the same time he turns his, and our gazes clash. Lifting my arm to wrap around his neck, I pull him into me. "You were worth every second, too."

I kiss him, and it's deep and slow and all-consuming. I still taste myself on his lips, and I know he can taste us too. I give him all the words I don't know how to say, let him feel them through the breathless moans that filter into his mouth through my own, through the feel of my tongue and teeth against his lips.

"Can I show you how much I've missed you, Honeysuckle?" he asks.

I laugh softly. "You've been doing a pretty good job of that already."

I feel him smile. "I'm not done yet, baby."

"Give me everything," I whisper.

Like a tether being snapped, his eyes go dark. He wraps his arms around my waist and tugs us both backward so we fall into the armchair next to the bed. His cock is rock hard against my ass as I sit down on him.

I realize our bodies are still visible in the mirror when he says, "Lean back against my chest and spread your legs over the arms of the chair."

I listen, watching myself as I lift my knees and open my legs. Leo shifts, lifting himself before tugging my back tighter against his chest and repositioning my hips.

I'm completely bared and soaking wet. The head of his cock emerges through my slit as he slowly thrusts forward, nudging at my entrance.

"Now reach down and put me inside you. Feed that pretty pussy with my cock. Watch as I fill you."

I dip my arm between my legs, grasping his length as he hisses at my touch. Angling my hips slightly, I press his cock into my center, and he thrusts to slide all the way in.

"That's my good little slut."

I watch both our faces—parted lips and hooded eyes—as he seats himself inside me. He moves slowly, ensuring I feel every inch of him, and pressure builds as he continues to fuck me deep and slow. I let my head fall against his shoulder as I look at our reflections. He wants me to watch myself, but I can't take my eyes off him.

When I look at my face, I only see him behind it, watching me through the mirror. The raw desire in his features consumes me.

When my eyes dart to my body, I only see his hands: one gripping my thigh and holding me open, the other palming my breast. I feel the sensation against my nipple, his fingers dancing along my skin. And when I look to where we're joined, I only see the way he moves in and out of me.

The connection between the two of us is like a bridge between souls.

I only see him branding me, claiming me.

The view of us is incredibly erotic, entirely wanton: my legs spread open, his cock pumping into me raw and hard. My wetness coats his length with each thrust he makes, the sound of our skin meeting loud and rough.

One of my hands is wrapped around the back of his neck, tangling in the hair at his nape, while the other holds my trembling leg open. He lifts his arm to remove my hand, covering it with his own as he slides both of them down my body and to the spot between my thighs.

The pressure is intense, tension building as I inch closer to another release. He dips our hands between us, hovering over the place where he moves in and out of me.

"What does it look like, Darby?"

He rubs my fingers over my center as we feel the way I'm stretched around him. He never ceases movement, his cock pumping into me with a steady rhythm that has me tumbling toward the stars.

"Answer me, Honeysuckle."

"It looks like coming home." I'm breathless, hardly able to speak as I begin to writhe and clench around him, desperate for that tension to break.

He brings our fingers upward, pressing them against my clit and rubbing them in soft circles. My eyes fall closed as I buck against our hands, his cock. I'm so close, yet somehow, I want him deeper. I want more of him. More sensation, more feeling.

I want him to claim me in a way that's impossible to erase.

"Faster," I whisper. "Harder."

"You need more?"

I nod, writhing against our hands. "More. Please."

He lets out a rough laugh against my ear. "You don't need to beg, baby. This cock is yours. These hands are yours. This mouth is yours. My fucking soul. It's all yours. Take what you want. Be the bad girl I know you are."

He removes his hand from mine, and I feel like I'm falling through clouds. My stomach tightens at the loss of feeling there, at the loss of his touch. I open my eyes to find him smirking at me through the mirror.

I find myself lifting off him, deciding his reflection isn't enough. I need to see his face up close, need to feel his lips against mine as we fall together.

He slides out of me as I turn around and straddle him, gripping the back of the chair and dropping back down onto his cock. He lets out a moan as I sink down, taking every inch.

I bring my mouth to him, sucking his bottom lip between my teeth and biting down. "Touch me," I demand. "Touch me everywhere."

He immediately grips my waist, running his hands down my spine before grasping my ass. Palming it hard, he moves me up and down at a faster pace. He groans into my mouth as I moan against his lips. Every inch of our bodies comes together, aligning flawlessly as we move in sync.

"More." I nip at his jaw. "More."

"Fuck." He lets go of my ass, reaching up to grab both of my arms. He pins them behind my back, causing my chest to arch upward. Gathering my wrists in one hand, he holds me still, smirking as he dips his head and takes one of my breasts into his mouth.

His eyes blaze as he bares his teeth, taking my nipple between them and biting down. A moan tears through me, my body tightening around him as my spine goes rigid. I work to move my body, but he's got me pinned tight as he thrusts up into me, moving faster with every buck of his hips.

He raises his free hand to my lips and, pulling away from my chest, he growls, "Suck," before sticking two fingers into my mouth. I listen, and he closes his lips back around my breast as I run my tongue along the rough pads of his fingers, savoring the taste of salt and myself on his skin. "I'm the only one to have this pussy, and I'll be the one who takes your ass, too," he murmurs around my nipple, teeth nipping at my sensitive peak.

My entire body begins to tremble as that tension reaches its break. "Leo," I whimper. He keeps his eyes on me as he moves to my other breast and plays with it in the same delicious way. "Yes, Leo."

"I love the way you say my name." He pulls his fingers from my mouth and continues to keep my back bowed, holding my wrists tightly as his free hand skates down my back, finger dancing between my cheeks, dangerously close to my ass. "But I want your mouth on mine when you come." I feel his middle finger playfully circle my tight entrance. "I want to fill you entirely, be inside every inch of your body when I send you spiraling toward stars."

"Oh, God," I throw my head back, moaning.

He dips his finger just inside my ass, stretching it slowly. "Is this the more you wanted, baby?"

"Yes," I hiss. The pressure is intense, and I feel so full, but the movement of his finger sends shocks to my core, heightening the pleasure gathering in the pit of my stomach and the center of my thighs. "Deeper."

"Filthy fucking girl." He lets go of my hands, and I fall forward, rounding my hips to force him deeper. "Kiss me, Honeysuckle," he whispers against my jaw.

I wrap my hands around his neck, sealing our bodies together once more. He surges forward, capturing my mouth with his. His kiss is frenzied and desperate, his thrusts into my body moving in time with his finger. My hips rock into him, faster with each passing second as we both near that edge, ready to tumble into oblivion together.

He swipes his tongue into my mouth, and I feel his body

tensing. "Leo," I moan. "Come inside me."

"Fuck. Fuck." He takes my mouth again as his cock pulses. The feel of him spilling so deep, filling me entirely, sends me falling off the edge with him. My body quivers as stars explode behind my eyes, and I can't see or think. I can only feel—feel him. I swallow the moans he lets out inside my mouth. I savor his hand tangling in my hair, straining as his body goes tight. I revel in him releasing inside me, wet and warm. My core throbs, my toes curl, and my soul shatters as I ride out my orgasm.

Leo doesn't stop moving, riding through it with me. His finger is still inside me as his cock continues to pump slowly while we both float through the cosmos together.

We stop kissing, but neither of us pulls away as we take a moment to recover. He cups my face, wiping the damp hair from my forehead. I run my nose along the length of his, leaning into his touch. I feel him smiling against my jaw, and I can't help but return it.

I pull back slightly so I can see his eyes. They're sparkling in the night, hazed with lust and passion. I brush my fingers along the chain around his neck, up his throat, across his jaw. He shivers beneath my touch.

"Leo," I whisper, studying all the planes of his handsome face. "That was..."

He rubs his thumb across my lip. "Incredible. Unbelievable. Un-fucking-real."

"Yes, all of that." I laugh breathlessly. "But it was...it was real. It was raw. It was..." I shake my head. "We've only been back in each other's lives for a number of days after years of silence." My chest heaves against his through my panting breath. "How is this feeling so strong again so soon?"

The smile that spreads across his face is blazing and beautiful. "That's because this is meant to be, Honeysuckle."

Thirty-Five

Honeysuckle

Then. August 11th.

The house is dark and quiet as I sneak inside, though I'm not sure sneak is the right word anymore. Grandma knows I come and go with Leo, Elena, and the rest of them.

I spent tonight at the Ramoses' shop with the rest of Leo's friends. Apparently, they have a room in the back that's supposed to be an employee lounge, but the boys like to sneak in beer and play pool there when they're able to steal the keys from Everett's dad.

Elena brought me a stack of her darkest, most taboo, and highly erotic romance books. I told her there was no way I could take any of those books home with me to Kansas. My parents would definitely order an exorcism, possibly just force me to become a nun altogether.

Elena told me I better get a head start on reading them before the summer ends, then.

The books are still heavy in my bag as I bound up the stairs and slip inside my bedroom. I slide the backpack under the bed, far away from my grandma's prying eyes, and flip on the lamp on my desk. My room illuminates in a soft, warm glow.

My grandmother tells me not to get myself in too much trouble, and what she doesn't know about, she can't tell my parents.

My parents, whom I haven't spoken to in a month.

I've never gone so long in my life without speaking to them, but I told them I wouldn't talk to them until I could talk to Dahlia too. My dad nearly popped a blood vessel when I told them that, but to my surprise, he hasn't called me and hasn't demanded I come home. I know he's been checking in with my grandmother, religiously checking my credit card statements to track what I'm up to, and confirming with my teachers to ensure I'm taking my online summer classes.

From what he can see, I'm still the same perfect child I've always been.

He must have his hands full with Dahlia and decided that if I'm doing fine here, there is no point in demanding I come home or punishing me for my insolence. I've never been grateful for my sister's rebellion, but right now, I kind of am.

I still miss her deeply. I even kind of miss my parents. In a weird way, I miss impressing them, miss hearing them validate what I'm doing, praising me for my accomplishments. Somehow, though, I don't miss them as people. I don't miss the pressure. I don't miss their love and affection, because I don't think they've ever given me any to begin with.

It's like all of the things they give me—direction, instruction, praise, and pride—I've found here, in my grandmother and in Leo. But all the things I've been missing—love, acceptance, support, friendship—I've found here in California too.

The only thing missing is Dahlia, the one person who's ever given me all those things and then some.

My phone begins to buzz next to me, but assuming it's Elena checking in on where I'm at in the stalker romance she lent me, I ignore it. After padding into the bathroom adjoining my bedroom, I wash my face, remove my makeup, brush my teeth, and get ready for bed.

Once I'm settled beneath my comforter, I grab my phone to respond to Elena's messages.

Leo never texts me. He rarely calls, either. He prefers to have all our conversations face-to-face. After I had to explain to him who John Hughes was, he decided he wanted our summer to feel as much like an eighties movie as possible, which meant sneaking into the backyard and throwing rocks at my window or writing me notes telling me to meet him at the beach.

Our phones are in case of emergency only.

Swiping it off the table next to my bed, I tap my screen, expecting to see Elena's name. Instead, my phone goes tumbling onto the mattress next to me as my hand covers my mouth in a gasp.

I have five missed calls from my sister.

I immediately call her back, my stomach twisting in fear as I wait for her to answer, losing hope by the second as it continues to ring and ring. I feel my eyes stinging with tears, fear coating the back of my throat and making it hard to breathe.

Finally, the line clicks, and her shaky voice comes through the speaker. "Darby?"

"Dal," I breathe. "Oh, my God. Are you okay?"

"No." Her voice cracks, and I hear her trying to contain what sounds like sobs as she whispers, "Everything is not okay."

I try to keep my own tone steady as I feel hot tears run down my cheeks at the fear in my sister's voice. "What's going on? What happened?"

"I...I stole my phone..." She pauses like she's trying to catch her breath. She continues, much clearer, "I broke into Dad's office and picked the lock on his desk drawers until I found my phone. I can't risk waking them, but I needed to talk to you. I couldn't take it anymore." Her voice cracks again. "I can't take any of this anymore."

"Dal, what happened? Why did he take your phone? Send me away? Not let me talk to you?"

She's quiet for what feels like years before she finally says, in a voice strong and sure, "I'm pregnant, Darby."

My mouth is open, but I can't seem to form words. I don't know if there *are* words for the shock I feel. The stomach plummeting realization of what Dahlia just told me.

"I thought it would be smart to tell Mom and Dad before I

told Jason. I thought...despite everything, I thought they'd help me. I thought they'd support me, want to be there for their..." She begins to cry again. "Their grandchild."

"But they didn't?" I finally find the words to ask.

I hear shuffling as if she's shaking her head. "No. They wouldn't even let me tell him. They told me I had to get an... abortion before anyone in town found out. That is all they cared about, Darby—how this would make them look."

"But Dad is vehemently against abortion." I'm not even sure why I say that. It doesn't matter. "He's been at the forefront of promoting anti-abortion legislation in Kansas for years."

"I know," she snaps. "Because, like every other powerful man in America, he wants to police a woman's body, shame her for her choices until those choices affect him. Then, of course, he needs his options open."

Something about that resonates with me, feels familiar. It's something Leo would say.

"What is it you want to do, Dahlia ?"

She sniffles again. "I don't know. I don't know." Her voice breaks. "I just... I can't make a decision like this because they told me to, because of their reputation. I need to make it for myself. But... I'm running out of time, Darby. My options are rapidly closing in on me, and I think..." She sighs. "I think I might want it. To have a baby."

"Okay," I tell her. "We'll figure it out together, and if you want to keep it, I'll be with you every step of the way. We won't let Dad force you into anything you don't want for yourself."

"I can't do this alone, Darby," she whispers.

Something cold and harsh pricks in my gut. "Dahlia, where is Jason?"

The sobs erupt again, harder and louder than before, as if she's forgotten she's supposed to be quiet. She's choking on her tears, and it's as if I can feel her body tremble through the phone as she gasps for air.

I can't do anything for her.

I feel a million miles away. My own heart seizes in my chest at the sound right inside my ear of my sister breaking down. Not before my eyes, not in my arms, because I'm not there with her. She's falling apart on the floor of my father's office in the middle of the night. Alone.

Because our parents care more about themselves—their reputations and their businesses—than their own child. Because I may have spent my summer finding Leo. Finding Elena. Becoming close with our grandmother.

But my sister has spent the last two and a half months alone. Disintegrating little by little. Losing herself. Because the only person Dahlia has ever had in this world is me, and I haven't been there for her like she's needed me to.

"I just called him before I spoke with you," she says finally. "He didn't ask where I've been for months, why my phone has been turned off and I haven't returned his calls. He told me that he has no interest in having a baby with me." She sucks in a breath. "Of being with me at all anymore. That he moved on." She continues to cry but somehow finds the strength to speak through her tears. "When I told him I was pregnant, he... God. He told me to get rid of it. Those were his exact words: 'Get rid of it.'"

"Dal..." It's all I can say. I can't imagine how alone she feels, how scared.

"I just wish I could run away, go somewhere nobody knows me, where nobody cares if I'm nineteen and pregnant. Where I can make a decision for myself. Where I can fucking breathe. I can't breathe here, Darby. I haven't left this house in weeks. Dad won't let me until I make up my mind...but you know what he means by that. Until I do what he wants. He won't let me leave."

My mind is made up instantly.

"I'm coming home, Dal. I'm coming home right away, and we'll leave together. We'll find somewhere to go together until you can get this all figured out. Until you can breathe again."

She only cries harder. After a long moment, she finally says, "I can't drag you into this, too, Darby. It doesn't matter anyway. Even if you fly home tomorrow, Dad won't let you see me."

"There is no dragging me. I can't stomach you hurting like this, and I know you'd do the same for me. Don't worry about Dad. I'll work around him." Somehow.

"I think you're the only person in the world who loves me," she whispers.

My chest splits open because I think she's right. I think I felt a lot like that before I came here, before I met Leo. Dahlia and I were all each other had, and even though I was ignorant of it, I abandoned her this summer.

"I'm coming home, Dal. We're going to figure it out together, I promise."

Thirty-Six

Heathen

Now. June 2nd.

She's the source of warmth for my incandescent soul.

Last night, as I watched the moon wash against her skin, casting her in an ethereal glow, I decided I most cherished the dark. Though now, as I wake in the morning to find the sun's rays reflecting across her face, setting her hazel eyes on fire, I find myself savoring the daylight.

It feels like an endless cycle of hoping each second becomes infinite, yet anticipating every future moment I haven't seen yet, where I'll find something new to love about her.

I didn't want to disturb her sleeping as her heavy breath landed against my neck, her hair splayed across the pillows, but I couldn't help myself. I missed her, even when she was lying right next to me. Just as I brushed wild hair from her cheek and behind her ear, those bright eyes fluttered open.

We haven't said anything yet, and she only smiles at me softly as she traces her index finger from my forehead, down over my nose, along my lips. Soft sunlight filters through the curtains behind me, shrouding her in gold.

She watches where her finger lays against my bottom lip as I ask, "Did you mean everything you said last night?"

Her eyes dart up to mine, wide and blinking. They knit together as she studies my face, taking a moment to respond. A flash of terror rips through me until she says, "Yes." She removes her fingers from my mouth, running along the column of my neck until they meet the necklace there. She rotates the ring between her thumb and forefinger. "Did you mean everything you said last night?"

"I already told you: I mean every word I've ever said to you."

She leans her head against my chest, hot breath fanning out against my skin as she sighs. "I'm never going to feel like I deserve you, you know."

We're both lying on our sides, facing inward on the bed, our naked bodies flushed together, her knee in between both my legs. Her skin is soft, smooth, and warm. Her floral and honey scent envelops the sheets like a spring garden.

I'm imagining that this is exactly what heaven looks, feels, and smells like when I grab her chin and lift her head so her eyes meet mine. "Then I'll spend the rest of my life showing you exactly why you do. Why you deserve everything."

I lean in and brush my mouth against hers, soft and unhurried, like I have forever to do this. And damn if I won't do everything in my power to make that true. Because I've been destroyed, and in holding her against me now—I'm re-created, brought back to life by the taste of her lips.

As I pull away, I watch her eyes dart back and forth between mine, as if they're searching for hesitation, for a lie. But I know all she'll find here is every promise I've ever made on my face, including that one.

"You're the one who chases my ghosts away now," she whispers.

I lean into her, laughing against her lips. "You're still the sunlight shining through the cracks of my shattered soul."

I kiss her softly, but as I pull back, I glimpse a flash of confusion on her face. Whatever she's thinking, she doesn't voice it. Instead, she asks, "Where are we going today?"

"Well, we have options." I chuckle, sitting up in bed and stretching. Darby follows suit. "We can drive straight through to Pacific Shores. It's about a nine-hour drive." She sits up to face me, covering her bare body with the sheets as her wild hair flies in a million directions around her head. "Or"—I smile as I tuck a piece behind her ear—"we can take a drive through Zion, find somewhere to spend the night, and go home tomorrow."

I expect her to smile back at me. I expect her to want to extend this trip as long as possible. I have no intention of letting her go when we make it to Pacific Shores, but I know that once we land back in real life, she'll have consequences she has to face. I intend on holding her hand through every one of them, but I know the adjustment—starting over—won't be easy for her. One more day in this bubble we've created for ourselves is what I think she needs, and I hope she'll agree to it.

Instead, her brows furrow, and a faraway look glazes over her face, as if she's thinking deeply about something. I give her a moment to consider things before she looks at me again. "Isn't Zion near"—she swallows—"St. George?"

I cock my head. "Yeah, I think so."

She lets out a long sigh, drumming her fingers against her leg almost nervously. Another moment of silence passes before she nods to herself and lifts her head to look at me. "Okay, let's go to Zion and stay in St. George tonight."

"What's in St. George?"

Her face is serious, her eyes almost sad. She gives me a soft smile. "I'll tell you when we get there. I promise."

My stomach drops, and I suddenly feel as if the town of St. George holds some part of our story, some part I'm not aware of yet. It's as if some memory there is the reason behind the haunted look in Darby's eyes.

Not wanting to push her for more information before she's ready to share it, I simply nod. A tug in my gut tells me tonight might be painful for us, and that makes me determined to make our day beautiful.

I leap from the bed in a flash, scooping Darby up into my arms princess style—the entire sheet still wrapped around her—before she has a chance to realize what I'm doing.

She giggles against my neck. "Where are we going?"

"Bathroom, Honeysuckle. This time, you're the one who's going to be making me come in the shower."

She definitely made me come in the shower. On her knees, mouth hot and soft against my hard cock as the water beat down over us, drenching her smooth skin in beads of moisture.

Then, she screamed my name as she rode my face while I held her up against the wall.

She let me wash her soft blond hair, and I let her wash my body. Then, I grabbed her face underneath the falling water and kissed her until we were both breathless and dizzy, feeling like the first time my lips landed on hers.

Another moment that felt like coming home.

Darby wraps one white towel around her body and another in her hair as she steps out of the shower and into the motel room, fumbling through her bag for clothes.

I wrap a towel around my waist and wipe away the steam fogging the mirror before brushing my teeth and washing my face. The bathroom is still doused in steam when I finish, so I scrawl *Darby and Leo* across the glass, ending it with a heart.

"That is so cheesy."

I turn around to find Darby, still towel-clad but with her hair down, leaning against the doorway with her arms crossed, smirking at me.

I shrug. "You bring it out in me."

She rolls her eyes, hiding a smile as she turns back into the room. I follow her out, hovering over her shoulder as she lays out a pink sundress, a pair of athletic shorts, a white bra, and a pair of lacy white panties.

She turns her head slightly, watching me from the corner of her eye as she slowly plucks the towel from her chest and lets it fall to the floor. As she reaches out to grab her underwear from the bed, I swoop around her and snatch it first.

She turns to face me with an exasperated yet amused look on her face. She crosses her arms over her chest, kicking out a hip as she waits for me to finish whatever game she thinks I'm playing.

Truthfully, it's no game at all. I just want to touch her. I want to dress her as much as I want to undress her. I want to remind her what it feels like to be cared for and cherished. The caveman part of my brain believes she should never lift a finger again, never want for anything, never be inconvenienced, even so much as bending down to put on her panties.

I can't say that to her, though. That would annoy her.

I can't say Darby is independent, mostly because I don't think she's ever been given the opportunity to be. But I think she wants to be, and I want to give her that too.

I'll let my caveman brain win just this one time.

She blinks up at me with those big honey eyes, and I stare right back as I slowly lower to my knees in front of her, worshiping at her altar like I promised I would.

I hold her underwear out and nod at her to step into them. She seems a bit breathless but listens. I hook my thumbs into the waistband, letting my other fingers trail along her soft skin as I lift them up her legs, kissing her tattoo before fastening them around her hips.

I repeat the movements with her shorts and then make her lift her arms above her head while I slip her bra on, only taking a brief moment to brush my lips across her pebbled nipples. Once I drop her dress over her head, I dip my head and kiss her softly.

I smile as I pull away, taking in her heavy breathing and pink cheeks, the way she looks at me like she's not sure I'm real.

Like I'm worth something to her. Worth something to the world. Darby looks at me like I'm loved—something I haven't felt in a long, long time.

With my career, a lot of people want something from me. They want my money. They want my sponsorship. They want me to help *them* make money. My status. My fame. My attention.

But nobody—nobody—has ever looked into my fucking soul the way Darby does. Nobody has looked at me so deeply and still decided they wanted me, still decided I was enough. I know that if I hadn't become the surfer I am, I'd be nothing to anyone.

But she's always looked at me like I'm enough for just simply being me, not for what I can provide her. I think it's because when I met her, I had nothing to offer but myself, and that had been all she wanted.

Knowing that, it makes me want to give her the entire goddamn world and then some.

That thought has me surging forward, desperate to taste her again. She smiles against my lips, and I want so badly to tell her that I love her, that I always have, that I've never stopped.

But while I've been in love with her this whole time, I think it's possible she may have fallen out of love with me. I feel like I'm having to convince her to fall back in love with me, and if she doesn't...I'm not sure what losing her for the second time will look like, and it fucking terrifies me.

So, I won't say those words until she does.

As I pull back from Darby's mouth, I push all thoughts of fear from my head. I'm determined to savor every moment I do have with her, every smile she gives me.

"Do you want to wear your hair up or down today?"

"Up," she whispers.

I lean around her, digging through her bag for a scrunchie when my hand lands on something rough and frayed. I keep searching for a hair tie, finding one and wrapping it around my wrist while also holding onto the necklace I noticed in the pocket of her duffel bag. I catch a glimpse of the twine, the small black stone nestled in the middle of the braided rope.

Folding it into my hand, I spin her and begin to brush her hair with my fingers, pulling it behind her head and gathering it in my fist. It reminds me of the way I held her hair while her mouth was wrapped around me in the shower. She sighs contently, and I wonder if she's thinking of that too.

I finish tying her hair up, and before she can turn around, I wrap the necklace around her neck and tie it in the back. Her hand lifts swiftly, fingers brushing over the stone at her throat.

She spins, looking up at me with wide, confused eyes.

"You kept it all this time."

Her face is solemn as she nods. She drops her head and looks at the necklace, her hand still covering the stone there. "She hates me, doesn't she?"

I huff an unconvincing laugh, my stomach suddenly feeling tight. "I think hated, past tense, would be more suitable. Now..." I sigh. "Now, I think the word would likely be indifferent."

Darby looks up at me, and I see the flash of hurt in her eyes. I reach out and cup her cheek while her hand lands on the center of my chest. I realize I'm still in nothing but a towel.

I didn't think things through before pulling out that necklace, realizing *this* conversation would likely follow.

Elena was hurt when Darby left without a trace, hurt that she never wrote and never called, never contacted any of us again. Where my hurt manifested as heartbreak, Elena's manifested in anger. It was strenuous on our own relationship for a while because, despite my confusion and my pain, I couldn't make myself stop loving Darby. I couldn't talk negatively about her. I couldn't even blame her. I just missed her.

Elena wanted to vent. She wanted to voice her pain, loudly, and I couldn't stand it. I couldn't stand when she'd tell me I was better off. When she'd tell me Darby wasn't worth my time or my thoughts. When she'd encourage me to move on or tell me Darby wasn't good enough for me anyway.

We both knew none of those things were true, but I think convincing herself to believe them made her feel better. They only made me feel worse.

Eventually, Elena moved on with her life, but she's also one to hold a grudge. Darby became a gray area in our relationship, and we didn't speak of her, but I always knew Elena never truly got over what she felt was a betrayal by her first real female friend.

"Somehow, indifference feels worse than hatred," Darby whispers. "But I get it. I'd feel the same way."

I shake my head. "I'm not sure that's even a reflection on you, Honeysuckle. I think it's more of a reflection on her." Darby cocks her head, willing me to go on. My hands are beginning to feel clammy, and my heart rate picks up, the way it does when you know you're about to confront something that brings you pain. "She's...Elena isn't the same person she was when you knew her. I don't think she has the capacity to hate anyone, but I'm not sure she has the capacity to love anymore, either."

My eyes start to burn as I think about my sister's devastated face and sunken, haunted eyes. The scream she let out in the emergency room that day, piercing and grating and destroying. The way she looked in bed for weeks on end.

She eventually got out of bed. After weeks of silence, she learned to speak again, went back to work, even moved away. By all appearances, she's moved on with her life, but that light never returned. She just seems...haunted.

My face must be giving my thoughts away, because Darby runs her hand along my jaw, pulling my attention back to her. "Leo, what happened?"

I try to give her a smile, but I know I likely just ruined our entire day. I had a feeling today was going to end up being painful, but this wasn't what I meant. Still, I suppose Darby deserves to know this as much as anyone, and she'll find out anyway if she plans on staying in Pacific Shores.

"Is she still with Zach? You..." She swallows. "You don't talk about him and August. Haven't mentioned them once."

I bite my lip, casting my eyes downward. That burn in the back of them returns, and I realize my hands are beginning to shake. Every time I think I've healed enough to speak it out loud, think I've moved on enough to address it, I come right back to this feeling, like I'm being choked and cut and scarred all over again.

"I'm sorry I didn't tell you before. We've been...preoccupied, and I honestly didn't know how to bring it up. Actually, I wasn't sure I wanted to."

She pulls me down onto the edge of the bed and sits next to me, placing her hand in mine and twining our fingers as we sit in silence. She doesn't push for information but sits with me until I feel like I'm capable of speaking without breaking.

I grab her hand with both of mine, running my thumb along her skin to ground myself. "Zach...uh." Fuck. I can't even say it. It's been years, and I still can't. Fucking. Say. It. "Zach was out surfing one morning a few years ago, and he..." I tip my head to the ceiling, blinking back tears.

"Drowned?"

The word comes out a hollow whisper, but not from my mouth. She finishes the sentence for me because she knows I can't finish it myself. My throat is too tight.

I just nod.

I hear her gasp, but I'm not looking at her. I can't yet.

When I think about the day that it happened, I break down. It's an indescribable feeling—the raw terror that washed through me when I got a call from August, the panic in his voice as he described to me over the phone watching his brother's body being pulled from the water.

At that moment, we still had hope. We all rushed to the hospital, convinced it wasn't too late. We'd all been wrong.

I can't think about their mom's face, about the harsh, unforgiving words their father spewed at August in that waiting room. I don't let myself picture Everett's devastation when he walked in.

But what's always destroyed me most—rendered me speechless—was the way it felt to watch Elena walk into the hospital. Confused. Eyes swollen and red, though at that time, she hadn't even known what happened, who she was even arriving at the hospital for.

It was a stroke of bad luck that the moment the doors shut behind her, the doctor was speaking the words, "We did everything we could..." I remember everyone else looking at the doctor, but

I was looking at her. I watched her eyes rapidly dart around the room, taking count of everyone there. I saw the exact moment she realized the one person who was missing. I watched her hear the sob rip from Zach's mother as the doctor finished the sentence.

I watched Elena's soul shatter right in front of me, and I realized I wouldn't just be losing a best friend that day, a brother. I'd also lose my sister. She'd never recover from that.

Darby's head falls against my shoulder, pulling me from the memory. "I'm so sorry," she whispers. I pull my hand from hers and wrap it around her shoulder, tugging her to me as I brush my lips against the top of her head. "We don't have to talk about it, but if you want to, we can."

"I've never been able to talk about it. To anyone," I admit.

She nods thoughtfully. "You don't have to talk about the way it makes *you* feel if you're not ready." She's quiet for a moment. "Tell me about Elena. How is she?"

I shrug. "Things were really...really bad for a while. We didn't know how to help her. We still don't, honestly. We just gave her time and space. Eventually, she seemed to kind of come back to us, but she's just not the same. A few months after...everything, she moved to New York, but truthfully, I think she just couldn't stomach living in Pacific Shores anymore."

"Were they together when it happened?"

I appreciate that Darby doesn't say the word she knows I can't stomach. She follows my lead, only crossing lines she knows I can handle.

"I have no idea." I sigh. "The way you saw things with them? Yeah, that never changed. Zach had left for a while to work on some ranch in Wyoming. He didn't tell Elena before he left. He came back shortly before it happened and found out Elena had decided to move on while he was gone." I shrug. "I don't know what came of that, and I just know they saw each other the night before. She's never told us what happened that night or where things stood when she found out."

I hear Darby sniffle, and I rub her head. "Regardless, if they had still been...involved up until just a couple of years ago, that's like...what? Eight? Nine years? It doesn't matter what the last few months were like. She loved him. I know she did. I just... I can't imagine that kind of loss." Darby looks up at me, her eyes shimmering with heavy tears. "I'm sorry. I know I didn't know him well, and it's not my loss to mourn, but...God, it's just devastating." She wipes under her eyes. "I guess I just want to grieve for you. For her."

I brush her hand away and replace it with my own, swiping it down her cheek. "It's comforting to see someone want to grieve for me." I force myself to smile. "I think I have so much trouble talking about it because I've been mourning for everyone else all this time. For August. For Elena. For Everett. I'm not sure I've allowed myself to feel my own grief, like I don't deserve to feel it as much as others do."

Darby shakes her head. "Did you love him?"

"Yes," I say without hesitation.

"Then you deserve to grieve."

My smile becomes genuine as I lean in and press my lips against her forehead.

"What about August?" she whispers.

My throat bobs. "August owns a tattoo parlor—"

"Oh, that's great, right? That was his dream."

I nod. "Yeah. His shop is four doors down from Heathens, actually. August lives two blocks from me. I haven't seen him in six months." Darby frowns. "Elena's haunted in a different way, but August is no less broken. He was there...when they found Zach. He was supposed to be surfing with him. I don't know if he was late, or if he left early and came back..." I bite my lip, letting out a breath. "Their dad blamed him for it, for not being there. Then, Elena did too. She still does, actually. I think August blames himself."

"That's awful," Darby whispers.

"Everett and I have tried to help him, to help them both. It's like...he and I leaned on each other. Grieved together. Healed together. But August and Elena fell apart in solitude, and we don't know how to put them back together."

Darby blinks. She's quiet for a minute, holding her head against my chest. "Don't take this the wrong way..." She pulls back and looks at me. "Maybe they don't need you and Everett. Maybe they need each other. They were closest with him, the last people to be with him. Maybe they need each other to heal." She shrugs.

I chuckle. "That's a good theory, Honeysuckle. Maybe you can let them know when we get home."

She rolls her eyes as I tug her back into me. I place my chin atop her head, inhaling her floral scent, grounding myself to her, letting myself bask in her sunlight until my darkness disappears. "Thank you," I whisper into her hair. "For letting me...for just letting me be."

She grips my forearm, sighing quietly. "Thank you for letting me just be too."

I hold onto her for a while longer, realizing that Darby is—has always been—the force that keeps my feet on the ground. I'm simply just better with her around.

We're better together than apart.

And I can only hope she knows it too.

Then. August 11th.

Honeysuckle,

I know it's pretty clear already, but I'm in love with you.

I haven't said it yet, but to be fair, you haven't either. I'm kind of waiting on you, because I don't want to scare you away. I realize that's silly, considering I have your name tattooed on my chest.

That reminds me: tomorrow is the day you promised I'd get to finally see your tattoo. I still can't believe the most beautiful girl I've ever seen, the kindest soul, the smartest woman, the sunlight that chases my ghosts away—I can't believe she chose me, that you see something in me that's worth loving.

You make me feel alive in a way I've never felt before, like any dream I have is possible. It's as if the whole world doubts me, but you believe in me, and that's all I need to keep going.

The best decision I've ever made was to provoke you that day, to throw rocks at your window and tell you your music sucks. The country has kind of grown on me in the last couple of months, though—please, don't tell my friends that.

The next best decision I've ever made was giving you all these broken pieces of myself.

I don't think they'll ever be fully repaired, but I think you've glued them back together, kind of like that stained glass artwork. When your sunlight shines through the patched-up shards of my shattered soul, it feels like my body radiates with color, colors I couldn't see until I met you.

You've changed my life, Darby. I've never trusted someone with so much of myself, never taken a risk like this, but the reward of you has been worth every second of fear.

This is the real deal, Honeysuckle. You and me. No matter where life takes us, I need you to remember that I'm always going to be your rock. Your protector. Your shoulder to cry on. You say the word, and I'm there.

I love you. I know the future feels scary right now, but I have faith in us. Distance is finite. It can be conquered. But you and I, Honeysuckle, we are infinite. We are destined. Written in the stars. Proof of the divine.

We're meant to be.

I'm going to slip this letter into your backpack tonight while we're at the shop and not tell you about it. I want you to find it at the time the divine decides you need to read it most. Maybe it'll be twenty years from now when we're happily married and one of our kids wants to use that totally vintage JanSport backpack for school. They'll find this letter inside and be reminded just how in love their parents still are after all these years.

Wouldn't that be something?

P.S. I secretly hope you tattooed my name on your ass. (I hope our kids read this, too).

Baby, I'm yours,

Leo

Thirty-Seven

Honeysuckle

Now. June 2nd.

I slide the box of emergency contraceptives across the counter, avoiding eye contact with the gas station attendant who takes it from me.

The scanner beeps, and the total appears on the screen. I sigh as I fish my wallet from my purse, moving swiftly to complete the transaction before Leo returns from the bathroom.

I don't know why I'm being weird about it. It's not like he wasn't present last night. Still, I don't want Leo to know just how deeply that act affects me, how much it took for me to ask him to do that.

In the moment, it was the closeness I longed for. The feeling of being connected to him again in that way. The knowledge that he's the only person who's ever seen me like that, heard those types of words from my mouth, had a piece of his body inside mine.

He doesn't know how much of a risk it is for me to allow him to finish inside me. He doesn't understand how stressed out I am about it now, how even though I don't regret it—not for one second—it scares me to know the consequences of it.

I don't want him to read that fear and mistake it for regret.

I pull my credit card out of my wallet when something warm, hard, and citrus-scented washes over me. His long arm stretches beyond my shoulder, sliding a card across the counter.

"It's okay; I can pay for it," I murmur.

Both of his hands come down on either side of my body, pressing against the counter as he leans into me. He laughs against my ear. "I'm the one who came inside you twice last night. The least I can do is pay for your Plan B."

"Leo," I breathe, my eyes darting up to the attendant.

She smiles to herself, not even bothering to look at me. "Honey, I've heard worse. Trust me."

I roll my eyes and push back against him. He chuckles as he steps away to give me space, tossing a bag of Cheetos onto the counter alongside his card.

I spin around to face him. "Cheetos?"

He shrugs. "You love Cheetos."

That softens me. He remembers my favorite snack from when I was a teenager. I don't have the heart to tell him I haven't eaten a Cheeto in years.

Processed food makes one gluttonous, according to my mother. Plus, Jackson wasn't a big fan of anything that had to be eaten with your hands.

"You've been paying for everything," I murmur. "It makes me feel bad."

He leans down, blue eyes studying me intensely. "I'm a millionaire, Darby." Those eyes narrow slightly as he grasps my chin. "I have more money than I know what to do with, and you know what I've been wanting to spend it on all these years?"

"You are not a millionaire."

He scoffs. "Yes, I am. I make good money in my profession and with my sponsorships, but I'm also more intelligent than people make me out to be. I've made some good investment decisions over the last few years, and they're paying off now."

"I think you're intelligent." My voice is a hollow whisper.

"Thank you. Now, answer my question. What do you think it is I've been dying to spend all this money on?"

"What?" I ask, my head still reeling.

I mean, I knew he had money. I may have Googled the salary of professional surfers the first time I noticed his face gracing the cover of a magazine in the grocery store years ago, but it wasn't millions. He doesn't operate like you assume millionaires do. He's still himself.

My parents aren't even millionaires, and they're the greediest, snobbiest, most elitist people I've ever known.

"You." He leans in, his eyes never leaving mine as he feathers his lips against my mouth, pulling me from my thoughts. "I've made all of this for you. Because of you." He kisses me swiftly before pulling away. "Plus, I'm a fucking gentleman, and the fact that you think for one second I would ever expect you to buy your own birth control is insulting."

I'm breathless as he reaches around me and takes his card, along with the bag of Plan B and Cheetos, from the gas station attendant.

"You sure you wanna take that?" she asks me with a laugh.

Leo gives me a slow smile, raising one brow. "Yeah, you sure about that, Honeysuckle?"

He winks, and my knees go weak.

He has no idea what he's saying. If I were going to have anyone's babies in this world, I'd want them to be his, but...I shake off the intrusive thoughts, plastering a smirk on my face.

I turn to the attendant. "I'm unemployed, homeless, and technically engaged to another man, so yeah."

Truthfully, I was deflecting from my own thoughts, but I did think the joke was funny. However, as I spin toward the exit of the store, I catch Leo's eyes narrowed, his mouth in a frown. I let out a forced chuckle as I brush past him.

He catches me with a quick stride, grabbing the door handle as if to hold it open for me. I step into it, but he keeps the bar in place, not allowing me to move.

"You're not unemployed. You're a teacher, and it's summer break. You're not homeless. I'm your home." He leans into my ear. "And you're not engaged to that man. The next time you want to refer to yourself as engaged, you let me know, because the only person you're marrying in this life is me."

I swallow as those words cascade over my body, skating along my bones, drenching my soul like a waterfall of intention.

I shiver at the seriousness in his voice.

"Are we understood, Honeysuckle?"

I nod, and Leo opens the door, saying nothing as we walk out into the bright midday sun toward the classic Mustang, red paint glittering in the light.

The next hour of our drive is mostly silent, but I don't think it's entirely because of what Leo said in the gas station. He wasn't angry at me for making that joke. He was just...fervent in his feelings for me.

I want to tell him how passionate I am too. How serious I am about him. How much I want to talk about a future beyond this trip—a future with the two of us together.

How badly I want to simply just *date* him. Lazy Sundays. Going to the movies. Eating dinner on the living room floor while we binge some television show we both love. I want to do laundry with him. I want to do his laundry.

I hate laundry.

I just want to be normal and domestic with him. It's weird and crazy and impulsive to be so serious about someone I've spent three days with, but the last three days of my life have been the most peaceful, insightful, and restorative of the last decade. I've been more myself with him than I have with anyone else.

The foundation of our past has solidified us as paired souls, I think. So now, despite how much we've changed and what our past looks like, we're perfect complements of one another.

I feel safe with him. I feel at home with him.

And I want—need—to tell him this, but first, I need to tell him the truth. I need him to know the truth of my leaving all those years ago, and I know St. George will be the place for that to happen. Once he knows the whole story, he'll need to make his decision.

If he chooses me, then I'll make sure he knows exactly how much I'm choosing him, too, but I know that I need to give him the freedom to walk away if he decides I can't be forgiven.

This whole day has been weird. Maybe that's why I made that dumb-ass joke in the gas station anyway.

I've been on edge since we left the motel. Leo thinks it's because of the news he dropped about Zach, which, in part, it is. I only knew Zach for a few short months when I was seventeen, but I know he's as deeply ingrained into Leo as I am, a best friend who was more like a brother.

That kind of loss weighs heavy on the people you love, so much so that it seeps from them and into you, too.

I feel heavier than I did when I woke up this morning, but I'll happily take on the extra weight if it means Leo can breathe a little easier than he did before.

As we fly down the highway, the red and orange landscape gives way to rolling hills and blue-green mountains. Leo has the top down, the roaring wind drowning out the soft, beachy, indie playlist he has on flowing through his stereo. He drives with one hand as the other casually drapes across the back of my seat. Every so often, he brushes his fingers across the nape of my neck, as if to remind himself I'm still here.

He looks relaxed, but we don't talk. It's not a tense or hard silence, though—more like the soft, comfortable kind that means you feel safe with the person next to you.

It's not just the news about Zach or confessions in gas station parking lots that have us in silence. I also have my own selfish reasons for being so quiet, for feeling so heavy.

My memories of St. George, Utah, are not pleasant ones, and I'm not sure what it's going to feel like to be back there again. I also know there are things I've avoided telling Leo, things that I'm still not convinced he'll be able to come back from.

I know that's what he's been doing—convincing me to trust him, to give him all my pieces all over again. He's been trying to show me that whatever my reasons for leaving all those years ago are, he forgives them without even knowing them.

I want to believe him.

But it doesn't change the fear so deeply ingrained in me. It doesn't change all the things I was told back then, the way I was manipulated. I'm still scared the truth will be too much for him.

We turn off the main freeway onto the one-lane highway that's supposed to lead us toward Zion National Park. The speed limit is lower here, and there are few other cars on the road. Despite the top being down, the roar of the wind isn't as loud as it was; the music comes through more clearly.

Leo reaches out and turns it down. "You don't plan on staying, do you?"

I look at him, but his eyes aren't on me—they're on the road. His jaw is relaxed, but I can see the crinkle of worry in his features, the reason he's afraid to face me. "I don't know yet," I admit.

I watch his fingers flex around the steering wheel and his jaw tighten as he thinks through my response. Finally, he nods.

It's not just the things I know Leo and I still need to work through that are keeping me from committing to staying in Pacific Shores. It's also the fact that, regardless of what Leo said, I don't have a job, not if I don't go back to Kansas. I won't have a place to live once my dad sells my grandma's house. I don't want to go back to Kansas, but if I can't figure out a way to make things work in California, I may have no choice.

I know Leo could take care of all those obstacles with a snap of his fingers, but the truth is, I don't want him to. I've been taken care of my entire life, and I want to take care of myself now.

"I've been left behind my whole life, Darby," he says quietly.

Those words hurt me. Kill me. My hands itch to reach across the seat and grab his, but I don't.

"By my mom when she died. By my dad when he decided it was my fault and abandoned me. I was left by Zach when he died, too, by Elena and August when they couldn't recover." He swallows thickly before turning his head, and blue waves wash over me. "I was left by you."

It's those words that make my eyes sting. I can't hold his gaze, so I look down at my lap. "I'm sorry."

"I'm not asking you to be sorry. I just..." He sighs. "I'm terrified. I'm fucking terrified, Darby." The road is straight, narrow, and empty, so I reach out and pull one of his hands off the wheel, wrapping it in my own. "I've never been enough to make someone stay before. I think that might be why I've fought so hard to be successful, to make money, to have a name. I've been fighting to be enough for someone." His voice cracks. "To be enough for you."

I crack open, too, tears cascading down my face. "You've always been enough for me."

"You left. You left me."

A strangled sob wrangles itself out of my throat. I'm not able to make words happen yet, so I just tighten my palm around his fingers four times.

"The possibility of having you has always been worth the risk of losing you. I didn't think twice before booking that flight to Kansas when I got your letter. Not just because you needed me or because the thought of you being married to someone else makes me sick, but because I knew seeing you again would lead to possibility, and that was worth the fear of losing you again." He inhales a shaky breath. "But I can't wake up one morning and just find you gone. I can't watch you disappear into thin air, into nothing. I can't spend another decade wondering if I'd made everything up in my head. I can't let myself believe that I have you, only to end up in a reality where I don't."

I can't see through my tears, but I can feel us flying down the highway. "Leo, pull over."

"What?"

"Pull over. Please, pull over."

He doesn't say another word, but I can feel the trepidation dripping from him as he exits the highway onto a narrow dirt road. He stops the car next to a barbed wire fence with grasslands and rolling hills on the other side. The deserted highway sits on an embankment just above us, allowing us to be somewhat secluded beneath it.

We're quiet for a second before he turns to face me completely. "I'm not giving you any ultimatums. I'll hold onto you as long as you let me. But if you're going to leave again, I just..." He licks his lip, ocean eyes bright with tears. "Give me the opportunity to walk away."

I close my eyes, my body trembling with every breath I take. "I don't want to go anywhere, Leo. I don't want to leave you. I never wanted to leave you. If you believe nothing else that comes from my mouth, please believe that." He reaches over the seat, pulling his hand from mine and cupping my cheek. His eyes flash back and forth between mine, as if willing me to keep speaking. "But you're right. You deserve the opportunity to walk away. You deserve the whole story. The whole truth. In the end, it'll be you who needs to decide if you want to stay with me."

"I'll always—"

I cut him off. "Can I drive? There is somewhere I need to show you."

Confusion ripples across his face, but he just nods as he takes my face in both hands and leans in, kissing along my nose and my cheeks. He kisses away my tears before his lips find mine, and we're both shaking as we hold each other through the moment.

He pulls his mouth away but rests his forehead against my own. A thumb brushes against my jaw as he whispers, "We'll be okay." Another sob bubbles from me, and he lifts his head to press his mouth against my temple. "We're gonna be okay, Honeysuckle. This was meant to be."

I can only nod in his arms. I hold on tightly to his shoulders, soaking in his warmth, his scent, his soul. As we sit there on the side of a deserted Utah road, it feels like healing.

After our tears have dried and our hearts have been patched, he pulls away from me. Running a hand down my arm, he laces his fingers with mine and squeezes them four times before throwing open the driver-side door and walking around the backside of the Mustang.

Something dings, and I glance over at his phone as the screen lights up with an incoming call.

"Can you see who that is?" Leo asks from behind the car. "It might be my agent, Lynn. She's pissed at me, and I've been dodging her calls for days."

I pull his phone from the center console. The call coming through is from a number not saved in Leo's phone, but it's one I recognize anyway.

My stomach drops, and my throat feels like it's trying to swallow my lungs. I feel my hands begin to tremble as the number flashes across his screen, shaking with my movements.

I don't hear him talking, but I think he is. The crunch of gravel beneath his feet starts roaring in my ears, bringing me back to the moment. I look up to find wide, blue eyes peering down at me under furrowed brows. "What's going on, Honeysuckle?"

"It's..." My voice is shaking. "It's my dad."

I look at him, and his eyes are narrowed in concern. "Calling me?"

I nod. My dad hasn't called me once since I ran away from my wedding. Neither has my mother—only Jackson and Dahlia. A few concerned text messages from friends and coworkers sprinkled in the first day or so, but after I didn't respond, they swiftly stopped.

Leo huffs, pulling the phone from my hand. I open my mouth to protest, but his thumb is sliding across the screen before he's pressing it to his ear.

I didn't have enough time to come down from the emotions of our previous conversation in order to prepare myself for this one.

"Leo, hang up," I hiss quietly.

He crosses his arms, leaning against the passenger door and looking out at the landscape as he answers. "Mr. Andrews, what can I do for you?"

I bite my lip so hard, I think it may bleed. My stomach is a funnel of despair and anxiousness.

To my surprise, Leo laughs. "That may have been the wrong phrasing of the question, because I will not be doing that." He turns to me slightly, winking. "I think what I meant to ask was: what the fuck do you want?"

I hear angry rumbling on the other end of the line, but I can't make out what my dad is saying.

"She is not a piece of property to be 'returned' to you, asshole. She's a human fucking being. Your *child*. Your child whom you haven't contacted one single time since she left that church." I hear my dad's voice interrupt him, but Leo presses on. "Do you give one shit about her happiness? About whether or not she feels fulfilled as a person? Do you even love her? Does *he*? The answer to that last question is no. That man does not love her, not the way she deserves, and that should be your priority. The fact that it's not is telling about who you are as a person."

The other end of the line is roaring now, and I can picture my father's face, red and angry, crinkled eyes so brown that they're nearly black. Dane Andrews is a man who isn't used to being told no. To having his flaws exposed. To being the lesser man in a conversation. To not having the power in an exchange.

If I know anything about my father, he did significant research into Leo the moment he found out I ran away with him. He likely knows exactly who Leo is now, exactly what he's worth. I'm sure he's intimidated by that, probably thinking he could play the scary dad role by calling Leo directly.

But Leo isn't even fazed.

No, he's laughing as he turns to me, a slow smile spreading across his mouth as muffled noise filters through his ear. "Your first mistake is assuming I give one iota of a fuck about my career."

That sentence has me pausing.

"The *only* thing I care about is your daughter. Ruin my name and my reputation, I don't give a shit. I'll retire tomorrow if it means protecting her from you."

Leo's jaw tightens as his hand shakes at his side. "Your daughter is not ruined. She is kind, smart, resilient, and strong. She's fucking incredible," he spits into the phone. "The only person who's ever tried ruining her is you, and you've failed every goddamn time. Every time you've pushed her down, she's gotten back up. She's figured out how to escape you, and she's going to be a better person for it." He pauses, letting out a rough laugh. "I'll spend the rest of my fucking life making sure you don't ever hurt her again.

"So, know this: I am not afraid of you. Throw whatever you want at me—at us—but she's not a piece of property, and she does not belong to you. She's a human being, and she's the love of my life. I'll do whatever I have to do to keep her safe."

He pulls the phone from his ear and hangs up before he spins to face me, chest heaving and eyes wild.

I move quickly as I open the door and get out of the car. He's still leaning against it as I step into him and wrap my arms around his waist. He kisses the top of my head, but I can still feel his body trembling.

"That was hot," I say as I pull back.

He licks his lips, fighting a smile as he runs a shaking hand through his hair, his eyes roaming over my body, turning from frantic to hungry. "Good." He nods toward the hood of the car. "Now bend over the hood and lift that little dress up so I can fuck out my frustrations, will you?"

He doesn't need to say more. I'm already folding my body over the tire, flipping my dress up over my hips and baring my backside to him. He steps up behind me, running a hand down my back and over the curve of my ass. His fingers play with the band of my underwear before he swipes through my center.

"Did that make you wet, Honeysuckle?"

"Yes," I whimper.

"Does it make you wet to know I'm about to fuck you out here in the open, where anyone could see us?"

"Yes."

He leans forward, and all of him presses into all of me. "You gonna put on a show for them? For anyone who drives by?"

I nod, feeling my body flush with heat. Anticipation buzzes in my core, my skin on fire in all the places he touches me.

"You're such a filthy girl." He moves quickly, pulling my underwear down my hips and to my ankles, restraining me from spreading my legs any wider. "Fuck. Look at you, bent over the hood of my car and dripping for me. This looks like my teenage dream."

"What?" I laugh, bracing my forearms on the hood. "Fucking a girl on the hood of your dream car?"

"No, Honeysuckle." I hear the sound of a zipper and the shuffling of clothes. Then, his cock is suddenly at my entrance, pressing into me and making my eyes roll as he groans, "Fucking you against the hood of my dream car."

Thirty-Eight

Honeysuckle

Then. August 11th.

I brought three suitcases with me, but I didn't have time to pack them back up. Plus, I have clothes in the dryer, and I'm trying to be as quiet as I can.

It's considerably harder when I can't breathe through my sobs. I can't see through my stream of tears as I frantically throw whatever clothes I can find into one suitcase.

Dahlia was right: I can't fly home without making it known to my dad. Not only does he own my credit card and routinely checks my statements, but he's also alerted of any charge over two hundred dollars. He'd be notified immediately if I booked a last-minute flight.

Not to mention, even if I figured out a way to pay with cash and get there undetected, Crestwell doesn't have an airport. The nearest airport is Wichita, an hour and a half away.

My only option is to drive. Driving will take longer, likely about three days. It's undoubtedly more dangerous, considering half the distance between Crestwell, Kansas, and Pacific Shores, California, is desert and ghost towns. There are lots of places to bury a body if I break down in the middle of nowhere and a serial killer happens upon me.

But it's a risk I've got to take.

I've been risky all summer, and I've never felt more brave. I can be brave in this too. I can be brave for my sister.

Plus, having a car means I have more freedom to sneak onto our property and get Dahlia out while our parents are away from home. More freedom to get her away from town.

I'll take Dahlia wherever she wants to go, but I'm hoping she'll agree to come back here.

I know Grandma will take her in. She'll do what she can to protect us from our dad, at least for a little while, until Dahlia can make her own decisions. Maybe long enough for my dad to give up on trying to rein us in and just let us stay with her.

Grandma doesn't work, so Dahlia could go to school, and Grandma could help with the baby while she's in class. I could help too. We could make it work.

If we can just get out from under my father's iron grip.

I shakily wipe my eyes and zip up my bags before I creep down the stairs and then set my suitcase near the door to the garage before sneaking inside the kitchen and swiping her car keys from the bowl she keeps on the counter. In their place, I leave a note:

Please don't report the car as stolen, and please don't tell my dad. Things are bad at home. Real bad. I need to go get Dahlia. I will drive back with her and return your car. I'm hoping we can both stay for a while. Maybe forever?

I will text you when I get to Crestwell and have Dahlia with me so that you know we're safe.

Love, sunshine

I wince as the garage door opens, praying it doesn't wake my grandma. I wait several minutes to ensure she hasn't stirred and then step out into the wind-chilled night. Throwing my suitcase into the trunk, I brace myself for what I have to do next.

The tears I've just begun to keep at bay spill over as I shuffle down the driveway and make a left. I wring my hands, thinking of how I'll explain all of this to him once I make it the six-house distance that separates Leo's home and my grandmother's.

I pause, chest seizing.

I can't tell him any of this.

I can't tell him about Dahlia's pregnancy. It's not my right to tell anyone else about what my sister is going through. She doesn't even know Leo exists. I also can't tell him I plan on stealing my grandmother's car to make the three-day drive back to Kansas by myself.

God, it sounds so stupid.

It is stupid, but what choice do I have?

Dahlia needs me, and that's the only thing I can let consume me right now, the only thing that matters. I know if I told Leo my plan, he wouldn't chastise me for it. He wouldn't tell me no, but he would demand to come with me.

I inhale a shaky breath, tears falling again. He would never condemn my stupid decisions, but he'd demand to be a part of them. Because at the end of the day, all he wants is to be with me. It doesn't matter where we are or what we're doing, as long as we're together.

Because he loves me.

I know he loves me, and suddenly, I feel overwhelmed with that love. I feel it all over me, and for a moment, it feels like too much.

I'm about to betray him. Leave him.

He can't come with me, because if things don't work out the way I expect them to, if my dad finds out...he'd ruin us, ruin Leo, ensure there would be no chance of us ever seeing each other again. He'd take Leo's dreams of surfing professionally and find a way to crush them. That's a risk I'm not willing to take.

I'll make this drive alone. I'll go a week without him if that means not having to go a lifetime without him instead.

I find my hand over my chest as I stand in the middle of the street, attempting to catch my breath. Tears stream down my face, soul heavy and heartbroken, as I make every effort to compose myself.

What I do next will hurt most.

I finish the walk to Leo's house, realizing the garage door is open and illuminated. Soft music flows through the speakers. As I reach the end of the driveway, I see Leo's sandy blond hair hanging in front of his face, his body bent over the hood of an old jeep. He's got on a red cut-off T-shirt, his muscle flexing where he braces one arm on the side of the car, his other inside the hood, working away at something.

Everett stands across from him, dark hair swiped out of his eyes, a streak of oil across his cheekbone. He's smiling the carefree grin as he holds a flashlight pointed down into the hood where Leo works.

They're laughing at something, and my heart swells at the sound, so carefree and childlike. It's the kind of laughter that sounds like salvation.

I slowly climb their driveway, but neither of them notices me.

It's not until I reach the edge of the garage that Everett lifts the flashlight to my face, squinting as he makes out my figure. "Darby?" he asks.

Leo's head snaps up, an immediate smile gracing his handsome face. "Hey, hon—" As soon as his eyes land on mine, I know he must see the devastation in them that's impossible for me to hide, the red-rimmed eyes and puffy cheeks. That smile falls. "Baby, what's wrong?"

I give myself the opportunity to take one final deep breath, plastering the most genuine smile on my face I can manage. "Hi," I say softly. "Nothing is wrong. I just...wanted to see if I could talk to you for a minute?"

His brows knit together, but he says, "Of course." Everett walks around the side of the Jeep and brushes past the stereo, pressing a button that abruptly changes the song, notching up the volume before swiping the tool out of Leo's hand and taking over for him.

That same old-fashioned melody from our first date flows

through the speakers in the garage as Leo walks up to me, worry still gracing his features, and grabs me by the hand. He pulls me down the driveway and into the empty residential road.

"This is the same song you played in the car on our date." I force a chuckle. "You guys are really into that old-timey, Beach Boys vibe, huh?" I ask, attempting to lighten the darkness of my mood before he can sense it.

He wraps his arms around my waist, pulling me against his chest. On instinct, I reach around his neck and interlace my fingers together.

Tears prick in my eyes as we begin to sway, feet slowly spinning around the pavement. In the middle of the night, on a deserted road, in a quiet neighborhood, my heart splits right open as we—unbeknownst to him—have our first and last dance.

Leo's smiling widely at me as the chorus of the song begins to play again. Those lyrics that caught my ears all those weeks ago feel so much more significant now. "It makes me think of you," he says with a smile.

I don't realize I'm crying again until I feel the tears drip off my face and roll down my neck, until Leo's brows knit and he reaches up to wipe them off my face.

"What's the song called?" I ask, willing the devastation out of my voice. "I want to remember it."

The sapphire stars in his eyes sparkle as he smiles at me, but I can see a hint of worry behind them. "It's called 'Baby I'm Yours.'" Another tear spills down my cheek at that. "Talk to me, Honeysuckle."

I lean into the warmth of his hand against my face. "I talked to my sister."

"Is everything okay?"

I give him a smile. "Yeah," I lie as more tears fall. "I just...miss her." My voice grows shaky as I sigh. "And I just want you to know that..." I look up at him, making sure our eyes lock, the way he told me he wanted me to do all those weeks ago. "I love you," I whisper.

His gaze softens, and his eyes rapidly search mine, as if

looking for some ounce of hesitation, some part of me that's not telling the truth. I'm lying about so many things tonight, keeping so much from him, but that statement is the one place he won't find doubt.

"I'm in love with you, Leo Graham." My voice comes out clearer—stronger—than it has all night, maybe all my life. I've never been surer of anything before. For what he'll come to remember of this night, for all the lies I've told, for all the hurt I'm about to cause, I need him to remember this. I need him to see the sincerity in my stare.

I need him to hear these words in his head when I'm gone so he can feel the confidence of knowing I'll come back.

He runs his thumb across my jaw, stretching over to my lower lip and brushing his finger there too. "The most beautiful sentence I've ever heard, coming from the most beautiful mouth of the most beautiful girl I've ever known." He smiles, tugging my lip down with his thumb. "I'm just checking to make sure this is real life."

Tears fall in heavy streams down my face, but I keep my voice steady. "It's real. We're real. And I love you."

Cupping my jaw, he drops his head so our foreheads press together. "I love you, too, Honeysuckle. With every single shard of my broken soul."

His lips delicately land on mine, and I feel myself ripping apart as the warmth of his mouth moves against my own. He softly runs his tongue along the seam of my lips as his familiar citrus taste mixes with the salt of my tears. The flavor of heartbreak.

I knot my fingers into the hair at the base of his neck, pulling him tighter into me. He groans, his mouth opening, his tongue sweeping in to claim mine. I'm desperate for him, falling apart beneath his hands, his heat, his kiss, knowing this is the last one—at least for a while. I need him deeper, longer, tighter. I want to sink into his skin, imprint him on me so I can continue feeling him, even with the distance between us.

"Darby," he moans into my mouth. I swallow it, knowing this is the last time, forging a place in my brain for that exact sound, for this exact moment, desperately grasping at a way to remember this.

"I love you," I whisper against his lips. "I love you." I run my hands along his jaw, down his chest and stomach, then back up to his heart, to the spot where my name is inked. "I love you." My voice cracks on the last statement.

And as I feel him smile against my mouth, my heart collapses in on itself.

"I love you."

I curl my fingers into the fabric of his T-shirt as he pulls his mouth from mine. My head drops against his chest as I inhale his scent one final time. "It's late, and I...have class in the morning. I should probably get home."

He's got one hand cradling the back of my head, the other on the familiar spot of my hip. It stings as he gives a light squeeze. "Okay, baby. I'll see you after work tomorrow."

I can't respond, I can't bear one more lie. So, I just nod.

I begin to step back, and he lets me go. His hand runs down my arm, but he grabs hold of my palm before I can put enough space between us. He interlaces our fingers and smiles at me, squeezing four times, the secret message only the two of us understand. "Always, Darby," he says.

"Always," I whisper back.

I slowly turn around and make my way back to my grandma's house, knowing his eyes remain on me until I'm out of sight.

I stand in front of the house that's quickly and irreplaceably becoming my home. Tears fall again as I say my silent goodbye.

I quietly climb into the car and turn it on. Closing the garage door as I reverse down the driveway, I begin my journey back to the wolf's den.

Thirty-Nine

Heathen

Now. June 2nd.

The world around me fades away as I slide into her tight, wet warmth. Nothing else exists except for the feel of her silken hair around my fist, the sound of my name falling off her soft lips, the way her flesh feels wrapped around my cock.

She's got her hands braced on the hood of my car, fingers spread wide to balance herself as I pound into her from behind. She takes every inch so perfectly. As if we're not outside for any passerby to see. As if she's so lost in me that she doesn't give a fuck. She drives me fucking mad.

I tighten my hold on her hair and pull her up so she's flush against my chest. With the way her underwear binds around her ankles, she can't move. I have complete control over her in this moment, and the way she quivers tells me that's exactly how she wants it.

"I've traveled all over the world, you know that, right? I've seen crystal clear beaches, roaring waterfalls, and sparkling cities." I remove my hand from her hair and bring it around her neck. She trembles as I pull out slowly, only my tip remaining inside her. "But there is nothing on this planet more beautiful than the sight of my cock"—I lift her dress and slip my free hand between her legs, brushing my fingers across her swollen clit—"sliding inside your pretty little pussy."

I slam back into her to the hilt. Her entire body shudders

around it, and her head falls back against my shoulder as those soft cries become screams of pleasure, of my name. I continue whispering against her ear between each thrust.

"Nothing." Thrust. "So beautiful." Thrust. "As you." I pause deep, holding her in place. "You're heaven on Earth, baby."

Her nails dig into my thigh as her body shudders, tenses, and then goes slack. "Leo," she whimpers as her climax rushes through her. I wrap my arm around her waist and hold her upright as she pulses around me, and her release floods my cock.

I begin moving again, knowing I'm about to chase her orgasm with my own. "Do you want me to fill this hot, tight pussy up again, Honeysuckle? Or do you want me to paint you in my—"

"Paint me in it," she moans.

Fuck me.

She pulls forward, and I slip out of her, stepping back as she spins and drops to the ground in front of me. It's the desperate look in her eyes telling me exactly what she wants that has me losing myself. I erupt, ropes of cum shooting across her cheeks and dripping onto her sweet, pink lips.

Darby smiles up at me softly, eyelashes fluttering as she swipes her thumb across her bottom lip, wiping away my release before sticking it in her mouth and sucking it clean.

Fucking Christ.

Her smile widens, and I now realize I may have said that out loud. Just when I thought she couldn't be more of a fucking dream come true.

I tuck myself into my pants and grab her arm, pulling her to stand and feeling proud at the tremble that shoots through her legs as she attempts to hold herself up. I bend over the back seat of the car, searching for a T-shirt I can wipe her face with.

I find one, and as I turn back around, she's leaning casually against the door, dragging a finger down her cheek and sticking it into her mouth too. "I like it when you claim me like that." She grins innocently, as if she doesn't already have my cock stirring again.

My head falls between my shoulders as I let out a strained groan. "You're something fucking else, Honeysuckle."

She laughs as I straighten and brush my old T-shirt against the soft skin of her face. I study the freckles dotted across her nose as I finish cleaning her up.

"Do you feel better?" she asks.

"I feel like your dad is a piece of shit. I feel like it would give him a heart attack to know I just fucked his daughter on the hood of my car in the middle of an open highway, and that does kind of make me feel better."

"Yeah, me too." She huffs a laugh, crossing her arms. "But I have daddy issues, so..."

I snort. "As do I."

She tilts her head, her ponytail brushing off her shoulder and falling down her back. "Have you ever heard from him?"

I nod. "Yeah, a few years after I started making a name for myself." I let my gaze fall to the mountains around us. "I assumed he was trying to get money out of me, so I ignored him for a while."

"But he wasn't?" she asks.

"Nope." I sigh, running a hand through my hair. "He just wanted to apologize for the way he left me, the way he handled my mom's death. Told me he was proud of the man I became, no thanks to him. He didn't ask me for anything at all."

"How do things stand now?" She leans into me, brushing her shoulder against my arm, as if she knows her touch alone helps keep me grounded.

"I forgave him, but I told him it was too late for a relationship, that I didn't have the capacity to allow that into my life." I shrug. "I just had to set a boundary. I wanted closure, but I wasn't interested in trying to rebuild something he so easily let fall apart to begin with."

She sucks in a swift breath. "I didn't realize people could just do that with their parents, choose not to have a relationship with them."

I turn and grab her face between my hands. "Of course you

can, Darby. You're your own person. You choose who you want to be part of your life. If someone isn't loving you the way you deserve, if they're not giving you the respect you deserve, if they're not putting into the relationship what you are, then you owe them nothing. It doesn't matter if you share blood."

She nods as I lean in to kiss her hard.

"Let's stop making today about other people, yeah? Today is about us."

"Today is about us," she whispers. She closes her eyes, placing her hands over mine. "I'm gonna drive us somewhere. There's somewhere I have to show you."

"Okay, baby," I say against her lips.

"Do you actually know where we're going?" I ask.

"I have a general idea. It's not a place. More like...a spot."

"Okay?" I'm trying to remain calm, but her sudden solemn expression is giving me pause. She's been on edge all day, bouncing back and forth between emotions rapidly.

I expected this to happen as we got closer to Pacific Shores. The escape we've been having the last few days is about to close in around us, and that phone call from her dad was definitely proof of that. The asshole just cut directly to the chase. He requested that I "return" her to him, like she's a borrowed lawnmower or something.

Then, when I not-so-politely refused, he resorted to threatening me, telling me he knew there was no point in offering to pay me off—which tells me I make more money than him—so he would just have to make a call to ruin my career. That he has "friends in high places."

He's a fucking idiot.

Surprisingly, though, Darby didn't seem all that put off by her dad's call—at least, not after I was finished with him. It was even before that—all day, really. She's been acting...afraid? Confused?

Now, she just seems determined.

As if she's been struggling to make a choice, and she's finally made her decision.

And that terrifies me.

"Do you remember that I told you my sister has a daughter?" she asks. Her golden hair flies back behind her, and her hands twist on the wheel as we drive down the highway.

I nod.

"Did I tell you how old she is? Lou?"

"No."

She chews on her lip. "Lou is nine. Nine and a half, actually. Her birthday is in January."

Nine years old. God, Darby's sister was young when she had her. I'm pretty sure Darby told me her sister was only a year or two older. By looks alone, they could almost be twins.

My mind starts doing the math as I think back on the last decade.

"She found out she was pregnant just before I was sent to live here," Darby says, answering the question before I can ask. "That's why I came to stay with my grandmother. My parents wanted Dahlia to get an abortion, and they didn't want me to know about any of it. They thought sending me away would keep me from finding out." Her voice is completely emotionless as she speaks, as if she's numb to it.

"When did you find out?" I ask, swallowing down my anger at her father.

"About twenty minutes before I came and told you I loved you the night I left."

That sentence slams into my gut so hard I lose all the air in my lungs. I feel like a cinder block just landed on my chest. My head whips to face her from the passenger seat, but she keeps her eyes on the road.

"She called me that night when we got home from the Ramoses' shop with everyone," she continues. "My dad had taken away her phone, essentially locked her in the house for months until she agreed to the abortion."

That's when I felt it: the cracking in her armor.

I remember her fear that summer, how she went weeks and weeks without hearing from her sister. The excuses her parents always had for Dahlia not being around. The pride I felt when she finally stood up to them, but they responded by ignoring her too.

"She was so scared, Leo. And when I think about that night... about the decision I made..." *The decision to leave.* "There are parts of me that wish I would've done things a million different ways. I hoped for a million different outcomes." She turns her head briefly, tearful eyes burning through me. "But I think that if I hadn't left..." She swallows. "I think that maybe we wouldn't have Lou." I watch one tear drip down her cheek and off her chin. "I love her more than anything."

I nod in understanding. "What happened that night, Honeysuckle?"

"My sister needed me, and I needed to be there for her before she was backed into a corner she couldn't get out of, forced to make a decision she didn't want to make." Darby's face is dead serious when she says, "All those things you told me, about having control over my body? Making my own decisions about it? Dahlia fought that battle, too, for a whole slew of different reasons."

I reach across the seat and grip her thigh, brushing my thumb across her soft skin, attempting to provide whatever comfort I can. "I understand that, Darby. Of course, I understand that. I..." I sigh. I don't want to make everything about me. I know that it's a heavy memory for her and her sister, but they've had ten years to process their side of things. I haven't. "I would've understood that back then, too."

She immediately nods. "I know you would. I know that." She lifts a hand from the wheel and wipes her eyes. "I planned to come back. Both Dahlia and I were going to come back together and live with my grandma. I took my grandma's car that night. I was supposed to drive from Pacific Shores back to Kansas, get Dahlia, and we were going to drive back together, before my dad ever found out." She looks at me again, ensuring my eyes are on hers as she says, "I was going to come back for you. I always planned on coming back to you."

She looks ahead, her eyes darting around our surroundings as if searching for something. We begin driving through a narrow canyon, red rocks towering over us on all sides. At the far end of the canyon, the road curves sharply. I feel the car begin to slow as if she's easing off the accelerator.

"Why didn't you?"

She doesn't answer me as we close in on the curve ahead. She begins to turn the wheel, but rather than rolling along the edge of the canyon, she slows to a crawl and pulls off the highway entirely, stopping the car right against the guardrail and throwing it in park.

She lifts out of her seat and looks around again before shrugging and settling down in the back of the car. I turn to face her, hazel eyes on fire behind the desert sun.

"I didn't come back because my father couldn't know about you, Leo. That was how I protected you, by keeping you away from that world, locked inside me. He would've *destroyed* you. Destroyed *us*." Her jaw tenses. "Just like he's going to try to do now."

I crawl over the passenger seat, settling in beside her as I bring her cheeks between my hands and kiss away her tears for the second time today. "I'm not going to let him touch us, Honeysuckle."

She turns her head, wrestling herself from my grip, her face falling into her hands as if she can't bear to look at me.

Reluctantly, I let her go. "Why did you let a decade go by?

Why didn't you come back when you were eighteen? Or just even call me? Send a text? Respond to my—?"

She turns to face me, harsh devastation on her face. "Because losing you was my punishment, Leo."

"Punishment for what?"

Then. August 15th.

Honeysuckle,

I'm thinking about your eyes right now, and I'm a little afraid that eventually, I'm going to forget what they look like. But right now, I can see them in my head.

They're so bright, so golden. Multitudes of colors dance whenever sunlight filters across your face.

Stars aren't just born in your eyes; I think they die there, too, exploding flashes of brightness that soar throughout eternity. I've been crawling through darkness all this time, searching for the light, and when you look at me, I feel I'm shrouded in sunshine after living in shadow.

When I touch you, it feels as if every question ever asked is written across your skin, as if the end of galaxies and the dark side of the moon are discovered within your arms.

My soul finds gravity in your body. I'm sucked into your sunlight. Now you're gone, and I feel untethered, floating through the cosmos on my own. Aimless, soulless. Lost.

I've tried calling so many times. Your phone was going straight to voicemail, and now it says your number is disconnected. I've tried talking to your grandma. She'll only tell me that you're safe, that you've gone back home... and that you're not coming back.

I don't believe her. I don't believe that you would do this to me. To us.

I know that wasn't home to you, Darby. This is your home. I am your home.

I don't know what happened, but I need you to know that I'll keep trying to reach you. I won't give up. Not on you. Not on us. Not until you tell me to leave you alone. Maybe not even then.

I don't know why you didn't tell me you had to leave. I would've understood. I thought you knew that, but maybe I wasn't clear enough. I don't know where things went wrong, what I did wrong.

All I know is that I love you so goddamn much it hurts, and I feel empty without you here.

I'm desperate for anything, some kind of response from you. Something to let me know I haven't imagined all of this. I'm falling apart over here, Darby. I think you took my soul with you when you left. I'm not just haunted by ghosts anymore; I think I am one.

I'm out of options. I've been leaving letters with your grandma to mail you, but each day that passes without a response splits my chest open a little wider.

You don't want to break my heart, do you, Honeysuckle?

I love you.

Leo

Forty

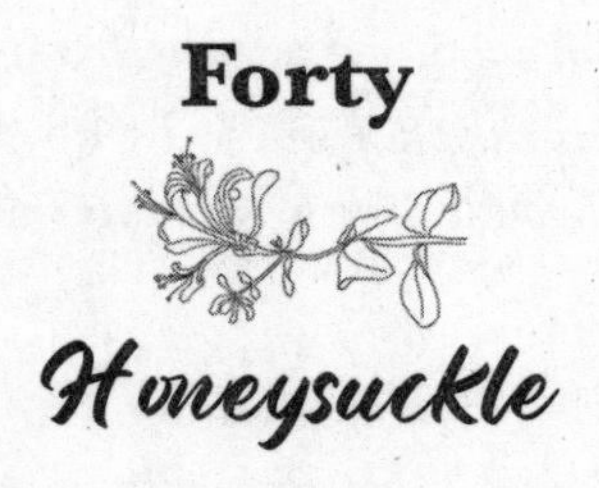

Honeysuckle

Then. August 12th.

My eyes droop as I attempt to focus on the road ahead of me. They're heavy with both unshed tears and exhaustion, and I can hardly keep them open.

The sun sets over the red rocks of Utah as I enter the seventh hour of my drive. The sky is a piercing azure, the horizon glowing with bright pink and vivid orange, the red landscape shimmering underneath the light. For a moment, I allow myself to clear my haze of anxiety and fear and admire the beauty in front of me. My first thought is that Dahlia would love this view. She always dreamed of traveling.

She went through a phase where she was entirely convinced she was going to buy herself a school bus after graduating high school and renovate it into a tiny home so she could travel wherever she wanted.

I think she'd love the Southwest. She'd love this landscape—rough and dry but undeniably beautiful, like something from another world. Plants that have the ability to thrive in the harshest conditions. All things that remind me of Dahlia.

I smile to myself. I'll bring her back here. Once I get her out of our parents' house, we'll come back here. We'll take this same route, and we'll stay the night, spend a whole day exploring the canyons and the arches, watching the incomparable sunsets that paint the sky.

One more day.

One more day until I can hug my sister. Until I can get her out. Until I can turn around and go back to Leo, to the home I've made for myself. The only piece missing from the puzzle of my life is Dahlia, and while I may be going to extremes to get that piece, I know it'll be worth it once we're together—once we're free.

I let my mind wander toward Leo, toward the beautiful, deep blue eyes that match the sky above me, that sweet spot where the sun is just lifting into the sky. I think I may take him back here someday too. Plan a whole road trip, just the two of us.

My eyes swell with tears, as has been the norm over the past day. I'll survive a few hours without crying, but they threaten each time Leo crosses my mind. I imagine him finding out I'm gone, imagine him calling me—though I've turned off my phone, afraid my dad will track me with it. I imagine him being so, so angry with me.

I imagine a future where he doesn't forgive me for this. Where I can't convince him to understand. Where he moves on before I have the chance to make it back to him. A world where I lose him forever. Where last night's kiss was the last. Where I'll never feel his heartbeat against my ear as we lie on the beach, or the way he squeezes my hips and my hands. His promises to keep me safe. His laugh and the way he calls me honeysuckle.

Being with him has become as normal to me as breathing, as simply waking up in the morning. A day doesn't pass where I don't expect to see him, to hear his voice.

I feel tears drip off my cheeks and onto my neck. My breathing becomes heavy, and my vision blurs as I let the possibility of losing him—well and truly losing him—settle into my bones.

A heavy wariness envelops me like a blanket, my stomach plummeting to my feet as I sink into that possibility. Suddenly, I wonder if this was all a mistake. Maybe I should have just called my parents, just flown home and tried to talk it through with them. Maybe there was some way I could've saved my sister and also saved myself.

I realize I've chosen my sister over the boy I've fallen in love with, and I'm not sure if he'll ever forgive me for that. While I don't regret going to the ends of the world to get my sister out of her despair, I now wonder if I could've chosen a different route. If there might've been a way to save all of us.

I furiously swipe at my eyes as the world goes blurry.

A sharp curve in the winding canyon roads appears.

I blink away the stinging moisture, placing my hand back on the wheel to catch the car before I drive headfirst into the rock face towering above me.

Too late I realize I turned too hard. I'm driving too fast.

The last thing I see is the flash of my own headlights against the guardrail.

The last thing I feel is gravity pulling me down the embankment.

Forty-One

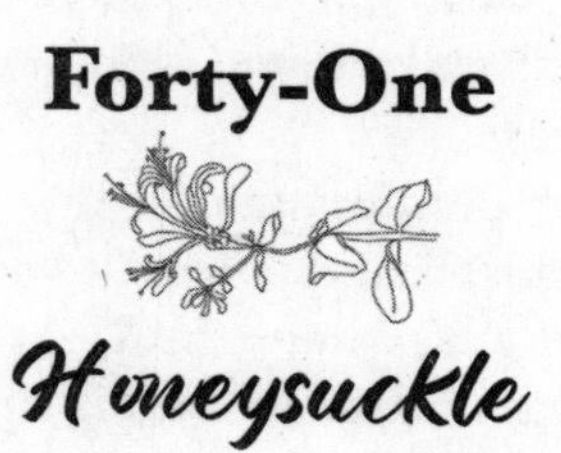

Honeysuckle

Now. June 2nd.

"This is the place you crashed?" he asks.

I lift my head from between my knees and glance around the canyon again. The sun is just beginning to lower over the rocks, casting them in a crimson hue. Rays of light filter in through the narrow valley between the towering cliffs, casting the world around us in gold.

"Somewhere in this area. I remember driving through this canyon. I remember the curve in the road." I shiver at the memory.

Leo leans closer to me, letting his hand rest on my thigh. "What happened after, Darby?"

My eyes are heavy, and I know the moment I open my mouth, the tears will begin to flow. I take a deep breath, facing Leo. He told me to look him in the eyes all those years ago, and I'll do it now, too.

"I'm in love with you, Leo." I see his face flare with surprise, and I see his eyes explode with color and longing. Still, he only smiles at me softly and tightens his hold on my thigh.

"I've always been in love with you. I never fell out of it, never stopped. Not for one moment." I feel my chest tightening as my heart pounds against it, begging to be set free. "Being with you again...it feels like my heart hasn't been beating, not since the moment I walked away from you. And now, I feel like it's bleeding out for you, flooding through me stronger and harder than I ever could've imagined at seventeen."

Tears flow freely down my face, and I don't try to hide them. I let him see every emotion there, every piece of my shattered heart, every storm I've weathered without him, how badly I wished he'd been there.

"I want to drive headfirst into it. Into us. I want to believe there was a reason for all of this pain. I want a happy ending. I want to believe that we're meant to be."

"We are." He leans across the seat, swiping his thumb along my cheek, taking my tears with it. "I love you just as deeply today as I did then. More, even. Give me your bleeding heart, Darby. I've been waiting for it all this time."

I shake my head, my body riddled with tremors as I fight back heaving sobs. "I can't let us have that future yet—not until you know the truth. The *whole* truth." I take a deep breath to steady myself. "Then, you need to decide, and I'll understand if you can't forgive me for it."

"Forgive what?" he asks.

I close my eyes, inhaling before letting them fall open. His hand on my knee squeezes four times. *You're safe with me.* I'm trying to look at his face, but I know the fear, confusion, and trepidation I'll find there may scare me into changing my mind.

Instead, I look out to the desert. "I was afraid my father would destroy us, but he didn't." I swallow, willing the courage to look at him now. His ocean eyes clash against mine. "I destroyed us, Leo."

Forty-Two

Honeysuckle

Then. August 13th.

My eyes flutter open at the sound of the beeping machine, at the hushed voices in the corner of the dark room. I can see the specks of light filtering through the blinds of the window.

"It looks like she's just beginning to wake up, so I'll go ahead and give you two a moment. The doctor will be back in a little while to speak with her."

All the hair on my skin rises, my limbs going numb and my hands beginning to tremble beneath the blanket of the hospital bed as the memories come flooding back.

By the time I stirred to consciousness yesterday, I was already in the ambulance being sped toward the small community hospital in St. George. I was informed that my driver's license had been found in the car and that my parents had been contacted.

My father was on his way.

I was rushed to the hospital and immediately put into surgery. I've spent much of the time since under anesthesia or blitzed out on pain meds, nearly unaware of my surroundings. Unfortunately, my mind now feels clear, at least clear enough for the realization of what's about to happen to settle in my bones.

"Thank you." His stern, hard, professional voice carries over to me, my body racking with nausea at the sound of it.

I squint my eyes shut and brace myself as the rough, clipped footsteps close the distance between the door and the bed I'm lying in. My brain immediately goes into flight mode, desperate for an escape, a way to get out of here.

"Darby." My father's voice is rough, grating against me with disappointment and cold rage.

I realize I haven't opened my eyes. I'm too afraid to see his face, to see my own features in him. To be reminded that no matter where I go, what I do, or who I try to become, I'm always going to belong to him first. I'll never escape him.

"Open your eyes and look at me, sweetie."

I let all the air expel from my lungs as I slowly turn to him, letting my eyes flutter open. He looks tired. His clothes are worn and stained. His hair is slicked with sweat, a five o'clock shadow filling in the normally clean-shaven space of his jaw. His eyes are bloodshot and seem to be rimmed with tears.

He steps up to me, hovering where I lie back against the pillows. His broad hand hovers over the top of my head, thumb rubbing across my hairline. I wince, realizing the bandaged cut there. "What were you thinking?" His voice is rough, full of emotion I've never seen from him before. "Do you know how scared we were?" I notice his lip trembling, his jaw tight. "To get a call from your grandmother that you ran away? To find your phone off? Having no idea where you were, who you were with?" He shakes his head, swallowing his emotion. "Then, to get a call that you're in the hospital with a broken leg, a concussion, and..." He sighs.

Unexpected guilt immediately pricks at my stomach. I never considered that my plan could potentially cause my parents fear or pain. Or maybe I just hadn't cared, because I never thought I'd see what I see in my dad's eyes right now. Genuine concern. Fear. Maybe even love.

"I'm sorry," I croak, feeling tears behind my eyes.

"Why?" he asks.

I can only shake my head. "I don't... Where's Dahlia?"

"She's at home with your mother."

I nod.

My dad takes a deep breath, pulls a chair up to the bedside and sits down before lacing his fingers through my own. "Why?"

I'm still trembling beneath his hand. "I was trying...to get back to..."

"How long have you known?"

Assuming he's referring to my sister, I say, "She called me the night I left and told me everything. I just..." I feel myself beginning to cry again. "I wanted to get back to her. I was afraid you wouldn't let me see her after I found out about the pregnancy."

"Her pregnancy?" he asks.

I nod.

"And what about your own?"

My head snaps to him. "What?"

I see it then. The mask of concern slowly begins to slip from his face, and that glacial rage replaces it. I feel the blood drain from my face, the goosebumps on my flesh prickling beneath his stare. My mind races at the accusation he's just made as I rapidly think through every moment of the last two months, every possibility I had never considered before.

"Is that why you were running back home, Darby? Did you think I was going to fix all your problems? Help you after you've been ruined by that boy?"

"I..." My breathing increases, and suddenly, I feel very, very sick. "I don't..."

His eyes narrow. "You're telling me you didn't know?" He scoffs. "You had no idea that you were pregnant after you'd been tramping around California all summer like a fucking whore?"

His words slice through me.

I cover my mouth with one hand as my body racks with sobs. Unable to look my father in the face, I slowly drop my gaze to my stomach hidden beneath the blankets. My free hand crawls out of my dad's grip and over to my midsection as I run my thumb across it.

This can't be real.

"I'm..." Unable to get the words out through my tears, I inhale shaky breaths in an attempt to compose myself.

"Enough with the dramatics," my father snaps.

Just then, knuckles rap on the hospital room door. A moment later, it creaks open as a tall brunette middle-aged woman in a white coat walks in. She's got a clipboard in one hand, and kind eyes rake over me from behind her black-rimmed glasses.

"Darby Andrews?" she asks.

I nod.

"That's a beautiful name." She smiles. "I'm Dr. Montgomery, and I'm here to talk to you about your injuries. Is that all right?" She looks back and forth between my dad and me.

He settles back in his chair, crossing his arms and nodding. The doctor then looks at me, as if asking for my permission too. I nod once more.

"Great. I'd like to speak with you both about your recovery process for your leg and your concussion. The cut on your head is minor and should heal on its own in a few days." She nods toward my forehead. "But I'd like to talk with you specifically about your miscarriage."

Miscarriage.

I blink, clearing my mind of all other thoughts but that singular word. I let it ring through my brain again, unable to fathom how I could've possibly been pregnant and subsequently lost it, all without knowing.

I wonder if the hollow ache spreading throughout my chest is because I was pregnant, or because I no longer am, if I'm shaking in fear or in grief, if I'm longing for something I never asked for but somehow had and lost anyway.

But the thought taking up the most space at the forefront of my mind is: *is this my fault*?

Did I do this? To myself? To Leo? To the potential baby who had just begun to take root in my body? Baby. Mine. Leo's. Ours. His dimples. My eyes. His laugh. My nose.

My body feels like a funnel of emotion, none of which I'm able to grasp onto or process. I feel like I'm swirling along with them, no longer in control.

"Did I..." My throat grows tight as I voice the words out loud. "Is it my fault?"

Dr. Montgomery looks at my dad, and I follow her gaze. That anger is still present on his face, but I swear, I can see it lighten–just slightly, as if he was unaware I didn't know. It's as if he can sense my guilt, and even just the smallest part of him hopes to comfort me with that glimpse of softness.

"It's possible that the trauma and stress of the accident could have caused it, yes, but miscarriages so early on in pregnancy are extremely common. It's impossible to know for sure."

"How...how far along wa...was I?" My voice trembles with each sob.

"Well, it's hard to say. Do you remember when your last menstrual cycle was?"

I try to remember the start of summer, the last time I remember buying tampons at the store. *How did I not notice?* "Mid-June, I think."

The doctor nods as she makes a note on the chart in her hands. "That would've put you at about six weeks." She tilts her head at me. "Does that line up with you..." She glances at my dad. "Your schedule?"

My eyes fall to my lap, unable to look either of them in the eye. I think back to that perfect night on our private beach. The math works itself out in my brain, and I realize that so much more must've come to life that night than just Leo and I.

I nod.

"I'd like to do a quick ultrasound to make sure everything is okay before you go home." She holds a handful of pamphlets out to my dad. "Miscarriage, while common, is its own version of loss. It can be a difficult thing to heal from. These are resources we recommend she utilize if she has any trouble coping..." She continues speaking, but I don't hear her.

She walks through my recovery, how to care for my broken leg, the type of pain and bleeding I can expect to experience from the loss of the pregnancy. I don't register any of that either. I can't bear to think about it.

I only think of him.

Of what he'd think of this. Think of me.

If this would be something he'd be able to love me through. He promised to always keep me safe, but what would he think of what I've done? How incapable I was of extending that same protection to a life he and I created together?

Would he be able to forgive me for it?

I cry in silence throughout the duration of the doctor's spiel, only realizing she's gone because of the sound of the door clicking shut and the sudden shadow engulfing me as my father stands.

"Enough of that," he snaps. "You don't get to do that. You don't get to cry anymore."

I turn my head, looking up at him, but I don't have words.

I don't have anything left to fight with, to fight for.

"You've brought this upon yourself, Darby. Now, pull it together. We're going home as soon as they discharge you."

"I need my phone," I say shakily. "I need to tell Leo."

My dad paces in front of the bed as he lets out a sarcastic laugh. "Leo? That his name?" He runs a hand down his face. "Your phone was lost in the wreck. I've already disconnected your number. You'll have no need for one for quite some time."

I only blink at him.

He blinks back at me. "What do you expect me to do, Darby? You're cut off. Your grandmother will inform that boy that whatever he thinks happened between you two is over, and he's free to move on."

"She wouldn't do that."

Giving me a cold smile, he says, "If she wants to keep her fucking house, she will." He shakes his head. "Plus, after that shit you pulled, she agreed with me that it's best you never see that boy or step foot in that town again. You stole her fucking car, Darby. Whatever ally you thought you had in your grandmother changed the moment you ran away like that."

I only sink further into myself, burying my face in my hands, letting the sorrow all but consume me. I don't look at him. I don't look anywhere. I let myself fall into the dark despair as the last twenty-four hours settle around me.

My dad continues, his voice softer now, "It's for the best, sweetie. This boy corrupted you all summer, made you believe things weren't true. Like he loved you, like he cared. All he wanted—all any of them ever want—is exactly what you gave him. Now that he's had it, he won't want anything to do with you."

No. That's not him. You're wrong.

"If I'm wrong, and he's everything you think he is and more, I'm doing you a favor. Because as soon as that boy finds out what you've done, he'll want nothing to do with you."

That conclusion makes much more sense.

Suddenly, my tears stop falling, as if my body ran out of them. As if I'm numb to all of it.

Irreparably broken. Hopeless. Soulless.

"Either way, it's best we wash our hands of it," he says finally.

"Do you really think he'd hate me?" I ask, more to myself than to him.

"I would," my dad says nonchalantly. "You ran away in the middle of the night. Abandoned him. Lied to him. Abandoned him. You were incredibly reckless and stupid. You put yourself in danger and killed his baby in the process." He laughs darkly. "I'd never forgive your mother if she pulled something like that."

Abandoned him.

It dawns on me that there is no coming back from this. From what I've done.

I finally lift my head, my father frowning at me. I wonder if

he can see the irreparable heartbreak in my eyes, see just how devastated, lost, and shattered I am.

He leans over the bed, and I wince as he brings his hand to my face, but he softly cups my cheek. "Maybe this was all a way of showing you that you weren't ready for all this, Darby. You weren't prepared for the mess you got yourself into, but maybe this is all a sign for you to come home, start over. You're a good girl, sweetie. You don't need to let this one summer ruin you for good."

I reach back into myself, searching for his voice, all those reminders he left me during our weeks together, but all I feel is emptiness where he used to be.

I think I may have left all the pieces of both of our souls on the side of that road in the canyons of Utah, because I can't seem to find them now. I think I may have broken both of us.

"I think we've lost enough in this family, don't you? Don't you want to go home and see your sister? Let's do what we can to help her get through this. She's going to need us, you know. You'll need to be around to help take care of your niece or nephew here in a few months." He gives me a smile.

I read the hidden message in his face.

It's Dahlia and the baby, or it's me and Leo.

But I know, deep down, that Leo's already lost to me. I'm already lost to him. There is no coming back from this, what I've done. There is no survival for the two of us.

But for Dahlia... There might be hope.

So, I gather up my soulless body and my heartless chest as I prepae myself to return to the house that never felt like home.

Forty-Three

Heathen

Now. June 2nd.

I breathe in through my nose and out through my mouth.

My head falls in between my legs where they're planted on the back seat of my car, Darby and I both sitting atop the trunk lid. I hear her sniffling next to me, and I feel her hand gently rubbing circles along my back. I smell the dust and the interstate, and I open my eyes to study the red leather of my seat.

I'm working to bring myself back to the moment. All the fibers of who I am suddenly mean something different now.

It's like I'm witnessing the course of my life change right in front of me, and there is nothing I can do about it. I'm looking down the barrel of a future I never got to have but I now know would have existed if everything had just been a little different.

My soul feels like it's being shredded at the seams.

"I'm so sorry," Darby cries quietly next to me.

That wakes me up enough to sit straight and pull her into me. I cradle her head against my chest, and she only cries harder. I feel her tears soaking my shirt right through my skin, seeping into my chest and drowning my soul.

"You were pregnant," I whisper.

She nods. "I didn't know. I swear to you, I didn't know."

I hush her. "I believe you, baby. I believe you."

Her fingers twist into the fabric of my shirt, hanging on tightly. I tuck her head beneath my chin and look out to the setting sun.

"I don't know why it still hurts so much, why I feel so broken over losing something I never really had."

I understand the feeling. It's something instinctual. Biological. Unexplainable yet no less devastating. "You might not have known, but your body did. It began preparing you for this huge thing to happen, something that would alter your chemistry, your instincts, your purpose for the rest of time. That existed inside you, and then suddenly, it didn't." She sucks in a swift, shaky breath at that. "That's always going to have an effect on someone, but I think the miscarriage represented something else for us. It wasn't just the loss of the pregnancy. It was what you believed was the loss of us. The loss of me." I feel tears sting my own eyes as I consider where we're supposed to go from here. "For me, it represents the loss of ten years we won't get back, an entire life we can't get back." Tears drip off my chin and into her hair. My stomach feels hollow, but I know it's nothing in comparison to what she must be feeling.

I think about her keeping this secret for so many years, grieving this loss alone, blaming herself for it.

"I'm sorry you went through this alone, Darby."

Her voice is broken and trembling as she whispers, "I brought it upon myself."

I pull her away from me, holding her by her forearms as I force her to look at me. "Do not ever say that again."

Her face crumbles entirely, her eyes swollen, her nose red, and her cheeks streaked in tears. Her entire body feels limp in my arms, as if everything she's held back for ten years, she's finally allowing herself to feel.

I lift her onto my lap and let her head fall into my neck. "You're home now, baby. You're here with me. You're safe. Allow yourself to feel it." I hold her against me tightly, letting my own voice shake as I whisper reassurances in her ear. "I've got you. I'm here. I promise."

"I'm sorry," she croaks.

"I know, love. I know." I break down with her, my body trembling against hers. "What do you need? What can I do?"

"Tell me it's not my fault." She pulls back, straddling my legs as she looks down at me. Cars pass on the freeway, but they don't exist to me, not really. It's just us.

"It is not your fault, Darby." I know what she's feeling; I felt it for years after I lost my mom. That kind of guilt is heavy and hard, but it can be overcome, accepted. "You were desperate, scared, and young. You were manipulated by someone who was supposed to love you unconditionally. It was an accident. It was not your fault, and you do not deserve to be punished. I never would've thought that of you." She seems to calm down the longer she looks at me. "He knew that. He told you exactly what would break you so that you'd never try coming back to me." She drops her head so her nose brushes against mine. "But you escaped. You got away, and I'll never let you go back to that. I'm going to keep you safe. I've got you now."

The smallest of smiles lifts at the corner of her mouth, and I follow suit with my own. "We're gonna be okay, Honeysuckle." I brush a piece of hair from her forehead. "We'll heal together."

She nods against my forehead, and I lean in to seal our lips together. I taste our tears and feel her trembling as she wraps her arms around my neck and presses us tighter. "I love you, Leo."

"I love you, Darby. I've always loved you." And as I say it, I mean it, though there is still one piece of the puzzle that doesn't quite fit. "Even after you got my letters, you still thought I couldn't love you through this?"

Her body stills, and I feel her breath halt against my lips. I swear, her entire heart has stopped beating too.

She pulls back suddenly, and her jaw tightens, her nostrils flare, her brows cinching at the center of her forehead. Those hazel eyes become golden fire, like raging flames of iridescent despair.

"What letters?"

Then. November 11th.

Honeysuckle,

Today's your birthday. Your eighteenth.

I haven't written in two months, not since I started losing hope you'd ever respond.

I dropped ten letters to your grandmother; she told me she'd send all ten to you, but you've never sent one back. You've never returned my calls, turned your phone back on.

I didn't want to give up hope on us. I know there are forces outside our control at play here. I know you're in the wolf's den, but I guess I just thought you would fight harder to get out of it. Fight harder for me.

Maybe that's why I'm writing you today. Today, you're finally an adult. Maybe now, you'll have your chance to get out. To become your own person. To find your way home.

And if that's true, then I want you to know that I'm still here. I'm still waiting. I think I'll always be waiting for you, even if you never come back.

It's been three months to the day since I last saw you. Last touched you. Yet somehow, it's still your face I see when I close my eyes at night. Still your lips I feel against my own. Still your name my heart beats for.

I still don't know where your tattoo is. I don't know whether you still have it, whether you still hear my voice in your head, whether you see my face when you close your eyes. Whether you miss me—if you even think of me. If you even care.

I don't want to believe that last statement could ever be true. I don't want to believe our summer could've meant so little to you that you'd throw it away without a second thought. Throw me away. Throw away every moment we had. Everything we gave one another. I don't want to believe that, but every day, I lose a little more hope.

Despite this, I haven't given up on us. I'm still searching for you in every place I go, in every person I meet.

I'm aimlessly wandering until I find you again.

I'm still yours.

Leo

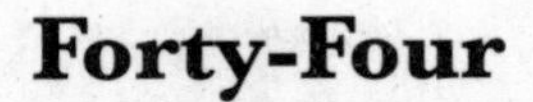

Forty-Four

Now. June 2nd.

I feel the anger—the hatred—coursing through my veins. I feel my blood burning. I feel myself being shred apart by the knowledge that the people who bore me are well and truly evil.

"I wrote you letters," Leo whispers. "Eleven. From the time you left up until your eighteenth birthday. I stopped after that because you hadn't...." His jaw sets as he swallows thickly. "I thought that you had received them and didn't want to respond. I thought when I got your letter about your wedding, you had finally decided to."

I shake my head, feeling the tears fall again.

Fuck. How many times today am I going to cry? How many times in a twenty-four-hour period can one's heart be shattered and repaired before the pieces no longer fit together?

"I never got them, Leo. I never got them." My voice is breaking. "I never would've left you unanswered like that. I thought...I thought you'd just moved on with your life, forgotten about me."

He folds me against his chest. "Never."

"We were doomed from the start," I murmur.

"No, love," he whispers against my temple. "I still believe we were meant to be."

"Why did all this happen? Why'd we lose all this time? Why'd I lose..." I trail off, not wanting to finish the sentence.

"I don't have answers for that, Honeysuckle. Sometimes,

things just happen. All I know is at this moment, in the reality we're living in right now, I'm sure we're supposed to be right here. Healing together." He pulls my head from him so he can look into my eyes.

"You're my 'it for me' person. You were my first love. Then, the one who got away. Now, you're my 'it was always you.' And it doesn't matter what happened in between, because you're gonna be my forever person too." He cups my face, bringing his mouth to mine. "You're my once-in-a-lifetime kind of love, Darby."

His lips move against mine. Soft, savoring, like it'll be this way forever. His warmth seeps into me, and it feels like he's the liferaft I cling to when I've been set adrift. He keeps me from drowning in myself.

I think about the man who made me and all the things he kept from me, all the strings he pulled and the hurt he caused to retain his power. I think about my grandmother, knowing that—at least part of her—was a victim in all this too.

"My grandma told you she was mailing the letters."

"Yeah." He sighs. "She did."

So either she lied to him, or my father intercepted them before they could reach me and got rid of them himself. I allow myself to think about what they may have said, about the imprint of heartbreak Leo likely left all over them.

I think about how hard he would've tried to convince me to come back, how deeply he loved me and how desperate he was to prove that.

"I wish I could read them."

He runs his hand down the back of my head in a comforting touch as we watch the sunset beyond the canyons. "When we get home, we can look through your grandma's house and see if she hid them somewhere. If not, I'll rewrite them for you."

"You'll rewrite eleven love letters for me?"

He looks down at me just as I look up at him. His blue eyes are rimmed with red, appearing fluorescent in the setting sun.

"I'll write you a love letter every day for the rest of my life if you just come home, Honeysuckle. Stay with me."

I see everything in those blue eyes. I see the first sparks of love, the first comfort I'd ever felt. I see my best friend. I see crashing waves and wind chime laughter. I see my past.

I also see my future. I see those lazy Sundays. I see quiet evenings on the beach. I see the sunset against the ocean, and I see us floating through the cosmos. I see his skin on mine, those whispered promises in the dark of night. I see the place I've been searching for and never thought I'd find again.

"I'm already home, Leo."

He smiles, cupping my face as I feather my lips against his.

Years ago, I thought I lost us here in this canyon, thought I left us behind in the desert, never to be recovered. But as Leo kisses me fervently, with every ounce of himself, it feels like two shattered souls healing together, bound by golden light.

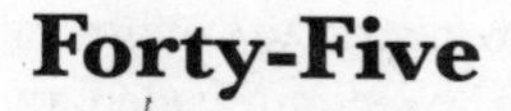

Forty-Five

Honeysuckle

Now. June 3rd.

Welcome to Pacific Shores greets me as we begin our descent over the hilly cliffside.

I see the Pacific Ocean for the first time in ten years. Bright blue horizon stretches as far as my eyes can track it. Palm trees tower over us on either side of the road, and the midday sun is warm above us. I can see the boardwalk at the bottom of the hill Leo's driving down. Everything is different, and yet the same somehow.

Maybe that's what home is supposed to feel like.

Kacey Musgraves flows through the stereo, and I find it fitting, considering that "Golden Hour" on my radio is the entire reason we met in the first place. Plus, I've listened to Leo's indie-pop-surfer-douche music for the last six days, and I'll always be a country girl at heart.

We head toward the boardwalk, toward Leo's apartment. We didn't end up making it to Zion, but we still stayed the night in St. George. We got takeout, checked into our hotel, and made a plan. I'm going to move in with Leo in his apartment. Five days is entirely too soon to take such a step, but the truth is, I've been committed to him my entire life, even when he wasn't in it.

Still, I've made it clear to him that leaving Kansas and starting over here in California isn't just about him—that it can't be just about him. I'm going to be looking for a new job—on my own.

He's not allowed to be involved in any capacity. He's not allowed to put in a word for me with his contacts at the school district, because, of course, he has contacts at the school district.

Though, he's now trying to convince me to step away from teaching altogether. He recommended that I try looking into being a florist again, except Pacific Shores doesn't have a flower shop. The closest one is like twenty minutes away, and the local elementary school is only two.

I also insisted I pay him rent, even though he owns the building and doesn't have a mortgage. Doesn't matter. I want to feel like I'm pulling my weight. He only laughed as he kissed my nose, agreeing but promising that all my rent money would go into a wedding fund anyway. That's fine by me, because when I do get married for real, I'm going to make sure it's extravagant and beautiful and everything *I* always imagined for myself.

And everything Leo imagined, too, I suppose.

As we reach the bottom of the hill and stop at a red light, I can see the boardwalk just a block ahead of us, a garage across the street where nearby residents park their cars. Instead of turning left toward the garage, though, Leo takes a right. He begins ascending up an all-too-familiar hill, and I know exactly where he's going.

"Leo," I say.

He cuts me off with a laugh as we reach the top, and he pulls into the driveway of the familiar white-washed, two-story home with the fading blue door and white wrap-around porch.

When I lived here, there were hydrangeas crowding the front bay window that looked into the living room. Now, it's honeysuckles that flourish there, bright pink and white and yellow.

Honeysuckles that I planted ten years ago. Planted for him.

The lawn is still manicured, and despite the peeling paint, the home looks to be in good shape. I let my eyes roam across the front yard before they land on the sign planted in the ground at the curb.

SOLD.

It's the first time I realize a tear is slipping down my

cheek. "I can't believe he really did it. Sold it without a second thought." I sniffle, turning my head to look at Leo. "What about all her things? Are they all still in there? Are they going to be sold with the house? Or did he already send people to clear it out?"

He gives me a smile, and it's not soft and sympathetic. It's... excited? Which is annoying. I know he's elated that I've come home with him, that I'm moving in with him, but I mean...my dad sold the only house that ever felt like home to me out of spite.

"Why don't we go check?"

I roll my eyes. "I'm not breaking and entering."

He grabs my hand, eyes glittering as he kisses my fingers. "Just trust me, Honeysuckle."

With that, he throws open the car door and steps out, walking right up to the front porch like he owns the damn place. I watch him pull out his phone and press it to his ear as I reluctantly step out of the passenger side and follow him.

"Hey, man," he greets whoever is on the other end of the line. "Yeah, I just got back into town. Thank you for making everything happen so quickly. I know that's damn near impossible." He laughs into the phone easily, and I can't help but wonder who he's talking to. "Do you have the code?"

That piques my interest.

I pick up my pace and head toward the steps as Leo leans against the door and says aloud, "One...two...three...one..." I hear something pop as Leo stands up straight. "All right, thanks. I'll see you at the Open next month, yeah?" He turns back to me and winks. "Cool. Thanks again, Dom."

I slowly begin to climb the steps up to the house, a comfortable familiarity washing over me, but something keeps me at the threshold of that last stair.

I see a box with a keypad hanging around the door handle, propped open and empty. My eyes find Leo, and he's beaming at me with pure joy. He looks so beautiful like this: board shorts, a blue T-shirt with some surfing brand printed on the front, black-and-white checkerboard sneakers and sandy-blond hair that hangs off his forehead. The chain and my ring hang off his neck, catching the sunlight, glittering with his eyes as he smiles at me.

He doesn't look haunted anymore.

He looks like Leo. *My* Leo.

He extends his hand, and a ring with two small keys dangles from his fingers. "Welcome home, Honeysuckle."

Forty-Six

Heathen

Now. June 3rd.

Darby's mouth drops open as her watery eyes rapidly dart between my face and my outstretched hand. She shakes her head in disbelief, but no words come.

I give her a moment to process, but as soon as her knees begin to buckle and she falls forward on the porch, I swiftly bend down and swoop her into my arms. She's sobbing into my shoulder, and I can only hope they're happy tears.

I shift her weight, slipping one of the keys into the lock and opening the door. It creaks as I step inside and shut it behind me. The house smells sterile, but it looks exactly as it did when her grandmother lived here.

I know that after Diane's funeral, Darby's dad had cleaners coming every two weeks or so. They've kept up with it for years, but as far as I know, he's never come here. Nobody has. All of Diane's furniture is exactly how I imagined it was the day she had the stroke that landed her in the hospital—the stroke she never woke up from.

Darby peeks her head out from my shoulder, hazel eyes wide as she looks around the space, cataloging all the differences and similarities. "What do you want to see first, baby?" I whisper against her head as I still hold her in my arms.

"How?" she asks.

I chuckle. "Dominic, the friend I was just talking to, is a

realtor. The day we were at that bar and you told me your father was going to try and sell the house, I called Dom and told him to make an offer for me. He stayed within legal parameters, but essentially, he made an anonymous offer that looked like a real estate tycoon—someone just like your father—was going to purchase the house to tear it down and build vacation condos. We made the offer anonymous because there are a lot of residents here in Pacific Shores boycotting against that kind of thing. Dane Andrews ate it right up." I snicker under my breath. "I paid extra to have the escrow expedited, and I paid to keep everything in the house. I promised that any personal documents of your grandmother's discovered would be returned to him, but he didn't seem to care much about that, I guess. Just wanted the house off his hands." I shrug. "I met Dom a few years ago while surfing out in Venice Beach. He's a good guy, but he's a great fucking realtor."

She doesn't seem to register any of it, which is okay. She can be shocked, as long as it's the good kind. Her eyes are still darting around the house as I hold her in the entryway. Finally, those pretty gold eyes land on my face.

"You bought me a house."

"No, Honeysuckle." I smile. "I bought us a house."

I set her down, and once she's steady on her feet, she moves in a slow circle around the room before landing back on me. "We're gonna live here?" Her voice is shaky.

"Yep."

"Both of us?"

I hear the question she isn't asking. I knew that somehow, moving into my apartment felt temporary for her, but buying us a house...that's permanent. That scares her. But that's all right, because I'm about to clear up any confusion she may have.

"I'm not spending another moment of my life away from you, Darby. We lost ten years, and I won't question the universe for that. Not anymore. I accept it for what it is, for whatever lessons we needed to learn or experiences we needed to have, whatever free-willed decisions we made that caused that. I won't waste my time wondering that anymore, but I also won't waste another night apart from you. You're it for me. I've known that since I was seventeen years old. I bought this house for us.

"For you to plant a garden in. For us to build a path down to our beach with, so you can watch me surf, and I can watch you suck my dick with the ocean in the background." Her lips twitch at that, and I smile brighter. "I bought a house for you to line with books and flowers and to fill with babies and laughter and happiness. To give you the home you've always deserved and never got to have."

She nods rapidly, tears dripping down her face. Without answering, she takes a sharp left and trudges into the kitchen, opening cabinets and drawers. She says nothing.

Now I know for sure I've stunned her into a state of shock.

"Yeah...yeah." She sighs. She slams a drawer shut and leans her hip against it, facing me. "Except, logically, we've really only been together for two months and like...five days? I mean, what if we both hate doing the same chores, and then we both refuse to do those chores, and we spend the next five years resenting each other and living in squalor?"

Despite the serious look on her face, I burst out laughing. I decide I'll entertain her small breakdown simply because it's cute to watch her freak out.

"What's your least favorite household chore?" I ask.

"Dishes."

"Great. How do you feel about folding laundry?"

She cocks her head, seeming to calm a little. "I mean...I wouldn't say I'm enthusiastic about it, but I don't hate it."

"Okay, so I'll do the dishes, and you can fold the laundry. I hate laundry."

She chews on her lip. "I can't cook."

"Neither can I." I take a step toward her. "We'll take lessons. We'll order takeout. I really don't give a shit as long as I'm eating my meals with you." She leans farther into the counter as I close the distance between us. "I'll take out the trash, and you can close the lid on the toilet seat when I inevitably leave it up. I won't even be mad at you when you yell at me about it. You'll water the plants because they'll die if I touch them, and I'll mow the lawn. You'll decorate the house, and I'll hang things on the wall." I brace my arms on either side of the counter behind her, pressing our bodies together. Her eyes are wide, chest heaving, as she looks at me. I let myself melt into her warmth. "We'll figure it out each day. We'll keep growing together. We'll change, we'll fight, and we'll have hard days, and that will all be okay." I drop my head, running my nose along hers. "You know why, Honeysuckle?"

She shudders at the feel of my lips against her jaw. I drag them up until they feather against her mouth.

"Because nothing is so bad when I'm with you, Heathen."

"If she still had them, they'd be in here, I think," Darby says as we enter the study off the dining room that her grandmother used as an office.

All that remains in the space is a wooden desk set in front of a long, narrow window and a small green couch across from it. Two tall bookshelves fit into each corner by the desk, but both are empty.

Darby walks around the desk, pulling open every drawer she can find. Once they're all emptied out, she sighs defeatedly. "It's empty. My dad must've had it cleaned out after she passed."

"It's okay, baby," I say as I step up behind her. I double-check the drawers Darby already opened, because if I know anything about Diane Andrews, it's that she was clever and intelligent and just as much a victim of the men in her life as Darby. I know that people in these situations have to think a step ahead. They have to be smarter than they let on.

I press down on the bottom of a few drawers, and sure enough, the shallow one right beneath the center of the desk pops open, revealing a secret compartment beneath it.

Darby gasps, and I smile.

There are a few large yellow envelopes tucked inside. I pull them out and hand them over to Darby. She chews her lip as she glances down at them. "Do you think it's an invasion of privacy?"

I shake my head but say, "I can't make that decision for you, Honeysuckle. You've got to decide how important it is for you to know what's inside those."

She contemplates for a moment before sighing and ripping one open. Her brows furrow as she checks inside before wide eyes dart up to me. "Holy shit." She flips the envelope and dumps the contents on the desk. Multiple stacks of banded hundred-dollar bills fall out. "Cash."

"Huh," I huff. "Wasn't expecting that."

"What do I do with it?"

I shrug. "Open the other envelope, and maybe it'll tell you."

She rips it open and immediately dumps the contents on top of the cash. About a dozen or so smaller envelopes come fluttering out. "Oh God," she murmurs as she lunges for them, beginning to flip them over. I see her eyes well up as she lifts her head. "It's them, Leo. The letters."

She shakily holds her hand out to me, and I take them. I count all of mine plus an additional two. The eleven I wrote her to have the return address in the top corner in my writing, along with Darby's name in the center of the envelope, but the mail-to address was filled in by Diane. I didn't know where Darby's parents lived, and she never told me. I see now that may have been to protect me.

The twelfth envelope is addressed to Diane from Darby's dad, and the last one doesn't have any address at all, just the word *sunshine* scribed across the center.

"This is all of them," I say, handing them back to her. "I think you should open the one from your dad first and then the one she addressed to you."

Darby nods, silent tears still streaming down her cheeks. She tears open the one from her dad, and I watch as her eyes scan across the page. Her nostrils flare the way they always do when she's angry, and she lets out a confirming grunt before wordlessly passing the paper off to me.

I unfold it. In Diane's writing, at the top of the page, is:

He isn't what you think he is. Just give them a chance.

The letter was returned with a one-sentence, handwritten response:

SEND ONE MORE OF THESE, AND YOUR HOUSE IS GOING ON THE MARKET.

I refold the letter when Darby hands me the second one. She's crying a little harder now, peeking over my shoulder to read it through again as I do.

Sunshine,

I'm sorry for how things turned out. I told you I didn't want you to let the years pass you by while you live a life that isn't really yours, and I'm afraid that's what I'm watching happen now. I'm afraid it's partially my fault. I've told you before that there are powers outside of my control, just like yours. Regardless, I still hope you'll make it back here someday, hope we'll have a chance to talk at some point without your parents hovering over our shoulders.

I hope you'll find a life that is entirely yours. I hope you'll do great things with it. I hope you'll find love someday too—the right kind of love.

I wanted to make sure you read these letters, but there were roadblocks in the way. I feel bad telling the boy I'd get them to you when I knew, deep down, I likely couldn't. But I'll keep trying, because most people don't get to be loved the way you are. And you know what's more powerful than fear, sunshine?

Love.

Love is brave. Love is courageous.

That's terrifying to people who are incapable of it.

I may not have the bravery and courage I need to play my part here. I'm afraid it's a bit too late for me, but I hope you find it. All of it.

Bravery. Courage. Freedom. Most of all–love.

Hope you find your way home, too.

Grandma

I realize I'm crying, too, as Darby wraps her arms around my waist, pressing her head against my arm. We're quiet for a while, reading and rereading her grandmother's letter.

I was angry with her for so many years. She was short with me. Avoided me. Wouldn't tell me where Darby was or why she wasn't responding to me. I wanted to blame her.

Then, after she died, I just felt a lot of guilt, and that hurt too. I know Darby felt affected by it in many of the same ways.

This is another piece of closure she never thought she'd have, another piece of her being fitted back into the puzzle of her soul. Mine too.

So, she cries against my arm. She mourns. She heals. And I let her. I hold her through all of it until she quietly whispers, "I want to read your letters, Leo."

I nod against the top of her head. "Okay, but let's go

somewhere else first."

I gather the papers and take her hand. She says nothing as I weave her through the house—our house—and out the back door, down the steps of the porch where she asked me to kiss her ten years ago and I said no. Beneath the window where I threw rocks the day I met her. Through the yard where I snuck in the middle of the night and stared up at her window because I couldn't stop thinking about the girl who looked a little haunted like me.

We carefully scale the cliffside that leads to the cove where we went on the night she gave me the ring that still sits at the base of my neck. As we step down onto the beach, I'm still pulling her through the sand behind me, but suddenly, her hand drops from mine, and she goes barreling toward the water.

She tilts her head up toward the sky, moving in a slow circle with her arms out at her sides as the waves lap against her ankles. A salt breeze flows through her hair, whipping it around her and shaking the trees within the cove. The sun just begins its descent behind her, shrouding her in gold.

It's the most beautiful thing I've ever seen.

My entire being comes alive at the sight of her.

"I love you, Darby!" I shout out to her.

She drops her head and smiles at me, tucking a wild strand of golden hair behind her ear. "Come show me how much!"

With that, I tuck my letters beneath a rock and jog toward the ocean, joining her in the water. She laughs as I lift her into my arms and spin her around. Legs locking behind my waist, she drops her nose to brush against mine.

The sun erupts behind her head like a halo.

"You're an angel," I whisper.

"An angel and her demon." She sighs against my lips.

"A heathen and his honeysuckle," I respond.

Within the waves, beneath the palms, and under the gold of the setting sun, I kiss her.

Two lost souls find their way home.

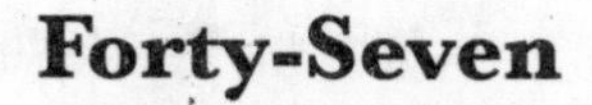

Forty-Seven

Honeysuckle

Now. June 6th.

"All the flowers in the hanging baskets on the porch are dying," Dahlia says on the other end of the line.

"Have you been watering them?"

I can hear her roll her eyes. "Yes, Darby."

I laugh. "I don't know what to tell you then."

"You sound happy, you know? You never really sounded happy before. Not like this."

"I am happy."

Leo and I watched the sunset in the cove while I read his letters. I cried the entire time, and he held me through it. It eventually led me to my knees with the ocean in the background, just like he said. Then, we had to climb back up the cliffside in the dark.

He was having a panic attack the entire time because we didn't have flashlights, but I couldn't stop laughing. We ended up going back to his apartment to sleep, since we weren't sure the last time the sheets were washed at my grandma's house. And because...well, we want a place that feels like our home.

We've been staying in his apartment the last few nights, but I've been coming to my grandma's each day to begin sorting through her things. I'll keep a few items that remind me of her, but otherwise, I plan on stripping the house clean and starting fresh.

Leo's back at work, catching up on the week he took off and

preparing for the U.S. Open in Huntington Beach next month. I'm still job searching, but for the summer, I'm going to focus on my grandma's house.

Which is what I'm doing now while I talk to Dahlia and sort through my old room. There are some things I know I'll give away, some I know I want to keep, and others I'm not sure about, so I have a box for those that I'll throw into the garage.

"Speaking of happy," I say, "I think you and Lou should come out here." I take a deep breath, preparing for my sister's response. "I know it's hard to uproot her, but I don't think there is anything for you there, and if I'm honest, I'm a little afraid of how Dad will retaliate with all you did to get me away from the wedding."

Dahlia snorts. "Don't worry about Dad. Trust me, I've got that handled. But I think you're right. It's time for a change." She lets out a small laugh. "Which is why my house is already on the market."

I all but squeal. "Are you serious?"

"Yep!" she chimes. "If I'm going to make the jump, I should do it before Lou has to go back to school."

"That's smart." I try to remain cool, but truthfully, I'm so giddy I could be sick. Dahlia and Lou are the only things missing from this new life, the final two pieces. "What about Jason?"

Darby scoffs. "The guy hasn't seen his daughter in two years, hasn't called her on her birthday or Christmas. I'm not even sure he remembers her name. He won't even notice."

My heart breaks at that. We all knew Jason wasn't a winner long before Dahlia got pregnant, but once she was, we held out hope that he'd step up. But it's been almost a decade, and we're still waiting for that to happen.

Dahlia deserves the opportunity to begin anew, no longer being the boss' daughter or the pregnant teenager. She deserves to thrive as herself, maybe even fall in love.

If I said that out loud, she'd probably call me a sensitive little bitch or something. She's got her emotions locked up tight. She has zero faith in relationships—in a happy ending for herself.

She's entirely dedicated to Lou, extremely protective, nurturing, and determined to give her daughter more than we had, but I think, in the process, she's forgotten who she is.

"I'll make sure I bring all your stuff out with us, too, but in the meantime, I did express ship your passport, birth certificate, and all that shit you'll need to get a job," she says. "Oh, and Leo asked me to convince you to let him take you shopping for a new wardrobe instead of wearing the same five things over and over again," she huffs. "So, this is me convincing you to stop being a dumb bitch and let the rich man spoil you."

There it is. She calls me a bitch at least once per conversation.

I roll my eyes. "Thanks, Dal. I'll consider it."

We're both laughing, excitement bubbling through the line at the thought of being reunited, when my phone beeps. I pull it away from my head and see I have another call coming through. "Shit. It's Jackson. Again."

He's still calling me every day.

"You gonna finally answer?"

I bite my lip. I keep telling myself every time that I'll answer the next time he calls, and then I never do. But if there is one thing holding me back from truly closing that chapter of my life, it's this.

I take a deep breath. "Yeah, I am. I'll call you back, Dal."

"Just remember, Darby, he can't hurt you. Trust me when I tell you that there is nothing he—or Dad—can hold over you. Do not let them make their threats."

I'm itching to ask her to explain, but I only say, "Okay, love you. Bye." I end her call and accept the incoming one. "Hi," I say softly.

"Darby?" He sounds surprised. "Jesus Christ. Do you know how hard I've been trying to get ahold of you?"

"I know," I mutter.

There is a weird comfortability here, like even though I now understand that I don't love Jackson, that I don't want to be with him, he's still someone I spent many years with. I've been telling myself I can't face him, but truthfully, he's the same person I've always known. He deserves more than I've given him.

"What the fuck, Darby? Where are you?"

I climb off the bed and head downstairs, suddenly feeling like I need a glass of water. "I'm not telling you, but I'm not coming back. I'm not sure what my dad has said, but I do mean it when I say it's over. And it's not you—"

"Is this because of Annie? I mean, you were pulling the whole virgin act on me. What was I supposed to do?"

Annie. His assistant. Huh. So, he was cheating on me.

His tone is harsher than I've ever heard it, which makes it easier to say, "I don't love you, Jackson."

"It's not about love!" he snaps. "It's about responsibility. It's about keeping your fucking promises."

His tone is harsher than I've ever heard it. He has always treated me with nothing more than tolerance, but I never saw us as a strict business transaction. I thought we had at least some semblance of friendship. It's clear now that it couldn't be further from the truth. And yet, I feel nothing as he speaks to me.

No sadness. No fear. No heartbreak.

"I gave you everything, you spoiled fucking brat. I was going to take care of you. The house, the cars, the babies. Do you know how many women out there would die for what I've given you, Darby?"

I huff a laugh just as the front door opens. Jackson continues to rant, but I'm not really listening. Better to let him get it all out if it means closure in the end.

Leo steps through the door, hair still wet with seawater. My heart picks up in my chest, and suddenly, that nothing becomes everything.

Contentment. Safety. Love.

I hold my finger up to my lips, motioning for him to stay quiet. His eyes narrow as he listens to Jackson, stepping up to me and pressing his lips against mine.

"Do you know what your dad is telling me, Darby? He's telling me that if I don't convince you to come home and put this Godforsaken wedding back on, he's going to make me pay for it myself. Do you know how much *your* wedding cost? Thirty thousand fucking dollars, Darby!"

Leo raises a brow, mouthing: *child's play.*

I roll my eyes, but he boxes me in on the counter, letting his lips feather along my jaw. Tension rolls off me as he continues down my neck and along the collar of my T-shirt.

"You humiliated me! Humiliated yourself. Your family," Jackson continues. "Running off with another man, no less? You look like a whore. I suppose you're fucking him too? So much for the innocent virgin, huh?"

Leo goes rigid, jaw tightening with anger. I shake my head, and he blinks the emotion away before swiftly dropping to his knees in front of me.

What are you doing? I mouth at him.

He only smiles, slowly unbuttoning my jeans and tugging them down my legs. I'm forced to bite the backside of my hand as he leans in, tugging my underwear to the side and fluttering a teasing lick against my clit.

"*My* whore," he whispers.

My eyes roll back, and I fight the moan in my throat. Leo then presses his mouth against me, closing it entirely around my clit and sucking hard. A low groan rips from my lips as I slap my hand over it. He chuckles against my center, flicking across me again with his tongue as a finger begins to tease my opening.

"What the fuck was that?" Jackson asks.

Leo doesn't stop. He moves faster, and I'm panting against the hand over my mouth. Heat races through my veins as he continues to lap at me. I start to clench around his fingers, feeling the crest of my climax climb over me.

"Darby? Do you want to fucking respond? At least acknowledge me and all that you've put me through?"

That wave retreats, and I let out a defeated sigh.

Leo shoots to his feet and leans over the counter, placing his mouth in the phone. "Look, man, I'm trying to have my post-workout snack right now, and you're interrupting. Can you get to whatever the fuck your point is so I can get back to my meal?"

Silence. Only silence greets us from the other side of the line.

"Oh, and if you ever dare to refer to my fiancée as a whore again, I'll fucking end you. Understood?"

Leo smiles, lips glistening with me.

"Wha...I...Who..." Jackson stutters. "Fiancée?"

"Did she not get the chance to tell you yet?" He chuckles. "The only person Darby's going to be marrying in this lifetime—in any lifetime, in fact—is me."

"What the fuck?" Jackson's practically shrieking now, and Leo is fighting back tears of laughter.

I'm mostly just stunned—stunned and wet and aching.

"Oh, and if money's an issue, I'd be happy to front the thirty thousand if that'll get you to shut the fuck up and leave her alone." With that, Leo sinks back down to his knees and doesn't hesitate as his tongue dives between my legs.

He devours me, gripping my ass and tugging me against him, fingers finding their way back inside and curling slightly, hitting the spot he knows will set me off.

I press the mute button on my phone just as a moan tears from my throat—one I can't keep at bay.

Leo sucks my clit and pulls back. "Don't mute us, baby. I want him to hear as I make you come so that he'll never be mistaken again." His eyes flare, and he nods at my phone as I shakily press the button once more. "First and foremost, I want that asshole to know that you belong to yourself. You're done being controlled by others." He flicks his tongue against me again, and I whimper. "But this pussy, Honeysuckle, this pussy belongs to me."

"Are you... Is he... Jesus, Darby. Are you fucking kidding me right now?"

"Look, Jackson," I huff. "How about this? You try and start any shit, and I'll tell my friends back in Crestwell that I ran away because you're fucking your assistant. I have proof." I pause but don't wait for him to respond. "And just so you know, the money for the wedding was taken out of my trust fund. You don't owe my dad a penny. It's not my fucking fault that your promotion in the company is conditional on marrying me; that's on my dad. Figure it out with him and let me move on with my life."

I hang up just as Leo's fingers hit the right spot, and his tongue presses against me, his lips sucking around me with enough pressure to send me bursting through the stars.

I cry out his name, rocking my hips against him as I come down. He doesn't stop too soon—doesn't pull away until he knows I'm completely spent.

"That's my girl." He stands, slowly slipping his fingers into his mouth and sucking them clean. "I'm so proud of you."

"What're we doing here?" I ask as we stand in front of the vacant building next to Heathen's, Everett and Leo's surf shop.

I haven't seen Everett yet, but I know he's been around. Leo leaves for his workouts and training early in the morning, and I'm too afraid to go see Everett alone. By the time we make it back to his apartment in the evenings, the shop is closed, and Everett is gone. Leo assured me his brother doesn't hold grudges like Elena does; he's just giving us some space to adjust to our life together, but we'll see him soon.

We normally enter the apartment through a set of stairs in the back, so I haven't seen the front of the building that faces the boardwalk yet.

The emblem of a cresting wave within a circle, something that looks like the tattoo on Leo's stomach, sits above the door. *Heathen's Surf Co.* is written next to it in bold lettering.

There are five units side by side, all dark except for lights on the opposite end of the row from Heathen's.

"What's down there?"

"August's shop," he says. "We'll... We'll meet up with him soon."

I nod as Leo pulls me into the empty unit in front of us. We walk inside to find the same wood finishings on the floor and walls that exist throughout the entire building, as well as the upstairs apartment. There is a bar that runs along the wall to the right of the front door, and some shelving on the opposite side of the room. Otherwise, it's barren.

"Why are we here?" I ask.

Leo spins, taking in the space slowly. "I'm part of an initiative with the city to boost small businesses. That's why I bought this building. My goal is to fill each unit with a small business that will attract locals and beachgoers alike."

"What were you thinking about putting here?"

He shrugs nonchalantly. "Wasn't sure. Figured I could rent it out to someone with an idea, or I could wait until my own inspiration struck."

"I'm assuming inspiration has struck?"

"You tell me."

I raise my brows at him, confused as to where this is going. Leo leans against the bar, giving me that boyish, mischievous smile I've missed for so many years as he pulls something out from underneath the counter, plopping it onto the bar.

It's all the cash we found in my grandma's desk.

"I've been thinking a cute flower shop would do well here. Would appeal to locals and tourists." He shrugs. "If only I knew someone with a green thumb and a love for botany."

"Leo." I sigh and look around, seeing all the possibilities in the space. My fingers suddenly itch for the feel of stems and petals, the sweet, soft smell I remember walking into each morning during college, and the peace I found in the colors and the creativity of the arrangements. The look on someone's face when their husband surprised them with a bouquet. The comfort the blooms provide at funerals, the excitement of weddings.

I swallow. "I told you I wanted to figure it out on my own."

"I know." He nods. "That's why I'll charge you rent." He slides the cash toward me. "Your grandmother would've wanted you to have this. I think she would've been proud to see you making a name for yourself in the town she loved so much—doing something you love so much." My chest swells at that. "So, I've taken enough out to cover three months' rent. The rest you'll use for start-up, and once you're open, you're gonna pay me every month. It's going to be your business, Darby. In your name."

He steps into me, placing his hand on my hips. "You're going to make it incredible, and that'll be on you. It doesn't have to be all or nothing, Honeysuckle. You don't need to be obedient and dependent on others or entirely on your own. You can accept support and be independent, too."

I don't know what to say; I'm not sure there are words. I simply fall into him—like gravity. I crash my lips against his, and his grip tightens as he spins me, pressing me against the counter and lifting me on top of it.

"Was thinking we could call it Honeysuckle," he says between my lips.

I hum. "Heathen and Honeysuckle. That'd be something."

He pulls back, running his thumb along my jaw, his other hand resting at my hip, right over the tattoo there. He squeezes it four times.

"It would be everything."

Forty-Eight

Honeysuckle

Now. July 10th.

Hundreds, if not thousands, of people litter the sand to get a glimpse of the surfers dotting the waves in the distance. Behind us, stretching far on either side, the beach is lined with white sponsor tents. An announcer's voice roars through the speakers, and it feels as if he's saying Leo's name a few times every minute.

Everett and I watch him intently from our elevated position in one of the spaces reserved for the families of the athletes. We're on a platform beneath an extra-large white tent that towers over the sand, where beachgoers and attendees alike settle in to watch the U.S. Open.

Everett's fingers tap against his forearm impatiently as we watch Leo on the waves. His bright green board flashes in the sunlight. I know it's got the Heathen's Surf Co. logo printed down the side, even though he lost out on some money using the board from his own business over one from his sponsors.

His agent, Lynn, is short, blonde, and kind of mean. She was unhappy with Leo's decision to forgo his board sponsor. She's in our tent, too, along with his assistant, Adam, and his Public Relations Manager, Kate. Lynn stands at the back of the tent, sucking on a cigarette, even though I'm fairly certain that's not permitted here. I think everyone's just too afraid of her to say something.

Adam and Kate watch from the opposite corner of the room while Everett and I stand on our own end. Everyone was pleasant enough when they met me, but it was as if I had "distraction" written across my forehead, as if I'm the one thing that can pull Leo's focus from surfing, the one who will be solely responsible for cutting down the amount of money each of them brings in.

I was a little insecure about being around his team. Everett was reassuring, though, telling me that they're all assholes. They don't like him, either, don't like that Leo wants to take time away from surfing to focus on their business. He told me he was happy to have someone here he actually liked, so when we arrived, he whisked me away to our own little corner, and we've mostly blocked out the rest of them.

I saw Everett for the first time about a week after Leo and I got to Pacific Shores. He'd been giving us some space to settle in together. I was nervous about seeing him, afraid he might give me the same cold shoulder I've come to expect from Elena—whenever I happen to see her again. She doesn't come home often, apparently—but Everett just tossed me up into a bear hug and told me he was happy to have me home. He's so much bigger than I remember. Huge, really. He must be at least a foot taller than I am at five foot four. Thick beard, corded muscles down his neck and arms, resembling some kind of tattooed motorcycle gang—Hercules. He still has that wicked gleam in his eye that tells you he's got a wild side. It almost reminds me of my sister.

He's the kind of guy Dahlia would say she wanted to climb like a tree, her favorite expression when it comes to big, bearded men. They're her cup of tea—for a one-night stand, at least. Dahlia doesn't do relationships, and she especially doesn't allow any of her conquests to meet her daughter.

Leo, Everett, and I get dinner together at least once a week, and Everett has been helping Leo with renovations on the building next door to Heathen's, which will soon become Honeysuckle Florals. Our goal is to open early next year, maybe even sooner.

I've only seen August once. Leo's told me not to take it personally; August keeps his distance from everyone, apparently. One night a few weeks ago, we were taking a walk along the pier at sunset and glimpsed August through the window of his tattoo shop. He happened to glance up as Leo and I strolled by, hand in hand. He did a double take as his eyes narrowed in on me.

We only waved through the window. He smiled, but it didn't reach his eyes. After a moment, he simply turned back to the client laid out on his table and continued his work.

Later that week, I brought him cookies and a bouquet of seasonal flowers: sunflowers, orange poppies, and a mixture of California golden and sweet violets. I thought the color mixture would look good on the reception desk of his shop.

I always remember August as quiet, a bit shy, but I also remember a hidden humor about him, a light in his eyes. Neither of those exist anymore. While I understand why, understand his reasons for shutting out those still left in his life, my heart broke all the same. I asked him if he'd be willing to have lunch with me once a month or so, without Leo or Everett, just the two of us. I guess I hope that having a relationship with someone who wasn't so heavily involved in his brother's death and the aftermath would help him. He agreed initially, but it's been about a month since that day, and he won't return my text messages.

August doesn't come to Leo's competitions anymore, either, though none of us can blame him for that. I can imagine how painful it would be to watch one brother get swallowed up by the waves over and over again, knowing another was swallowed the same way and never made it out.

My own heart stalls in my chest every time I watch Leo out on those waves. Even with an audience, even with lifeguards littered along the beach and the Coast Guard on standby, I can't help the jolt of fear that runs through my veins every time he disappears beneath the surface. The seconds feel like years as we wait for him to emerge. I know Everett feels the same way. He quietly mutters to himself any time Leo goes under, digs his nails into his skin every time Leo pops up on his board. I can't read the waves the way the boys can, but I know something's about to happen when Everett inhales swiftly and grabs my arm. His eyes are wide as I look up to him, my gaze following his toward the water.

Leo's paddling swiftly into the horizon line. He's the only surfer out there in action, all the others pausing simply to watch him.

In the distance, I see the swell of a large wave barreling toward him as he meets it head-on. Just as it begins to crest, Leo jumps up on his board effortlessly. He swivels his hips and bends his legs as his surfboard cuts sideways, and he begins to skim along the white caps.

He pumps the back of the board with his ankles, rotating his upper body as he moves up and down the wave. He cuts up rapidly, launching himself into the air before gliding back down the wave without missing a step. His movements are fluid and graceful, like he's the water himself.

As the ocean tunnels over him, I'm sure he's going to sink down with it, but he doesn't. He continues swiveling his board along the collapsing wave, riding it all the way to shore, keeping his balance in the shallow water until he literally hops right off the board and onto the beach.

I can't hear what the announcer is saying, but I do hear his excitement ringing inside my ears. The crowd goes wild, and nearly every person along the pier has rushed to the side of it, leaning over the railing to get a glimpse of the legendary surfer.

I remember Leo being good when we were younger. I remember him being mesmerizing, but it was nothing in comparison to what I've just seen him do now. I'm breathless.

As he steps out onto the sand not far from us, he grabs his board from the shore and looks up directly at our tent—at me. His smile is big, bright, and prideful as the rest of the world—the clapping of the crowd, the flash of cameras, and the roar of the announcer in the speaker—fades away, and he zones in on me.

He raises one arm, holding up his pointer finger and his pinky, sticking out his thumb. I immediately make the same gesture back. "I still don't know what that means." I laugh.

"It means *I love you*," Everett responds.

Tears well up in my eyes as that settles in me. I remember him making that gesture every morning as he surfed and I watched him on the shore all those summers ago, before we ever said those words. He'd been telling me back then. Every day. He loved me.

He loves me.

He always has.

The next thing I know, I'm bursting through the flaps of the tent and down the platform stairs. The sand is hot beneath my feet as I land on the ground, but it doesn't stop me from running toward him. Leo's smiling as he bends down to unstrap his board from his ankle, and then he's moving toward me, too, closing the distance between us.

His laughter chimes against my chest as he sweeps me into his arms. He's soaking wet, and I feel the water seeping into the fabric of my blue dress, but I don't care in the slightest.

"I love you too," I murmur against his neck as he wraps me around him. "And you're amazing. Watching you surf is the hottest thing I've ever seen, and I need you to do all those moves again later when you're on top of me."

The laughter that bursts out of him is roaring and beautiful. "You're somethin' else, Honeysuckle." He sets me on my feet, kissing my forehead. "Maybe retiring was a bad idea."

He's still laughing, but I'm rearing back, confused. "What?"

Just then, unfamiliar voices close in on us, and I watch Leo's eyes focus on something behind me before lighting up with amusement. "Hey, fuckers. Nice of you to show your faces."

I slowly turn in Leo's arms as he tugs me against his chest, wrapping one arm around my collarbone. Two men tower over me, one with dark skin and short black hair. His laugh is silky and rough, golden-brown eyes glimmering in the sunlight. The other has slightly lighter skin, a head of dark curls, and striking hazel eyes. A camera hangs around his neck, dangling at his chest.

Leo gestures to the brown-eyed man. "This is Dom and"—he waves at the man with the camera next to him—"Carter."

They're both pretty—like...really pretty. I feel like I'm

suddenly the character in a why-choose romance novel who somehow ends up surrounded by unnaturally attractive men, even though we all know there aren't that many supermodel-type guys just walking around in everyday life.

Except apparently there are in mine, because my professional surfer boyfriend has graced the cover of several magazines over the years. And now I'm being stared down at by his two Greek god-looking friends, just as his Herculean brother steps off the platforms and joins us.

"Hi, Honeysuckle," Dom says with a smile. I realize he must be our realtor. "Nice to finally meet you."

"You too," I murmur, feeling flustered for some reason. "Thank you for everything with the house."

"Thank you for the commission." He winks.

"All right, enough of that," Leo mutters. "And call her Darby."

"Hi, Honeysuckle," Carter drawls, his voice practically a purr. He winks at me too, and now I know I'm blushing.

"Assholes."

Everett laughs.

I tilt my head toward Leo, glancing up at him. "What's your deal?"

He points at Dom. "That douchebag's voice is pure sex. I don't like it when he calls you that." He then points at Carter. "And he's too pretty. It bothers me. Plus, he has bedroom eyes."

All of those statements are true, and the longer they look at me, the more alert I feel, but I can't help laughing at Leo too.

He's hot when he's jealous.

"Thanks, baby." Carter smiles. "I think I got some great pictures of you out there today."

Leo snorts. "I thought you didn't take photos of people."

"You're too pretty. Can't help myself." Carter shrugs. "Guess the feeling's mutual."

Leo flips him off, but I can tell he's smiling.

"The girls are at the gallery today, but we're gonna pick them up when it closes and go grab dinner. Do you want to come?" Dom asks. "You'll buy, of course, rich boy."

Carter shoves him, laughing under his breath. "You should come, though. Darby can meet Macie and Pep. They need more friends."

Dom grunts in agreement.

I open my mouth to accept, but Leo beats me to it. "Rain check? We've actually got plans tonight."

"We do?" I ask.

Leo tightens his hold on me, looking down with those sapphire eyes as his dimples pop.

We mumble goodbyes to Leo's friends, and Everett tells us he's taking off, too, but we'll see him at the shop tomorrow. As we turn to wave everyone off, I notice for the first time the sea of photographers, fans, and reporters waiting for a second of Leo's attention. I gasp, realizing the audience surrounding our entire interaction.

Lynn and Kate are standing at the forefront, giving Leo stern looks. He sighs. "I gotta give an interview before we go. Go stand with Adam for a second."

I glance over at the base of the tent we'd been watching the competition in and notice Leo's assistant is standing by the stairs, speaking into his phone. I kiss Leo's cheek, noting the shutter sound of cameras as I step away from the crowd, attempting to ignore the lingering looks of confusion before huddling up next to Adam.

I'm far enough away that I'm not in line of the cameras crowding him, but close enough that I can still hear his interview. A woman in a black sundress with short black hair steps up to Leo. She holds a microphone to her chest that has ESPN written down the side.

"Mr. Graham," she says brightly.

"Call me Leo."

"Leo." She smiles. "How does it feel knowing you've placed with the highest score in Huntington Beach here today?"

"I feel incredibly lucky," he responds humbly.

The reporter laughs. "We all know better than to assume it's all luck that's gotten you this far in your career. Tell us a little about your process and what training looked like for you leading up to this season."

Leo talks through his routine and how he prepared for the competition today. He again praises the weather, the conditions, and the other athletes, because if there is anything to know about him, it's that he is genuinely humble. I can tell he doesn't want to boast, even though he should.

"Speaking of luck, I notice you're not wearing the staple chain around your neck that you normally keep tucked into your wetsuit. Is it no longer your good luck charm?"

I expect to see him stiffen under questions regarding his personal life, but Leo smiles now instead. "My good luck charm is here with me today, actually." His eyes dart to mine as he winks, and I blush as dozens of curious stares fall on me. "The necklace was only ever a representation of something greater, and now that I have the greater thing, I don't need a token of it."

Myself, the reporter, and every other person on this beach swoon.

Leo told me he was going to put the necklace away for safekeeping somewhere, which I thought was strange, considering he'd worn it for a decade and hadn't lost it yet.

As Leo and the reporter finish the interview, she asks one final question. "What can we expect to see from you this upcoming season?"

Leo smiles brightly, and I only slightly catch the scowl of his agent behind him. "You can expect this season to be my last."

Gasps echo throughout the world, including my own.

The reporter sputters. "But you're only twenty-seven. You have years of your career in front of you."

Leo nods, taking on a serious look. "You're right. I'll always be a surfer. You'll never get me out of the waves entirely. But I've been running my entire career, traveling the world, and pushing my body to the limit. I've had the time of my life doing it, but I'm ready to settle down at home and focus on my business." His eyes flick to me again, softening as a small smile highlights his lips. "And my family. I want to be present in the lives of the people I love." He then turns toward the crowd, addressing them directly. "You'll still catch me out on the waves, just maybe not so often. I hope you'll come to stop by Heathen's down at the Pacific Shores boardwalk when you're in the area."

The crowd cheers as he walks toward me with purpose. I watch the world around him fade away as his sapphire gaze narrows on me. He reaches me in a number of strides, and his hands immediately come to my cheeks, lifting my face toward his.

"I've already committed to competitions and appearances this year in Honolulu, South Africa, and Portugal. Come with me?"

"Always," I breathe.

"How do you feel about being on the news tomorrow?"

"Scared, but less so if it's going to be with you."

He smiles, and those boyish dimples I fell in love with appear on his cheeks. Without leaving my gaze, he shouts, "Adam! The box."

I can't look away from him, either, but I feel the presence of his assistant and the shuffle of something exchanging hands. I'm too afraid to look at what it is, because I'm afraid if I stop staring into Leo's eyes, this moment will pass all too quickly, and I know I need it to last forever.

He slowly sinks to one knee, and I feel my heart rate speeding through my body. It lifts straight from my chest, taking my soul with it until it feels like I'm hovering above the two of us, watching from a distance.

"There have been times where I've struggled with faith and fate, where I've had a lot of questions I never thought I'd get the answers to. Where I've felt like a soulless ghost, lost and wandering." He takes my trembling hand in his steady one. "But meeting you made me believe in things I never thought were real. Knowing you answered every question I've ever had about the world. Finding you again brought me back to life."

Tears stream down both our cheeks, those blue eyes brighter than the ocean behind them as they shimmer through his emotion.

"You're my once-in-a-lifetime love, Darby, and I don't want to live another moment without the entire world, all the universe and the heavens above it, knowing that we're meant to be." He lifts the black velvet box, revealing a golden ring, now studded with diamonds that catch the sunlight. "Will you marry me?"

The familiar gold band now holds a round diamond, accented by smaller tear-drop diamonds around it. Vines of gold wrap around the band, looking almost like stems.

The entire ring looks like a flower.

"Leo," I gasp.

"I got the idea to add a diamond to this ring the night you gave it to me all those years ago. I've always known it was gonna be you, Honeysuckle."

He's still on his knees, gazing up at me with so much emotion, I feel myself dissolve as tears drip onto the sand below.

"It's the most beautiful thing I've ever seen." I find myself falling onto the ground, too, leveling my face with his. Despite this technically being my second proposal, nothing in my life has ever felt more real. Nothing else will ever compare to this moment, and I know with certainty that every decision I've ever made has led me right here, back to him. "Yes, of course, I'll marry you, Leo. I've wanted to marry you my whole life."

He slips the ring onto my left hand, and though it's not the first time I've had this ring there, it feels more comforting than ever. "You're the most beautiful thing I've ever seen." Leo raises his hands to my face and cups my cheeks. "I love you, Honeysuckle."

As he closes the gap between us and feathers his lips against mine, I whisper, "I love you, Heathen."

While I'm faintly aware of the flash of cameras and the cheer of crowds, the only thing that exists in this moment is him, the two of us alone, floating through the stars.

And when he kisses me in a way that feels like crashing waves and blooming flowers, I know I'm home.

Epilogue

Leo

Fifteen Years Later. August 11th.

"Hey, Mom?" Willow calls out from somewhere in the house.

I'm at the stove, stirring a pot of pasta sauce. Darby's at the kitchen island, assembling a bouquet of sunflowers, irises, and dahlias for Everett to pick up later. "Yeah?"

A moment later, our daughter comes around the doorway. Willow Maeve. Her middle name is after my mom. She's got Darby's honey-colored hair, rosy cheeks, and freckled nose, but she's got my blue eyes and dimples.

She's the best of both of us.

She holds up a familiar-looking yellow backpack. "I just found this in the garage. Can I paint it?"

Willow's nervous for the school year to start. She's in her freshman year of high school, and I know she wants to go into the new phase of life with a sense of identity.

She's got the creative gene like her mom, but she's also an athlete like me. She's got zero interest in flowers or surfing, much to our dismay. She's a great volleyball player, and she's been exploring different art mediums over the last couple of years. It appears she's found her groove in painting after spending the summer working under a friend of ours, who owns a gallery in Venice Beach.

Darby's head snaps up, a soft smile on her face. Her eyes narrow as she studies the backpack, trying to place it. I know exactly what it is. I distinctly remember the last time I saw it.

"Sure, I don't see why not," she says, turning back to her flowers. "Is there anything inside?"

A smile spreads across my cheeks now.

I turn back to the stove and say nothing as Willow walks across the kitchen and sets the backpack on the island. "Actually, yeah. There are some weird old books in here."

I glance back to watch Willow pull out four stacks of dark-colored books and set them on the counter.

"Oh, my God." Darby laughs. "These are your aunt's. She gave them to me like a hundred years ago." My wife looks up at me with a smile. "Grandma must've thrown this backpack in the garage at some point, and we just never got rid of it."

That's not entirely true. I noticed the backpack in the garage, but I promised myself that the divine would intervene when the time was right. I made sure Darby never accidentally got rid of it, but I also didn't give it to her myself.

"I'll have to give these to Elena when I see her this week." Darby stacks the books on the counter by the doorway where she keeps her keys.

I nod toward our daughter. "You should probably check all the side pockets and stuff too."

Okay, maybe I'm influencing fate a tiny bit.

Willow shuffles through the backpack, coming up empty until she unzips the front pocket, brows knitting together when she pulls out a faded piece of paper.

I smile to myself as my daughter unfolds the yellowed letter, my wife hovering over her shoulder as they read it through.

Willow looks up at me, and I can see the emotion shining in her eyes, though she doesn't let the tears fall. Some kids don't get to see parents who love each other. Some kids don't get to have parents at all, or they get really shitty ones. We knew we were never going to give her that. We were going to make up for everything we never got to have. We were going to make sure our daughter knew exactly what love looked like, how much fight it took, and how real it could be.

"When did you write this?" Willow asks.

Darby glances up at me too, tears streaming down her cheeks. Her brows cinch together, her nose red, and she's sniffling, but there's a sparkle in her eyes, filled with so much love, it makes my knees buckle.

"Twenty-five years ago." My eyes are on my wife. "Right after we got our tattoos."

Willow's head whips around to face her mom. "Oh, my God, you actually have Dad's name tattooed on your ass?"

Darby ignores her, eyes on me as she rounds the island and flings herself straight into my arms. "Wouldn't that be something?" She sobs into my shoulder as I cup the back of her head and nuzzle my face in her hair. I inhale her floral and honey scent.

"I love you, Honeysuckle."

I lift my gaze to find our daughter leaning against the counter with tears in her eyes. "Wow, Dad," she whispers. "You really manifested your whole life, huh?"

I smile at her, spreading out one arm and beckoning her toward me. She crosses the room and joins her mom. "Nah, sugar, I just always knew this was meant to be."

With both my girls in my arms, I know I'm home.

Acknowledgments

Each story I write, the list of my gratitude grows exponentially, but what a wonderful problem to have?

First, my Bubs. I'm sorry you didn't like Chapter 22 (how dare you?) but I'm eternally grateful that you exist. I wouldn't be able to write love stories or soulmates or one true love if I didn't have my own. Thank you for giving me that. For always reading my books even though they're not about astrophysics. For cooking me dinner and forcing me to drink water. Thank you for being you, and for loving me.

Emily and Lexi. Heathen & Honeysuckle led me to both of you, and I'll never be convinced that it wasn't all written in the stars. If this book does nothing else than give me your friendship, I'll consider it the most successful thing I've ever done. You're my atoms and my stardust and my shared brain cell. Thank you for being so intrinsic to Pacific Shores. This series truly belongs to both of you, methinks.

My agent, Dani, and SBR Media for helping this series reach places I never dreamed they could go.

The Page & Vine Team for taking a chance on my little universe and bringing it to stores all over the world. You make me feel like the luckiest author alive.

My parents and my step parents for all your support, and my brother, Robert, too. You're truly the king of word-of-mouth marketing.

Kes, Julie, Lauren, and Lil. I'll never not put you in the acknowledgments for my books. Thanks for loving me my whole life— including all the times I thought nobody else ever would.

My street team. For validating my love for this story in times I really needed to hear it, and helping me have the courage to put it out there. For loving this book and sharing that love widely and loudly. I appreciate you more than I'll ever be capable of expressing, but I hope you can feel all my love.

Tori Ann Harris, because I don't think there would be a trade version of this book if you'd never found it. You're my #1 Leo bully forever.

My ARC readers. Thank you for taking a chance on my story and helping me share it with the world. I'm so grateful for your support.

Darby & Leo's Playlist

Cardigan | Taylor Swift
I miss you, I'm sorry | Gracie Abrams
Golden Hour | Kacey Musgraves
champagne problems | Taylor Swift
Softcore | The Neighbourhood
exile (feat. Bon Iver) | Taylor Swift
I Wanna Be Yours | Arctic Monkeys
Two Ghosts | Harry Styles
Summer | Calvin Harris
Sad Beautiful Tragic (Taylor's Version) | Taylor Swift
Chemtrails Over The Country Club | Lana Del Rey
Baby I'm Yours | Arctic Monkeys
American Money | Børns
Fall In Love With You. | Montell Fish
Honeysuckle | Fulton Lee
Heathen | Colouring
Holy Ghost | Børns
Sunlight | Hozier
Fine Line | Harry Styles
Out Of The Woods (Taylor's Version) | Taylor Swift
Yellow | Coldplay

About the Author

Sarah fell in love with reading as a child. She quickly learned that books can take her to all the places she always dreamed of going, and allow her to live endless lifetimes in the one that she was given.

Sarah believes that to be seen is to be loved, and that's why romance is such an important genre. She believes romance novels offer readers reflection and relatability, ultimately helping us understand ourselves, and the world around us, a little better. She prides herself on crafting healing, raw, and uplifting stories that explore the complexities of the human spirit through the guise of love.

Sarah was born in California and raised in Southern Oregon, and still considers herself to be a Pacific Northwest gal at heart; right down to being a coffee snob, collecting hydro flasks, adamantly believing in Sasquatch, and never having owned an umbrella.

She now resides in Arizona with her husband and their pup, Rue. When she's not writing, she's reading, and if she's not reading, she's probably out searching for a decent cup of coffee or binging Vanderpump Rules for the millionth time.

Connect with Sarah on social media: @sarahabaileyauthor

Sign up for her newsletter to be the first to know about updates and announcements: sarahabaileyauthor.com/newsletter